Book 1 of the Treasured Lives

borrowed lives

Endorsements

In *Borrowed Lives*, McClain takes readers on a journey through artisan Meredith Jaynes's struggles, joys, and rewards of fostering three needy sisters. In the process, she finds healing in herself from her own tragic loss. Readers of women's fiction and foster parents will especially enjoy this book.
—**June Foster**, author of *Dreams Deferred* and *Ryan's Father.*

This is a heart-warming story featuring ornery goats, children in need of a home, and a no-nonsense widow learning to live life again. I love how McClain isn't afraid to show her Christian characters struggling in everyday situations. Grief is a hard subject, but McClain's wit and the thread of romance makes it the perfect blend for a wonderful fiction read.
—**Joy Massenburge**, best-selling author of *A Heart Surrendered.*

Carol McClain has written a touching story of human struggle laced with humor and imbued with the enduring, childlike faith that overcomes. If you are a fan of women's fiction, add this book to your reading list.
—**MaryAnn Diorio, Ph.D.**, novelist, DMin, MFA, author, life coach, licensed minister, Association of Biblical Counselors

I'm not usually a fan of women's fiction because I rarely enjoy reading books that deal with grief, drugs, and abandoned children. But Carol McClain has dealt with extremely tough situations in a sweet, witty way. Her characters are memorable and charming. I fell in love with them. The life situations are realistic enough to make the reader think Ms. McClain has lived through them herself. I highly recommend this well-written, well-characterized novel not only to people who enjoy women's fiction, but to those who love a happy ending of a truly, delightful story.

—**Anne Greene**, award-winning author of *Shadow of the Dagger* and *Red Is For Rookie*

Carol McClain doesn't disappoint. She pulls hard on readers' emotional strings in *Borrowed Lives,* thoroughly investing us in the lives and well-being of Meredith Jaynes and the severely neglected children in her care. Even though I couldn't quit turning pages, I also couldn't quell some deep introspection. If you like multi-faceted women's fiction with a cast of characters who live off the page, a romantic thread that will keep you wondering, and a story that will at times bludgeon your heart, then make it soar, read Carol McClain's *Borrowed Lives.*

—**Naomi Musch**, author of the *Echoes of the Heart* and *Empire in Pine* series.

Book 1 of the Treasured Lives

borrowed lives

CAROL McCLAIN

PUBLISHING THE POSITIVE
Plymouth, Massachusetts
A Christian Company

Copyright Notice

Cover and Interior Design: Derinda Babcock

Editor(s): Peggy Ellis, Deb Haggerty

PUBLISHED BY: Elk Lake Publishing, Inc., 35 Dogwood Drive, Plymouth, MA 02360, 2021

Library Cataloging Data

Names: McClain, Carol (Carol McClain)

Borrowed Lives / Carol McClain

420 p. 23cm × 15cm (9in × 6 in.)

Identifiers: ISBN-13: 978-1-64949-143-5 (paperback) | 978-1-64949-144-2 (trade paperback) | 978-1-64949-145-9 (e-book)

Key Words: foster children, adoption, child abuse, drugs, relationships, romance, values & virtues

Library of Congress Control Number: 2021933890 Fiction

Dedication

I dedicate this book to Caroline Vozzo. She's bright, engaged, compassionate, and loves God with all her heart. I couldn't ask for a better granddaughter.

Acknowledgments

The first thing God did when he created our universe was to speak the world into existence. I am eternally grateful he shared his gift of creating worlds with me. Mine will never be as complex, intriguing, or unique as his, but he allows me to be a part of his creation.

I also want to thank Liz Lay White and Steve Rondeau for the information they shared about our current Social Services system. In the county where I live, sixty percent of all children do not live with their biological parents. I've seen and heard of situations like the ones Bean and her sisters lived in. I'm grateful for the men and women who sacrifice their lives to be good foster parents. My work strove to be true to the operations of the Department of Social Services. Any errors are mine and not those of White and Rondeau.

I've worked extensively with ministries helping those lost to addiction. Without their dedicated service, few would recover.

I also could not write as well as I do without the faithful prodding of my critique group. They refuse to let sloppy writing or wrong assumptions slide. These women provoke me to be my best, and I love them to pieces.

ACFW Knoxville and The Author's Guild of Tennessee have also encouraged me and moved me forward in my writing career.

I also wouldn't be writing without the encouragement of my husband and my friends. When things get hard, they reinforce my resolve and support my endeavors.

My editor, Peggy Ellis, Elk Lake Publishing, Inc., and acquisition editor Linda Rondeau have championed me. Without them, this work wouldn't be as polished as it is.

Chapter 1

Something crashed downstairs.

Meredith Jaynes bolted up in bed. *John? Rosemary?*

She shook sleep from her head and listened for another sound.

Nothing.

Just a dream.

Then porcelain shattered.

Not a dream.

She tossed off her covers. Out of habit, not onto John's side. While her heart hammered, she slid open the bedside table to grab her Walther .22. Meredith strained to hear. She prayed for silence. She slipped in the cartridge then ratcheted a shell into the chamber and released the safety.

Once more, something clattered like a tipping chair or a marionette tap dancing on the hardwood floor.

She tiptoed into the hallway.

Below her, the distinct bleating of goats wafted up the stairwell.

Goats? Inside?

She reengaged the safety on her .22 as she scurried down the stairwell.

In the kitchen, Oreo, her black and white Nubian who looked like her cookie namesake, eyeballed her with cocked head and slit pupils. With a bleat from her perch on the table, she dug into the loaf of bread Meredith had brought home from the farmers' market.

Meredith leaned against the doorjamb and breathed again. The metal of the gun she held chilled her through John's shirt—one she hadn't washed, so his scent would surround her. She shook terror out of the way and slipped the gun onto the countertop where the weapon clacked against the toaster.

"Oreo, off my table!" She strode to the nanny and grabbed her collar.

Oreo skidded across the golden oak surface gouging the wood with her keratin hooves.

Meredith clenched her teeth and groaned. "Oreo, Daddy finished this tabletop only ten months ago." *Before Rosie ...*

She shook the thought away and let out a breath. Another sanding and polyurethane would mend the scratches.

But her heart? Nothing would fix the gouges and scars.

Oreo thudded to the floor. Meredith dragged her out into the gray dawn, dense with fog.

Across the yard, the pen's fence stood ajar. Not a goat milled in the enclosure. Off to her left in her garden, Cappuccino and Mocha munched on the carrot and beet tops.

"No!" She scurried to the goat run, shoved Oreo inside and latched the gate. Next, she ran to her garden. She grabbed Cap, but Mocha gamboled across the rows and settled at the pole beans.

A goat in hand was worth more than one in the veggies. She led Cappuccino back to the fenced-in yard.

How would she wrangle the rest of her herd? They'd be like grabbing fish—nab one, two would escape.

Only one thing would lure them back from wherever they frisked. Inside the barn, she grabbed the galvanized pail where she stored their grain and rattled the cover. Making as much noise as she could, she scooped the molasses-scented pellets into her bucket. By the time she tramped to the trough outside, the nannies bleated hungrily as they skipped toward their breakfast.

She counted as they entered the enclosure. *Three, four, five, six.* Only six. Vivienne Van Goat and the two kids were AWOL.

She left the herd happily munching on grainy goodness and stepped toward the house then skidded to a stop. Billie Jean danced on the roof of her truck with Bobbi-Jo Riggs. Bobbi-Jo spied her and hopped onto the truck's back cap.

"No, no, no." Meredith broke into a run.

At the vehicle, she lifted Bobbi-Jo and put her down to grab Billie Jean. Bobbi-Jo jumped back up.

Sharp hooves scratched the paint.

She couldn't wrestle both. Meredith hauled Billie Jean into her arms and lugged the forty-pounder to the goat run. Her breath came heavy from toting the wayward kid.

Bobbi-Jo didn't want to play on the truck alone. She scrambled after Meredith like Merry's little lamb. Or goat, as this case warranted.

Both kids romped in the pen.

Meredith stepped inside the enclosure and latched the gate. Now out of breath, she leaned against the sturdy fencing. Two by fours pressed into her back. She counted. Six nannies. Two kids. Only Vivienne missing.

Still leaning on the gate, Meredith scanned the yard. At her garden, one triad of bean poles had been knocked over. The vines holding her newly ripened vegetables splayed over the ground. The beans she had hoped to freeze this evening for winter's bounty.

Hooves had torn up the root vegetables.

Vivienne must be munching berries somewhere. Thorns or thickets, nothing stopped Vivienne Van Goat. Once out where fresh rippling water kept algae away from her pond. Beyond the pond, the fields belonging to her in-laws rose in a patchwork of green topped by the purple Cumberland Mountains. Her father-in-law's cattle munched serenely in their barbed-wired pasture. Few ever escaped. Pa might work in a bank by day, but his cattle were his passion. If he could've made a living as a cowboy, he'd never need to die to be in heaven.

Meredith stepped into the kitchen, which lay in disarray. Goat marbles scattered across her floor. After sweeping the waste and disinfecting the table, she picked up the gun lying next to the toaster.

John was the protector. He insisted she learn to shoot.

She closed her eyes and inhaled, fought the pain behind her eyelids.

When the feeling eased, she trekked upstairs and stashed the weapon in the bedside table. She changed into jeans and a T-shirt.

The ache didn't ease.

Only one thing helped. Goats.

Back in the barn, the top to her freezer stood slightly ajar, caught against a bag of milk frozen for her soap making. Several from the pile she had stacked to the freezer's brim were missing. Frost formed along the edge of the appliance.

She frowned. Her nannies were intelligent, but they didn't know how to reclaim their own milk—milk she needed for her soap. With market season in full swing, she couldn't afford to lose her product.

Parker Snow pulled into Christ Church's parking lot.

In five minutes, he'd silence his cell. He prefer to turn off the phone. But he was on.

On call. Vibrate would be as quiet as he could keep his phone.

This had been a long, sad weekend. He had to remove twelve-year-old Steve from his home. No relatives would take the boy, and he ended up in an overcrowded foster home. The child's suppressed tears and silent rage tore at Parker. Sometimes being a man stunk. Men didn't cry. Had to be strong for the kid. But ...

He slammed the door to his ancient Cherokee. As though the sound woke his phone, his cell shrilled his mother's ring. He silenced the ringer and shoved the cell into his back pocket. He'd let voice mail pick up. If he refused the call, she'd know he ignored her by the instant disconnect. She'd complain until he got on his knees and begged forgiveness.

He chuckled. *Yes, Mom nagged. In the end, she was kind.* No sense in irritating her. He'd let Ms. Samantha Snow assume he had the volume down.

The phone buzzed. The vibration in his back pocket made him jump. *A voice mail. Another matchmaking? Here I am, nearly thirty, single, driving a soccer mom vehicle and harried by Mommy to date her friends.* Disgust roiled his stomach.

Something had to give.

Church. He needed a refreshing, hope-filled service.

Pastor would probably talk about Christian duty or tithing. Still, he hoped.

Parker stepped into Christ Church's foyer. His phone vibrated once more. He closed his eyes. Inhaled. Mommy dearest was a nag but didn't badger. Usually. He checked.

Sure enough—work.

He stepped back into the warm June sunshine to take the call.

"Parker, the kid you placed yesterday. He's got to go someplace else. He punched the foster mom and threatened to run away. You need to pick him up."

"Where do I bring him?"

"Try the group home out in Jellico."

"That place is an abyss—the Hades of houses."

"He lives in Jellico or with you."

"Fine." Five minutes later, he headed up to the home in Fincastle to destroy whatever he didn't ruin in Steve yesterday.

His job hurt.

He destroyed children's lives.

Chapter 2

The soap emulsified. Meredith added lavender oil and swirled in lilac dye. Once the pattern pleased her, she poured the product into the molds. To the top of the soap, Meredith sprinkled lavender flowers and swirls of trimmed soap. She covered the molds. After stashing the unused bagged milk into the freezer, she herded her flock, milked, and fed them. With her bucket of drinking milk in her hand, Meredith stepped into the fenced-in goat run. She turned and made sure she closed the freezer properly.

She double-checked the lock on the fence, then headed toward the house.

As she reached the porch, her sister's van pulled up behind her cabin, and the doors slid open. Meredith placed her bucket of milk on the decking as she shielded her eyes with her palm to better watch the circus spectacle she knew was coming. Out popped two of her sister's kids. The human variety of kid, not the goat type.

"Aunt Merry." Seven-year-old Anissa, who was born the year before Rosemary and had the same ginger hair, leapt into Meredith's arms and wrapped her legs around her hips. "Daddy's a bonny-fido preacher. I wished you might could've been there."

"Say 'could have' not 'might could've.'"

"You ain't an English teacher."

Phoebe trotted over, thumb in her mouth. With her free arm, she hugged Meredith's thigh.

Meredith pulled on Phoebe's arm. "Four-year-olds shouldn't suck their thumbs."

"I'm three." Phoebe held up three fingers. "I stop when I'm four." She plopped her thumb back into her mouth.

Meredith waddled toward her sister. Both girls clung to her like Mom's cat fur on Velcro.

Sunny Buchanan mumbled something as she bent over Owen strapped in his car seat. When she stood grasping her son, she turned and bumped into Meredith.

"What did you say, Sunny? You were mumbling into Owen's head." Meredith unwound Anissa and Phoebe from her legs. "Your kids need Static Guard. They're clingy."

Sunny grinned. And probably because Meredith was currently childless, she handed Owen off to her. "Did you listen to my voice mail?" She grabbed her girls' hands and stepped toward the house.

"Voice mail?" Meredith offered a sheepish grin. "No. Goats got loose this morning. Haven't checked the phone."

"That's why you weren't in when we stopped by before church." They stepped into Meredith's tiny kitchen. Sunny picked up and handed Meredith a piece of paper decorated with soft floral designs. "Have you been in your own house at all?"

She grinned. "Worked all day."

Sunny glanced at the clock on the stove. "Nearly five. Have you eaten anything?"

Again, Meredith grinned. "Drank a little milk. Ate fresh yogurt and whatever blackberries the goats didn't devour." She dumped the milk through the strainer.

"Out in the barn?"

Meredith nodded.

"Baby sister, what am I going to do with you? Sometimes I think you live out there."

"My office has a cot and a kitchenette. I stash my preserved veggies and frozen goods in my office. I should live in my barn." Meredith read the note. Another invite to Blake's ordination as youth pastor. "Oreo had unhooked the pen. All nine of them were rambling."

"We didn't go searching the fields and barns to find you. Blake was antsy to arrive at Trinity on time."

"Sorry I missed the ordination."

"From your smirk, I know you lie." Sunny stooped at the bottom cupboards. "Hey, where'd you move your plastic bowls?"

"They should be in the cupboard."

"Nope." Sunny opened the dishwasher. "You're the only person I know who empties the dishwasher as soon as the dishes are clean."

"If you don't, dirty tableware sits in the sink." Meredith put Owen on the floor and fished through the cabinets. She brought out two bowls and handed them to her sister.

Sunny gave them to Owen with a wooden spoon she took from Meredith's utensil caddy.

"I don't know where the other plasticware is. So, what brings you here now?"

"Can't a sister see her sister? Someone's got to feed her. I swan you lost another five pounds." She looked at her daughter. "Anissa, bring in the casserole. Phoebe, you can help 'Nissa carry in the last of the coconut cake Miss Nell made."

The girls ran out the back door. "Before I forget. Our van must go into the shop on Wednesday for a recall. They said they couldn't finish the repairs until late in the afternoon. Can we borrow your truck?

"I don't need my truck until the weekend. Go ahead."

"I hope seven isn't too early for us to stop by?"

Meredith leveled her eyes at her sister. "Allison Buchanan, you know. Four a.m. would be too early. Five or later is fine."

"Thanks, but don't call me Allison."

"Right. You're sunshine and knockout roses."

Sunny hugged her sister. Owen pounded the plastic as Sunny settled into the rustic captain's chair at the small table. "I'm sorry you missed the service. Everything was beautiful."

"Is Deacon Mills still attending?"

"You need to drop your attitude, Merry."

"When Hades freezes over."

"For a year, you—"

"Nine months."

"You've wallowed for nine months, and you should move on."

Meredith inhaled as her pulse pounded in her temple. She bit her lip. *Don't say anything—* "Since I was little, you've told me how to live. Stop."

Sunny shook her head. "Sometimes your temper pops like an overblown balloon."

Meredith hiked a hand on her hip. "And what does that mean?"

Sunny kissed Meredith's cheek. "It means I love you, and I'll see you Wednesday."

Parker pulled up to his modest white clapboard house and parked his Cherokee under the metal carport. "We're home, Steve."

The twelve-year-old scowled as he pressed himself into the seat. Anger narrowed his eyes, and his nostrils flared. He said nothing.

"Every place is full. You'll stay with me until we can find a home."

"And change schools. Again."

"We've got all summer to find a place in this district. We won't change schools." Parker winced. *I shouldn't promise what I may not be able to deliver.* He turned to hide his face clouded with doubt. He shoved open his door and walked to the back of the SUV where he pulled out the plastic bag containing Steve's few belongings.

The boy hadn't emerged from the vehicle.

Parker pulled at the door. "Let's go." He nodded toward the house. "You have your own room. The guest bath is yours alone."

"For how long?" Still Steve sat. Sullen. With good reason.

"I've got to be honest. My days are chaotic. They'll let me work more regular hours now with you here. When we find a permanent place—"

"I got a home." He crossed his arms and leaned back into his seat as though to glue himself to the upholstery. "With my mother."

Parker's jaw tightened. Telling Steve why living with his mother wasn't a good idea wouldn't change the child's mind. She and her current boyfriend were all the stability he knew—or what Steve thought was stability. But the boy's bruises told the real tale of his home life. "You'll stay here for a short while, until we find you a good home."

He dragged himself out of the van. "I've heard the lies before."

Without giving Parker a hand with his stuff, Steve shuffled behind him. Inside, Parker let Steve settle in the room. Time to return his mother's call.

"Mom. Sorry I missed your call."

"I figured you had your hands full with work. IsWednesday okay?"

"Wednesday?"

"Didn't you listen to your voice mail?"

He shook his head.

"Can't see you shake your head."

He chuckled. *Mom, you're a prophetess. You see all.*

"At six, I'll have dinner for you."

"I have a kid with me."

"A kid?"

"His name's Steve. All our foster homes are filled."

"You'd think someone in this county would help a young boy. Someone besides a single male."

"How about you?"

"Your father's the only wayward male I can handle." She chuckled.

"Sixty percent of the kids in our county are not with their biological parents."

"I know. You tell me regularly. Bring this one on Wednesday, but take him home again." Her voice muffled something Parker didn't make out. "Got to go. You know your needy dad."

She tried to sound tough. Still, Parker heard the tenderness in her voice. Her affection tied her apron strings tighter. Parker had to unknot them.

Chapter 3

Meredith swiped the sweat dripping from her forehead with the end of her T-shirt and squinted against the sky. Wednesday's sun rose high and erased any shade her two-foot-high tomatoes and stakes of pole beans had given her. She needed to cool off in the air conditioning and escape the Tennessee mugginess. After she tossed the last of the weeds into the wheelbarrow, she arched her back and stretched her shoulder blades. The tension from hours of stripping weeds from her garden slipped away.

Time for lunch. She had a half loaf of bread from the farmers' market—the loaf Oreo didn't eat last Sunday.

After lobbing her gardening gloves into the half-filled barrow, Meredith headed for the house. She stepped up on the porch as her backdoor swung open.

"Who ...?" She peered into the light blue, oversized eyes of a little girl. A filthy little girl with strawberry-blonde hair. From her size, not much older than Rosemary was ...

The girl's eyes widened. She dropped the plastic bag she held.

"What are you doing in my house?"

The child's gaze shifted to Meredith's right.

Meredith grabbed her shoulder. "Don't think about running. You're not going anywhere until you answer me. Who are you?"

The child studied the porch slats.

Meredith lifted the child's bony chin. "Your name is?"

"Bean."

"Well, Bean, why are you in my house?"

"I didn't see your truck, so I thought you was gone."

Meredith dropped her hand. "If I were gone, you could enter my house?"

Bean shook her head while keeping her eyes focused on the porch.

"Don't you know trespassing is illegal? I could have you arrested." Even as she said the words, she fought her smile.

Bean's head jerked up, and she held Meredith's gaze. "Please don't arrest me. I—"

"Easy." Meredith's smile refused to stay concealed. The child was a high-strung filly. Too ready to bolt.

"I needed to borrow some stuff." She looked at the bag lying on the porch.

Meredith scooped up the plastic sack and opened the bag. *No.*

No, no, no, no.

Her heart constricted so tightly Meredith was certain it'd crack in two. She clenched her fists and stared at the summer dresses. A pink one lay on top—*the* pink dress. Rosemary's favorite. Studded in rhinestones and ruffles. The princess dress that ended everything. The clothes blurred before her eyes. She blinked several times and inhaled. Her heart refused to beat. "What right do you have ...?" The words sizzled. Her palm itched to slap the child. She had no right.

But ... Instead of exploding, her heart hemorrhaged. Pain flowed in tears along the line of her nose. She swiped them away and dared to study Bean.

The child looked like a kicked stray. She scuffed her filthy flip flops against the porch and scratched her braided head.

Her chin ducked and nearly touched her collarbone as her shoulders hunched. Could she melt into the decking?

"You should've asked me. Not taken Rosie's ..." Meredith swallowed hard. She tied the handles of the plastic bag. Her sister's words rose unbidden: *You've wallowed for nine months, and you should move on.*

Meredith inhaled and looked up at the blue sky shining beyond the porch roof. A calm cerulean color. Her heart beat again—or at least thudded hollowly against her ribs. She reached out and once more lifted the child's chin with her index finger. She scrutinized Bean's frightened eyes. "You want lunch? I'm about to eat." *Lunch? What am I thinking?* Meredith studied the sky again. Without looking back at Bean, she could sense the child perking up. She turned her attention back to the waif.

Bean's shoulders straightened, and her eyes glistened. "You're not gonna arrest me?"

"Not today." *I'll feed you. Clothe you. Won't arrest you.* With a gentle hand, Meredith turned the child back into the house.

Bean nearly skipped to the table. "Thanks. I was afraid you was gonna arrest me. I might could've run, but I know you're—"

"Slow down." Meredith used a long, serrated knife to slice the loaf of bread.

Bean plopped onto the kitchen chair. The tip of her toes brushed the floor, and she folded her hands in front of her. Her lips quirked into a grin. Her eyes danced.

"You look like you're waiting for Santa Claus."

"Ain't no such thing as Santa Claus."

"True." Meredith slid the bread onto two plates. "Why do people call you Bean?" She diced an onion for the tuna salad. "You like tuna, I hope? I have peanut butter if fish is too yucky."

"I like tuna." Bean bobbed her head.

"Your name?"

Bean's eyebrows rose in question.

"What's your real name?"

"Bean." The child scrunched her forehead as though Meredith's brain synapses snapped.

"Bean's a pet name."

"Like a dog?" The child's mouth dropped.

Meredith grinned. "No. A diminutive—a fun name. Like mine. My family calls me Merry and my sister Sunny. They're not the names on our birth certificates. My real one's Meredith and Sunny's is Allison—although she'd deck anyone who called her Allison. Bean sounds like a nickname."

Bean shrugged. "My name's Bean."

"Okay."

Meredith piled tuna on the homemade bread, added the last of her garden's lettuce and sliced the sandwich diagonally. "I'm sorry the tomatoes aren't ripe. The lettuce has gone by—"

"Where?" Bean twisted her neck looking for something. "I don't see no lettuce."

Meredith had to bite her lips to keep from laughing. "The weather's too hot, so the lettuce became bitter. Also, my bread's dry but tasted great this weekend." *Or so Oreo tells me.* She slid the plate in front of the child.

Bean bit into the sandwich. Her eyes darted from side to side. Her shoulders hiked again. She looked like a stray dog guarding her treasure. Before she swallowed, she took another bite.

"Slow down. I have plenty more."

"Do you think I can take some home?"

"I'll give you the leftovers. Stale bread, bitter lettuce and all." She winked.

"This is good." Bean spoke around a mouthful of food. "I could do chores for you. You can pay me with food."

"With food?" Meredith stiffened. "You don't have to work for food."

"I don't want to go to jail." She bit into her sandwich. "I want to make restitution."

"Restitution? Do you know what the word means?"

Bean placed the sandwich carefully on the plate and leveled her eyes at Meredith. She looked like Meredith's mother when Cora Crabtree decided to act all motherly.

"I'm eight, Miss Meredith."

"All of eight?" Meredith studied the girl. So small. *I thought you were Rosie's age.* "You know what. I'd like restitution. You help me weed the garden, and I'll let you have those clothes." Her heart clenched. Her baby's clothes.

Maybe all but the sundress.

For the next two hours, after sugar cookies and a pound of grapes, Bean knelt next to Meredith and weeded. "I like green beans. Especially when Mama cooks them with bacon."

"Green beans? I could never make Rosemary eat them. Or my husband."

"When will they come home? I've never seen them around."

Meredith bit her lip to stop its quivering.

"I'd give you green beans, but my goats got into them last weekend."

Bean's head jerked. Her shoulders hunched.

"Ah. So, I blamed my kids when you ate all my veggies? No wonder your mama calls you Bean." Meredith tickled the child. "How long have you been coming here and borrowing green beans?"

"I'll pay you for them."

"No need." Meredith eyed the child. "Your company is good payment."

With the garden free of weeds, Meredith stood. "I'm tired. How about you?"

Bean got up and wiped her grimy hands against her equally filthy slacks. "I probably need to go home. Mama worries."

"Let's clean up, then I'll walk you home. I'd like to meet your mother."

Bean shook her head like a bobble-head. "You don't got to."

"Really?"

She tilted her chin. "I know the way myself."

The child splashed away most of her dirt in the sink in the powder room next to the kitchen.

Meredith took out the glittery sundress from the bag of clothes Bean had taken. She clutched it to her and inhaled. Smelled only laundry detergent from the last washing. Nothing of Rosemary remained. At last, she folded the outfit and stuffed it back in. She added their leftover lunch and double bagged the whole shebang.

"I'm clean." Bean held out her hands. "See."

Meredith took the child's hands and inspected them. "Good job." She handed the plastic bag to her. "There's a lot of stuff here. I'll drive you home when my sister returns my truck."

"No, thank you, Miss Meredith. I use a shortcut and will be home lickety-split."

Meredith stepped out the front door and watched the child trot up the front walk. At the road, she turned left. She'd give Bean a head start and then follow. Something was up. No eight-year-old willingly weeded a field of vegetables for restitution. Heaven have mercy. What child loved green beans?

Bean disappeared down the hill.

As Meredith stepped off the front porch, a vehicle rumbled up Hen Waddle Hollow. Her truck and her sister's van turned into the driveway.

Meredith studied the road Bean walked. *I'll have to talk to your mama another time.*

The van door rattled. Sunny yelled, "Stay put, girls."

Meredith smiled at her rollicking family.

"Thanks, Merry." Her brother-in-law, Blake, hopped out of her truck. "Do you want it here or back by the barn?"

"I'll take care of the truck." Meredith reached for the keys he offered. "Did you see a little girl down the road?"

"Nope. No one walks in Tennessee."

Two tornadoes scrambled out of the van. "Aunt Merry, can we pet the goats?" 'Nissa and Phoebe didn't wait for an answer. They raced toward the pen.

Sunny lowered the vehicle's window. "No, girls. We need to go home so Daddy can go back to the bank. If he doesn't work, we don't eat."

The girls looked as though someone poked them with a pin, and the air buoying them leaked out. If they could pout any deeper, they'd trip on their bottom lips.

Blake pecked Meredith on the cheek. "You want a couple of human kids?"

"I love them but can't deny you their zest."

"Thanks again for the truck. See you later this week?"

"I can't hide from you, and especially not from your obnoxious wife. When I try, you always find me."

Sunny thumbed her nose at Meredith as she rounded the van. She climbed into the passenger side, and Blake took the wheel.

Meredith waved as they drove off. When they disappeared, she climbed into her truck. Turning left, she crawled down

Hen Waddle Hollow. At every path, behind every trailer, she slowed—any slower and she'd be parked.

No Bean.

Parker pulled his jeep behind a Mercedes in his family's circular driveway. *Fancy company.* Of course, his mother failed to mention she'd invited someone else to Wednesday's dinner.

He stepped up to the door of the brick house perched on an outcropping of rock high in the Cumberlands. People drooled over this view.

They wouldn't when snow fell.

The thought of a flurry, or a flake or two, made the town's people hunker down for Armageddon. Up here? The s-word was a four-letter atrocity.

He turned and studied Jacksboro below. The hills rose on the east side hiding the hollers and lanes tucked into the landscape edging the cockamamie Norris Lake. When the Tennessee Valley Authority, the TVA, flooded the hollers, the rivers ran into a million inlets and curved around the high ground. He inhaled. His mother's roses scented the area like a woman's cloying perfume. With a sigh, he turned to face his fate. Or whatever awful spinster from one of her clubs Mom wanted him to meet.

He stepped into the foyer.

"We're in the living room, Parker. Is Steve with you?" His mother's voice sounded perky and sunshiny, a pitch or two higher than her normal tone.

He stepped into the living room. Seated in front of the picture window which displayed the valley below, were his mother and father and, as he figured, a lone woman.

But!

What a woman! Thirtyish, if he had to guess. Slim but womanly. She curved in all the right places. Her fitted jeans and tank top made him wonder if he'd be able to concentrate on anything she said or did. She had more curves than Lily.

"No Steve?" His mother asked.

"Nope." His mother's question brought him back to reality. "We found a home. Probably the last one in the Jacksboro school district."

"Who'd you con?" His father asked. "The Andersons?"

Parker shook his head.

"Then the Baskins gave in."

"Bingo." He turned to the stranger. "I'm Parker Snow. I imagine you figured that out already."

"This is Felicity Murphy. She joined the quilting guild last week, so I wanted to get to know her better," his mother said. "We love having a young'un working with us."

Felicity smiled and rose from the love seat. "I'm not so young." She nodded her head toward his mother. "And Miss Samantha, you're not old."

Mom waved her off, but her grin said the compliment delighted her.

Parker shook Felicity's hand.

Her handshake was firm, but her skin soft.

He shivered and hoped no one noticed.

"Sit." His mother indicated the seat next to their guest.

Seeing as the only other chairs here were spindly, uncomfortable ones, he settled next to Felicity on the loveseat.

"Felicity is a master quilter."

Parker smiled, then glanced at Dad who fiddled with his cell. He caught his father's attention.

His dad's eyes seemed to say, "Sorry, Son. Sewing? Can't help with the conversation."

"What line of work are you in, Parker?" Felicity shifted in the seat and faced him.

His heart skipped a beat. She might be her mother's acquaintance, but she was cute. Her eyes, light blue, rimmed with dark brown around the irises like they couldn't decide what color they should be, made him forget her trim shape.

"Parker?" His mother asked. "Are you going to answer Felicity?" His mother smirked a half-smile. His tongue-tied actions let her know she'd discovered someone who could take his mind off Lily.

"I'm sorry. Work has me absentminded. What did you ask?" He tried not to look at her eyes. Such a contrast to her dark skin and hair.

"Your job?" Felicity tilted her head.

"Social worker."

"In what area?"

"My mother hasn't filled you in?"

Felicity's chin dipped, and she shifted in her seat. "Samantha said something about social work and children. Do you have a hard job?"

"Yes." He offered no more.

They sat in silence for several awkward beats.

His mother looked at her watch. "Dinner will be ready in about five minutes." She stood and turned to her husband. "Darrick, can you give me a hand?"

His father rose and tossed his phone onto the coffee table. He winked at Parker and trailed his wife.

"Beautiful view," Felicity said.

Parker nodded. "I don't notice it much anymore. Grew up in this house."

Silence yawned between them. Coworkers and kids comprised Parker's conversation. With a non-coworker, privacy issues sealed his lips. What did you say to a pretty woman? Child abuse would be a relationship killer.

"I work at Weston's Funeral Home in LaFollette." Felicity's matter-of-fact tone made Parker think she did clerical work.

"Receptionist? Secretary?"

"Funeral director."

He jolted forward. "Pardon?"

"Surprised?"

He nodded.

"I'm mostly Kit Weston's mortician. He greets the people and arranges the funeral details. I make the parlor and the deceased beautiful." She laughed. "I guess you didn't expect me to say this."

He shook his head.

"We have lots in common. Both of us deal with sad endings."

You understand.

"Tell me about this Steve."

The tale of the angry boy who no one would take spilled out. Or at least the points he could reveal.

Tears brimmed Felicity's widened eyes. Thankfully, she didn't take his hand or say anything. She simply listened as he told his tale.

A timer dinged. After a few seconds, Parker's father stepped into the living room. "We've got about ten minutes until dinner, not five." Again. he winked at his son. "You know your mother and her timing."

Parker twisted his lips. After nine months home, this wasn't his first set-up.

"What would you like to tide you over until dinner's ready?"

"Nothing for me. Let me hunger for bloody rare meat." Felicity laughed, a pleasant sound, a woman with a warm sense of humor.

Her chuckle melted Parker and erased the thoughts of another child he couldn't help. He wasn't going to mind this evening.

Chapter 4

As Meredith slipped the first wrapper around her lavender-lemon soap, the barn door creaked open splaying sunlight across the hay-strewn floor. Dust motes danced in the quiet air.

"Sunny, you know I have to pack for the festival tomorrow. If you're going to bug me, help." Meredith tied a lavender ribbon around The Merry Goat label then turned when she placed the bar into the box.

Bean stood in the doorway backlit by the June sunshine.

Without thinking, Meredith grinned. She puffed out air and blew a wayward strand of hair off her face. "Here for more restitution?"

As though the word restitution set her free, Bean skipped to Meredith trailing the stench of cigarettes on her clothes. "Can I help?"

"Does your mama know you're here?"

The kid looked down. "I asked her. She says fine."

Meredith stretched her legs under her worktable and cocked her head. *Today, I'm going to talk with your mama, little Bean.*

"What do you want me to do?" Bean dragged a nearby chair close to Meredith.

"How are you at tying bows?" Meredith picked up a bar of soap from the container. "Can you make them as nice as this?"

Bean bobbed her head. She leaned so close their shoulders touched.

"Let me see."

The girl snatched a strand of lavender ribbon and wrapped the slim strand of grosgrain around the bar. Once tied, she studied the box half-full of finished product and frowned. With quick movements, Bean untied then refastened the ribbon. "See. Just as good."

Meredith cocked her head and puckered her lips. She faked studying the result. "Yep. You're now a master." She handed Bean the bag holding the cut ribbons. "Start tying. When we run out of ribbons, cut more."

The child's eyes widened. "You'll need more than this?"

"Yep. Gotta sell a boatload of soap and lotion, or some little Bean will go hungry."

"Where're you gonna sell them?" Bean bit her lip as she focused on the ribbon.

"During the summer, I sell at the farmers' market on Market Square. When there's a festival, I take The Merry Goat there."

The child squinted at Meredith.

"You look confused. What're you thinking?"

"Why do you take your goats to parties? And how do you tell which goat's happy? They look the same to me."

Meredith covered her mouth to hide her laugh. "I don't take the goats to parties. Why do you think they go?"

"Ain't a festival a party?"

Meredith nodded. "Sometimes, but these are fancy markets where people gather to buy local goods."

"You said you'd take a merry goat to them?" Bean puckered her lips as though she were trying to make a kindergartener understand.

"I'm not talking about happy nannies. My company's name is The Merry Goat. See?" She ran her finger under the logo on the cardboard wrapping her soap.

"Why do you call your soap The Merry Goat?" Bean peered at the bar she held upside down as though reading the label.

Meredith turned the soap right side up. She frowned. *Can she read?* "Merry is short for Meredith." She pointed at herself. "Goat ..." She hitched a thumb toward the pasture. "Do you see the joke?"

Bean nodded and tied her third ribbon in half the time she took on the first two. "Lookit!"

"Great job, Little Bean."

"Ain't little. Can I go to the farmers' market with you tomorrow?"

"Not going to the market. Tomorrow's the Lavender Festival out in Oak Ridge. Festivals pay my bills and let me have fun. The Market keeps me from bankruptcy."

"Huh?"

"Never mind. I'll ask your mother if you can go to the next market."

Bean bent over another bar to work on the ribbon.

After an hour packing soap, Meredith helped Bean tie the remaining bars. At last, she stood. "Aren't you sore from sitting so long?"

"No. I like helping."

"Want lunch?"

The girl nearly leapt to her feet.

"I'll take that as a yes. Peanut butter okay?"

"Do you have jelly?"

"As a matter of fact, I made a fresh batch of blackberry jam. If you don't mind seeds and chunks of fruit, we can use the jam.

"I like blackberries." Bean scratched her head, then slipped her hand into Meredith's.

It felt warm but rough, like Cinderella's. Meredith squeezed the hand and inhaled. Mingled with the smell of tobacco, she caught whiffs of strawberry wafting up.

Hand in hand, they walked toward the barn door.

Bean stopped next to a bicycle hanging beside the door. "That's pretty."

"Thank you." Meredith tugged the child, and they stepped out of the barn and into the light.

The sun highlighted the rosy hue of Bean's hair. Strands of strawberry-blonde blew in the wind making Meredith chuckle.

"What's so funny?"

"Not funny. Fun. Your hair smells like strawberry and matches the color."

"Mama washed it for me with strawberry shampoo at the lake."

"At the lake?"

Bean nodded. The action made the oddity of washing her hair in a lake seem normal. "I like to swim and wash and play all at the same time. Except, the shampoo sure doesn't taste like strawberries."

"I imagine not."

"Shampoo tastes like orange peel."

"Because you're not supposed to eat shampoo. They've got to make the flavor bad."

In the house, Meredith picked up her bread. "Today, all I have is store-bought."

Bean knelt on a chair near her at the counter. "I'll help. Store-bought's what Mama uses. She buys bread from the outlet in LaFollette."

Meredith eyed the child. So sad to be so poor. Her own insurance money didn't stretch as far as John's salary had, but she lived comfortably. When she finished her degree ...

More than finances, she missed John's help around the farm. Meredith got the work done without too much meddling from her mother. Or from Sunny. Still, her life oozed prosperity compared to Bean's.

Meredith untwisted the bread tie and placed two slices on a plate.

"Why's the bread brown?" Bean crinkled her nose as she pulled a sunflower seed off the crust. "Why're there so many seeds?"

"I use whole grain."

"We eat white bread."

"You didn't complain last Wednesday."

Bean pooched her lips. "That bread was homemade and didn't have no seeds."

"Here, we eat this or nothing."

"Then I'll eat this." Without being asked, Bean picked up the knife and carefully spread the creamy peanut butter over the bread in a thin, smooth layer—like Rosemary used to. On the opposite piece of bread, she layered the jam, then slapped the two sides together.

Meredith pulled out a quart of goat's milk while Bean placed both plates on the table. Bean sipped the milk but made no comment about the gamey flavor unlike Sunny. *Ew. Your milk smells like goat.* Her kids held their noses. Bean drank the milk like she slugged down the stuff every day.

Probably did. Meredith hadn't misplaced bags of frozen milk. A little "restitution-worker" had been helping herself.

After lunch, Bean rinsed the plates and slipped them into the dishwasher.

While the child worked, Meredith found her mixer and a pint of cream.

"What're you doing?" Bean asked.

"Making whipped cream.

"You can make whipped cream with milk?"

"Not the milk, but the cream." She turned on the mixer. With wide eyes, Bean studied Meredith.

"Hand me the sugar." Meredith nodded to the bowl.

"My mama uses the cream in a can. Me and my sisters squirt it in our mouths."

"You sound like my husband."

"Where is he?"

"He only ate like that when we went to his folks. I always make my own here." Meredith sprinkled a little sugar into the froth and beat the mixture for thirty seconds. "Grab a banana." She nodded toward the bunch on the counter. "I'll fetch the ice cream."

"Ice cream! I love ice cream. Especially from Dairy Queen. You know we got one in town now."

"I know."

Bean handed over the banana she twisted from the bunch.

Meredith sliced the fruit over the ice cream. She thought she'd given Bean first place in a beauty pageant with the way her eyes lit up and her shoulders straightened.

The child didn't eat like a beauty queen, though. More like a hungry puppy. She hunched over and curled her arm around the bowl as though protecting her treasure from predators.

After licking the bowl, Bean shoved it away. "Thank you, Miss Meredith. Ice cream is delicious."

"I hadn't noticed." Meredith smiled. "Your mama's going to worry. Don't you need to go home?"

The child sat upright. "What's the time?"

Meredith pointed at the clock on the stove.

Bean looked in the general direction. Scratched her head, then stared at Meredith.

"Four. Time for you to take me to your mother."

"She's at my aunt's right now. I'll take you there next time."

"At your aunt's? She left you alone all afternoon?"

Bean studied the window overlooking the back porch. "I'm not alone. I'm with you."

"Let me walk with you."

"No. She's not home. We'll go next time I come here."

"Promise?"

"Yep."

Meredith frowned as she watched Bean trot down the road. Meredith longed to trail her, but then the bleats from her flock reminded her she had too much to do to prep for the Lavender Festival. Bean helped immensely, but not as much as her family did.

The sun set behind the Cumberlands as Parker drove Felicity home from their first date Friday night. Light lingered until after nine o'clock during the summer months. You could watch the sun set in the cool of late evening. Parker drove Felicity past Cove Lake. Before them, the best view of the mountains rose. He pointed to an outcropping of rock. "My folks' place perches right there."

Felicity nestled back in the seat and said nothing.

He glanced her way.

With her hands on her lap, she let out a long sigh. Everything about her spoke of contentment. She didn't need to say anything. He heard her agreement in her posture and quiet. Had Lily ever acted this way?

Too soon, he pulled in front of her house. Her brick home with manicured lawn and gardens put his to shame. Despite her obvious prosperity, she didn't seem to mind riding in his jeep cluttered with clipboards, fast-food wrappers, and emergency supplies. He hurried around to her side and opened the door.

Felicity smiled. Full, natural lips—not like those of actresses who looked as though bees stung them. Her large smile revealed perfect teeth and crinkled her eyes. She offered him her hand. She didn't pull it away once she stepped out.

Electricity pulsated up his arm. His breath caught. Had a year passed since Lily left him? The pain prickled the back of his neck. His stomach tightened as memories he couldn't squash pressed against his heart. One week before their wedding, she claimed she wasn't called to marriage. One month later, she married the music minister from their church. After they settled the wedding debacle, life dragged him from Paducah back to mommy and Jacksboro's Department of Children's Services. His move made him low man on the DCS totem pole. He didn't think his life would heal.

Still grasping his hand, Felicity turned to him and tilted her head. "Thank you. I had a wonderful time." Her breath puffed against his cheek. So close. So pleasant.

Should he? His heart hammered like a teenager's. He leaned toward her.

She arched upward.

He slipped his arms around her waist, and her arms encircled his shoulders. He kissed her warm lips. He couldn't let his mother know she found someone who appealed to him. Samantha Snow would preen as she prepared for his wedding to Felicity Murphy.

Back in the jeep, he grinned, feeling like the village idiot. Something about this mortician unsettled him.

Maybe he could love again.

He thought of Lily, and an unpleasant shiver shook his spine.

Chapter 5

At the beginning of the week, Meredith removed the screen from her bedroom window, leaned it against the wall and climbed out of the dormer. Watching the sun waken in the cool mornings made her glad to be alive. Here she'd forget that God abandoned her.

More than a year passed after their marriage before John accepted her weird roof sitting—even on warm winter days. He finally gave in and began to hand coffee or her Bible out to her.

He'd balked when Rosie, as a toddler, joined her mother. But he lost the battle long before Rosemary was born.

On this Monday, though, the sun had climbed well into the sky. Meredith leaned against the building and cupped her steaming mug of java. After the insane weekend, lying in late felt decadent. Divine.

Meredith tipped her head to the sky and smiled at her use of decadent and divine in the same thought. Existence twined good and evil like tares and wheat.

Too bad all hints of sunrise vanished. At least the fog danced as usual early in the day. Out beyond the tree line, the mist swayed over the water, making obvious where the green waters of Norris Lake lay.

Where Bean and her sisters had bathed.

The brush moved across the road. She leaned forward. *A deer? No, too much movement in the weeds. My goats?* The leaves moved again, and the back of a strawberry-blonde head came into view. *Bean, why didn't you let me know you'd been here? Have I denied you anything once I realized you were the one who pilfered every morsel of food I owned?*

Bean emerged beyond the grasses of the overgrown field and hit the abandoned road to the old Wheeler place. Moss and weeds now crowded the abandoned road. Instead of heading toward her home, or where Bean hinted her home lay, she turned to the right, toward the Wheeler house.

Time to find out what's true about your life.

Meredith scrambled into her room and threw on her jeans and a long-sleeved shirt. If she was going to jog through a pasture filled with ticks, poison ivy, and brambles, she'd protect her extremities.

She loped out of the house—glad to see her goats safely tucked behind the sturdy fence. From their bleats, they weren't happy about her heading away from them. Away from their milking, and perhaps more, away from their food.

After trotting across the road and snaking through the trees separating Hen Waddle Hollow from the field, she picked her way through blackberry bushes and sumac while scoping the ground for shiny, three-leaved vines. Within minutes, she found a well-worn path in the overgrown field. *Bean had visited me long enough to wear a path?* Soon the trail opened to the Wheeler Road. Bean had turned to the right this morning. So did Meredith.

In a few minutes, a dilapidated house came into view.

The front porch listed to the right. Slats of pressure-treated wood pulled loose from the frame. Above the porch, the overhang which supported a couple of rooms canted to the side. Collapse seemed imminent.

Old appliances and a sodden mattress, probably filled with rodents, littered the porch. Ripped garbage bags spilled their guts, further blocking the front door.

Meredith studied the precarious overhang. Even when well-kept, the addition didn't meet code. This current state threatened an avalanche.

Following the well-worn track to the back, she skirted the house. The path ended. "Bean? Where are you?"

Shushing drifted from the inside. Typical of urchins. When they tried to keep their peers quiet, they were always louder than the ones they wanted to silence.

Without knocking, Meredith stepped into the derelict kitchen. She gasped.

Dishes piled in the sink. Old food cleaved to the counters, and something blue and smelly stuck to her Tupperware bowls, the ones Sunny couldn't find a week ago. Candle wax-coated wine bottles.

A table stacked with papers and a Coleman camp stove and lantern sat under a window streaked with years of rain and dust. A hole pierced the top of the window like someone had shot through the glass. The place literally, or maybe litter-ly, smelled like a dump.

A child's cry brought Meredith into the living room.

Here Bean cowered against the stairs, her hand over a toddler's mouth. The child, hugged tight to Bean's chest, couldn't be older than eighteen months or a malnourished two-year-old.

Another girl hunkered next to Bean. At least Meredith thought the ragged child was female. The kid looked to be four or five. She clawed at her head.

Meredith shuddered. *What's in your tangled mop, child?*

"Bean, where are your parents?" Meredith crossed her arms. Anger at the absent parents churned her stomach.

"I don't know." Her voice choked in a pathetic whisper. Her hand dropped from the crying baby's mouth.

"Give me your brother?"

"She's my sister. Crystal."

Meredith picked up the child. A makeshift diaper, one of Meredith's missing dishtowels, did little to stop the seepage from her sodden bottom. Two safety pins barely held the improvised diaper in place. Meredith grimaced.

"Why didn't you tell me you lived like this? I thought we were friends."

Bean leapt to her feet. Her itchy sister clung to her. Bean's wide eyes shone with tears. They begged Meredith. "We are friends. My mama said we had to be secret or the police would arrest us."

"No one will arrest little children."

"But—"

"Do you trust me?"

Bean nodded.

Meredith bobbed the toddler in her arms. The baby quieted and found her thumb. She lay her head on Meredith's shoulder. Meredith shivered and looked through the thin blonde, baby hair. Did she see a louse? She knelt before Bean and laid Crystal down and removed the sodden towel. A bare bum repulsed her less than the filthy cloth. As she picked Crystal up once more, she leveled her eyes at Bean. "Do they always leave you alone?"

"Only at night, sometimes. They go to a party when we're safe asleep. Mama makes sure I know to take care of my sisters. Sometimes if Mama has to run to the store with Danny, she has me watch them. She pays me with Tootsie Pops."

"When did you see them last?"

"They went to a party in Caryville after I got home from your house. The day we wrapped soap. They never leave Crystal and Roxie alone without me."

"Come." She offered her free hand. "Take Roxie's hand." Meredith's nose crinkled as she uttered the name. *I thought Bean was a bad name. But Roxie and Crystal? Too close to drug names.* "We're going to my house. We'll clean you up."

"You're not going to arrest us?"

"No." *You are obsessed with being incarcerated.* She struggled to steady her voice. "No police officer will take you into custody. I promise." *I'm calling DCS, but no one will imprison you.*

Roxie scratched again.

Meredith's shoulders scrunched with Roxie's action. *After I call the DCS, I'll hose you off in the barn.*

Life moved perfectly for Parker. No calls came in at work. He could catch up on his paperwork. Today he'd check in on Steve. He thumped his file cabinet closed. His phone rang. "Parker Snow."

"This is Meredith Jaynes. I live at 518 Hen Waddle Hollow."

"How can I help you?" Although he already knew. If she was patched through to him, she had kids with questionable lives.

"I found three girls living in a house without water or electric. Probably filled with mold and bubonic plague."

He doubted the plague, but mold was a certainty. "Go ahead."

"I hope I'm not out of line, but the oldest two are in the tub, and I'm going to shave the middle girl's hair."

"Whoa. No shaving."

"Okay. But she's full of jumping critters. The youngest has a diaper rash that makes leprosy look good."

He smiled at her exaggeration. He liked a sense of humor. "Where are their parents?"

"The oldest, who calls herself Bean, hasn't seen her mother or Danny, her mother's boyfriend, since Friday evening. The child spent Friday here, helping me."

"You knew about ..." He clamped his teeth together.

"No. I thought they were poor. I didn't know where Bean lived until this morning." She paused.

He could almost see her swallow hard.

"I had no idea *how* she lived, or I never would've allowed the girls to stay in *that* place a second after I'd met Bean. My stomach wanted to hurl." Her voice, although soft, seethed with anger. "You have no idea how awful their home is."

I know. Believe me. I've seen everything. "Okay." Parker blew out his cheeks and blinked. "Five-one-eight Hen Waddle Hollow, you said. In Jacksboro?" He scribbled the address on a sticky note from his desk.

"Yes."

"I'll be there in twenty." He disconnected the call. No foster homes opened up since Wednesday. Where was he going to stow three kids? Siblings always wanted to stay together. Life would work better if they stayed as a unit.

Crystal, dry, fed, and her bottom slathered in udder balm, and diapered in another dishcloth, slept on the couch. Meredith laid cushions from a chair on the floor to soften any fall the toddler might take. Now she needed to check on the older girls.

And take care of the lice.

She'd nipped a few nits from Crystal's head. Thin blonde hair made black bugs easy to spot. Hopefully the sleeping toddler wouldn't infest Meredith's couch.

How do I eliminate them?

Mayo? Where'd she hear that mayonnaise worked?

Ah. TV.

In an old episode of *The Office*, Pam and Jim's kids had lice. Pam infected the whole office, so she brought in a jar of mayo and smeared the goop over everyone's head.

Meredith had mayonnaise.

She knocked on the bathroom door. *Should she enter? Would their parents or these kids think she was kinky?*

"Come in, Miss Meredith."

She opened the door a crack and averted her eyes. "Have you washed?"

"We're playing."

"I'll be right back." She opened the door to Rosemary's room. As always, when she stepped inside her daughter's room, breathing came hard. She hadn't changed a thing since before hospice. Rosie's quilt lay, unwrinkled, on the bed. Bright squares in pink—her favorite color—interspersed with sky blue, sunshine yellow, and grass green. She loved brightness. Was sunshine personified. Rosemary's Baby Alive doll perched on the pillow as if the doll would open its eyes and cry for Rosemary. Baby Alive. Meredith gulped. The irony of the name of her child's favorite toy stung like glass shards in her heart.

She closed her eyes and tried to breathe. Wished God would heal her. Knew he wouldn't. When the feeling passed, Meredith opened the dresser drawer.

She found underwear in one. Nightshirts in another. They'd swim on Roxie, probably be a little snug on Bean. But they'd only wear them until DCS took them. *I'm sure they've got stashes of clothes. And lice remover.*

Back at the bathroom, she nudged the door open a crack and tossed in the clothes. "Have you washed your hair?"

"We need help."

She entered, knelt by the tub. With Roxie braced against her arm, she tilted the child and scooped handfuls of water over her head. The discomfort of bathing a stranger fled as though she'd known these kids from birth. After lathering and scrubbing Roxie's head until her hair squeaked between her fingers, she washed Bean's.

Ten minutes later, two girls with tangled mops and damp skin tottered behind her like baby chicks into the kitchen.

"Sit here, Roxie." Meredith lifted her and sat her on the table.

The comb slid easily through her thin hair. Then Meredith massaged mayo into the child's scalp.

Bean, kneeling on the kitchen chair, leaned in close. "What're you doing?" Her puzzled eyes looked more like a quizzical old lady than a child.

"Killing lice." She coated every square inch. "Checking you next."

Someone knocked at the front door.

"Come in." She should check, but no one ever wandered out here without reason. The guy at DCS said he'd be here in twenty. And that's exactly how much time had passed.

"Hello," a man called from the living room.

"Back here. In the kitchen." *Where I can fumigate easily.*

A tall, lean man with a square chin stepped inside. He stuck out his hand. "I'm Parker Snow from DCS. He held

42

out his identification." His head tilted as his eyes squinted. "Are you making a salad?" He eyed Roxie, who now sat in the chair next to Bean.

"Yep. Lice-salad."

"Vinegar works too."

"This worked on *The Office*. That's good enough for me." She chuckled as she picked up the jar and squinted at the label then handed him the mayo. "See? Vinegar is a main ingredient."

He grinned.

"I saw a child dozing on the couch. Is she one of the three you told me about?"

"Yes." *His chin's not like John's.* Meredith flushed. Nine months. Shouldn't notice another man. "And these two munchkins." Without thinking, she bent and kissed Roxie's mayo-coated-louse-infested head. She wiped mayonnaise from her lips and screwed up her lips. "Ew. I forgot."

"You said they were living in an abandoned house."

She nodded as she wrapped Roxie's head in a towel. "Come here, Bean."

Bean nearly leapt into her lap as though Meredith offered the kid a trip to Dollywood. Bean leaned against Meredith as she worked the comb through her hair. This one tangled more than Roxie's.

Parker Snow tapped at his iPad, then fumbled through his briefcase.

Meredith bent close to Bean's hair and moved strands around. Found a few creepy-crawlies and nipped them with her fingernails. *Gross, little buggers.* She continued working the hair but found no more lice. Fortunately.

"Where is this house?"

She looked up at Parker Snow. He wore dorky round glasses, but they contrasted with his long, narrow face. The glasses made him look smart and hip. She ducked when heat rose up her neck. She tugged on Bean's tangle-free hair. The child didn't seem to mind the extra combing. "There are two ways to go there. Head south for about a quarter mile and pick up the actual road or cut across there." She pointed toward the front of the house, then slathered mayo over Bean's head.

Parker shuffled his paperwork. "The cops will be here any minute—"

"Cops!" Bean jumped up and clutched her hands over her chest. "Miss Meredith, you promised."

"You won't be arrested. I promise."

Parker grinned. His too perfectly aligned teeth paid homage to years of orthodontics. "No. I can promise too. You won't be arrested." He turned his attention back to Meredith. "When the sheriffs arrive, we'll need to see the girls' home."

"Sure." She wrapped Bean's head in a towel, stood and took their hands. In the living room, she shifted Crystal who snuffled slightly, but didn't wake. "Bean says Crystal is two. I haven't seen her walk. Roxie's said nothing since I've had her. They're going to need PT and probably other therapies." She turned to Roxie. "Sit here and watch your sister, so she doesn't roll off the couch."

Roxie nodded. The towel shifted, and she grabbed it.

"Let me." Meredith's heart melted as the girl ducked her head.

Roxie looked up from under long eyelashes.

Meredith re-tightened the turban as a vehicle rumbled up the front drive.

Car doors slammed. Meredith moved the curtain away from the picture window. Two cruisers parked in her driveway. A couple of cops faced each other and chatted.

"The ..." she gazed at Bean, "our friends are here."

A knock announced the officers.

"Come in."

A short, lithe officer and a taller, bulkier one, stepped inside.

"DCS called," the short officer said.

"Here are the kids, Robin." Parker Snow turned to Meredith. "This is Sergeant Robin Calhoun." He then pointed to the heavyset one. "Detective Drew Carroll."

"The sleeping beauty is Crystal," Meredith said. "Our lice-ridden Carmen Mirandas in the turbans are Roxie and Bean."

"Where did you find them?" Detective Carroll asked.

Meredith gave directions, but the cops cocked their heads and looked at each other.

Officer Carroll pursed his lips. "Where?"

"I can show you." She lifted Crystal, who didn't move.

Parker took the child from her and laid her back down. "You stay here with the little ones." He knelt before Bean. "Can you show us where you live?"

The child trembled and pressed herself against the back of the sofa.

"We have to see if your parents are there," Parker Snow said.

Bean looked up at Meredith.

"Go with Mr. Snow, honey. He's safe, and he'll bring you right back to me." She inhaled a sharp breath. *They'd be taken away once they returned. No need to tell her now.* "I absolutely promise. You're not going to jail. Right, Mr. Snow?"

Parker held out his hand. "No jail for you."

"We'll be here when you return." She gave the cops directions to the road a vehicle could maneuver. Sort of. Her heart filled with rocks as she watched them leave.

"You live here?" Parker asked.

Bean nodded.

"For how long?" As if the duration mattered. He'd never seen worse conditions.

The girl shrugged.

"Where do you go to school?" If he knew their school, he could find out her name.

"Mama homeschools us. She doesn't want the government to arrest us."

He licked his lips. *Right.* He raised his iPad and took photos, especially the pile of clothes and toys and Coleman apparatus. Proof the girls stayed here.

The cops scribbled notes. "We've got most of what we need." Detective Carroll looked at Bean. "You don't know your real name."

"Bean."

"Bean what?" Sergeant Robin Calhoun asked.

She shrugged.

He glanced at Parker. "Going to be hard to trace." He looked back at the child. "And your sisters' last names?"

"Just Roxie and Crystal."

He nodded. "Well, Snow, we'll leave them with you. As soon as we find something out, we'll let you know."

Parker returned to Meredith's, and the cops drove off.

Within ten minutes, the girls, still sealed in towel turbans, ate ice cream on Meredith's back porch. Bean's delighted chatter made the children sound like they attended a birthday party.

Parker leaned against the kitchen counter.

Meredith stood with her back to him and fussed with the coffee pot. "Did you find anything out from the sheriffs?"

"No." He picked up an 8x10 photo of Meredith posed with a man and a pretty little girl who reminded him of the

Wendy's mascot, given her tight, reddish braids and freckled face. The man looked familiar. "You know more than we do right now."

Meredith turned as she reached for a cupboard. She stumbled back. Her eyes remained fixed on the photo in his hands.

"I know him." Parker tapped the glass. "Isn't this John, John ...?" He grinned. "Of course. John Jaynes. Given your last name, you married him. Where is he now?"

Meredith handed him a mug bearing a slogan, 'I know men, so I keep goats.' She turned back to the coffee maker and poured another cup that said, 'My home's a barn.' A picture of a black and white goat with floppy ears graced this one. "Have a seat. Do you want milk or cream? And a disclaimer. I only serve goat milk."

He studied her back. *Avoiding my question? Why?* "Sugar and goat milk is fine." Parker placed the frame back on the shelf and sat in a captain's chair at the small round table. He fished out his papers and his iPad again as Meredith got the coffee condiments.

"Here's the deal," Parker said. "We don't have a home capable of taking three children."

"You can't separate them." Meredith sat across from him.

He gave his head several long, slow shakes. "How about you taking them in?" He glanced around the kitchen. "Your house is small but clean and pleasant."

She jerked upright. "I'm not prepared to care for three kids. I live alone. In six weeks, I start school. Need to finish my Vet Health Science degree at LMU. Insurance and soap making only do so much. I need a more stable income."

"Your husband?"

She shuddered.

He blinked. Something niggled at the back of his mind. Suddenly, he remembered. His jaw dropped, and words stuck in his throat. He took a deep breath. Exhaled. "I'm sorry. I didn't mean to be insensitive."

The slim woman sipped her coffee. Long sleeves hung halfway over her hands, giving her a vulnerable, little girl look. Reddish-blonde strands of hair had slipped from her ponytail. She looked as though she tried to hide behind them. Her downcast eyes wouldn't meet his.

"John's accident happened about the time I came back to Jacksboro." He looked away. An awkward silence filled the room. "I can't recall the details, though." He turned back to Meredith and studied every movement.

Meredith stared at her finger rimming her cup.

"I knew John a little in school. He was a few years ahead of me. I don't remember you, though."

"Went to Norris. Met John at LMU."

Bean clattered in through the back door carrying three bowls. "I'll put them in the dishwasher for you."

"Leave them for now, and go keep your sisters busy."

They sipped coffee silently as Bean rejoined her sisters on the porch.

"Can you take any of them?" Parker asked. "Bean? Seeing as you're closest to her?"

Her mouth worked as though fighting with herself. Her eyes turned glassy. She looked at Parker. "Bean can stay. I already love her, but I don't know how I can handle the other two. They seem to have special needs. My tuition's been paid. As I said—"

"School."

She studied her cup sitting on the table grasped in her hands.

"Can you take them for a little while? A week or two? We have no homes available."

"I'm not certified as a foster parent. Don't you have to take classes?"

"I can check your home now. By Thursday, the judge can rule on placement. From there we'll work our way to certification."

"I'm barely solvent now."

"Social Services supplies an EBT card, Tenncare, and a stipend."

"Money's not the issue. I ..."

Parker tapped information on the iPad.

Meredith drew designs in pooled condensation on the table. "If I don't take them, they won't stay together?"

Parker Snow shook his head.

She looked beyond him as though eyeing the girls.

"I'll be honest. We have almost no homes open in the county, and none that will take in three girls. They will be separated."

"No."

He jerked at her vehemence.

"Sorry. I didn't mean to be so brusque, but they have to stay together."

Parker shrugged.

"We ... um, I have a day bed with a trundle in John's study downstairs. If I don't raise the trundle, Crystal can sleep close to the floor. Roxie will sleep on the raised bed." She shuddered and peeked up at him. Her luminous eyes talked of pain he didn't understand. "Rosie's room has a bed."

"Rosie? Who's Rosie?"

"My late daughter." She stirred her coffee furiously as though cream and sugar hadn't yet dissolved. Her breaths came fast, and she didn't meet Parker's eyes. Finally, she peered up at him. "*Please* find their parents—" She held up a hand and stood. Meredith turned her back to Parker. While staring at something, or nothing, on the ceiling, she crossed her arms. "If you find those awful people, lock them up. How could they have treated these girls this way? Find them a good home. Until then, they'll live here."

Parker's muscles softened. He wasn't sure if he grinned, but inside, he was jigging like Bo Jangles. "Do you want to show me around?"

"Look all you want."

Checking out the tiny house didn't take long. Two bedrooms and a full bathroom upstairs—towels and water still damp lay on the floor. A study, living room, kitchen, and half-bath downstairs. Maybe twelve hundred square feet. Clean. Well maintained. He finished his check and went to his jeep.

There, he dug through emergency supplies and filled a few plastic bags. In one, he tucked a bottle of Rid Lice and an electric lice comb.

Mayo may help the girls now, but this would eliminate all louse infestation.

He returned to Mrs. Jaynes's home. "Here." He offered the bag to Meredith.

"What's this?" She looked inside. "I passed inspection?"

He couldn't tell if her smile was one of joy or fear.

Chapter 6

The girls romped along the fence to the goat pen, or rather, Roxie and Bean romped. Crystal sat in the shade. She laughed and clapped her hands.

Meredith headed back to the house at one o'clock. The girls had only eaten ice cream while Parker Snow completed his paperwork, but they didn't complain. The kids should've been nagging her for food hours ago.

Priorities had a demanding order. She milked her goats, so mastitis didn't ruin the herd and wash away her livelihood. They ate their grain and hay because unlike her newfound daughters, they complained about the lack of food. Third on the list—hungry children.

In the kitchen, she slathered peanut butter and jam on bread. After slicing the sandwiches into quarters, she grabbed a quart jar of milk and slid the food to the center of her pedestal table. "Bean," she called from the porch, "Wash and help your sisters to the table."

Meredith picked up her phone to call her sister. Fourth on the list—clothing and diapers. Especially diapers.

Sunny picked up. "Is that you, Merry?"

She rolled her eyes. "Nope. Caller ID absconded with my name. What do you think?"

"Silly little sis." Sunny's chuckle resonated like a mama's arms wrapping Meredith in a hug.

"Do you have clothes from your kids I can have? And extra diapers of Owen's. New ones—not his used ones. Dish towels don't work well as diapers."

"Since when do you need diapers?"

The girls clattered into the kitchen. Bean carried Crystal on her hip, and Roxie squeezed a barn cat in her arms. The cat, one Meredith could never corner, seemed content. Roxie's eyes watered. She sneezed.

Meredith stooped toward Roxie. "Do you have a cold, sweetie?"

"A cold, sweetie?" Sunny's cheerful laugh reminded Meredith her sister was on the line.

"Wait a minute, sis." Meredith took the cat who promptly clawed her. "Out of here." She tossed the cat out the back door.

"You called me, so don't tell me to get out of here." Sunny sounded less than cheerful. "What're you talking about?"

"Sorry. The ..." Meredith inhaled. *What do I call the girls?* "Talking to the neighbor's kids." This wasn't a lie. The Wheeler house was the closest to hers. "Go wash, girls." Meredith pointed to the powder room.

"What girls?" Sunny asked.

"The neighbor's kids. They need clothes, and your kids are the perfect size. I think Owen's diapers would fit Crystal."

"Who's Crystal?"

Meredith rolled her eyes. Allison Buchanan learned nagging from the best. Mom could badger gold out of Midas's clutch.

The girls trooped back into the kitchen, their hands dripping water. They'd barely sat when they plowed into their sandwiches as though they hadn't eaten in days. Probably hadn't.

"I told you. She's—"

Roxie dropped the Mason jar of milk she was attempting to pour. She cowered and covered her head. "Sowry. Not mean to make mess."

"So, you do talk!"

"You know I do," Sunny said. "Ergo—"

"Ergo? Who says ergo nowadays?"

"Ergo, you're not speaking to me. What's up?"

"I'll tell you when you come over. I've got to go." She disconnected.

The three girls trembled.

After grabbing a roll of paper towels, Meredith knelt next to Roxie. She ran her hand over the child's hair. "Don't worry. We never lack for milk. You helped me collect a couple of gallons this morning. Remember?"

Roxie peered up from under her arms clasped over her head.

Meredith picked up the Mason jar. "Look. These jars are sturdy." She snapped her fingers against its side. "Not even chipped a little."

Slowly, Roxie dropped her arms. Her trembling stopped.

Meredith sopped up the spilled milk while the other two shoved food into their mouths once more.

We can add psychotherapy to the occupational, physical, and speech ones. How many other therapies exist?

After lunch, they hit the barn once more. Meredith couldn't tell who cavorted more—the girls or the goats. The girls leapt. The goats bounded. Crystal rode on Bean's hip as the older two raced the nannies. Mocha nibbled their hands, and they laughed as though a circus clown entertained them.

"Lookit those long-haired goats!" Bean jogged toward one of the Angoras. "I didn't see you milk this one."

"The Angoras aren't bred."

Bean looked at Meredith as though she sported cotton candy for brains.

"I know goats ain't bread. Bread comes from the grocery store. Not farms."

Meredith grinned. "Not bread you eat. My mother shears them and weaves their wool into fabric. Makes sweaters and hats from them."

"She's weird." Bean bounded toward the two Angoras who pranced away.

You don't know the half of Mom's oddities.

Meredith tossed the last of the soiled goat bedding into the wheelbarrow as Sunny's car pulled up. She leaned against the fence and waited for the crazy crew to erupt from the van.

Before Sunny killed the motor, the doors slid open, and Anissa and Phoebe scurried to the field.

"See. I told you," Phoebe said around her thumb. She stood almost nose to nose with Roxie. "Wanna play?"

The girls skipped off as though they'd been friends from birth.

'Nissa, old enough to be shy around strangers, eyed Bean who stepped back.

Sunny carried Owen on her hip. "Hello there." She ducked and addressed Crystal. "This is Owen. Who are you?"

Crystal dipped her head.

Sunny sat Owen next to Crystal. "Play nice with the little girl, buddy-boy." She turned toward her sister.

"Are you going to hang out in the goat pen like a satyress or are you going to tell me who these kids—and I don't mean your goats—are?"

"Watch your sisters, Bean." Meredith looked up. "'Nissa, mind your brother and sister. If you guys stay out of trouble, I might have cookies and milk—"

"Real milk?" Anissa's eyes held hope only a seven-year-old could hold.

Meredith knew what she meant. Cow milk bought from Food City. "Yep. Real milk." Her goats produced bona fide lactose-laden liquid. 'Nissa would figure out Meredith's definition of real milk as soon as she raised her glass and caught a whiff.

By the time she reached her kitchen with Roxie and Phoebe trailing behind her, Sunny had the tea kettle whistling and the cookies on the table. Along with three cups.

"Can't you count?" Meredith asked. Then she heard the truck. She puffed her cheeks and blew out a long breath. She didn't look at her sister. "You called Mom?"

"I've got ears. Heard the kids. You needed clothes and diapers and worried about lice. Mom has radar. She called right after you. When I told her what you needed, she said she was coming too."

Without knocking, Meredith's mother sashayed into the room like a fashion model on a runway. Her slim wrists sported bracelets woven from rabbit fur. Angora earrings swung from her lobes. Fabric artist extraordinaire, Mom didn't look her fifty years. Didn't look like anyone's idea of a grandmother. She wore her favorite neck scarf woven from cat hair and Angora goat. Not that she needed a wool covering, given the eighty-five-degree temp with a hundred percent humidity. She bent toward Roxie, and one end of the scarf flopped on the child's shoulder.

Roxie sneezed.

Not a cold. Cat allergies! We're in trouble. Barn cats and Mom with her corps of kitties.

"Who are you?" Mom didn't connect the sneezing to her scarf.

"Rowsie." She glanced at Mom then returned to studying the table.

"Rosie? Like ..."

Meredith's heart tightened. She took a breath. "Rock-see." She emphasized the words.

"Where did you come from?" Mom's face hovered inches from the frightened child.

Meredith took her shoulder. "Sit, Mom. I'll fill you in." She took her mother's scarf.

"Hey." Her mother reached for her wrap.

"Roxie appears to have cat allergies. You play with Roxie or wear your scarf. Not both."

"Cat allergies? Well, we'll give her exposure therapy, and the allergies will vanish." Mom lifted Roxie and sat the girl on her lap. "You are a boney little thing. Miss Cora's going to fatten you up." She glanced at Meredith. "Give this girl something to eat."

"A half-hour ago they each ate a sandwich, peaches, milk, crackers and soup. If I feed them something else, they're going to upchuck."

Mom dunked her tea bag in her cup of hot water. "Who're the others? Where did you find them? What're they—"

"Stop, Mom." Meredith sat. "I'll tell you." She filled her mother in as her mother jounced Roxie on her knee.

"This is a God thing," her mother said when Meredith paused.

"A God thing?"

"Yes. He's helping you get through your pain—"

"Stop." Meredith lurched to her feet, nearly knocking over her chair. "Do. Not." She inhaled a deep breath and leaned over her mother.

Mom looked up at her daughter with wide eyes and a direct stare.

Meredith read their concern and steadied her voice. "Please, Mom." She turned to her sister. "And you, Allison. Don't tell me how to heal. You don't know."

Bean, carrying Crystal, and 'Nissa, lugging her brother, barged into the kitchen. They pulled out chairs and wedged themselves around the table designed to seat four, not nine, people, even if most of them were pint-sized humans.

Thank you, Lord, for interruptions.

"Cookies." Anissa grabbed one and knocked over the hot mug of tea in front of Sunny. The steaming liquid flowed off the table and onto Crystal's lap.

The child didn't jump, but Meredith did. She knocked into Sunny as they rushed to Crystal's aid.

Crystal's eyes widened, but she didn't pull away to cool her legs.

Why aren't you crying? Meredith mopped the hot tea off the toddler, then hoisted Crystal to the powder room. After stripping away the wet dress she had fashioned from one of Rosemary's T-shirts, Meredith wet the cloth with cool water and wrapped Crystal's legs. They bore the red stain of the burn. *You should be screaming, kiddo.* Whoever raised these kids was going to have her hands full. What kind of therapy rehabilitates neuropathy? Could she ever walk? What had Crystal's mother done to destroy her kids?

She returned to the kitchen to find Roxie wiping her running nose on her arm, still sitting stiffly on Mom's lap. Her mother, unaware of the child's discomfort, chatted with Sunny while running her fingers through the child's hair.

"Careful," Meredith said.

Mom questioned with her eyes.

"Lice."

Meredith would've thought she told Mom that June was hot.

She continued to weave Roxie's hair like she wove everything her fingers touched.

Finally full, 'Nissa grabbed Crystal and Bean lugged Owen, and they ran outside once more. Roxie slid from Mom's lap and hurried after them.

"Are you going to adopt them?" Her mother asked after the screen slammed behind the kids. "Adoption would get your mind off Rosemary. You need to move on."

Meredith sipped her tea. She had to do something with her mouth before she retorted. If Mom didn't have her say sooner, she'd speak her mind later.

"She found them this weekend," Sunny said. "She can't decide on adoption yet." She looked at Meredith. "You couldn't possibly take them on. Without John—"

"I couldn't ...?" Meredith swallowed her words, but her thoughts sputtered. *How dare you tell me again what I can or cannot do? I will adopt them if I want.* She sipped tea in a vain attempt to rein in her emotions. *Or I'll let you think I'll adopt them. Only a crazy lady would take on three neglected children.*

Sunny gave their mother a knowing look. "Blake and I have our hands full, and there are two of us and no goats."

Sunny and Mom chatted about their theories on adopting three waifs like stray barn cats.

Meredith kept silent. The Bible said, "He who guards his mouth and his tongue, Guards his soul from troubles." Sometimes Scripture came in handy. Once in a while.

Rather than listening to her family babble, Meredith stepped into the living room and sorted through the clothes and diapers Sunny had brought. Pretty dresses and jeans sparkled with rhinestones. T-shirts bore pictures of Disney princesses. Poor little Crystal. She only had Owen's old clothes. Boy stuff, but if she didn't mind boiling water, she wouldn't mind the Thomas the Engine or the Sponge Bob Square Pants characters decorating her apparel.

Meredith would find something better at Walmart once she got her first stipend.

My first what?

You're not keeping them long enough to earn a stipend. Remember that, Meredith Jaynes.

Night fell. After combing Roxie's hair and removing every dead nit, Meredith tucked her into the daybed.

Crystal snored lightly on the bottom trundle.

Upstairs, she stopped outside Rosemary's door. The old sorrow welled up from the pit of her stomach and gripped her heart as she grasped the doorknob. She closed her eyes. Wished, vainly, to feel God's healing presence.

As usual, only pain engulfed her.

She opened the door.

No one lay on the bed.

"Bean?"

"In here." The little voice came from across the hall. From her room.

Under the covers, on John's side of the bed, lay the child.

"What are you doing? You sleep in the other room." She worked to make her voice strong. Surely Social Services wouldn't look fondly on a stranger sharing a bed with a child, even though said stranger was a surrogate mom.

"I want a sleepover. I never had one."

Meredith stepped toward the queen-sized bed and held out her hands. "Come on. You need to sleep in your own bed."

Bean pouted and slunk further under the covers.

Meredith didn't move.

At last, Bean crawled under the comforter to the end of the bed. After tumbling to the floor, she stomped to Rosemary's room, slamming the door behind her.

Meredith tried to bite off her laugh.

This time she opened the door without her stomach knotting. "I need to tuck you in."

She might have been promising the child a meeting with Cinderella. Bean beamed and sat up, throwing off quilt and sheet. She clasped her hands in front of her. "For real?"

"Lay down. I can't tuck you in when you're upright.

Bean flopped down as if her bones turned to pudding.

Meredith pulled the sheet over the child and tucked the blanket under the little body. Next, she opened the window. "I like fresh air. If you're too hot with the window open, let me know. I'll turn on the air for you."

"We ain't got any air conditioner at our house."

Your house wasn't fit for wild boars.

As though Bean heard her thoughts, she scowled and turned away from Meredith.

"What's wrong?"

"Nothing." Bean whispered.

"Suddenly you're sulking." Meredith pulled on Bean's shoulder to make her face her. Tears streaked the child's cheeks. With her index finger, Meredith wiped them away. "These tell me you're sad."

"I miss Mama. Why'd she forget to come home?"

"I don't know. Those two cops and the nice man from Social Services are looking for them. I'm sure they have a good reason for staying away so long."

Bean sat up suddenly and flung her arms around Meredith.

Meredith laid the child down and stretched out next to her. "I'll stay with you until you feel better. Okay?"

The child nodded.

They lay stiffly together.

"How about I sing for you?" Meredith asked.

Bean nodded.

Meredith sang "Reindeer are Better than People," Rosemary's favorite song from her favorite Disney movie *Frozen*. As Bean slipped off into sleep, Meredith couldn't help but believe the truth of the lyrics seeing as Bean's parents abandoned their three girls.

When Bean snored softly, Meredith kissed her forehead. "Goodnight."

In her own bed, sleep came quickly. And deeply.

The room was dark. No moon shone, and Meredith shifted. She bumped into something. *John?* The thought jolted her awake, and she opened her eyes. A body lay curled against her. *Bean?* She moved back. Bumped into something—or someone—else. Roxie? Crystal?

Three girls curled into her. Her bed had never been so crowded but felt so secure. Maybe for their first night, a little human comfort would be okay with DCS?

Chapter 7

Parker scuttled to his desk then flipped through his Excel program. Only Tuesday. He yawned. After sleeping through two alarms—and his breakfast time—he shouldn't be so tired.

The cursor blinked on his computer. Only one child welfare check today. *Good.* His relief lasted until he read the next item. He had a supervised visitation in twenty minutes.

He drummed his fingers on his desk as he organized his schedule. Two homes opened up last night, so he could put Meredith Jaynes's kids in them. All three couldn't live together, but two could. A list of chores glowed on the screen in front of him. He'd squeeze in a call to the sheriff's office. Hopefully, something developed with the missing parents from Wheeler Road.

"Parker?" His supervisor stepped over to his desk and handed him several forms. "Fred Dinsmore's been diagnosed with pancreatic cancer."

"Dinsmore?" Parker tapped his fingers on the desk. "They're the ones with Dale?" He tabbed over to the next spreadsheet on his computer and scanned the document. "Right."

"We've got to find a place for their boy," she said.

"I've got a home in Duff." *Down to one home for the Jaynes's kids.* He smiled up at his boss. If he acted positive, perhaps things would work out.

She pivoted and left as his phone rang.

"Parker Snow speaking."

"Parker, Mom here."

He rolled his eyes and sighed. With the exhale, he wanted to flop over and bang his head on the desk. *Mothers!*

"Parker? I know you're still on the line."

"Mom, I'm at work."

"I'm on your work number, so I know where you are."

Then shouldn't she honor his time? His schedule didn't fit into an eight-hour day, let alone a twenty-four-hour one.

"I wanted to tell you Felicity went to quilt guild last night. She's got a funeral today and tomorrow, but you can call her after nine."

"She said I could call her?" *What kind of woman goes telling a man's mother to make his son call?*

"Of course not." His mother's snort told him how stupid he was. "When I asked, she told me you had a good time Friday night. You both got along well. I don't want you to miss out. You're still mooning over Lily."

Mooning? College sweethearts. Engaged. One week before the wedding she cancels our life together. "I've got a mess here at work. If I don't leave now, I'll be late for a supervised visitation at the courthouse. Thanks for calling." He hung up. His brother, Hayes, gave Mom a grandson. She wanted a grandchild from Hayes's *older* brother. She always emphasized their age differences when recounting Parker's failings.

He grabbed his coat and dashed to his meeting.

In the parking lot by the sheriff's office, he wedged his jeep into the last available space and hopped out of his vehicle.

"Snow."

Parker turned to see Drew Carroll lumber out of his patrol car. Parker glanced at his watch. *Five minutes late.* Once more, he plastered on a smile and joined Detective Carroll. "News on the parents of those kids?"

"Probably. We found two bodies off the closed section of Cove Lake in the off-limits area."

"The fisherman access?"

Carroll nodded. "Fish by day. Shoot up at night."

"All-access services—legal and illegal." Parker chuckled sardonically. "So, you don't know their identities?"

"No identification, no vehicle. Male and female—mid-twenties. Both pretty ripe. Coroner's got them down in Knoxville."

Parker rubbed the back of his neck. "You think the kids belong to the ... the deceased?"

"Right sex and age. Have the parents shown up?"

He shook his head.

"Do those kids have a photo of their folks?" Carroll asked.

"I don't think so. You saw the dump they lived in. I'll ask Mrs. Jaynes."

"Taking a bit of work to find usable prints. The lady was submerged, and both provided a feast for the scavengers. They'll be running the prints through IAFIS. DNA will take longer."

Again, Parker glanced at his watch. Nearly fifteen minutes late. "Keep me posted?"

Carroll saluted and turned toward the jail as Parker trudged to the courthouse.

A little after four, Parker called Meredith Jaynes then headed up Hen Waddle Hollow. He could've done business over the phone, but this got him out of the office. Also, telling her the kids' parents may, or may not, have been found, and devoured, needed to be told face to face. Mrs. Jaynes seemed so fragile. His he-man genes wanted to spare her more pain. Whatever load she carried weighed more than his.

Besides, a twenty-minute drive there and back would close out his day. He'd hit Pizza Hut.

Pizza. The perfect food: carbs, protein, veggies. Eaten daily, he'd be fatter than Miss Piggy. *A Mr. Piggy? Wilbur? Napoleon?* Before he finished scouring his mind for all the pigs of media, he pulled into Mrs. Jaynes's driveway.

The family gathered in the vegetable garden. The two younger kids played by a checked tablecloth spread out on the ground. Bean knelt by the vegetable bed and helped Mrs. Jaynes. Sunlight splayed over the scene. Too bad he'd be yanking two of the kids out of here. The Tiptons said they'd take the two oldest children. Two, they claimed, were more than they could handle.

"Mrs. Jaynes." He waved.

Mrs. Jaynes shielded her eyes with her hands, then smiled. After throwing down her gardening gloves, she stepped toward him. "Howdy, Mr. Snow."

"Call me Parker." He shook her hand. "Mr. Snow is for old fogies."

Meredith cocked her head. "And yet you call me Missus? You're saying I'm old?"

Her joke melted his muscles. "Touché. Meredith."

"Any news on the parents?"

His good news about the Tiptons evaporated like rain on a steamy pavement. He came out here to tell her about them and about the parents, but seeing her, the kids ... the news was too gruesome. He'd wait until he knew definitively. No need to tell her the parents probably lay in the morgue in Knoxville until he knew for sure. He shook his head.

"What's happening with the girls?"

"I've got a home." He expected a grin. Thought he'd see tension ooze out of her.

"This home can only take the two oldest girls."

"Bean and Roxie?"

He nodded.

"But what about Crystal? You can't separate ..." She glanced back toward the garden.

"They won't consider Crystal with her medical issues and age." *I was lucky they agreed to Bean, let alone Roxie.*

Meredith crossed her arms and studied the ground. "When would they go?"

"I can take them now."

She jolted. Her lips mouthed the word now.

"How about in the morning? We planned on homemade pizza for tonight. We've got the dough rising in the kitchen."

He bobbed his head while studying Meredith's face. Keeping the kids here would allow his workday to end on time. "Works for me."

"Besides, I've got one more nit-combing to do."

"I'll see you in the morning."

"They'll be lice free and ready." She scratched her head then offered a half-smile. "Saying the l-word makes me itch."

He scratched his arm. "Yep." He turned to go, then he remembered. "Do the kids have pictures of their folks?"

"I've washed everything they had. Found no evidence of paper in the washer."

"At the house?"

"I'll check in the morning. I'm doubtful."

"A picture might help."

"Help what?"

Parker swallowed hard. Maybe he should've told her about the bloated bodies. "In the search for their families. I'll be by for the kids around nine-thirty."

Meredith looked away and sighed. After a moment, she turned her eyes back to Parker. "I've only known Bean a little. Giving her up will be hard."

"The problem with foster care is the kids live with you for a lot less time than the love lasts."

Twenty minutes later, Parker sipped a Coke at his table in Pizza Hut and waited for a stuffed-crust-everything pie. Sometimes his job stunk. Abused—or abandoned—kids. Tearful parents. Grandparents too old and infirm to care for little ones.

Occasionally, after years of red tape and searching and paperwork, he got a happily-ever-after adoption or permanent placement. Some foster kids stayed on long after the stipends quit coming even though the parents never got to adopt them.

Sometimes.

Not often.

Usually, he had to yank kids out of good foster homes and send them to distant relatives who demanded their rights. When the foster parents only wanted the compensation, the kids got stuck with them until they turned eighteen and began abusing their own kids.

What was wrong with this world?

How long before the whole system imploded?

"Watch your sisters, Bean." Meredith strode into the house and into the bathroom. She needed five minutes. Two girls would leave in the morning. How could she let them go? What about Crystal?

Of course, she couldn't care for them. Not with Crystal's special needs. The child had limited feeling in her legs. Hours of googling leg neuropathy produced lists of causes like hip dysplasia, Myasthenia gravis, spina bifida, cerebral palsy.

She washed the grime off her hands and splashed water on her face. Parental neglect. That was what was wrong with Crystal. Nothing she wouldn't grow out of. Crystal had been raised by her older sister. Carried everywhere. With a little therapy, she'd be running marathons.

Or at least a 5K.

And Bean?

She'd lose Bean. *I'll never find out her real name. Never see her again.*

She dried the water dripping off her face and stared into the mirror seeing only the afternoon which passed so quickly. The girls giggled as they kneaded dough. Bean sliced her finger on the cheese grater. Pain didn't faze her. Meredith made her stop and wash the wound. At this demand, Bean had sulked and crossed her arms smearing the oozing blood on her filthy shirt. She smiled and agreed to wash only after Meredith promised she'd buy her bandages with *Frozen* characters on them. Then every time she hurt herself, she could cover the wound with something fun and pretty.

Tonight, they'd sprinkle the pizza with the peppers, mushrooms, and pepperoni they'd sliced up this afternoon. Not one complaint floated in the kitchen as they prepped. Even her sweet Rosemary had groused about peppers and mushrooms. She and John wanted meat and more meat. Venison, pork, bacon. No vegetables on pizza.

These three? They'd gobble down anything, even liver.

Sweet girls.

Abused children.

They needed love.

Roxie talked more. Two full days here and her shyness ebbed. Thank heavens, she'd go with Bean who could interpret her words. She spoke in "other tongues." Didn't know the Bible claimed little girls couldn't speak in tongues if there wasn't an interpreter.

With Bean gone, she'd have no help with Crystal. How could she raise the child alone and keep her household afloat? But maybe they'd have a home for her soon, or she could cajole Sunny into helping. Allison loved telling her what to do and showing her how to do everything correctly.

The kitchen door clattered. "Miss Meredith? Where are you?" Bean called. The other girls chatted, and chairs scraped against the floor.

"I'm right here." Meredith blew her nose and washed her hands again. Squaring her shoulders, she stepped into the kitchen.

"What did that man want? Are we going to live with you forever?" Bean looked at her with hopeful eyes. "Did he find Mama and Danny?"

"Do you have any pictures of them?"

"Yep." Bean grinned. "On Mama's phone. They took lots of selfies."

"Where're their phones?"

"They always take their cells with them. When you find Mama and Danny, they'll show you."

Meredith's heart sank. She knew what she wouldn't find in the Wheeler house. "Go help your sisters wash."

"Kin do bupples?" Roxie asked.

Meredith looked to Bean.

"She wants a bubble bath."

"Right after dinner." Meredith kissed the top of her head then jolted back. Lice.

No. They were gone. Tonight, she'd know for sure.

What would happen if their new family didn't watch out for lice? "For now, wash yourselves thoroughly. You'll have to pass my inspection." Meredith hiked a thumb at herself. "Then we'll start dinner."

The girls scurried out.

Meredith picked up her phone and dialed Parker Snow's cell.

Parker laid his phone face down on the table, making sitting in the red upholstered booth a mite more comfortable. If he was lucky, he'd forget the cell. With no emergency calls from the office, he'd have a peaceful evening. He ate half a slice of pizza then threw the remains on his plate. He'd been hungry an hour ago. Now?

He waved down the waitress as she bolted past his table with a loaded tray. She smiled at him. "Can I have a takeout box and the bill?"

She eyed the uneaten pie. "Was everything okay?"

"Fine." *With the food.* "Don't know where my appetite went."

He tapped his foot and leaned against the back of the booth while he waited for the server to return. Funeral tonight. Can't call Felicity. He hadn't talked to her since their date. He plucked a piece of pepperoni from his discarded slice and bit the spicy meat. He didn't want to be alone.

Solitude made him think about Lily. His chest constricted with the old, unrelenting hurt.

His muted cell, on vibrate, rattled on the tabletop. The thought of answering galled, but duty forced him to. Mom or work. No luck for anything else. "Parker Snow."

"This is Meredith Jaynes. The one with the three girls."

He grinned. Having a voice more sultry than her fragile frame hinted at—she had no need to identify herself.

"They've got to stay together. With Bean's help, I can handle all three until you find a place for them together."

"Sounds great." Parker leaned against his booth.

The waitress slid the takeout box and check tray in front of him.

"I'll tell the family they'll have breathing room before the next kids arrive."

"You know, two full days here, they're doing much better. Tomorrow we'll scour the Wheeler house for any identification. If we find pictures, I'll bring them with us to court on Thursday."

"Sounds good."

"Oh. Wait."

"Yes?"

"No more bugs in the little goldie locks." She laughed and disconnected.

Hunger assaulted Parker. He shoved aside the to-go box and gobbled half the pie.

Bean bounded up the stairs.

"I'll be up in a minute." Meredith stood at the bottom of the stairs next to Roxie and Crystal's room. Her heart suddenly hammered like a full-blown panic attack. She palmed her chest. She made a mistake—couldn't care for three challenging children.

"Miss Mewedith?"

Roxie sounded so cute. Her lisping voice tugged Meredith into their room. "I'll tuck you in." Meredith pulled the covers up on Roxie and Crystal. "You stay here tonight, you understand?"

Both bobbed their heads.

She leaned over and kissed them. Earthy lavender from the bubble bath clung to their damp hair and skin. "Tomorrow we'll look for ..." Heavy eyelids closed before she finished her sentence.

She straightened and studied the sleeping cherubs. *No. I can do this.* She smiled, and her heart quieted. Could she love them already? She left to settle Bean for the night.

In Rosemary's room, Bean kneeled at the open window.

"What're you doing?"

"Wishing on a star."

"For?"

"That the nice guy finds Mama and Danny."

Abused. Still, children longed for their parents.

"Into bed."

"Will you sing again?"

"What do you want to hear?"

"The funny reindeer song. Sometimes animals *are nicer* than people."

"I've got goats. I understand what you're saying."

Bean hopped into bed as though she'd slept there all the days of her life.

Meredith smoothed the blankets around her as she sang.

With the closing line, Bean asked for another song. Then another.

Meredith sang her favorite jazz tunes until soft snores rose from Bean's parted lips. She bent and kissed her reddish curls. In her mind, she pictured Rosie, tucked in a hospital bed, white sheets around her thin body. The only color was her red hair plastered against white skin.

With Bean here, maybe she could heal.

Back in her own bed, Meredith picked up a book. Towels and puddles littered the bathroom floor. The dishes lay in the kitchen sink while the clean tableware stuffed the dishwasher. Who cared?

The girls slept, and for the first time in nine months, Meredith wanted to savor the quiet.

Chapter 8

On Thursday morning, after the third pass along the courthouse corridor, the third time past her overbearing family wedged onto one bench, Meredith wiped her sweaty hands on her skirt.

She glanced down. A stain on her skirt? Oatmeal? She licked her finger and rubbed. The stain didn't fade. Hot chocolate? Hopefully, the judge wouldn't notice and think her a slob.

If he did spot the smudge, perhaps he'd assume she'd be a good mommy.

Mom sang to the girls as she tickled them. Meredith's daughters—um, her wards—giggled. Sunny and her kids jammed themselves on the same bench. Nothing like family togetherness. Eight people thronged the seat designed for four. With no room for eight, they literally sat on one another, ignoring the nearby empty bench.

Chatter down the hall made her look up.

Parker Snow hurried toward her, his shoes squishing on the tile. A smile etched his face.

"Sorry." She swiped her hands on her skirt once more before she took his proffered hand. "I scoured the house. No pictures of their parents. Nothing worth salvaging unless you want moldy dishes and mildew."

"Got enough of them at my place."

His warm chuckle heated her stomach. She glanced at the floor. "Bean says their cell phones have pictures. If you find—

Parker took a handkerchief out of his pocket and polished his glasses. He shrugged as he resettled them on his nose. "We found two adults down at Cove Lake."

"Do they want to take the girls?" Meredith glanced at her family. Her eyes ached, but she was done with tears.

"Deceased. Apparent overdose. We won't know the cause of death until the coroner completes the autopsies."

Meredith's hand covered her open mouth, her eyes wide. "Their parents?"

"We don't know. Whoever took their car and wallets also helped themselves to cell phones."

"Nothing like love among thieves." She shivered. To OD and *then* be robbed was a worse indignity. "Who are ... were they?"

"Both have records. Daniel Harrison—"

"Daniel?"

He nodded.

Meredith inhaled a slow, deep breath. Breathed out. "Bean calls her mother's boyfriend Danny." She stared into the distance, only half hearing Parker's words.

The children giggled, unaware of the tragedy.

"Meredith?"

She blinked and refocused.

"Did you hear me?"

She offered a smile, hoped it looked real, not sheepish. "I got distracted. What about Bean?"

"The woman's name is Beth Willoughby. We assume she's the mother. Can you bring in their toothbrushes? We're hoping to find a DNA match with the deceased."

"Hoping to—"

He chuckled and held up his hand. "No. Not in 'Whoopie. We got a match.' If we know definitively, we can find their families."

"When do you need them? Where do I bring them?"

"Drop them at the office."

"But what about today? Do we still—"

His grin sparkled his eyes, intensified by the lenses of his glasses.

She cringed. *Why'd I notice this now?*

Parker reached over and held her arm. "Don't worry. Finding next of kin and making a positive connection will take time. Today will be a formality."

"When will classes for foster care begin?"

"Soon. I need to double-check the exact time."

"His Honor, Judge Peyton, can see you in his office now," a guard called.

Meredith breathed in. Couldn't exhale. She straightened her spine and plastered on a smile. Turning to her wards, she held out her hand. "Ready, girls?"

Bean skipped to her side and grabbed one hand. Roxie, with red eyes and runny nose from Mom's cat-hair coated clothing, grasped the other.

"Want Mamaw with us," Roxie said, then sneezed.

Her mother held Crystal on a hip and joined her.

Sunny and her crew trailed behind.

Terror at the sight of the mob wanting to follow buckled Meredith's legs. Speech caught in her throat.

The guard stood by the door to the judge's chambers without saying a word.

"No." Meredith's head shook back and forth. "I'm a big girl. I face the judge alone."

"But," Sunny tucked a wayward strand of Meredith's hair behind her ear, "we want to support you."

"No." Meredith pulled the strand free, even though hair hanging in her eyes annoyed her. "I do this myself."

The guard coughed.

Meredith dropped Roxie's hand and took Crystal from her mother. "Bean, hold onto Roxie for me."

Bean grasped Roxie's hand. If she squeezed any harder, Roxie's little fingers would bulge like a pinched balloon.

Meredith wiggled a finger between the clutched hands. "Loosen your grip, munchkin. You don't want to amputate anything."

"Amputate?"

Meredith smiled. She nudged Bean's back, and the two girls trudged into the judge's chambers as though marching to their execution.

Inside, Parker already sat and chatted with Judge Peyton.

"Good afternoon." The judge half rose from behind his modest desk—not made from exotic wood. Just a simple metal one like she'd find in Staples. An open folder lay on the clean surface. Judge Peyton's graying hair and wire-rimmed glasses made him look like a college professor rather than a judge who held her life in his control. He extended his hand as though greeting a friend.

Meredith shook, amazed at the soft fingers and gentle touch.

He didn't overpower her. His firm grip comforted and said *I like you. I'm happy to meet you.* "Please have a seat."

Meredith pulled a chair forward for Roxie and another for Bean. She settled herself with Crystal on her lap in the seat closest to Parker.

Before she could lean back, Bean wiggled onto her lap, half shoving Crystal off. Roxie sat with her head bowed and played with the cloth of her dress.

Meredith nestled her chin against the top of Bean's head. *What if they take her away?* Another loss would kill her. God wouldn't care.

"We're looking for a good home."

Meredith's head jerked upright as though the judge's deep voice yanked a noose around her neck.

His warm smile quieted Meredith's racing heart to an almost normal rate.

"Tell me, Bean," he leveled warm brown eyes at the girl. "Do you like living with Mrs. Jaynes?"

Bean leapt off Meredith's lap and stepped to Judge Peyton's desk. She leaned toward him with her hands flat on the surface. "Oh, yes. She's the best mother I ever had."

He chuckled.

Bean's eyes widened. "I mean, not more than my mama, but the best second mother."

Judge Peyton smiled. "That says everything." He turned to Roxie. "How about you?"

Roxie lifted her shoulders and hunched her head, looking like a turtle ducking into its shell.

"Don't worry." Meredith gentled her voice. "Be honest."

A tear dripped down Roxie's cheek. She nodded without looking up.

"Are you saying yes?" the judge asked.

Roxie's nod barely nudged her head.

The judge's voice returned to its grown-up tone. "These girls need extra care. Are you up to it?"

"I've made an appointment at the rehab center for an evaluation on Roxie's speech. We plan to take Crystal to the doctor on Monday. Something's not right with her motor coordination. I've started reading to Bean every night. She can't read."

"Your actions confirm our assessment. The girls are clean, and they look happy to be with you. From your proactive actions with the girls' care and from your background check, you'd be a good foster mom. Are you willing to be trained?"

Meredith's heart leapt as hope resurrected. "Of course. I want to be what these girls need."

"You're widowed and have a farm. Are you able to care for them alone?"

"By any chance, did you see the horde in the hall?"

He grinned. The smile creased his eyes and made them sparkle. "You do have support."

"Or meddlers." Meredith bit her lip. This wasn't the time to crack a joke.

"I like your sense of humor." He rifled a few papers. "If you don't have concerns about the responsibility you're taking on, I see no reason to not give you temporary custody of the girls." He looked at the three children. "What about you? Do you want to live with Mrs. Jaynes?"

Roxie's head jerked upright. She swiped her cheek with the back of her hand and grinned.

Bean's jaw dropped.

Crystal played with Meredith's earrings.

"I think Roxie and Bean agree. Crystal wants to inherit your jewels." Again, the judge's smile warmed the room. "Until their biological family is found, they're free to stay with you providing you take the DCS training."

Meredith leaned forward and grinned. Suddenly aware that she must look like a circus clown, she composed her face into something a mite more sophisticated. "For real?"

"For real." The judge flipped the file closed and stood. He offered his hand once more. "Parker will have you fill out the forms. Then go and enjoy being a new mother."

In the hallway, Mom and Sunny thronged Meredith.

"What'd he say?"

"Are they staying?"

"Give us details."

"Can we go clothing shopping for them now?"

The questions bombarded her so quickly she couldn't tell who asked what or which to answer first.

Meredith held out her free hand and beckoned them to quiet. "We're celebrating at KFC. My daughters love chicken."

"Make sure you get them *baked* chicken," Mom said. "Fried isn't healthy."

"But I want ice cream," Bean said.

"Remember, you told me Jacksboro has a Dairy Queen now," Meredith said. "After *baked chicken*, we'll go there."

"They might offer frozen yogurt which is the better choice." Her mother hugged Meredith.

Sunny and her girls joined the group hug.

Being ganged-up on choked out any more speech.

"Ouch. No breathe," Roxie protested from under the web of arms and female bodies.

"We have a few papers to go over first." Parker Snow rifled through his briefcase.

The adults and a gaggle of frolicking children headed down the hall.

Ten minutes later, Meredith joined her new family on the courthouse lawn. Every child, but Owen and Crystal, ran around the flagpole like sprites with a Maypole.

Meredith took a step toward them.

"We have this." Mom turned toward the children. She hitched her head toward Sunny to follow.

Meredith and Parker continued down the few steps to the street and turned toward the parking lot.

"Thank you for your help." She peered up at him, and her face warmed. She looked away. He couldn't see her blush like a teenager.

"I'm the one who needs to thank you. I hate separating siblings. They do better—"

"Parker?" A tall, slim woman wearing straight-leg jeans and tank top bedecked with rhinestones crossed the street from the library. Several books were tucked into her arm. Mahogany-colored hair hung down her back in rich, thick waves.

Parker half-turned.

Meredith couldn't mistake his expression. After a year of dating and eight years of marriage, she still looked at John with the same silly grin and sultry eyes. Their bodies always leaned in toward each other as Parker and this woman's did.

He turned back to Meredith for a second. "This is Felicity Murphy." Quickly his gaze found Felicity's again. Without glancing back, he said, "This is Meredith Jaynes."

Felicity offered her hand. "Meredith Jaynes?" Her distinctive blue eyes darkened. "Sounds familiar."

The women shook hands. Felicity's delicate fingers wore no jewelry. Unpolished, trimmed nails seemed oddly juxtaposed with her regal bearing. She looked like a woman who would wear gold and diamonds and bejeweled rings on manicured hands. Like she should be dressed in Burberry jeans and carry a Prada purse.

Perhaps her jeans and tank top were designer labels. Meredith couldn't tell Prada from a Walmart brand. "Parker probably said something about us."

Felicity shook her head. "No. Not from Parker." Her perfectly plucked brows puckered over incredible blue eyes. "No, the name's from someplace else." She peered at Meredith.

Meredith's heart stuttered as recognition hit. Tie up Felicity's hair. Put on reading glasses. No way would she forget those eyes.

The six children with the adults in tow clambered down the sidewalk toward them.

Suddenly, Felicity's eyes widened, and her lips parted. "I remember now. What a sad situation. Not one easy to overcome. How're you doing?"

Meredith's blood cooled. "Good." Her voice whispered, and all other words caught in her chest. She glanced toward the girls who clamored around her and grabbed Roxie and lifted her. The child's legs wrapped around her hips comforted Meredith, made her feel like she hugged a teddy bear. Made breathing possible. "We've got to go. We promised the kids KFC for lunch."

"Ice cream," Bean said.

Meredith gazed down at the child. "I remember my promise." She turned to the crowd thronging her. "Ready?"

"Yeah!" screamed 'Nissa. "Come on, Bean. I'll race you."

"Watch out for—"

The girls ran off before Meredith could finish her caution. Sunny, clutching Owen, and Mom, holding Crystal, jogged after them. The two women tried, but failed, to corral the scattering children.

Roxie wriggled out of Meredith's arms and sprinted after the others.

As though her feet stuck to the pavement, Meredith trudged to the car. She forced herself to not look back at Parker and his pretty girlfriend. So much for healing.

Sunny's van, holding all the kids but Crystal, pulled next to Meredith's truck. "See you at the restaurant." She drove out of the lot.

Stepping back from strapping Crystal into her new car seat, Meredith bumped into her mother. "Sorry."

Mom wrapped her in her arms. The woven earrings tickled her nose.

"Mom. What're—?"

"I told you healing would happen."

She tried to pull away, but Mom held her tight. "What're you talking about?"

Mom released her bear hug but held Meredith by her shoulders. "You can love again, even if Parker's involved with the pretty funeral director."

So, you remembered her too.

"Because he's taken doesn't mean you can't love someone else."

"John and Rosie have only been gone—"

"Nine months. I know. Happiness will find you.

Mom climbed into the front and plopped her knitting tote on the console between them. The bag overflowed and crowded Meredith.

The truck felt empty. The girls legally belonged to her for less than an hour, and already, they chose to ride with Sunny.

Meredith started the engine and turned to leave the parking lot. On Main Street, Parker and the undertaker stood in the same spot. He leaned close to her. A small smile played over his lips.

She couldn't move on. John and Rosemary left a chasm too wide to bridge, and God didn't want to build one to cross the divide.

Chapter 9

Parker watched as Meredith's truck passed. "How do you know Mrs. Jaynes?"

"I performed her daughter's funeral. Ended up flying solo—my first solo wake—because the funeral got delayed. Kit had a cruise he couldn't cancel, so I managed the whole thing."

He refocused on Felicity. "I didn't think people delayed funerals."

"Mrs. Jaynes's husband had an accident—"

He stiffened. "He died with the daughter? I thought she was sick, and he died in a crash."

"True. As I said, the situation was unexpected and tragic."

"The poor woman." He shook his head as Felicity's words sank in. "They died close to each—"

A sheriff's car crossed the road. Facing the wrong way, the detective pulled into the parking space nearest Parker and Felicity. He rolled down the driver's side window. "Got a second, Snow?"

Parker glanced at the officer. "Sure." He turned to Felicity. "Give me a moment?"

"I've got to run." Felicity's fingers brushed his arm. "I'm free Saturday if you don't have to rustle up wayward families."

"For you," he winked, "I'm free too. I'll call."

Felicity strolled toward the parking lot. He kept his focus on her as he stepped toward Detective Carroll.

"Did the kids have any pictures?" Detective Carroll asked.

"None. Are the autopsies finished?"

"The medical examiner's backlogged. We'll contact you as soon as we can test the kids against the deceased." With a salute, he rolled up the window and drove off.

Parker straightened. His eyes tracked Carroll's vehicle, but he didn't see the car. His mind mulled Felicity's comment that the Jaynes funeral was 'tragic.' *An accident. An illness. A sad case.* He shook his head. All he remembered was a high school acquaintance died after being T-boned by a kid coming off Mount Hebron Road. He shook his head to clear it.

All funerals—especially of young people in the prime of life—were sad. *Why was this one a sad case? Or sadder than normal?*

And why had the funeral been delayed?

He'd ask Felicity on Saturday.

He grinned.

Felicity. What a woman. Gorgeous. Sophisticated. A woman with everything he desired. Not needy or self-absorbed.

The perfect lady.

He stopped and tilted his head and grinned at the sky. *Take that, Lily.*

Katydids whirred in the darkness, and a soft breeze wafted through the screened window.

The girls piled onto Meredith's bed.

"Stowy," Roxie begged. She held out the new book she'd picked out at Walmart after gorging on KFC and Dairy Queen.

Bean scurried out of bed.

"Where're you going?" Meredith asked.

"I want my book." Bean darted across the hall.

Meredith climbed into the middle of the girls. She propped up pillows—John's included—and pulled Crystal onto her lap. The child nestled back as though she wanted to melt into Meredith. Roxie, if she got any closer, would be on her legs as well. Meredith opened the book. "The moon will soon be full."

"Wait!" Bean wailed as she careened into the room. "Don't start without me!" She hopped onto the bed making the frame squeak in protest. "Start from the beginning." Bean wedged herself under Meredith's arm.

"We only read one line. You haven't missed—"

"Start over." Bean laid her head against Meredith.

She felt like a mommy sandwich wrapped in a bun of children. Contentment flowed in her veins, warmer than blood.

Meredith ran her finger under the words as she read. "The moon will soon be full—"

"Mewedith, lookit," Roxie jabbed her finger at the words moon and soon.

Bean leaned forward and squinted.

"Only the first letters change." Roxie looked up and grinned. Triumph shown in her eyes.

Bean scowled.

Crystal sucked her thumb. Her little hand shoved the page wanting to see the next one.

"You're one smart cookie, Roxie. Do you see what changed, Bean?"

Bean scowled and flopped back against Meredith's arm. "Looks the same to me."

"See," Meredith pointed to moon. "M-o-o-n." She glided her finger along the line. "And s-o-o-n. The oon is the same, only moon starts with an m and soon—"

Roxie tapped Meredith's cheek. "Read more."

"The moon will soon be full. It will pull the tide up high." She gazed down at Bean. "What letter did we change?" She held her finger under the p.

"P. P. Oops. I say naughty word. Roxie giggled. "I knowd my alphabet."

"I'm proud of you." She kissed the top of Roxie's head, keeping an eye out for lice. So far, she had defeated the bugs. "Do you girls want to sing the alphabet song?"

"There's a song?" Bean asked.

Words caught in Meredith's throat. *They don't know their alphabet song?* She hoped her shock didn't show. "Oh yes. And I know a bunch more songs you probably never heard before."

"Like the reindeer one?"

Meredith nodded. "Hmm, hmm."

"Will you teach us the alphabet song now?" Bean's face brightened.

"I'll sing it, "A, B, C, D..." Once they learned the melody and order, they sang the song.

Again.

And again.

At last, Crystal went limp on Meredith's lap as sleep overtook her. Meredith slipped her off and laid her down close to the wall on John's side of the bed.

Roxie crawled onto Crystal's vacated spot and nestled against Meredith's chest. Halfway through the next round of the alphabet song, her head fell back. Her soft snores made Meredith want to bury Roxie inside her and protect her forever.

Before the end, Bean's head fell forward—then jerked back.

"Time to sleep." Meredith crawled over the bodies littering her bed.

"Not tired." Bean's head twitched again.

"Then keep your sisters company." Meredith pulled up the covers. "I've got to clean up the kitchen."

"I can help."

At least Meredith thought the last word Bean said was help as sleep conquered the ragamuffin.

In the kitchen, Meredith hummed the alphabet song. *Enough kids' stuff.* She switched to Billie Holiday's "The Man I Love." She improvised the tune. Holiday sang jazz, so she could change the melody anyway she wanted, and her improv lifted her spirits. She leaned against the sink, the water seeping into the top of her jeans as the dampness soaked her T-shirt. Happiness? How long since she felt so good?

While tapping a rhythm with her foot, she sank her hands deep into the soothing, sudsy water and sang a little louder.

Billie Holiday morphed back into the ABCs. Meredith peered over her shoulder toward the stairs.

The three had sung until their little voices went hoarse. She needed to teach them a little scat singing. Spice up their quartet.

But not as spicy as Billy Holiday's repertoire.

She scrubbed her pot and smiled. Too much time had passed since she had a little spice. She and John promised each other when Rosemary got well, they'd do all their romantic things—nights at the Bijou for the Knoxville Jazz Orchestra, watch the baby gorillas at the zoo, kayak or hike the Smokies again. As soon as Rosie got well.

An hour later, as her girls weren't sleeping in their own beds, Meredith settled into Rosemary's single one.

Tomorrow.

She tossed onto her right side.

I have to start another batch of soap. She fluffed the pillow and made a nest for her head. *The finished products need to be removed from the molds and wrapped.* She flopped back on her back and started to fold back her fingers as she enumerated the rest of her chores.

Number four, pack for the farmers' market.

Five, apply for the fall craft shows. Six, the beets and Swiss chard and kale needed to be picked before the heat ruined the last leaves. Seven, replant them for a fall harvest.

Maybe next week once her girls were settled.

Her girls. It sounded so natural. Could they be her children?

God, if you like me at all, let me adopt them.

God? Could he ...?

She turned on her side. Maybe God would. He could. She closed her eyes and prayed. *Will you let me keep them?*

Parker warned her foster kids rarely stayed with foster parents. If adoption became possible, years often passed, many times ending in heartbreak. He said to guard her emotions.

Well then, Lord, if I can't have all three, please, never take Bean away.

Saturday she'd discover how to sell her product in Market Square while corralling three active kids. Not possible without Bean.

She wished she knew who they were.

Wished to make them hers.

Number eight, give Parker Snow their toothbrushes.

Being a foster mom was going to hurt.

Chapter 10

Only nine on a Saturday morning, and Meredith's head pounded like a jackhammer on asphalt. She maneuvered her truck down Union Street toward her booth at the farmers' market. Never had she been this late.

"Hold." A man in a bright yellow vest held out his hand to stop the truck.

She powered down her window and then rubbed her temple. "I'm late."

The man grinned. "I recognize you now. The street's officially closed, but if you promise to be careful, I'll let you through."

She held up her three middle fingers in salute. "Scout's honor."

With a chuckle, he waved her down the street packed with vendors' vehicles and parked as close to her site as she could get.

Customers strolled the pathways on Market Square in downtown Knoxville to view the wares from the vendors who arrived on time.

At least she arrived. Two hours ago, Meredith had doubted she would. Roxie hid in the barn loft, afraid Meredith would lose her.

Bean cried for her mother.

Crystal dropped her cereal bowl then scooted through the porcelain, unaware she cut her leg. Blood stained her new clothes—the ones Meredith bought from Walmart two days ago. These togs had never been worn by Owen, and were designed for a little girl, not a boy.

She tended Crystal's legs. Fortunately, the cuts weren't deep or abundant.

With Crystal bandaged, Roxie found, and Bean bribed, she thought she'd push the speed limit to make up for the delays and arrive at Market Square on time.

On the way to Knoxville? Her gas light pinged in her truck. She rolled into the gas station on fumes. Then, one full hour of bickering children. Three stops along the highway to quiet them and an "interview" with a police officer who had pulled her over when she swerved while yelling at the girls. She knew her head would burst, or the dam holding back her hysterics would fracture.

Still strapped in the car seat behind Meredith, Crystal kicked the seatback like Meredith's favorite percussionist—Futureman. Even he didn't bang as hard a tempo for Béla Fleck as Crystal's feeble legs did.

"You're in my space," Bean whined.

A slap.

"Ahh. Miss Mewedith, Bean mean." Roxie's whimper didn't need interpretation.

Meredith bit her lip. *No more shouting.* She leaned against her seat. *Why are they acting up? Rosemary never...*

No use going down that train wreck of thinking.

In a half an hour she'd be set up. Then she'd buy the girls a treat from Wookie Cookie. *Reward them for misbehavior?*

No. Bribe them.

She swung open her door and settled her baseball cap more securely on her head. "Let's go. I need your help to set up right over there." She pointed to a blank space on the pedestrian mall. "We need to hurry because we're late." Meredith hopped out of the truck and jogged to its bed. She wheeled her tent from under the cab cover to her site.

No girls tailed her. All week she couldn't shake the little shadows. First time in a crowded, strange place?

Meredith looked around. She craned her neck and yelled. "Bean! Roxie!" She stood on tiptoes but saw no strawberry blonde heads bobbing along the rows of vendors.

The back door of her truck stood ajar. The back seat—empty. Almost empty.

Someone cried. The two who absconded left Crystal behind.

No one answered her yell. Meredith's temples now throbbed. Thumped a zillion times worse than a jackhammer.

She unstrapped Crystal and hitched her onto her hip. *Thank heavens no one took you.*

Whoa. What a stench. She looked at the sulking child in her arms who was unaware of the toxic fumes emanating from her diaper. If OSHA showed up, she'd be in big ... diaper contents. Maybe this is why no one kidnapped her.

Meredith inhaled to settle her nerves.

Yikes. Wrong action.

She'd deal with the diaper later. Meredith strode the aisles of the market. "Bean. Roxie." She swiveled her head, searched between booths.

The owner of Wookie Cookie flagged her down. "Meredith, who're you looking for?"

"Two girls I'm fostering. One is eight, about this tall." She held her hand chest high. "The other is five." She lowered her hand toward her stomach.

"I thought so. Two girls ran off over there." The shopkeeper pointed in the direction Meredith had come.

"Thanks." Meredith pivoted. Her face heated, and her stomach churned. An official foster mother for two days, and she lost the kids. Surely DCS would take them away. She stopped and allowed herself a smile. At the moment, losing custody sounded divine. But ... they had to be found before they could be taken away. She hoisted Crystal more securely on her hip and retraced her steps.

"Bean. Ro Ro." Crystal pointed.

Meredith gazed in the direction the toddler—if you could call a child who couldn't toddle a toddler—pointed.

Back by her truck, the two wayward waifs sat.

Meredith broke into a jog.

Once back at her vehicle, she sat Crystal down, doubled over and inhaled, or tried to inhale. When her breathing quieted, she looked at the two runaways.

Chocolate smeared their faces.

Meredith glared and fisted her hands on her hips. "Where did you find chocolate? I packed plenty of healthy food for us. None of it contained chocolate."

"Over there." Bean pointed into the distance. "Don't worry. I got a cookie for Crystal and you." She reached into her pockets and brought out pieces of Wookie's distinctive Star Trek-themed cookies.

"How'd you pay? I haven't given you any money."

Bean stared at the pavement.

Meredith groaned. She tilted her chin and studied the rooftop bar on a vintage brick building across the square. She couldn't look at Bean. If she did, she'd explode—or at least her head would. She stepped to her truck's cab and fiddled in her purse for ibuprofen. After gulping two without water, she returned to the girls.

"Help me cart the wares to our site."

Bean leapt to her feet.

The three of them hauled boxes the few yards to where Meredith had dumped her tent. Together, they set up in a matter of minutes.

"I can get more for you," Bean said as Meredith opened her tables.

"More what?" Meredith spread out tablecloths.

"Cookies." She grinned. "I saw a place with honey. I love your—"

"Stop." Meredith's stomach ached like she'd swallowed a rock. When she could swallow again after the tension eased in her gut, she stared into Bean's wide eyes. "Stealing is wrong."

"But she had lots of cookies, and the other guy had a gobullion jars of honey, and we don't have any. They won't miss a few. Mama says to only take from people who have lots—"

"Shut up." She ran her knuckles over her aching chest. Surely, she was too young for a heart attack. "I'm sorry. I shouldn't talk to you like that."

"Like what?"

"Saying shut up."

"Mama and Danny say shut up all the time. Don't mean nothing. Just being mad. I gotta worry when they say naughty words like—"

"Stop." Meredith's breath quivered. A movement behind her distracted her. "Stay seated, Roxie."

"'Kay."

She heard Roxie's bottom hit the ground again.

"How'd you do that?"

"What?"

"See Roxie when you wasn't looking at her."

Bean's innocent question broke the spell. Meredith laughed. She took off her baseball cap and wiggled her ponytail. "My back eye is hidden in my hair." She pointed at Bean. "So, you better be good."

"I always am."

Meredith nodded. "Help me finish setting up. Then we're going to have a talk."

Twenty minutes later, while the two older girls hauled soap out of the truck, Meredith changed Crystal's diaper.

Finally clean, she plopped Crystal down, shoved the mess into an empty plastic bag and handed the nasty garbage to Bean. "The waste bin is there." She pointed toward Wall Street. "Use the can farthest away from all the vendors, and come back immediately. If you help yourself to anyone's goods, you'll be grounded for the rest of your life."

Bean trudged toward the road while keeping the arm with the plastic bag extended and the other hand holding her nose.

Meredith plunked her cooler with fresh goat milk under the front table. "Roxie, come here. Help."

The two arranged the soap display.

Bean returned.

Meredith studied her. She bit her lips to keep from asking what she stole on her way back. Nothing bulged in her jeans' pockets. Her face only held the smears from the pilfered chocolate cookie. She smiled at the child. "Here." She handed a disinfectant wipe to Bean. "Wipe your face, then pitch the cloth there." She pointed to a box under the side table where she'd tossed the wipes that she'd used to clean up Roxie and to wash her own hands. "Help us finish."

"Why's that *spasth* empty?" Roxie pointed at the bare spot in the booth.

"My mom's fabric art goes there." She looked over at Bean. "You'll find the box on the floor under Crystal's car seat."

Bean hiked toward the truck, which had to be moved.

Soon.

Customers began rearranging product even before all had been set up. Meredith made three sales then realized Bean hadn't returned.

She turned to discover Roxie, Bean, and Crystal had disappeared. About three booths away, three little blondes wandered.

"Girls!"

They turned.

Meredith pointed to the spot beside her. She watched them as they trudged back to the booth. "Sit." She pointed to the ground. "Don't go anywhere. I need to retrieve Mom's goods."

She ran to the truck, snagged the box, and strode back to her tent. "Set this up for me." Meredith tended to a few customers.

Five minutes later, Roxie sneezed. She wiped her nose with the end of her T-shirt.

As though the sneeze popped Meredith's anger, her muscles relaxed. The girls sat next to Mom's fabric art—made from Angora goat, cat fur, sheep wool, flax—anything Mom could spin, she wove. Did she have allergy medicine for Roxie? No.

Meredith hooked the tent curtain to the front of her booth, so customers would know she was closed.

And to deter other people who believed she had enough goods to share.

"Into the truck." She didn't care if she sounded gruff. Once she parked, bought Claritin, and sold enough soap and milk to pay her bills, the day would smooth out.

If not?

She'd give the girls back to Parker Snow.

She drove into the parking garage on Walnut Street and circled the levels. Up and up and up. Top tier. She shifted into an empty space and blew out a breath.

Bean and Roxie unsnapped their seatbelts.

"Stay. Sit." Meredith flopped her head against the headrest. *One. Two.* She counted to six before she unsnapped her belt and turned. "Stealing is wrong."

"But—"

"No buts. We will go to Wookie Cookie later and tell the vendor you took cookies. Since you have no money, I'll have to pay for them. I'd hoped to buy a treat for you at the end of the day. I guess you already bought it."

"But they have so much, and we don't—"

"Bean!" Meredith sliced her hand across her throat to silence the child. "People may look like they have a lot, but they don't. Like me, this is how the merchants here make a living. They work long hours and deserve to be paid."

Crystal kicked the back of Meredith's seat.

Roxie slouched.

Bean crossed her arms and slunk down. Defiance showed in every muscle of the two older girls. Crystal plugged her thumb in her mouth and broke wind.

The older sisters giggled.

Crystal grinned.

Meredith sniffed. *Hopefully just gas?* "Let's go. We apologize. I pay. Then you two work with me."

Once out of the car, Meredith checked Crystal's diaper. Clean. Then she handed the toddler to Bean, grabbed her hand and Roxie's.

Crisis over.

She hummed "Blue Skies." Ella Fitzgerald sang truth. Nothing but good from this moment on.

Her song proved prophetic. The girls acted like seraphims—the best of angels. At two, they helped tear down The Merry Goat. By three, they finished packing the truck. At four, they pulled up to the farm. The girls flung open the doors and ran.

"Get back here."

"Why?" Bean asked. "We're home."

Home? She frowned at the thought. *Shouldn't this make me happy? They think they're home.* She shuddered and shoved the thought away. "I need help."

"Tired." Roxie rubbed her eyes. She'd slept all the way home.

Tired? So was she. The two girls stood with arms drooping at their sides. They were children, and the day must have dragged for them. They weren't her slaves. Needed to be kids. "Go play."

They turned to run.

"Wait."

The girls stopped.

Meredith lifted Crystal who'd already unstrapped herself. "Take your sister. Stay out of trouble. I'll unload."

Meredith unpacked her truck and stored unsold items in the office in the barn. The sun drifted through the west-facing window.

How late? She checked her phone. *An hour passed?*

She straightened and cocked her head. It was too quiet. *What are the girls up to?*

She walked into the kitchen. And jolted to a stop.

Had a bomb gone off? Bits of bread scattered around the table like the girls had been feeding the pigeons. Peanut butter smeared the surface like they finger painted. Milk dripped from the counter and splatted the floor.

She stood at the bottom of the stairs and hollered. "Bean! Roxie! Crystal!"

No one responded. Meredith tromped up to the bedrooms.

Empty.

Down to John's study.

No girls.

She stepped onto the front porch and called.

Nothing.

Yelled some more.

Only a bird flew to the limb of the magnolia tree. Nothing else moved in the still air.

Silence.

"Bean? Roxie?" Meredith strode to the road.

The only movement now came from the yard spinning around her like she rode a merry-go-round. Her legs turned to rubber. They wouldn't hold her upright for long. *Where? Where would they be?* Meredith looked north. Then south.

She exhaled.

Where do I look for them? Should I call the cops? Parker Snow?

She twitched her lips. No. They'd say she had to wait before missing persons was alerted. *Wouldn't they? I don't know.*

"Bean! Roxie! Crystal!" She gritted her teeth and stomped down the road.

Called again.

Walked back up. Her face heated, and she wanted to smash something. Anything.

"Girls?"

Nothing.

She took a long, cleansing breath, and her nerves settled. *John, what do I do?*

A breeze caressed her face and told her everything would be okay.

Bean wandered all the time. She took care of her sisters. Had been left on her own for hours at a time, and she knew more about this area than Meredith did. Until a week ago, no one worried about the kids getting lost or abducted or taken by Social Services.

Bean and Roxie and Crystal would be okay.

They would.

She had to believe.

Her goats bleated. They needed milking. If the girls didn't return by the time she finished, she'd call Parker. He would know what to do.

Maybe I should call my sister?

Meredith gave a nervous chuckle. Desperation addled her brain if she considered adding Sunny to her line of defense.

Meredith tied Oreo into the milking stanchion. She leaned her cheek against Oreo's hide, and the goat's musky scent soothed her frayed nerves. The nanny's warmth and the sound of the milk hitting the pail unknotted the muscles in her back.

Roxie loved milking.

She stiffened. Looked around the barn as though she'd see the little imp and hear her lisp that she wanted to milk the cookie goat.

Meredith stood.

Oreo bleated.

She sat again and strained the milk from the bucket.

Cappuccino's turn. She tied Cap into the milking stanchion. But ...

She stepped out of the barn. *The truck. I could take the truck and look.*

From the hook in her kitchen, she nabbed her keys, climbed in the vehicle, and drove up and down Hen Waddle Hollow.

No kids.

Back in her kitchen, she dialed 911.

Hung up before the first ring.

911 didn't deal with lost kids.

Could the girls have returned to the old Wheeler place?

No. Who would want to step in there?

She sank down on a chair at the table and buried her head in her hands. *They'll come home.*

Home. The run-down house had to be where they went.

After rushing from the house, Meredith crossed the street.

She took a few strides into the field when the three urchins emerged from the Wheeler Road.

She strode toward them and crossed her arms. "Where were—?" She skidded to a halt. "Drop—" She shuddered. "No. Don't drop the gun. Put it down."

Bean stooped to place Meredith's pistol on the ground.

Meredith ran, scooped up the Walther and gasped. She'd never unloaded the semi after dumping the gun in her bedside table the day Oreo danced on her kitchen table. Her lips moved. She closed her eyes. Air wouldn't enter her lungs. She'd suffocate here on her road.

How could I?

I'm incompetent.

Incapable.

A horrible, miserable excuse for a mother. No wonder God took Rose—

No. She wouldn't believe any more lies. She checked the gun's safety.

On.

Relief swamped her as she released the cartridge and shoved it into her pocket and the empty gun into her waistband. "How could you?" Her voice barely rose above a whisper.

"We needed protection in case Danny's friends—"

"Do not *ever*, and I mean never-ever, go into my dressers again. You could've ..."

Bean scuffed her foot. She looked like she had when Meredith first found her slipping out of her house with a bag full of Rosemary's dresses.

"How could you run off and not tell me?" Meredith's voice shrilled, even to her own ears.

"Don't yell at us." Defiance laced Bean's voice.

"I'll scream all I want. What if you'd hurt someone?" *Why was I so stupid?*

"Leave me alone." Bean shoved Crystal toward Meredith.

The child slipped in Meredith's arm. She wrenched the toddler and secured her before she hit the ground. "You have to obey me—"

"No, I don't. You're not my mother." Bean ran across the road and into the house. The screen slammed behind her.

Meredith rubbed her neck.

Roxie stood beneath her, her bottom lip pouting, her eyes large and watery.

"Where did you go?"

"Home. No Mama." A tear escaped her liquid eyes, and she shuddered.

Meredith stooped to Roxie's level and sat Crystal on the path. "Come here."

The child flew into her arms. As she sobbed, her little body shook as though December froze her. "Want Ma. Pa." She shuddered. The late day humidity pressed in around them as the child's tears soaked Meredith's T-shirt.

Roxie's cries set Crystal wailing.

Meredith plopped on the ground and skootched the children onto her lap. She held them until the weeping stopped.

Then she held them a moment more.

Back in the house, she offered the two little ones mac and cheese.

"Not hungwy." Roxie skulked to the sofa, plopped down, and pulled up an afghan.

"Crystal, hungry?" Meredith shook the box.

Crystal shook her head and pointed at Roxie.

Meredith carried the toddler to her sister and turned on the TV. Reruns of Paw Patrol came to life. The girls huddled together.

Meredith trudged up the stairs. She clicked open the combo for the gun safe built into the bedside table. *Never again. Meredith Jaynes, never again take the lazy route. Even when these girls find homes, lock the gun up.* She slid in her semi and locked the safe.

In the bottom drawer, one fitted with a simple lock, she dumped the cartridge and turned the key. If a mass murderer broke into her home, he'd have to wait until she unlocked all the drawers and loaded.

She sunk onto the edge of her bed. Maybe she should sell the gun.

She wasn't cut out to be a mother. God made the fact abundantly clear. Maybe Deacon Mills was right.

What sin have I committed?

Revisiting Mills's accusation wouldn't help. He had no right to the title deacon.

She headed to Bean's room and tapped on the door.

"Leave me alone." Bean's voice muffled through the door.

Meredith stepped into the room.

"I said, go away."

Here one week and you act like you own this place. Was this a good thing or not?

The child lay on her bed, curled on her side.

Meredith sat next to her. How do you tell a child her mother's probably dead?

Silence settled.

Bean kept her back to Meredith.

Meredith caressed Bean's head. "Come downstairs when you're ready to talk. Or eat." She stepped away, then turned. She opened her mouth to tell Bean she loved her.

Bean lay with her back to Meredith.

In the kitchen, Meredith cleaned. Laughter from the TV wafted into the room, but the girls didn't join in the giggles.

Meredith stepped into the living room. The TV blared but the couch stood empty.

No footsteps had padded up the stairs.

Could they have run off?

She didn't hear the front door open. Or slam shut, as the girls preferred.

In John's study, she discovered both kids curled into each other on the bottom mattress of the daybed. She peeled the rumpled blanket from under them and tucked them in. She then kissed their little heads.

Safe. All of them. She returned to the kitchen, picked up a quart of milk and opened the fridge.

Milk? Her heart hammered.

My goats!

With bare feet, Meredith ran to the barn. Cappuccino bleated in the stanchion. The rest of the herd yelled at her from the pen. *She forgot her bleating goats. My babies. My livelihood.*

Everything in her said to throw herself on the floor, to kick her feet, and beat her head onto the cement. Instead, she straightened her back. Finished her chores.

Midnight approached. The house groaned as Meredith sank onto her bed. The girls slept in their own rooms for once. No one wanted to be a part of anyone else's family this evening.

Meredith stared at the darkness. Sleep wouldn't come.

She got up and fumbled through the closet for one of John's shirts. She sniffed each one. His scent had faded. Every day she found a little less of him even without washing his clothes.

At last, she found his favorite fleece, one with his strongest scent.

Back in bed, she clutched the jacket to her and waited for the familiar comfort.

To no avail.

She climbed out of bed and removed the screen from her window. She scrabbled onto the sloped roof and nestled against the dormer.

She couldn't do this. Foster damaged children.

Market day, the bread and butter of her business, was a bust. If she kept the girls, she'd be bankrupt in a week.

Worse than that, she'd forgotten the gun, the one she always kept locked when Rosemary lived. The weapon had become her safety valve after John died, something to fend off her fear of being alone.

The girls missed their abusive parents. She trembled. *Dreadful. How can they love those neglectful ...?*

She sniffed John's fleece. Outdoors and hay? Ink and leather? *Am I forgetting his smell? His arms and wisdom.*

And the girls? What would they do when they learned they'd never go home?

The girls loved those awful people. They hung out for more than an hour at the horrid, condemned building. *Why didn't I think to look there?* The skin on her forehead tightened, and her headache resurrected. Drug-addicted, neglectful parents were preferable to her.

What is wrong with me? She dashed a tear away with the heel of her palm.

But those parents? She'd left the toothbrushes at DCS yesterday. How long until they learned if the girls belonged to the two who overdosed? Those bodies at Cove Lake had to be their mother and father. According to Bean, they always came home, but a week had passed, and Bean's parents hadn't shown up.

Someone else had to take the girls.

She couldn't do this alone.

She couldn't.

John, what do I do? What do you want me to do?

She stared into the dark. In the distance, a streetlight glowed. Nothing moved. No car. Animal. Not even a breeze.

John?

Tomorrow I'll call Snow. He'd take them. Give them a home with someone who could take care of them the way the children needed.

Chapter 11

The world moved as it should. Parker walked Felicity to her front door. As she leaned against the wood, he framed her with his arms leaning against the jamb and kissed her.

Warm lips. At first touch, gentle and almost chaste.

Then he wrapped his arms around her and drew her close. The whole of her pressed against him, and he knew he could love again. However, if he continued to kiss and hold her like this, he wouldn't be able to stop. He stepped away, leaned his head towards her and touched her nose with his. "I enjoyed our evening."

"Even if I hate country music?"

He dropped his arms and drawled, "Been nice knowing you."

She laughed and slapped his arm. "If I don't give you the wrong idea, come in, and I'll show you the quilt your mother raved about."

"Which one? There were maybe thirty or forty she mentioned."

"The thirty-second one." Felicity turned and clicked the lock.

Her house matched her—dark polished furniture in a clean, modern style surrounded a comfy-looking pink couch with quilted pillows. Beyond the living room, a tall china vase with sunflowers sat on a rectangular dining table. Her talent adorned the table with appliquéd placemats. A TV perched on a quilted runner on an entertainment unit in the living room. The open floor plan was unpretentious but high-end.

Most amazing? Not a speck of dust.

"Beautiful home. Mine's decorated in my late grandmother's out-of-date furniture and a promise to clean on my day off."

Her eyes danced. "We call your style vintage which is quite hip these days. And I pay a cleaning lady. I can give you her name."

He held up his hand to decline and settled onto the sofa.

"Would you like wine? Coffee?"

"I'm driving. I need to sleep at some point tonight, so I'm good."

"I'll be right down." Felicity slipped up the stairs and into a room off a small balcony edging the vaulted living room.

Parker sank onto the rosy-colored sofa. The quilted pillows spiced up the solid color of the couch. He picked up one to study. Simple cross-shaped flowers in pinks and blues seemed to define her. Spiritual and down to earth. He inhaled. As though the pillows were a real garden, the fragrance of some sort of flower drifted up. He didn't think sunflowers, or the pillows, smelled like this. He took another deep breath. Peonies?

Soft. Understated. Like Felicity.

"Here you go." Felicity's heels clicked on the stairs.

He stood and turned.

In her arms, she carried a brightly colored bedspread.

After she laid the quilt over the back of the couch, his breath caught. He wasn't one for girly-girl stuff, but this one? His mother regaled him and his brother with her projects for nearly thirty years. He thought he was immune to the beauty of handmade quilts.

This one was museum quality.

"What kind of flower is this?" He pointed to the centerpiece—a burgundy, jagged-petaled flower with a similar one growing from the top.

"Bee balm."

"How long does this take to make?"

She hiked a shoulder. "I love solitude. With most of my family scattered, when I'm not working on the dead, I work with fabric."

Family. "Do you miss them?"

"Who?"

"Your folks? Your brothers?"

"We see each other from time to time. They're all as persnickety as me, so we're only good for short spurts. Of course, since I go to my brother's church, I see him and Gracie all the time. Too much time." She chuckled. "They're working on baby number five right now."

"Many kids in your family?"

"A gazillion. So, if I ever think I might want a child, I visit my brothers. Then I'm cured."

"You don't want children?" He tried to keep the query out of his voice. His age advanced, but he always dreamed of a houseful of children—a dozen. Or, at the least, one of his own. For the remaining eleven, he'd take them from the foster system or adopt them from someplace like Christmas or Easter Island. Have holiday children.

Maybe he'd create his own island, build a home to treat abused children with the love and respect they deserved.

"Sometimes," she said.

Her voice snapped him out of his reverie.

"Kids would be nice. But I'm thirty-two. Had two serious relationships. My first love broke my heart. The second was the wrong man, so I broke up with him. Married or single, childless or not, I'm content."

He ran his hand over the quilt. "You have so much patience. I bet you'd be good with children."

Her gaze held his. For a second, he thought she'd tell him to leave, that his obsession with kids turned her off.

Felicity folded the quilt and laid it aside. "Have a seat. Talk for a bit."

Here comes the get-lost speech. His legs warred against his will. His brain screamed, "Run, Parker, run." His legs revolted. He sat on the edge of the couch.

Felicity laughed and leaned against the arm of the sofa. "Relax, Mr. Snow. I don't bite."

He offered a close-lipped smile and leaned back. His stiff body refused to unwind.

"I'd have a child or two if I met someone that I loved who wanted one," Felicity said. "Seriously, though, I love the peace of my life. I love not worrying about someone's spirituality. What if my child didn't want to know Christ? The world's a mess." Here she shook her head. "I'd hate to bequeath the family I adored this awful planet with its Babylonian ideals."

He opened his mouth. Closed it again. Her reasoning? He didn't agree.

Before he could speak, she leaned toward him and placed a finger over his lips. "I know the arguments. My brothers told me, especially Bert."

"The pastor?"

She nodded. "He and Gracie gave me every biblical reason to have children. They're convinced their kids are the ones who will correct the ills of the world." She shrugged, then moved in next to him.

He pulled her closer. The heat of her body chased away the last of his tension. "Maybe one of them will be the next John Wesley."

She tilted her head and glanced at him. "John Wesley will have to be the one baking in Gracie's belly. The four already here? Not a chance." She laughed.

"Little firebrands?"

"Definitely. But is there any reason to not be happy with the abundance of beauty God's given us?"

Happy? Am I happy? He knew the answer and had no argument for Felicity. "I understand." He lifted her hand and kissed the smooth skin. Silk under his lips.

She lay her head on his shoulder, and they sat in silence.

Wind chimes tinkled from somewhere. The air conditioner clicked on. Signs the world still existed, but, at the moment, nothing mattered but the woman in his arms.

He closed his heavy eyes for a minute. Visions of children buried under paper filtered through his mind. Lost families scrambled over the piles of paper, crying. Someone screamed. With a snort, he bolted awake.

Felicity jolted in his arms.

"Sorry." He wiped his mouth and hoped he hadn't drooled on her.

"No problem. I nodded off too."

He stood. "I can go to church tomorrow—for the whole service. Would you like to come to Christ Church?"

"I'd love to, but ..." She stood and took his hands.

"Off to brother Bert's?"

She smiled.

Her full lips lured him in. He inhaled and held his breath to stop from taking her in her arms and making speech impossible. He behaved himself.

"I'd skip going to New Life, but we're on for the soup kitchen this week. Gracie gave me a list of chores." She draped her arms around his neck. Her long fingers twined themselves in his hair. She kissed him.

His stomach flipped, and he forced himself to step away. If he didn't? He managed to avoid compromising himself a few minutes ago. His self-control only went so far.

"I can go to Christ Church next week," she said.

"I'll be on call. The way work has gone, I probably won't go, myself."

She nodded, and they walked to the door. "I had a wonderful time."

"Me too. I'll call you early next week."

Parker didn't see much of the road as he drove home. He hummed his favorite country tunes. In his bathroom, he didn't see his reflection as he combed his wet hair and brushed his teeth.

His down comforter swaddled him, and dreamless sleep came quickly.

Light streaming through his window bolted him upright. *Nine already?* He missed the early service but had time to loll in bed and dream of Felicity. With the perfection of this weekend, life in Jacksboro would be doable.

He propped his arm behind his head and stared at the ceiling.

No emergency calls for kids in distress. A lazy Sunday morning. A beautiful woman waiting for his next call.

Felicity was right. In whatever state he found himself, he would be content. His gaze searched the ceiling as though looking for God. *I promise, Lord. You've blessed me beyond measure. If Lily was wrong for me, I'm glad we didn't marry.*

Sunday morning, Meredith and Bean returned from the barn to find the kitchen in disarray.

"Roxie!" Meredith called. "Come here."

The child skulked into the room looking like a kicked dog.

Meredith closed her eyes. If she looked at Roxie, she'd lose her resolve and keep them. She couldn't handle these girls. The rattling of dishes made her open her eyes once more.

Bean and Roxie put the dishes in the dishwasher while barely jangling a dish or clinking silverware.

Roxie worked with bowed shoulders, more like an abused child than a five-year-old.

Abused?

Of course. Tears bit Meredith's eyes. She blinked them away. Last night she allowed self-pity to hammer her. Nine months ago, grief about killed her.

She blinked some more. Her nose ran. *No. I will* not *cry.* Her emotions refused to listen. She ran up the stairs and into her room while sobs choked her chest. The screen from the window still leaned against the wall and the warming morning streamed into the room.

She crawled onto the roof. Leaning against the dormer, she tucked her knees into her chest. With a bowed head, tears racked her. She sobbed for an eternity. When her hysterics subsided into hiccupping sobs, she fished a tissue from her pocket and blew her nose. If she remembered right, Parker Snow went to church. She'd have to wait until noon or so before she called.

These girls deserved someone who could treat them as they should be treated. Someone who wouldn't think about goats when they went missing. Who'd know they wanted their mama and daddy. Someone who wouldn't lose her temper.

They need a mother in control of life. Someone to love them as they deserved.

Perhaps she was too sinful. God thought so.

Two hours later, the girls romped outside in the goat pen.

Oreo nibbled Roxie's hair, and Vivienne head-butted Bean. As though Billie Jean and Bobbi-Jo Riggs recognized a fellow baby, the kids danced around Crystal.

Despite herself, Meredith smiled. Like this, she could love the girls. Too bad the idyll always passed, and her malignant side took over.

She stepped into the house, found her cell, and scrolled through the contacts for Parker Snow's number. She pressed the call button, and the phone chirred as it dialed.

Of course, as voice mail picked up, a van pulled into her driveway.

Sunny and the Sunshine gang.

Her phone pinged, reminding her to leave a voice mail. She couldn't say, "Get these kids out of my hair" on voice mail.

Doors clanged. Little voices faded as their owners raced to the goats. Or more likely, ran to Meredith's human brood.

"Parker. Meredith Jaynes here. Sorry to call on Sunday. Call me."

"Hey, Merry." Sunny appeared on the porch, all smiles, with a pan of something steaming and hot.

Meredith clicked off her phone and shoved it onto the counter.

Blake held the door as his wife waltzed in.

"Mom's coming in a half-an-hour with dessert, probably something loaded with fruit and avocado—if she could find a recipe with those two items," Sunny said.

Blake grimaced.

"And a tame kitten for Roxie—"

"Roxie's allergic—"

"Sorry, Sis," Blake said as the screen bounced shut behind him. "You know Cora."

"I'll pop this in the oven on warm." Sunny shoved the pan into the oven and fussed with the controls. "While the girls play, tell me about your week. I bet you had loads of fun."

Loads.

"I've got sweet tea." Meredith poured a pitcher of tea and added ice. Grabbed the glasses. "Open the door for me. We'll sit outside before the sun hits the back porch.

As the sun slowly chased the shade away, the three sipped tea, chatted about their weeks. Meredith said nothing about the thievery at the farmers' market or losing the girls or forgetting to lock her loaded gun. Allison Buchanan would spit fire at the last two events. If she told Miss Sunshine Buchanan that she wanted to give the girls back to Social Services?

No sense riling big sis until the deed couldn't be undone.

"Why's Mom bringing a cat?" Meredith asked.

"She's seen how Roxie loves your barn cats. And those wild, clawing, yowling beasts don't let anyone touch them. She's good with animals."

"Do you see how she sneezes, her eyes water, and her nose runs whenever she's around Mom, let alone a physical cat?"

Blake gave a lopsided grin. "Exposure therapy. You know—eat dirt, forget hand sanitizers, snack on peanuts during pregnancy. Mom's ... well, she's Cora Crabtree."

As though Blake's words summoned his in-laws, Mom and Dad pulled into the driveway. Mom hopped out of their car. "Hey, baby ..." Her voice drifted away as her hand waved above her head, which she ducked into the back seat. She turned, clutching a kitten. "Roxie." Mom scuttled over to the pen, and six kids ran to her as though she were Santa Claus.

"Mom." Meredith stood and took a step toward the crew.

Sunny grabbed her arm. She nodded at Meredith's vacant chair. "Don't worry. The kitten's male, so you won't be saddled with kittens.

Meredith sat as Dad stepped onto the porch.

Despite the distance, Roxie's squeal of delight resonated. *I can buy stock in Claritin.*

Dad bent over and kissed Meredith's cheek. Did the same to Sunny. "Ain't kissing you, dude." He punched Blake's arm.

Blake saluted. "Have a seat."

Dad pulled up a wicker chair.

Meredith kept her eyes on Roxie.

She held the cat under its front legs, its back against her belly. The kitten's face was mostly white but had an orange stripe running down its nose, like an upside-down exclamation point. The child's grin seemed to straighten her posture. She looked in control.

Mom's Chacos thwacked up the porch step. "Why so somber?"

"You know she's allergic to cats, don't you?"

"Exposure will create antibodies." Mom peered at Meredith's glass. "Is your tea unsweet?"

Meredith gave a slow sweep of her head.

Mom groaned and shook a finger.

"Come on and eat, Cora." Blake stood. "Sunny made chicken and biscuits. Did you bring dessert?"

"Avocado fruit salad."

Meredith laughed.

"What's so funny," Mom asked.

Mom could find a way to combine avocados with anything— kale, mashed potatoes, or strawberries and melon. She looked at the five other kids in the field. Three currently were rolling down the hill. *Fruit salad—a good symbol for this crew.*

Owen and Crystal looked to be racing on their butts. Crystal led by several lengths. *Little, non-mobile Crystal. Are you going to be a racer? The athlete of your family?*

Roxie clutched the kitten to her and ran to the porch. "Lookit what Gamma gived me."

Gamma? Meredith eyed her mother.

"I'm gonna call him Olaf like the snowman." She ran her finger down the cat's face. "See his carrot nose?"

"He does have a carrot for a nose. And he's mostly white, like a snowman." Meredith took the cat. He clawed her.

"He wants me." Roxie took the kitten back. She squeezed the cat to her chest then sneezed. "I likes Olaf." She ran back to the crew romping in the field.

Meredith chuckled again. *You'll be the vet.*

Chapter 12

Monday, after doctors and therapists and tests and not eating since six a.m., Meredith pulled her truck into McDonald's overcrowded lot.

Inside, a blast of frigid air hit her. "Welcome to winter, girls."

The two older children skipped to an empty booth.

Meredith wedged her family in. "What do you want?"

"Happy Meal."

"With hamburgers and French fries."

"Chicken."

"Nogs," Crystal said.

"Crystal wants nuggets." Bean translated.

"Toys."

"And soda."

Meredith covered her grin with her index finger. "Shh. I can't tell who wants what if you all speak at once. Two nugget meals, one hamburger, and no soda."

The two older girls pouted. Crystal, who had been smiling, looked from one sister to the other. As though inspired by their sulk, Crystal stuck out her bottom lip.

"How about drinking chocolate milk?"

Bean and Roxie cheered.

After glancing from one sister to the other, Crystal grinned and clapped her hands.

They certainly were easy to please. "Watch your sisters, Bean."

She nodded.

As she stepped to the kiosk, Meredith looked over her shoulder at her family. *What a good girl Bean is. Could I have done everything today without her?* She punched in her order and added three apple pies. The kids hadn't asked for them, but they deserved a treat. They were so well-behaved. Too well-behaved.

She waited at the counter as orders came out. The girls sat obediently in the booth. A perfect trio of beauties.

The doctor had taken x-rays of Crystal's lower back and ordered an open MRI—the appointment in Oak Ridge would come through sometime this week. He mentioned spina bifida, but the case appeared to be mild. With therapy, she might walk and maintain bladder and bowel control.

Thank heavens for the last one. Whatever the kid had been eating produced enough methane to fuel a nuclear reactor.

Meredith didn't believe the child would be incontinent. Last night, Crystal demanded to sit on the potty after Roxie finished. Crystal preened when she peed. Meredith could hope for bladder control. What if the child never walked?

"Number 78."

Her food. Meredith grabbed the tray and headed back to the girls.

TennCare would cover a wheelchair. After the doctor, she'd taken Roxie to speech therapy at LaFollette Rehab. At the center, she'd seen a boy with a wheelchair with flashing lights around its tires. Maybe they made them with pink lights instead of the blue the boy used. Crystal would love the sparkles. Using a wheelchair would become an envious situation.

Would TennCare or DCS cover the cost of a fancy chair?

Regardless. She'd make sure Crystal had one.

Wait. Not keeping them. This is too much.

A lot of work.

"Happy Meal." Roxie squealed and grabbed a box, then she withdrew into her turtle posture. "Sowry." She swallowed hard—so hard Meredith couldn't help but notice her throat constrict. "I mean sorrwe." She grinned. "I said it wight."

"You did indeed improve your pronunciation. But you have nothing to be sorry about." Meredith put the tray on the table and ran her hand over the child's fine hair.

The girls sat with hunched shoulders and hands in their laps.

These poor kids.

"Eat." Meredith opened boxes of chicken nuggets and pushed the hamburger meal to Bean. She twisted off caps from the chocolate milks and sat them in front of the girls. "You've got to be hungry."

"Potty. Go potty."

Meredith's head jerked up. "Crystal, do you want to use the bathroom?"

"Potty." Crystal bobbed her head.

"Watch your sister, Bean." She hoisted Crystal and headed to the restroom. She sat Crystal on the john, and the little thing did what she wanted to do.

So, we definitely won't have to worry about bladder control!

Parker's stomach growled. That's what he got for arriving to work at eight to catch up on work. *Diet a la DCS.* No time to eat.

It was now after two o'clock. He squinted and tried to think where he needed to be next. A home visit up on Stinking Creek at three?

If he grabbed a Mickey D's takeout, he could eat on the way. Maybe return Mrs. Jaynes's call before he lost cell service.

The end of McDonald's drive-thru line stretched in a wild Mobius strip. Drive-thru would not save time today. He backed-up and parked across from McDonald's.

Ordering inside will be faster.

He jogged into the side door. A line formed at the ordering kiosk but moved quickly. He punched in his choice then stepped toward the counter and bumped into a customer. "I'm sorry." He glanced up. "Mrs. Jaynes. I was going to call you on the way to my three o'clock."

"Guess what?" Her grin lit up the room. "This little one went potty. We're going to celebrate with ice cream at Dairy Queen."

Parker chucked the child's chin. "Good job."

"Hungry." Crystal pointed toward the booth where her sisters played with their Happy Meal toys. "Bean. Ro Ro."

"Go eat," Parker said. "I'll catch you before I leave."

Mrs. Jaynes gave him her incredibly innocent smile before she stepped toward Crystal's sisters.

Once he had his order in hand, Parker headed toward the Jaynes's table. "Sorry I didn't return your call yesterday. I'd silenced the phone for church and forgot about it until this morning. How can I help you?"

Mrs. Jaynes licked her lips.

He waited.

"I'm having a hard time understanding the girls. They need a lot of help ..."

"Speech therapy can—"

"Not therapy. Roxie had her first session this morning. Crystal saw the doctor." Mrs. Jaynes poked her straw up and down in her drink cup. Her uneaten Big Mac lay on the tray in front of her. She didn't look at him. "Taking care of children of addicts is hard."

"Celebrate Recovery has programs. CR helps more than addicts. The organization assists families dealing with the fallout of addiction. The program comforts those suffering from hurts and hang-ups and …" He paused. "I forgot how CR's slogan goes."

At last, Mrs. Jaynes met his eyes.

Buoyed by what looked like a positive response, he barreled on. "CR helps those who are suffering—"

"Don't they meet at Trinity Church?"

He nodded.

"They'll open a resort on the moon before I step foot in there."

Her words felt like a slap. Mrs. Jaynes was a gentle, fragile woman. But this angry reaction?

He glanced away then back at Mrs. Jaynes. "Are you familiar with NA? Narcotics Anonymous meets at the Rec Center."

She hiked a shoulder and looked at him with large eyes.

For the first time he noticed their color—not brown particularly and not green. Hazel? Specked with gold.

"I—"

His phone rang. He glanced down. "Sorry, I have to take this, then I have thirty minutes to make the forty-minute ride to Stinking Creek. I'll call later?"

"Miss Mewedith, I gotta use the bafroom."

Parker shifted the bag of food to his left hand and held out his right to shake. "Honestly, CR is the best there is for recovery. But NA works too." He glanced at his watch.

His phone continued its ringing.

"Answer your phone." Mrs. Jaynes nodded in the direction of the ringing "Call me later."

Parker clicked on his cell and waved good-bye as he strode toward the door.

"Parker Snow."

No one spoke for twenty seconds or so. Then a woman's voice came on. "We've noticed an irregularity with your Discover Card—"

He hung up. Didn't have a Discover Card.

He shifted his phone and food, then turned at the door and watched Mrs. Jaynes walk Roxie to the ladies' room. Mrs. Jaynes didn't look relieved about NA or CR. *Did she have more to talk about? And her reaction about going to Celebrate Recovery at Trinity Church?* An overwhelming need to protect her surged from the pit of his stomach.

Caring parents are hard to come by. Lord, don't let me lose her.

"Wait, Mrs. Jaynes."

She turned and lifted her gentle eyes towards him.

He gripped his bag of food between his teeth and scribbled a note on the back of his business card. "Pffle trt."

She smiled. Took the card.

He grabbed his bag again. "The translation of pffle trt— foster care training starts Thursday night."

He opened the door to the overwhelming heat of non-air-conditioned Tennessee and dashed into the car.

"Miss Mewedith, why are we stopping at Dairy Queen?" Roxie called from the back seat.

"Crystal learned to use the potty."

"Me too."

She smiled. "But this was your sister's first time."

"Uh-uh. She didded powty last night. Like me!"

"But can all of us eat ice cream?" Bean leaned as far forward as the belt would allow her.

"Indeed."

"I get two." Roxie waved two fingers in Meredith's peripheral vision.

"No, you don't." Bean sounded like a typical older sister—bossy and know-it-all. Sort of like Sunny.

"I went to the bafroom too."

"No, Roxie. Crystal asked." Bean talked over Roxie's head. "If anyone gets extra ice cream, I do because—"

"Bean, enough." Meredith parked the car. Thank heavens they were fighting. She almost lost her resolve to give them to another home. She opened the back door to lift Crystal from her seat.

"My kitty, Olaf, wants ice cream." Roxie crossed her arms.

"Your cat doesn't eat ice—"

"Yes." Roxie slumped and banged her feet against the bottom of the seat. "He's used to the cold 'cause he's made of snow. He wants cold ice cream."

Knowing how the duo would react, Meredith slammed the door and stepped toward DQ,.

"Wait for me."

"And me."

"Bean. Ro Ro." Crystal strained in Meredith's arm and leaned toward the two repentant sisters standing at the car.

Meredith held out her hand, and the girls raced to her.

The air conditioning at Dairy Queen had turned the entire interior into a walk-in freezer. Meredith didn't relish living in the land of *Frozen*, so the four sat at an outside booth. To stop their whining, everyone got large sundaes. Meredith made hers a triple.

"But you didn't eat lunch, Miss Meredith." Bean crossed her arms, again looking like the matron of the family.

"I had a Big Mac."

"You didn't eat any."

"I did. Some." *Why am I arguing with an eight-year-old?*

Her phone rang. "Parker. Hello."

"I've got a minute or two here before I lose my connection. What's up?"

"What do you mean?"

"More than finding a support group bothered you. Is everything okay?"

"The girls ..." She glanced at them.

Bean had finished her ice cream and eyed Roxie's.

"Here." Roxie shoved her treat over.

"Wait a minute, Parker." She covered the mouthpiece of her phone. "Don't you like your ice cream, Roxie?"

She bobbed her head. "I love ice cream, but Bean always share wit me. Now *I* can."

Could a heart melt? Meredith's blood certainly warmed. "Parker?" She turned her attention back to the phone call. "Any news on the parents?"

"None."

"Let me know as soon as you have something. The girls need closure."

"Sure th—"

And the connection went dead.

Dead.

She studied her girls. Sweet, tragic, beautiful beings.

Was it a good thing we lost our connection before I gave them up?

Chapter 13

Meredith lay down for a minute after her shower. *Friday, already? Market tomorrow ...*

A warm bundle of flesh snuggled in close to her.

Meredith shifted and wrapped her arms around Roxie. The imp wriggled closer. A loud purr from Olaf said the kitten had joined them. She sighed. The warmth of Roxie and the kitten and her bed begged her to stay here all day. "Hey, Rox. I think I fell back asleep."

"You did. For a long time."

"You should've woken me."

"Miss Mewedith? Can I call you Mommy now?"

Meredith's eyelids popped open. "You always could until we find your real mom. Why are you asking?"

"Last night, you took a class to be our mommy." Roxie moved closer.

Meredith cupped her head in her hand. "Not exactly *to be* your mom. The training class allows you to stay with me until the police find your real one." Meredith's heart constricted. Nearly two weeks passed. Those bodies found at Cove Lake were likely these kids' parents, especially as the man's name was Daniel.

"Why don't my real Mama and Daddy come home?"

Meredith's fingers played with Roxie's hair while Olaf crawled over Meredith to swat at sunbeams splaying across the quilt from the open window. "Maybe they're sick?" With her index finger, she lifted Roxie's chin and grinned. "Have you been into chocolate?" With her thumb, she rubbed Roxie's mouth. "I haven't fed you yet."

Roxie sat up in bed.

"Don't worry. Bean cookeded us pancakes. With chocolate chips."

Meredith propped herself up on an elbow. "She cooked?" Meredith sniffed. Smelled only fried pancakes, not a house on fire or melting plastic. "She should've gotten me."

Little feet pounded her stairs, and, with a thud from a kick, her partially opened door swung wide.

Bean, hoisting a plate of misshapen pancakes in one hand and Crystal on the hip on the opposite side, stepped in.

"We made you flapjacks." Bean flopped her sister onto the bed, tilting the plate as she did. Syrup spilled from the plate into Roxie's hair and onto the pillow.

"Hey." Roxie's eyes pooled with tears, and her one-syllable word rang with indignation. "Mommy, Bean got me sticky."

"Mommy?" Bean's eyes widened. Meredith couldn't tell if Bean was angry or sad or confused.

Meredith leaned up against the headboard, took the plate, and patted the last spare spot on the bed. She kissed Roxie's head. "Your sister made you sweeter. We'll take a lavender bubble bath later."

The girls chattered while Meredith ate cold, leathery pancakes. The best she ever had.

The sun crept high as Bean and Roxie washed and dried the pots and pans. The scent of cinnamon from baking zucchini bread filled the room. Meredith's stomach rumbled. She'd eaten five of Bean's pancakes and snacked on the nuts destined for the sweet bread. Something shifted her appetite to high gear.

The rumble of vehicles outside brought Meredith to the back porch.

Sunny's van and Mom's truck pulled into the driveway—a guaranteed caravan of chaos. Engines stopped, and the usual storm of urchins tumbled out, stampeded to the porch, and burst into the kitchen.

Meredith watched the oddly dressed crew.

Phoebe wore a swimsuit. Her goggles perched over her eyes. Visible globs of sparkly sunscreen slathered her nose.

'Nissa wore an off-the-shoulder, pink suit with ruffles and pink water shoes.

"Y'all heading to the pool at Cove Lake?" Meredith asked.

"No." Mom made her grand entrance followed by Sunny holding Owen. Plastic Walmart bags hung from Mom and Sunny's arms like bangle bracelets.

Sunny plopped Owen on the floor. Immediately he crawled to Crystal. Sunny shimmied her bags off her arms and onto the table.

Mom pecked Meredith on the cheek. "We're taking Dad's pontoon out. Girls' day."

"Leaving Owen here?" Meredith laughed.

"Our only exception." The oven timer dinged. Sunny pulled out two pans of sweet bread. They clanked on the counter, and she fished for a knife in the utensil drawers.

"But none of us has bathing suits or towels or—"

"There." Sunny pointed to the bags covering the table with the butter knife she held.

"What're these?" Bean asked. Hope shimmered in her eyes as she clenched the back of a chair. "Is this for us?'

"Yes, ma'am." Sunny turned back to the cabinets and rattled dishes. "Well, not all for *you*, but for your sisters and you." She spoke facing the pans of hot bread.

"You know the zucchini bread is too hot," Meredith said.

131

"Ew, I hate zucchini," Anissa whined.

"Don't eat any." Sunny knifed into the steaming loaves.

"And this is for you." Mom handed Meredith a brightly printed bag decorated with images of fireworks.

"What's this?" Meredith asked. Knowing her mother, she probably knit a two-piece bathing suit out of rabbit fur.

"Open your gift."

Meredith removed the top tissue paper. True to her prediction, the bag contained a crocheted piece. She pulled out a tunic-length, open-knit bathing suit cover-up. Not rabbit fur or goat hair. Cotton yarn had been knitted in a drop stitch pattern in shades of pink and burgundy which morphed into blues. The colors deepened as they descended from bodice to hem of a pretty overshirt.

"How beautiful," she whispered. The magnificent garment swallowed her next breath.

"Lookit, Miss Meredith." Bean waved a pink bathing suit in the air. "I gots the same as Anissa's. And I got flipflops."

"I gotted a blue one." Roxie squealed and jumped. "Lookit, Mommy, with the real Olaf." She shoved the suit adorned with a giant snowman in Meredith's face. "And sparkles on my shoes." Roxie looked up at Mom. "Does kitty Olaf gotted a bathing suit?"

"No, honey." Mom sat and wriggled Roxie onto her lap—hugging her close.

The child sneezed.

"Kitty-cats don't like to swim."

"Is this for Crystal?" Bean held up a suit decked out with Paw Patrol characters.

"Indeed." Sunny kissed the top of Bean's head and slid two plates of steaming sweet bread on the square foot of clear table. "We left the towels and the coolers in the van. "Now, seeing as you'll have evening chores with your nannies, we're leaving as soon as you change, so we have lots of time. We've got Dad's pontoon all day. Blake gave me the credit card, so we'll have gas. We'll sail to Shanghai Marina and eat." She clapped her hands. "Chop, chop. Let's go."

"This is a beautiful cover-up, but I don't have a suit."

Sunny slid the next two plates of bread onto the table and leaned over the bag Meredith held. "Look under the rest of the tissue paper."

Meredith stared at her sister.

"Mom didn't only knit you a top." Sunny lifted the hem of her overshirt. Under the cover-up identical to Meredith's, only in shades of yellow and orange, she wore a two-piece bikini.

Meredith's jaw dropped. She plucked out the last piece of tissue paper from her bag and pulled out one identical to Sunny's, except for the color. "I'm not wearing this in public." Her face heated. "This is too ... risqué ... to even be worn in private."

Her mother lifted the hem of her sundress. She wore the identical get-up, only in purples. "We all are. Girls' day. We're swimming in our secret cove. The tunics make this demure enough even for a prude like you." She swatted Meredith's rump. "Go put on your new duds."

"But I have to be back to prep for market and take care of—"

"You won't miss a thing." Sunny rattled bottles in the fridge. "Who wants milk?"

"'Ew. I want real milk."

"Me."

"I want soda."

Meredith shook her head and left to change.

By the time she returned to the kitchen, Mom's truck had left, and Sunny was tooting the van's horn. Meredith grabbed her wallet and phone. Then she looked at her cell. *No service out on the lake*. She slid the phone on the counter. After clicking off the lights, Meredith ran out of the house like someone Bean and Roxie's ages.

An hour later, they sailed into their secret cove off a dead-end bay. Dad had found this spot when both she and Sunny were their kids' age. The inlet went nowhere. Wasn't known for fish. An uninhabited stretch of land belonging to the TVA surrounded their favorite swimming hole. With nothing to draw in boaters, the cove remained empty.

Mom and Sunny whipped off their wraps.

"Come on." 'Nissa tugged Bean by the hand to the front of the boat. "We're jumping."

"No!" Meredith lunged.

But both girls dove off the pontoon before she could stop them. They disappeared beneath the green waters of Norris Lake, then bobbed to the surface, buoyed by orange lifejackets.

"Come on, Roxie, Phoebe." Sunny already held Owen as she sat on the stern.

Phoebe crawled down the ladder. Roxie looked over her shoulder at Meredith.

In the water, the older girls screamed and splashed and laughed.

Roxie's shoulders hunched, and her lips trembled. Meredith guided her to the ladder. "Roxie, we won't let you drown. You can have fun like Bean and 'Nissa or sit on the boat with—" A splash interrupted her. She turned toward the noise.

Her mother and Crystal broke the surface of the water. Crystal's mouth opened in shock. Then she giggled. "'Gain. Do 'gain."

"Mom." Meredith ran to the stern. "Be careful. Crystal can't walk."

"But she can swim, I bet." Her mother let go of the child. Meredith gasped.

Crystal chortled. "Swim. I swim." Her legs, wavy in the refracted light of the water, paddled like a puppy's. Her arms splashed, and she blinked against the churning water.

Meredith stood at the edge of the pontoon. She could watch and swelter or join her family.

She looked down at her attire. Swimming in her cover-up would tangle her movements. Without the cover-up, she'd be free like Sunny and Mom.

She whipped off her overshirt and jumped feet first. Seconds seemed like hours as she hurled up into the sunlight and then crashed into the lake. The cool water shielded the ignominy of her microscopic bathing attire. She sunk into the darker depths, then breached the surface like a playful porpoise. Laughter greeted her. She held out her hands. "Roxie, I'll catch you."

Roxie crawled down the ladder. The water buoyed her. "I'm floating."

"That's why you have a life jacket. Go join Phoebe."

Roxie let go. Giggled.

Crystal and Mom paddled toward Meredith and stopped several feet away. "Swim to Miss Meredith." She let go of Crystal who propelled herself away.

"No! Mom. She's scared."

Crystal's mouth puckered, ready to cry. She turned her head and looked at Mom, then back at Meredith. She waved her arms and kicked her legs and thrust herself into Meredith's arms. "I swim!" She leaned toward Mom. "'Gain."

Meredith let go.

"No. 'Gain."

"Do you want me to throw you?"

Crystal looked up at her and nodded.

Meredith tossed the toddler toward her mother.

Mom tossed her back.

A half-hour later, both adults, cold and tired, swam to the pontoon to join Sunny and Owen who had given up on swimming. Mom climbed aboard.

"Roxie and Phoebe, swim where we can see you." Meredith tugged Crystal toward the ladder. "Let's dry off."

"No." Crystal splashed the water, dousing her eyes. Instead of crying, she grinned and slapped the lake again.

"Aren't you cold?"

"No." She splashed again and giggled.

"Bean, hold on to your sister. No tossing her. No letting her go."

"Miss Meredith." Bean's blue-tinged lips pouted.

Meredith arched her brow. "Either watch your sister or climb out of the water."

Up on the pontoon, Mom handed Meredith and Sunny a cup of unsweet tea while her eyes stayed focused on the girls frolicking in the water. "I'm tickled with how so much joy came out of so much sorrow."

Meredith crinkled her forehead. "The girls' situation?"

"Wasn't thinking of them, but yes."

"What were you thinking?" Sunny asked.

"Over eighty years ago, people lived down there." Mom pointed off into the water. "The government came in and made them leave their homes, dig up their dead and relocate so the land could be flooded. Leaving your heritage to be flooded for government purposes had to be hard."

"Out by my place, off Bluff Road," Meredith said, "you can see the steps leading to an old church when the TVA lowers the lake levels. Worlds existed down there now masked by the water."

"Didn't you and John hang out by the old church?" Mom asked.

Meredith nodded as she frowned.

"We're cold," Anissa whined.

"Then come back onto the pontoon," Mom said. "Roxie and Phoebe, you too."

"But ..." Phoebe whined.

"No backtalk."

All the girls kicked to the boat ladder, but Crystal pulled away.

"No. Swim." Crystal splashed the girls.

"Stop, Crystal." Meredith reached down and hauled the toddler out. "We need to dry off." Meredith rubbed the towel over Crystal's arms and torso. "After a snack, we're going to Shanghai for dinner."

Shortly, the older girls, their lips blue with cold, shivered under towels and ate veggie chips, Mom's supposed healthy alternative to regular chips.

The sun moved west. The wind cooled them as they motored toward the marina.

At Shanghai, Meredith's kids, Phoebe, and Owen agreed to eat Mom's suggestion of fish and mashed potatoes.

'Nissa refused. She and Sunny chowed down on hamburgers and French fries.

Mom ate half their fries.

Later, Meredith leaned against the front seat of Sunny's van. Her mood darkened with the dusk. She had chores. Goats. Packing for market.

"I forgot to tell you." Sunny pulled up to Meredith's house. "If you don't mind, the girls are coming to Mom's and my house for a sleepover."

"They'd love it. Give me a few minutes to pack pillowcases for overnight. I should buy the girls suitcases."

"Nope." Sunny slid the car into park. "Mom and I are making another Walmart run. If we're going to have regular sleepovers, we'll need caches of toiletries and clothes at our places."

"Wait until my mama and Danny hear about the boat and the sleepover." Bean unsnapped her seatbelt and leaned over the console. She tapped Sunny on the shoulder. "Do you think Grandpa Crabtree will take Mama and Danny on the boat? Danny always promised to take us. He loves boats."

Meredith's sister shifted in her seat and gave Bean the smile that earned her the Sunny nickname. "Anytime they want, sweet cheeks."

Meredith climbed out.

Mom's truck pulled in parallel to Sunny's. The passenger window lowered. "I'll race you to town."

"You go on ahead, Mom," Sunny said. "You've got two sleepyheads back there."

Mom turned and studied the sleeping Roxie and Phoebe. Both strapped in their seatbelts, holding hands, snored with opened lips. She revved her engine and backed out. After squealing her tires, Mom disappeared down Hen Waddle.

Meredith leaned through the van's open window and kissed Bean's head. "You keep 'Nissa, Owen and Crystal out of trouble. Okay?"

"'Kay." The window started to roll up, then opened once more. "If Mama comes home, tell them where I am."

"I promise I will."

The windows closed, and Sunny made a more decorous U-turn than her mother.

Meredith waved them off. Their absence weighted her like gravity and welded her feet to the ground. Without the girls, sorrow was too heavy to bear.

She stepped into her lit kitchen. *I'd turned off the lights.*

The kitchen was pristine. Dishes washed. Zucchini bread wrapped. Not filthy like this morning when they left.

She slipped into her work togs.

At the back of the barn, rolls of hay stood sentinel. *Pa Jaynes hayed today.* She stepped inside to silence. Not a nanny in sight. On her freezer, she found a note.

Ma will milk the herd, and we'll bring you the milk tomorrow. Your flock is working for me in the east lot eating their keep in weeds and brush.

Sweet Pa Jaynes. Works the bank all day. The farm the rest of the time. The man never slept.

She didn't need the milk, though, especially with the girls away and market tomorrow.

Market. I need to pack the truck.

In her workroom, no boxes of soap sat on shelves. The bars she needed to wrap had disappeared. *Where ...? The truck? They weren't in the house.*

At her truck, she opened the cab cover. There, in tidy stacks, stood all her supplies.

She smiled even as her heart weighted. Nothing to do. Before the girls, she yearned for free time. Now?

She returned to the house and turned on the burner to boil water for tea.

Her phone lay where she'd tossed it this morning. While the water boiled, Meredith called Pa Jaynes. Her in-laws could keep whatever milk they got.

No one answered, so she left a message, then discovered she had one herself. Parker Snow. His message was succinct.

Call me. Important.

She dialed as the kettle whistled.

"Parker Snow." Laughter and chatter sounded in the distance.

"I'm sorry if I'm interrupting. I just got in." Meredith turned off the screeching teapot. "What's up?"

"Excuse me." The words were faint as though Parker wasn't talking into the speaker. Things quieted on his end. "I've got bad news," he said. "Or at least definitive news."

Her mouth dried.

"We've got DNA matches. The man and woman we found last week were Crystal and Roxie's parents. Daniel Harrison and Beth Willoughby."

Her throat constricted. "What about Bean?"

"Harrison wasn't her father, but Willoughby was her mom."

Meredith sank into the kitchen chair.

"We can't locate birth certificates on the youngest two. We found Bean's out in Memphis. Her real name is Pearl Solomon."

"Have you found their families?"

"Sorry. I can't hear you." His voice muffled again as though he covered the receiver. "Be right there." The volume increased once more. "What did you say?"

Meredith inhaled. Wasn't this what she wanted? For the girls to go to their real homes and be loved by real relatives? "Have you located other members of their families?"

"Not yet. Call me whenever you need something. I've got to go. When I know more, I'll contact you."

Meredith sat for a long time with her cell in her hand.

My poor babies.

Chapter 14

Out the back window of the Snows' living room, the last rays of the sun vanished behind the mountains. Felicity lifted a tray of pastries like an offering before setting them on the coffee table. "These are from me."

Parker's stomach grumbled despite the fact he'd finished a course of grilled salmon, fresh asparagus, and a baked potato the size of Idaho with enough fixings to sate a Sumo wrestler. He fixed his attention on the variety of sweets. His mouth watered.

"My eyes are up here." Felicity laughed and pointed at her face with two fingers. She settled on the love seat. "And no, I didn't bake them. I stopped at Flour Child's on my way back from Knoxville."

"Who was on the phone?" His mother came into the living room with a tray of coffee and cups. She turned her head before Parker could answer and called to Dad who dawdled in the kitchen. "Darrick, bring in the sugar and half and half." She put the tray down.

His mother sat on the couch and poured coffee. "No worries about sleeping. Decaf." She handed Felicity a cup. As Parker's father returned with creamer, and sugar, and spoons tucked in his breast pocket, she poured a second cup. "So, who called?"

"Mrs. Jaynes."

"What a tragedy about those kids' parents," his father said.

"Mrs. Jaynes sounded distraught." Parker stirred in two teaspoons of sugar. "Almost like I said her folks died. She's such a fragile woman."

Felicity shook her head.

"What?" Parker asked.

"She's a lot tougher than you think," Felicity said.

Parker waited for more.

"What makes you say that?" his mother asked.

"The bits and pieces of the funeral nine months ago have fallen into place. What a fiasco." Felicity placed her cup on the coaster. "Heartbreaking and cruel on so many levels."

"Why was this one more tragic?" Parker asked, "aside from being a kid's funeral?"

Felicity leaned forward—her arms propped against her legs. Her abandoned coffee steamed on the table. "As I told you last week, Kit should've performed the funeral, but Mrs. Jaynes delayed it. Mr. Jaynes, what was his name ...?"

"John. He and I went to school together. He died about the time I got back to town."

She nodded. "John Jaynes was bringing in a different outfit for his daughter who had died after a long battle with cancer. As he drove to the funeral home, a kid ignored a stop sign and careened into his car killing Mr. Jaynes instantly."

The three Snows gasped almost in unison.

"You mean right after the child died?" His father asked.

Felicity nodded. "I think the next day. His death postponed the calling hours, so the family could combine the two. They had Mr. Jaynes cremated and tucked his urn in the little girl's arms." Tears sparkled in Felicity's eyes. "I see a lot of pain in my field, but this one? Can you imagine your baby holding her daddy's ashes?"

Parker pulled her into his arms. Her warmth and life dulled the horror of what Meredith Jaynes endured. No wonder sorrow swaddled her.

Dad leaned back in his chair.

"So how does this make Mrs. Jaynes strong?" Parker asked.

"During calling hours, someone bumped into a flower arrangement near the head of the receiving line. I was cleaning the mess as a man stepped forward. He said something to Mrs. Jaynes. I caught the weird words sin and befall—not the usual comfort offered at a wake.

"She yelled, 'what?' With her gentle demeanor, the volume shocked me. Mrs. Jaynes's body language spelled trouble. Before I could stand to usher the gentleman out, she hauled off and punched him in the nose. Blood flew everywhere. He shook his head, splattering those near him. Mrs. Jaynes's mother took Mrs. Jaynes to the family room, and I had to call 9-1-1. She broke the man's nose."

"Little Meredith?" Parker chuckled picturing the thin, delicate woman with the big heart socking an oaf and busting his schnoz.

Parker's mom and dad laughed.

Mom passed around the pastries.

The sight of them turned Parker's stomach.

Chapter 15

The morning sun startled Meredith awake. She bolted upright and patted the bed looking for the girls.

Not here. Having a good time.

For now.

She dressed for market and stepped into her kitchen. Granite glistened under the lights. The sun peaked through the back windows welcoming the new day. No goats or girls needed her.

The sunlight and gleaming kitchen suffocated her. She had to go someplace. Anyplace. But where? *Go see the girls?* The idea sounded right.

Halfway to Sunny's, she pulled off the road.

No. Let them play. One more day. Let them make believe their mother and Danny would join them on the next boat ride.

She turned and drove. Without paying attention, she wandered until she found herself on Bluff Road. Perhaps her conversation about this place yesterday subliminally directed her path.

Meredith maneuvered the large truck down a narrow, little-used dirt road and parked at the end where the road met the lake.

John and Rosie and she used to love to picnic here. Their checkered tablecloth covered the pine-shrouded earth under a huge tree. John strung up a hammock between the pine and a tulip poplar. He and Rosemary would lay in the hammock as he taught her bird calls. Rosie would practice until Meredith wanted to scream. After eating and bird-calling, they'd fall asleep in the soft breeze off the lake.

Meredith scanned the roadside for the tree. Where the pine last stood, lay an open patch in the woods. The tree had toppled, and the needles had fallen from the limbs. Shelf fungus clung to the bark. Moss began its crawl along the dead tree, turning the wood back to the earth.

Meredith sat on the trunk and squinted at the lake. Being mid-summer and prime boating season, Norris Lake stood at full pond hiding the sunken church. The TVA slowed the water of the dam in summer so life could frolic here.

In the distance, a bass boat purred.

A woodpecker worked a nearby tree. A crow cawed.

Peace settled here. Funny. She sat at the site of what once caused great sorrow as people left their heritage so the government could flood the hollows. Who lived here eighty years ago? By now, the children of the displaced had died and the great-grandchildren had no knowledge of what was lost.

Maybe the boater she saw several minutes ago had a great-papaw attending the meetings at the church beneath the calm waters.

Sorrow passes.

Dead trees become new growth.

She smiled. *And Meredith Jaynes becomes a philosopher.*

An early morning call had Parker following his GPS to a false alarm. Arguing neighbors saw child abuse where none existed.

But out here, deep in this hollow, his Waze refused to give him directions. GPS demanded cell service after losing him along the back roads. He'd have to drive until he picked up reception. Parker headed the way he thought he'd come. He turned down unfamiliar roads until he recognized Hen Waddle Hollow.

"Turn left then proceed for five miles," the computerized voice intoned.

"Now you talk to me," he lectured Waze, "once I know my way." Instead of heading to town, Parker turned right. Maybe he'd catch Mrs. Jaynes and see how the girls took the sad news.

He pulled into her yard as she climbed out of her truck. "You're galivanting early."

She smiled. "What brings you out here? If you're conducting a surprise welfare check, the girls are at Sunny's and my mom's."

"How'd they take the news?"

"I didn't have the heart to ruin their perfect day. We took Dad's pontoon on the lake. Then they got a 'real' sleepover. Figured tonight will be soon enough to ruin their lives."

"How're you dealing with this news?"

Meredith shrugged. "I feel so out of my league. How can people with addictions ...?"

"Organizations can help. Remember, I told you about Celebrate Rec—"

She held up her hand.

Parker's stomach growled. The noise had never been this loud since he was a kid and forgot his lunch for school. Maybe Mrs. Jaynes didn't notice.

"Hungry? I was going to fix myself oatmeal. Would you care to join me?"

"I couldn't bother you, Mrs.—"

She shook a finger at him and grinned. "My mother is missus. Please call me Meredith."

He opened his mouth to speak.

"And you're not bothering me. Actually, you're an answer to …" she bit her lips. "Was going to say prayer. Anyway, if oatmeal works for you, I'd love company. Seeing the lateness of the morning, I'm playing hooky from the farmers' market. Maybe you could coach me on how to break the news to them."

Chitchat filled the cozy kitchen as Meredith stirred the cereal. A white-faced cat with a startling orange nose matching the blotches on its torso wove figure eights around Meredith's legs.

"The cat's a new addition," Parker said.

"Mom believes Roxie needs exposure to her allergens. She gave Olaf to Roxie before I realized what she was doing. Taking the kitty away seemed crueler than letting Roxie sneeze." She reached for a bowl from the cabinet when her head jerked. She turned with her hand still raised. "I'm not going to lose my kids because I let her have a cat, am I?'

Parker laughed. "Can she breathe?"

Meredith nodded as she lowered her hand.

"Does she want the cat?"

"Most times, I can't peel Olaf from her arms. Roxie's destined to be an animal trainer or a snake venom milker, or hippo doula."

"If you keep her from venom milking, then you're fine." Parker's stomach growled again.

Meredith laughed then quickly covered her mouth. "Sorry. I'm rude."

"How so?"

"Laughing at your hunger."

Parker waved her apology away. "You'd think I didn't eat. Felicity, my girlfriend, and my mother prepared enough food last night to feed an Olympic marathoner. And I ate everything. I should still be digesting the banquet."

Meredith slipped a bowl of steaming oatmeal on the table and pushed the sugar and raisins toward Parker. "

"Can we pray?" Parker held out his hands as Meredith sat.

After a pause, she slipped her fine-boned fingers into his. Her skin was not as rough as he'd imagine farming and goat husbandry would make it.

"Thank you, Lord, for losing my way, then bringing me here. Thank you for the food I didn't need to prepare and the dishes I won't have to clean up. Amen."

Meredith laughed. "Prayer like yours will make me a praying woman again."

Parker dropped a healthy dollop of butter on the oatmeal. "'Again' implies you used to be. What happened? I'm sorry. Is my question too personal?"

"No. Like my mother and sister and father tell me, grow up and move on." Meredith salted her hot cereal. "Even my mother-in-law says I need to let God mend my heart. She lost a child too. If she could heal, perhaps I need to grow up."

"I heard John died a few days after your daughter?"

"The next day." Her eyes darkened. "I blame myself."

"How so?"

"Rosemary, my daughter, loved this ugly pink sundress with all sorts of ruffles and too much glitter. She wore the outfit ragged. When we prepped for her funeral, I brought a pretty dress I loved to Weston's Funeral Home." Her voice softened to a near whisper. "All the way home, not dressing her as she'd love nagged at me. The dress *I* wanted, she hated. The next day, I insisted John take the ugly dress and have the mortician—your girlfriend—put it on my baby. Rosie needed to rest in the clothes she loved. I was so distraught over her death, John made me take a Xanax to calm down which made

149

me insanely tired. He convinced me to go to sleep. John said he'd take care of everything. I agreed so readily. Now, I wish I'd gone with him because on his way …"

Parker waited.

Meredith's lips moved, and she blinked. "On his way to Weston's, a kid ignored a stop sign and T-boned John. My husband died instantly." She rubbed one eye with her finger. "I slept while he died. Alone."

Parker leaned forward. He yearned to take her hand and give comfort.

"With prepping my husband, we pushed the burial back a week. Your girlfriend ended up conducting the wake and burial."

"She told me the pieces she remembered."

"I thought then I lost everything. Little did I know Lester Mills would take the last of my heart."

Meredith stood and rinsed the plates. She filled the coffee carafe with water. "I'm making enough java to keep me going. Do you want some?" She faced the wall—unable to look at the pity sure to be shining in Parker's eyes. *Do I sound normal?* Meredith didn't hear tears in her voice.

"I'd love some."

She blinked several times then flipped on the coffee maker and turned. She leaned against the counter, waiting.

The scent of hot coffee filled the room, and she handed him a cup.

"Usually, I drink my morning joe before I eat," Parker said. "I need an eye-opener. The coffee smells wonderful."

They sipped coffee at the table, but Parker fidgeted.

"What's on your mind, Parker?" Meredith pushed her cup away and leaned forward. "You look confused."

"I know a Les Mills. He goes to Trinity and volunteers at CR. Is he the reason you don't want to go to Celebrate Recovery there?"

"If he's an example of Christianity ..."

Parker chewed his lip, and he glanced into the distance.

"What're you thinking?"

"There's more to your story. If you'll forgive me, bitterness doesn't match what I know of you. What did Les take from you?"

The companionable atmosphere evaporated. Did she want to share? Meredith studied Parker. Once they found the girls' families, which they would since they knew their parents' identities, she'd never see this man again.

She'd tell him. Let out the last of her grief. Maybe heal. Maybe she'd be able to handle the loss of her three little girls when the inevitable time came. She swallowed.

He tilted his head and studied her. No words were needed to understand he wanted to hear the rest of the story.

"Since your girlfriend did the funeral, you may already know."

He studied the table.

"She told you."

"Some."

Meredith clenched her hand. "The day of the funeral lasted forever. Lines of people and sorrow and small talk and the same, tired phrases, 'I'm sorry for your loss,' or 'God needed more angels.' I had no more tears left. Then Lester Mills approached. I never got on too well with the churl."

"He can be arrogant."

"I heard Xeres ordered the sea to be whipped because it disobeyed him. Mills makes Xeres look humble."

"Guess you don't like him."

She sipped her coffee. The cup clicked back onto the table. "As he neared me on the receiving line, he raised his chin in his egotistical manner. 'I'm sorry all this has happened.' He glanced at the casket, something I still couldn't do without falling apart. "'The Lord wants me to ask you something.'

"'Oh, God,' I prayed. My last prayer ever," Meredith said. "'If you have any love for me, please show me I didn't cause Rosemary and John's death.'"

"'The Lord is righteous. He wouldn't punish you without cause. What sin did you commit to make tragedy befall you?'

"I refused to hear any more. Guilt of not praying hard enough for Rosemary. Regret for letting John return to the funeral home. Hours of hearing other people's sorrow—my folks, his folks ..."

Parker leaned forward, his arms resting on the table.

"I belted him." She flexed her fist. "I thought I broke my hand. I know I broke his nose. God showed me what he thought of me. I was done with Trinity Church. Finished with God."

Chapter 16

Realizing he gaped, Parker shut his mouth. "You know you did nothing wrong." He studied her as she loaded their cups into the dishwasher. "I'm not going anywhere until we talk."

With the rattle of cups, the dishwasher door clanged shut. When Meredith turned, her face showed no turmoil.

Someone I want to protect? He shook his head to chase the inappropriate thought away. "You already told me you were playing hooky from farmers' market, so you have no place to be."

"I have nothing more to say." Sparks glinted in her eyes hinting at the anger she was capable of. "Like everyone tells me, I'm moving on."

Parker leaned back in his chair and crossed his arms.

Meredith quirked a half-smile. "I guess you mean what you say. You're settling in?"

He waved his phone in front of her. "Unless someone calls, I'm here until we talk."

"Then let's sit on the porch where there are beautiful views."

They sank into the white wicker chairs. Meredith stared into the distance.

"Amazing." Parker pointed to the mountains rising over the valley below. "Does this view ever bore you?"

"Never."

"'Though the mountains be shaken and the hills be removed, yet my unfailing love for you will not be shaken nor my covenant of peace be removed,' says the Lord, who has compassion on you.'" Parker shifted his attention from the mountains to Meredith. "Isaiah 54 something."

"Fifty-four, ten. John used to sing how the mountains and the hills would dance before the glory of God." Her chuckle sounded light. "He'd do a little jig. I'd scat sing, and we'd dance."

"He sounds like fun. You loved him very much."

Meredith smiled but remained focused on the distance. "He was a once-in-a-lifetime love. God knew what he was doing when he brought John into my life."

"I can understand leaving Trinity because they allow a judgmental boor in a leadership position. But why give up on God?"

She didn't answer.

"You didn't lose Rosemary and John because you did anything wrong. Bad things happen. Did the actions of Bean and her sisters cause their parents to die?"

"Of course not. If anything, Bean worked overtime to make sure her sisters stayed fed, clothed, and safe. And she's only eight. The other two? They're too young."

"Yet a fate, arguably worse than yours—"

Meredith leaned forward as though she wanted to leave. After a long second or two, she settled back in her chair.

"I'm not minimizing what happened to you. The girls, though, lived neglected in a hovel. Then one night, the parents didn't come home. The kids stayed there for the whole weekend without food or parental care. Crystal needs a lot more attention than an eight-year-old could provide. It took a lot of work to discover the names of those addicted parents," Parker air-quoted the last word. "To know for a fact the kids belonged to them."

Meredith dipped her head looking sheepish.

"Now, they live with a stranger. Crystal has spina bifida. Everything terrifies Roxie."

Meredith smiled. "Except Olaf and goats."

"And probably mountain lions." Parker grinned.

"My heart breaks because Roxie only feels safe with animals." Meredith's eyes glinted. "And my mother. Your life stinks when you only feel safe with Mom."

Parker laughed. "You have a good family."

"I do."

They sat in silence for a few minutes. "Bean became the parent and took on their responsibilities."

"Oh. You haven't stopped your lecture?" Meredith laughed.

"Not me. I'm a mean DCS child-taker."

Meredith slapped his arm lightly. For the first time, she leaned back in the chair as though she were comfortable.

"On top of their awful past, their future could be grim," Parker said. "They may be taken away from a home they love to live with people they've never met in a place unfamiliar to them. I don't know why God allows evil to happen. Cancer strikes down children. Car accidents kill. Parents work hard to destroy their children. These things happen, even when we're good and righteous and holy." Parker's phone rang. He glanced at the screen, then at Meredith. "Mull over my grand philosophical monologue. I'll be right back." He stepped into the kitchen and took his call.

Five minutes later, he returned to the porch.

Meredith was leaning on the railings, staring into the distance. She turned. "Emergency?"

Parker nodded. "One last thing about Les Mills. You know him better than I, but if anyone committed a sin, Mills did.

Don't let him ruin your life with Christ. There are a billion churches in Tennessee. Find another. Come to Christ Church with me or New Life with Felicity or, given Roxie's gift—one of the snake handling—"

"Never!" Meredith shuddered and laughed. "I'd reconcile with Mills before I stepped into one of those places."

"You are a wise woman." Parker laughed. "I've got to go. In the meantime, call if you need anything. I'm sorry I didn't help with telling the girls about their folks."

"When's the funeral? Surely not an open casket wake." Her voice lowered as if frozen in horror.

"No open caskets. Or funeral. The coroner will wait for a relative to step forward. If no one claims the bodies, they'll be cremated and buried."

"How awful for the girls."

He nodded.

"I'll figure out the best way to tell them. I understand grief and know what comforted me in my darkest moments."

Parker stepped off the porch. "I know you will." He drove off but watched Meredith in his rearview mirror as she waved goodbye. She didn't look sad, but not happy. He couldn't fix her. Only God could. If she let him.

The sun sat low in the west when Sunny's van drove up Meredith's driveway.

Three little girls bounced against their seatbelts.

Meredith opened the van's door as the kids spilled into the yard. "Look at y'all. So pretty."

Bean pirouetted. In her hand, she clutched a new Barbie doll, its hair already a tangled mess of synthetic strands.

Roxie ducked her head and sucked her thumb. She thrust out her other hand holding her own doll.

"A veterinarian Barbie. How wonderful. And all of you are wearing matching shorts and shirts. How can I tell you apart? Even the same sparkly headband." Meredith fingered Roxie's hair. "You're beautiful." She lifted Crystal from her car seat.

The child yanked off her headband and pushed it onto Meredith's head. The plastic band lay cockeyed, half over her forehead.

"Where are the rest of the crew?" Meredith asked Sunny who sat in the van.

"I left them home. This way, I'll have a half-hour of quiet." She waved and drove off.

"Can we go to Uncle Blake's church tomorrow? Did you know he's a preacher?" Bean's eyes begged so earnestly Meredith wanted to agree. Bean didn't wait for an answer as she skipped to the porch.

"Are you hungry?" Meredith asked.

"No." Bean called. "We ate at Pizza Pan. Did you know they make pizza covered with chocolate?" She ran into the house before Meredith could answer.

"Where's Olaf?" Roxie shoved her doll at Meredith, then skipped toward the barn. "And our goats?" She skidded to a stop and turned. Roxie's face seemed to scold, *Where'd you hide my animals?*

Meredith held out the hand clutching the doll. "Come here. Olaf's in the house. The herd's working for Pa Jaynes."

In the living room, the five of them, counting Olaf, crowded together on the couch.

"Miss Sunny fed us pancakes—"

"Grandma gived me bananas and granul ... gradu ...?" Roxie frowned. "I forgot the word. Crunchy cereal."

"Granola," Meredith said. "Hey, you," she called to Crystal who slid to the floor. She lifted her to her lap.

"We gots to eat healthy, Grandma said." Roxie grabbed the remote.

157

Meredith covered her hand and slipped the controller beneath the cushions. "Not now." She cradled Crystal's head against her chest.

The toddler leaned into Meredith and sucked her thumb. Her eyes closed as sleep conquered her.

The girls quieted.

"Why're we sitting here doing nothing?" Bean asked.

Meredith nuzzled Crystal's head with her chin as the other two snuggled into her sides.

I've got to tell them. Yet words froze.

Crystal's breaths puffed against Meredith's chest.

Olaf jumped out of Roxie's clutches and thudded onto the floor.

The waif started after him, but Meredith grabbed her arm. "Wait." She held her breath. Slowly, she exhaled. "I hate to end your wonderful weekend on a sad note, but I have bad news."

Roxie sat back on the sofa, and she slunk against the back as though she would disappear.

Bean stiffened next to Meredith.

"Your parents ..." The news needed to be told like tearing off a band-aid. Tell them quickly. Then deal with the pain. "The police found them, but they died."

Roxie looked up at Meredith. She gave no other reaction.

Bean stared off toward the television.

"I found out late yesterday. I didn't want to ruin your weekend, so I waited until you came home. The police are looking for your relatives—"

"No." Tears welled in Bean's eyes. "They're supposed to come home!" She punched the couch and wriggled to its edge.

Meredith grabbed Bean's forearm and wrestled her own arm around her while not dropping Crystal.

"Will they come home soon?" Roxie asked.

Bean shook herself free from Meredith and bolted off the couch. "No, stupid. Didn't you hear?" She bent forward and hissed the words. "They're dead. Like the skunks and 'possums we see in the road." She ran up the stairs, and the door to Rosemary's—no—to Bean's bedroom—slammed behind her.

Roxie's eyes teemed with tears. "Will buzzards eat them?"

"No, my sweet. They're in ..." H*ow does one explain a coroner to a five-year-old?* "They're in what we call a morgue, a place where the dead rest until we find relatives. When your aunts and uncles are found, your parents will be buried. You'll live with me until we find someone."

"I don't want to live with welatives, Miss Mewedith. I want to stay with you."

"Me, too, honey." She pulled the child close and sat until soft snores came from Roxie as well as Crystal.

Only a few short days had passed since she'd hoped to give the girls back to DCS. Now she'd die if they took the kids away.

In their bedroom, Meredith smoothed the sheets over Crystal and Roxie. Olaf curled at his mistress's feet. She gave her girls one last kiss. Then looked up at the ceiling.

Time to help Bean.

Once upstairs, she tapped on the door but got no answer. She opened it.

"Go away." Bean thwacked her Barbie doll against the floor where she sat. Her headband lay in pieces, scattered across the room.

Meredith sat next to her but said nothing.

Bean thrashed the doll a few more times.

At last, Meredith took hold of the Barbie.

Bean tugged.

Meredith held tight. "You know, I found out your real name."

"I'm Bean." She yanked the doll, and its head popped off. Bean flung the head across the room.

Meredith placed the doll's body behind her and pulled Bean close. "The police found your birth certificate. Your name's Pearl Solomon."

"That's an ugly name."

Meredith ran her hand over Bean's tangled hair. "I think Pearl's beautiful."

Bean slunk against the bed, but she didn't pull away from Meredith.

"One of my favorite Bible parables is about a pearl. They come from oysters. Do you know how the shellfish make them?"

Staring at the floor, Bean pouted.

"A little piece of sand slips into their shell and bugs them, so they coat the irritation with beautiful, white layers. The result is a fine pearl which jewelers make into earrings or rings or necklaces. Imagine. Beauty comes from an imperfection."

"What's an imperfe, imp ..."

"Imperfection means something irritating. Defective."

Bean didn't say anything, but she lost her stiffness.

"In the Bible," Meredith continued, "God tells us a merchant—that's a vendor like me—found this beautiful pearl in a market, maybe like the one we go to. Maybe there was a Wookie Cookie in this market tempting the vendor—"

"Hey." Bean attempted to pout, but a smile broke through. Her body softened against Meredith's.

"This merchant found a pearl. So, instead of buying cookies, he went home, gave up everything he had so he could buy the jewel."

"Why? I'd rather have chocolate cookies."

"I know you would." Meredith tapped Bean's nose. "Now listen closely. This is the important part of the parable. Since pearls are made from imperfections, they're like us. Jesus is the merchant. He died for us, so we could go to heaven. He gave up everything."

"Isn't Jesus God?" Bean asked.

"He is."

"Wow. He gave up everything?"

"What this story also says is sometimes a merchant who sells goat soap loves her Pearl so much, she'd do anything she could to help her."

"I don't like the name Pearl. And I miss my mama."

Meredith ran her fingers through the child's hair. "I understand a little. I miss my husband and my daughter. I can't imagine how I'd feel if I lost my mother. You'll always be my Bean." She leaned over and kissed her head. "And I won't call you Pearl if you don't want me to."

They sat in silence until Bean's head nodded and jerked upright.

"Let's go to sleep."

"I'm not tired." Her bottom lip trembled. "I broke my new doll."

"I can fix your Barbie."

Bean straightened. "Really?"

"Broken things can be mended." Meredith retrieved the doll's head and popped it back into place. "See."

A smile lit Bean's face.

Meredith stood next to the bed. "Time for sleep."

Bean shook her head. "But I'm not tired."

"How about I lay down with you?"

"Okay." Bean's eyes drooped.

Meredith climbed in and pulled the sheets over them. The two spooned together in the single bed until Bean slept.

Meredith stayed longer. What did the future hold for these kids? What comfort could she give?

Chapter 17

Soft light filtered through Meredith's closed eyelids. An unusual peace drifted in.

She blinked sleep from her eyes. Gray light filtered through the windows as she sat up and hugged her knees to her chest. She searched the ceiling. *Was God up there?* Perhaps Parker was right. Did faith burrow deep inside?

That awful deacon. If he hadn't ...

She closed her eyes and knew. Mills didn't wrench her from the Lord. Her attitude had. If she tried, could she find her faith again?

She waited and listened for a reply from God.

Nothing stirred inside her.

Maybe he was busy selling all he had for her like the merchant and the pearl.

For the first time in ten months, she felt good to be alive. No pain weighted her. Zilch. She stretched out her legs and grinned. Her girls would be up soon. Maybe she'd make them baked French toast.

A rooster crowed, and a hound bayed. Time to start the day.

She threw off her covers and stepped into her jeans and her worn T-shirt. As she loped down the stairs, she tied her hair into a ponytail.

Silence filled the house as she scooped coffee and water into the coffee maker. While it brewed, Meredith stepped out to milk and feed her goats. She stopped on the porch.

No goats. Vivienne Van Goat and the girls worked for Pa this weekend.

The sunrise pinked the sky. The morning air begged her to sit outdoors. After pouring sweet, hot coffee into a goat mug, Meredith sank into the porch chair Parker had occupied.

She wanted her kids to wake up. We know who you are, Pearl Solomon, Roxie and Crystal Harrison. Maybe the worst is over for you.

Steam wafted from her cup, and she sipped. Before she finished, little feet came padding out to her.

"Miss Mewedith?"

"Hey, Rox."

Roxie stood next to her.

Crystal clung to her sister's hip, her legs wrapped around Roxie's waist. Sort of. The child hung at a cockamamie angle. Meredith grabbed Crystal from Roxie's arms before Crystal plopped on her head.

"Crystal went potty alweady."

"Good girl."

"Where's Bean?" Roxie settled in the chair next to Meredith.

"She's sleeping." Meredith pointed up in the general direction of Bean's room while she pulled Crystal closer.

Roxie plugged her thumb in her mouth. "Uhh-uhh."

"What do you mean, 'uhh-uhh?'" Meredith pulled the thumb out of the tyke's mouth.

"I just been there. She's not in bed."

Meredith scrambled to her feet and strode into the kitchen. "Bean?"

No answer.

She loped up the stairs with Crystal glued on her hip and Roxie trailing a step or two behind. Bean's door remained closed. "Bean?" Meredith rapped on the wood, then she opened the door. The bed was rumpled but empty. "Bean!"

She looked down at Roxie. "Where'd she go?"

Roxie hiked her shoulders.

Where could she be? Back in the living room, she turned on the TV and sat Crystal on the couch. She took Roxie's chin in her fingers and stared into her eyes. "I'll be right back. Watch your sister."

Tears pooled as Roxie took her turtle posture.

Meredith slapped on a smile and forced confidence in her voice to calm both hers and Roxie's fear. "I need to check the barn and see if your sister's out there. I'll be right back." She stepped toward the kitchen and turned. "Make sure Crystal doesn't fall off the couch."

Once outside, she ran.

In the barn, dust motes danced in the early morning light seeping in through the windows. Sweet hay and molasses scented the air. No goats and no girl. Meredith stepped into her office. Closed freezer, clear desk, and made-up bed. Meredith scrunched her eyes and scratched her head. *Where could she be?*

She snapped her fingers. *The Wheeler house! Last time, Bean headed there.*

With a gun.

Her heart skipped a beat.

Maybe two.

No. Her gun remained locked in her bedside table. The last run-away taught her about caution. With no gun to worry about, Meredith had to figure out where the child would go. Only a few places existed here where Bean would feel safe.

She raced back into her home—her chest squeezed tight, gasping for air. She scooped Crystal from the couch. "Let's go, girls."

"Where we going?" Roxie asked.

"To find your sister."

After strapping Crystal in her car seat and making sure Roxie secured her seatbelt, Meredith gunned her engine and sped down the road toward the junction of Wheeler Road and Hen Waddle Hollow. Once on the Wheeler Road, the old pickup rattled over ruts. Branches scraped overhead, scratching the cab. *She'll be at her old house. She will.*

The morning light brightened the wreck of a building but didn't make the abandoned dump look any more appealing. Meredith turned off the truck and shoved the keys into her back pocket. She turned and pointed a finger at Roxie. "Stay put. Watch your sister. Promise me?"

The child nodded.

Meredith sprinted into a deserted house.

She ran through the kitchen and into the living room. Here, she turned around in circles as though if she looked again, Bean would materialize. Panic reached out its hand and seized Meredith's throat. *If not here, where?*

Upstairs?

Skirting the soft, rotted stairs, Meredith reached the bedrooms. They held nothing but discarded clothes. One pile looked ransacked. Or maybe they'd always been thrown around. This place horrified her so much she didn't spend much time studying the surroundings the last time she was here.

Dust on the dresser had been disturbed as though little fingers pawed through the trinkets strewn across the top.

"Bean!" She stood in place and listened but only heard her own panting.

After another mad dash, Meredith hopped into her truck and cranked the engine.

Heedless of the trees and the litter in the overgrown yard, Meredith swerved into a U-turn and gunned the engine. The truck jolted back over ruts, as she retraced her path.

Before she hit Hen Waddle Hollow, Meredith pressed her Bluetooth.

"Call Parker Snow."

"No phone is available," the sedate, mechanical voice replied.

Meredith slammed her hand against the steering wheel. She left her phone at home.

Leaving rubber as she swerved onto the paved road, Meredith sped home and skidded into her driveway.

With Crystal in her arms and Roxie jogging behind her, Meredith dashed into the kitchen.

"Bean!" Meredith skidded to a stop.

The child sat at the table with a bowl of cereal before her.

"Where were you?"

"Sleeping."

"Don't lie. You weren't in your room."

"I slept at Mama's."

"How long?" *Does it matter—one hour or eight?*

"After you fell asleep."

"You were gone all night?" Meredith sunk onto a chair. *All night, and I didn't know. Oh God, help me.* "How could ..." Meredith swallowed. If she spoke now, she'd scream. "We'll talk later. Feed your sisters."

Meredith's breaths came in short, sharp bursts. She had to breathe. She stepped out on the back porch and grasped the railing.

Her hands shook, and she gulped breaths. In part, anger vised her chest. Anger at Harrison and Willoughby—pathetic excuses for parents. At Bean for terrifying her. At herself for not hearing Bean leave the house.

More than anger, fear pressed down. *All night alone in that dump. Why?*

But she knew. Her girls—rather the children—belonged to another. She'd never be enough.

She hung her head. *Of course, they missed their parents. Even as bad as they were.* She lifted her eyes to the hills behind Pa Jaynes's valley and finally quieted.

For over nine months, grief, almost too much to bear, submerged her. At times, pain felt so heavy she couldn't breathe. Until a week or so ago, she slept with John's shirts.

She understood loss of loved ones. Healing took time. Lots of time.

These girls bore more than she ever had.

No chatter drifted from the kitchen. Only silverware clattered against bowls. Glasses clinked.

At least the children ate.

Finally, water ran as Bean and Roxie rinsed dishes at the sink.

Meredith returned to the kitchen.

Bean jumped back.

"Don't be scared. I'm not angry now. Sit down, girls."

The two dragged themselves to the table. Chairs scraped.

Bean hung her head as though avoiding Meredith's eyes.

Roxie hunched her shoulders again. Crystal held up her hands to Meredith.

"You want my lap?" She asked the toddler.

Her head bobbed, and Meredith settled Crystal on her knees. The weight and warmth of the child melted the last of her anger and fear. "Girls, I know you're sad, but you can't go back to the house. Things are falling apart, making it unsafe. I do have an idea that may help you."

Bean drew her finger through the damp rings on the table left from their cereal bowls.

Roxie sucked her thumb.

"Funerals comfort the ones left behind. We can't bury your parents. As I told you, they're in the morgue in Knoxville. But maybe we can go to your old house—"

"But you saided we can't." Roxie lifted sorrowful eyes to Meredith.

"With me. One last time. Y'all can pick out something you want to keep as a memory and one item we can bury."

Bean reached into her pocket and pulled out a tangle of necklaces and earrings. "I already found what I want."

Meredith fingered the jumble of metal. "Is there something here we can bury and never have again?"

Bean shook her head.

"If not, we'll go back one *last* time and pick out something that reminds us of your parents, maybe a shirt that smells like them. Then we'll have a funeral. We have a little cemetery where we buried our old dog and the kitties who died. We'll build a little cross—"

"Can Uncle Blake come?" Bean asked. "He's a preacher, and he can pray."

"Why do you want a preacher?"

"'Cause you gotta have a preacher for a funeral. When I was real little, my mamaw died. This was before Crystal was born. Mamaw's preacher prayed really nice things so she could go to heaven."

Meredith's heart tugged. She'd suffer anything for Bean. "Of course. But we'll have to wait until next Sunday. One week from now. Uncle Blake works at the bank with Pa Jaynes. And I work at the market on Saturday." She pinched Bean's ribs. "I need to earn money, so this little food-monster can eat. I'll call Uncle Blake when he gets home from church this afternoon. Okay?"

"Yeah." Bean bounded out of her chair and danced a little jig around the kitchen. "I like Uncle Blake's prayers."

Didn't take long for Sis to convert them. Her heart relaxed, and she smiled. She felt like God danced with Pearl Solomon.

The week flew by with no more drama. On Sunday, Mom carried out a bowl of tossed salad, complete with candied pecans, Craisins, and whole wheat croutons.

Meredith had given up trying to convince Mom her version of healthy needed tweaking. A salad loaded with sugared nuts and stale bread didn't pass as a health food.

Mom centered the bowl on a folding table under the canopy Meredith used at the market. "Don't bring out any of the mayonnaise salads. We don't want this to turn into a whole family burial." She laughed at her joke.

Meredith groaned.

Dad finagled a pint-sized wheelchair from the backseat of his car. LED lights blinked pink and purple with each rotation of the wheels. "Where's my little sparkler? I've got a glittering buggy for her."

Crystal clapped from where she sat under the table. "'Parkle. Pretty 'parkles."

"Come here, my jewel." Dad scooped her from the ground and settled her into the chair.

A rumble of a vehicle rattled across the field announced Pa and Ma Jaynes arrived on their Mule.

Ma Jaynes hopped out and rounded the Mule. "I made a peach cobbler." She pulled a 9x12 dish from the back of the open-air vehicle. "Pa brought chips and Mountain Dew."

Pa hauled out a cooler and kissed Meredith's cheek. "Your girls will be home tomorrow. We've brought their milk." He lifted the cooler to indicate he'd stashed the milk there.

"Can you put the milk in the freezer?" Meredith nodded toward the barn.

"Done." Pa walked off.

The Buchanans arrived in the van with their usual tumble of children.

By the time they headed to the plot where they'd bury their mementos, the table groaned beneath the weight of brownies and pasta salad, chips, and dip. Coolers overflowed with soft drinks and juice boxes. The aroma of smoking pork drifted from the smoker Blake set up before he left for church that morning, and chicken marinated in the kitchen where the fridge had been stuffed until the door barely shut.

Now they stood by a shallow hole Blake had dug yesterday while Meredith and the gang worked the farmers' market. Bean and Roxie held gift bags. Crystal and Owen squealed as they played a few feet away.

"What do you want to bury, Bean?" Meredith nudged her shoulder.

Bean stepped up to the hole. "Mama, I always liked this sweater of yours." She trembled and stepped away.

Meredith grabbed her and squatted, so she didn't tower over the child. "You can cry." She could hardly hear her voice. "Your mama knows you're sad."

Bean shoved the bag into Meredith's hands and pointed to the hole. "You put it there."

The bag rustled in Meredith's grasp. "Let's bury this together." She wiped Bean's tears with her knuckle. "Okay?"

Bean bobbed her head.

Meredith knelt at the gravesite. Now the idea of burying the clothes and mementos where the Jayneses had buried their pets felt coarse. The girls needed their parents' graves to be someplace other than a pet cemetery. Too late to change. "Beth Willoughby, your daughter loves you more than you can imagine." She pulled Bean, so she knelt next to her. "Do you think you can lay this in the hole now?"

Bean nodded and laid the memento down like she tucked a doll to bed. "Please, Mama, kiss Mamaw for me. I miss her too."

Bean's lips contorted. She turned and buried her head in Meredith's stomach.

Roxie dropped her bag and hugged her sister.

"Don't cwy, Bean." Roxie stroked her sister's hair. "I'm here."

Meredith expected sobs to shake Bean, but only a few tears escaped.

"Do you want to bury your daddy's hat now, Roxie?"

The child stood and picked up the bag. She dropped her father's hat into the hole. Roxie looked up at Blake. "Your turn."

Blake cleared his throat. "Lord, Father ..."

Oh Lord, Blake does know not to talk about hell, right? She looked up at him, and he winked at her.

Her face relaxed as peace surrounded her.

"You loved Beth and Danny more than their children did. We ask for your comfort and peace. Let these little ones know their worth. Amen."

With the amen, Meredith thought he said, "Let's party." Bean scooped up Crystal and ran with 'Nissa and Phoebe toward the picnic table.

The girls frolicked while pain rained down on Meredith where she still sat by the grave. She watched the children play—grief forgotten for the moment. But heartache had the habit of returning in waves. Pain would wash over them when they least expected and twist their lives.

At least they could play. For now.

Parker pulled up to New Life a half-hour later than he'd told Felicity.

With her stilettos tossed on the sidewalk, Felicity romped on the front lawn with a group of dark-haired children. Judging by their staggered heights and coloring, probably Gracie and Bert Murphy's crew.

No one turned toward him, so he watched.

The kids squealed as Felicity chased them. She grabbed one, held her upside down and tickled her. Then Felicity gently laid her down and chased a younger boy.

Parker smiled. *She says she doesn't like kids.*

Felicity looked up. Her expression changed from childlike delight to sophisticated contentment. She hugged a kid who got too close to her, then padded to the sidewalk. She picked up her shoes from the pavement and strode to the car. At the driver's side, she leaned in and pecked Parker's cheek. "Let me say goodbye, and I'll be right back." She hopped as she slipped on each shoe. Then with her sultry stroll, Felicity walked toward a pregnant woman, who had to be her sister-in-law. Felicity hugged Gracie and waved to a man wearing a clerical collar. She then made her way to Parker's car.

"Sorry I was late." After she settled in, Parker leaned over and kissed her cheek. "Service ran over. We had communion today. Then our pastor cornered me and got chatty about life."

"No problem." Felicity fumbled through her purse and pulled out a gold tube. She pulled down the visor and applied lipstick. "You can see the kids keep me busy." The lipstick tube thunked back into the pocketbook. "And make a mess of me." Felicity ran her brush through her hair.

Parker pulled away from the curb.

Felicity's laugh chimed. "I fixed myself *before* church, too, for your information."

"I figured as much." He glanced her way. "Do you want to walk the nature trails in Knoxville or hit the movies?"

"I've had enough of the great outdoors, and heels don't like soft earthen trails. So, movies at the Regal." She tilted her head and ran a finger under her eyes. "My mascara's running. You didn't tell me I looked like David Bowie." She flipped up the visor and flashed him her beautiful smile. "There's a new Chinese restaurant in Farragut. Wok It."

Parker settled against his seat as he neared the highway. He hadn't realized how tense he'd been since Felicity climbed into the car. "Sure."

Felicity scrolled through her cell.

Parker glanced at her as he maneuvered into traffic. *She loved those kids. Maybe she really wants a few. Foster a few. Like the ones up Hen Waddle. Everyone would love those critters. Maybe I should bring her … No.*

"Parker?"

He hit cruising speed. "What?"

"Which one?"

"Which what?"

"Movie. I named three."

"I'm sorry. I got distracted with traffic and merging."

Felicity twisted around in her seat. "Sunday. There's not even a cargo van on the road. Is something wrong?"

"No." He shook his head vigorously. "Nothing at all." Even as he wagged his head, something niggled at the back of his brain. "Long week, is all. So, what movie?"

Chapter 18

Meredith grabbed for Crystal as she maneuvered her new wheelchair back and forth in the tiny exam room. The lights on her tires flashed as she rolled backwards and hit the wall.

Crystal pushed forward, and giggles peppered the air.

In a plastic chair, Bean cuddled Roxie on her lap.

Roxie leaned into her sister's arm and ran her finger along the words as she read from a board book. Her lisping voice serenaded Meredith making the chaos of doctor visits almost fun.

At last, the door opened, and the orthopedic doctor strode in. In his arms, he held white plastic leg braces. Multi-colored butterflies adorned the plastic forms.

Crystal rolled into him.

"Oops." He smiled, much to Meredith's relief. He stooped to peer into Crystal's face. "You own a cool, new wheelchair."

"Bampa buy." She made a bye-bye wave with her little fingers.

The doctor straightened and looked at Meredith. His squinted eyes told her he needed a translation.

"Grandpa bought the ''parkly chair' for her," Meredith said.

"You have a good grandpa." He patted the exam table. "Hop on up here, kiddo."

Meredith lifted Crystal and sat her down with her legs outstretched.

"Flufferby." Crystal clapped and fingered the purple and pink butterflies decorating the white plastic.

"You like butterflies?" The orthopedic picked up a pink strap attached to the orthotic and looked at Meredith. "Attaching the brace is simple." He velcroed the next strap, then another.

"I think I can manage attaching straps" Meredith said.

The doctor kept his focus on a knob he turned at the orthotics' knee.

Meredith stiffened in a panic. "What are you doing now? How do I know how much to twist—"

"Don't worry. Once aligned, you won't need to readjust." Finally, he lifted Crystal from the table and stood her on the floor.

She grasped his fingers and swung her leg forward as though about to walk away. "I run."

"With these, she should eventually be able to hold onto furniture and walk like an ordinary toddler. Not run, though."

"You don't know Crystal." Meredith took the child's hands.

Crystal gripped the tips of Meredith's fingers and wobbled one more time. "I'm in trouble. I can't keep track of her when she scoots on the floor on her butt. Walking?"

The doctor laughed. "Continue with PT. I'll see you in six weeks." He handed her the appointment forms.

Forty minutes later, they pulled into a handicapped parking spot directly in front of the elementary school office.

Before Meredith could unhook her seatbelt, Roxie and Bean hopped out of the truck. They clasped hands and ran toward the door.

"Stop!" Meredith jumped from the cab, then paused. No cars approached, and the baby remained strapped in the vehicle, only one choice faced her. Crystal needed to come with them.

At the entrance, the girls yanked the school door. "They locked the door," Bean called.

"Stay there." Meredith trotted across the roadway while pushing the wheelchair. She grabbed Bean's hand. "They lock them so bad people don't come in."

Roxie widened her soulful blue eyes. "We not bad."

Sometimes I wonder. Meredith smiled at her thought. She pointed to a small button. "Ring this bell."

Bean poked the buzzer which echoed inside the school.

"No. Me." Roxie stood on tiptoes and jabbed the call button.

Bean rang a couple of more times. "I already—"

Meredith grabbed Bean's hand. "They heard you."

The door buzzed, and both Bean and Roxie grabbed the handle.

School can't start too soon.

The crew raced into a long foyer. Across the hallway, Meredith approached a small window and told the secretary what she needed then ushered her chaotic crew into a large room with several offices lining the back wall.

"I'll be with you in a sec." A middle-aged secretary glanced at Meredith's band of eager enrollees, then back down at her computer. A large counter walled the woman off from the zealous children shuffling from foot to foot in front of her.

Meredith tapped Bean and Roxie on the head. "I'd like to register these two girls."

The secretary clicked the computer keys again and spoke without stopping and without glancing up. "We need their birth certificates and medical records. Proof of residency." With a final clack at the keyboard, she looked at the family.

Meredith fumbled through the folder she prepared. "Roxie and Bean are my foster daughters. Since we don't know what their medical status is, we're redoing their immunizations." She handed the medical records to the secretary. "I have the residency forms." She passed them over the counter. "Pearl has a birth certificate." She plopped the paper on the growing pile. "DCS is looking for Roxie's."

The secretary peered through her glasses at the birth certificate. "This is a copy." She handed the paper back. "We've got to have an original birth certificate. We can't register her otherwise. And we need one for Roxie too."

A cement mixer dumped its load in Meredith's stomach. She stared at the empty folder in her hand.

"Ma'am?"

Meredith refocused on the secretary. "I'm sorry. This fostering overwhelms me."

Years vanished from the secretary's face when she grinned.

"We can work with DCS. You'll need a notarized form from Roxie's caseworker. If they have a copy of Pearl's—"

"My name's not Pearl." Bean crossed her arms.

Meredith pressed her lips together to stop her grin. Of all times for Bean to assert herself.

"Then what is your name if not Pearl?" Again, the secretary smiled as if the child's insistence was perfectly normal.

"Bean. I'm eight. My real mama calls me Bean." She jabbed a finger toward the papers on the counter. "I don't know why that paper calls me Pearl."

"When you start class, be sure to tell your teacher you want to be called Bean." The secretary tweaked the child's nose and looked at Meredith. "If DCS has a copy, they can obtain an original from the issuing courthouse." She peered at the paper. "A call to Memphis will do the trick."

"But school will start ..."

"Social service has done this before. They know the routine, and your kids won't miss a day of school."

"But we start in two weeks."

"No problem. Call their caseworker. She'll know—"

"He."

The secretary tilted her head.

"Parker Snow's their contact."

"I know him. He's a hottie."

Heat rose into Meredith's cheeks. He was cute. She noticed when he first showed up. Why was she flustered by his looks?

"Anything else you need?"

The secretary's voice brought Meredith's mind back to the school office. "Do you have a supply list? I can't go into Walmart without the three of them bugging me for the pretty things, especially the backpacks. Even though they'd never been sent to school, they sure know what they want."

"All three?"

"Yep. Even the tyke insists on a backpack."

Roxie gripped the counter with little hands and rested her chin on them. Her pretty eyes focused on the secretary. "I'm smart. I know'd my letters *and* numbers. Mama Mewedith's gonna buy me a Olaf backpack like my kitty."

"You have a cat named after my favorite snowman," the secretary said. "You have good taste." The secretary glanced at Crystal in her wheelchair. "And you have pretty braces."

"Look." Crystal rolled herself back and forward. "'Parkle."

The secretary looked at Meredith. Her eyes asked, "translation?"

"Sparkles. She loves the lights on her wheels. You need ESL training to understand Crystal and ..." She glanced down at Roxie who seemed mesmerized by the secretary. Meredith nodded toward her.

Again, the secretary's warm smile soothed. "I'll be right back" She walked down a hallway behind the counter.

And Crystal bumped into the counter. Again.

"Bean, could you take Crystal into the hall and let her roll around? Stay where I can watch you." Meredith pointed at the foyer outside the windows.

Bean left, and a minute later, the secretary returned with a photocopied paper. "Here you go. These are the basic needs. We send out a complete list when school starts. Each teacher has her own specifications." She scanned the office. "Did two of your girls run away?"

Meredith pointed at the window toward the entryway. "I couldn't do this without Bean. She watches her sisters, makes sure everybody is happy and loves to help." She paused then waved toward the corridor. "Can they play out ..."

"They're behaving. You're blessed." She answered the ringing phone.

Meredith waved goodbye and took Roxie's hand. "Let's go look for the school supplies we know you'll need."

"Do we go to school tomorrow?" Roxie cavorted like a happy puppy.

"Not tomorrow."

She stomped her feet and crossed her arms.

"If you stick your bottom lip out any further, you'll trip ..."

Roxie dashed toward Bean and grabbed her waist in a hug that must've squeezed the air out of her sister. "I'm getting a backpack with Olaf."

In Walmart, Meredith picked up a few notebooks and number two pencils. "Bean, come back here."

Bean raced up the aisle pushing the cart holding Crystal who squealed in delight.

"When do we buy good stuff?" Roxie pulled Meredith's hand, urging her to move to a more interesting section of the store.

Meredith held out a box of markers. "These are fun. They smell like oranges or roses or chocolate."

Roxie sniffed the box. "I don't smell noffing."

Meredith grinned and turned to toss them into her buggy.

Buggy. She scanned the aisles near her. *Where'd her cart go?*

She couldn't see Bean and Crystal, but the whole store heard them.

"Bean. Here now!"

They careened around a display and back into the stationery aisle.

Meredith waved for them to return. She glared and hoped her eyes' daggers would silently hush the girls.

A woman puttering by in the store's scooter gave her the evil eye and glared at the kids.

Bean now shoved the cart as though the wheels stuck to the tiles.

Meredith offered an apologetic grin to the grumpy scooter-lady.

In the backpack section, the girls studied the selection as though choosing a perfect wedding dress.

"Lookit, Roxie," Bean shouted. "Queen Elsa."

"I wants Olaf." Roxie dropped several backpacks off the rack as she swatted the one with Elsa's picture out of Bean's hands. The bag flew across the aisle and smacked Crystal who let out a screech. Her squawk probably startled the grumpy lady with the motorized buggy by the stationary.

Meredith stooped over the cart to comfort Crystal who stopped screeching as though someone flipped the off switch.

"Flufferby." She pointed.

Meredith turned. A Crystal-sized pack studded with glittery butterflies hung on a low rack. "Want this?"

For an answer, Crystal grabbed the satchel to her chest.

Meredith straightened. Her back creaked like Mom complained hers did. *Kids. They'll make a crotchety old lady out of me.* Children? She scanned the knapsack section.

No children stood nearby. Although, a quiet clapping sound told her they played somewhere nearby.

She clamped her teeth together. "Where are your sisters, Crystal?"

"Der." Little fingers pointed.

Meredith bent over.

Under a rack of clothes sat Roxie and Bean. Their new school bags piled in front of them barricaded them from sight. Together they worked an intricate clapping game along with its silly rhyme.

Should I scream? Maybe drag them out of here—forget supplies.

Meredith studied the girls. She took in a deep breath to quiet her nerves. "Time to go."

Without waiting for the wayward duo, Meredith strolled Crystal and their packages to the checkout.

Like puppies afraid of being left behind, the ornery sisters ran after Meredith and Crystal.

"Stop."

"Wait for me."

"Don't leave us."

They skidded into Meredith's back and nearly knocked her into the woman in front of her in line. "Sorry." She offered the woman a rueful grin—or she hoped her smile looked apologetic. *I need babying.* "What do you say we go to Aunt Sunny's?"

She bit her lips as the crew cheered. *Go to Sunny's? I've truly lost my mind.*

Chapter 19

The long, hot summer had browned the grass in the backyard of Sunny's house. The late afternoon sun still heated the air while the humidity amplified the heat.

Bean romped with 'Nissa. Phoebe and Roxie cavorted on the gym set while Meredith leaned back on the porch swing. Owen and Crystal crowded both sides of her.

"They look good on you." Sunny grinned and nodded to the two little ones wedged against Meredith. She handed her sister a cup of hot tea.

Meredith sipped and grimaced. "Herbal?" She sipped again. "I like it, but I expected real tea. With sugar since Mom's not here."

Sunny patted her belly. "Herbal for eight more months."

Meredith sat upright. "Really?"

"Yep. Number four."

The desire to hug Sunny overwhelmed Meredith, but the two tykes who now dozed on the swing stopped her. Dumping her hot tea on them would not be a good idea. "I'm so happy for you. When did you find out?"

"This morning. Don't tell Mom, yet."

"Are you kidding? She'll start plying you with vitamins that'll make prenatals look small."

"Mommy." Phoebe ran up the back-porch steps.

"What's all over your face?" Sunny licked her fingers, scrubbed, then studied her hand. "Where'd you find chocolate?"

Phoebe pointed behind her. "Bean shared."

"Bean?" Meredith wriggled away from the toddlers and put her cup on the deck. She stood. "Pearl Solomon! Come over here. Now."

Bean approached with head bowed and hands behind her back.

"What're you hiding?"

She shook her head. "Nothin'."

Meredith held out her hand. "Show me nothing."

Bean lifted her head. Her eyes hardened like flint. "I said nothin'. Why don't you never believe me?"

With her hand extended, Meredith remained silent.

Bean held out an almost empty bag of M&Ms.

"Where did you find candy?"

Bean hiked a shoulder.

Meredith closed her eyes and inhaled again. She opened her eyes and stared off into the distance. "Sunny, can you watch Crystal and Roxie? Pearl and—"

"I'm not Pearl. I—"

Meredith glared.

Bean scowled with pinched lips.

"Pearl and I are returning to Walmart. We have candy to pay for."

The two walked to Meredith's truck. She ground her teeth. *I need to talk to her.* Her words to Bean had to be gentle, but the child had to understand why she couldn't steal. Or wander away. Or ... behave the way her parents trained her to be. If she spoke now, her voice wouldn't be calm. Her anger would set back the patient work she'd done with Bean over the past month.

On their drive back to Walmart, the only noise came from passing traffic and her rattling truck.

Meredith parked in a spot away from all other vehicles. They climbed out, and Meredith stooped down to Bean's level. She took Bean's chin between two fingers and made her look at her. "Do you know why we're here?"

"'Cause you're mad."

Meredith stared into the child's eyes. "I'm mad, yes, but we're here because stealing is wrong."

"But Walmart has lots of stuff. They won't miss one pack of candy."

"Because a store has plenty to sell doesn't mean they can give everything away."

"You say that all the time—"

Meredith placed a finger over Bean's lips. "What if every girl in Jacksboro took a package of M&Ms?"

Bean ducked her head.

"Walmart wouldn't have any to sell. Right?"

Bean stood stiff and still.

"Let's go."

In the store, Meredith gripped Bean's hand and headed to the pocketbook aisle. She found a pink faux-leather change purse with a glittery strap. Clutching Bean's hand, she lined up at the service area and waited their turn. She looked down at Bean. "*You* are going to tell the woman why we're paying for an empty package of candy."

The child's eyes widened, and she tugged at Meredith's hand as she stepped away. "No."

Meredith gripped Bean's fingers and said nothing. They crept forward.

At last, their turn came.

"We have to pay for this." Meredith placed the empty M&M bag on the counter. "Bean, what do you say."

The child's scowl would melt Greenland. "I'm sorry. I ... borrowed the candy."

The clerk bit back her grin as she scanned the barcode.

Meredith handed her a twenty-dollar bill and took the change. She then handed the clerk the change purse. "Can I pay for this here?"

With her change and the receipt in one hand and Bean's hand clasped in the other, Meredith led Bean to a chair in a nearby kiosk and sat. She pulled Bean close and handed her the change purse. "This is for you."

Bean's bowed head jerked up. Her narrowed eyes asked questions.

"I'll give you an allowance for all the work you do for me—five dollars a week." She handed Bean the change. "You already bought the candy, so this is all you have left. You can spend the money any way you want, or you can save your allowance until you have enough for something special. When you spend everything, you have no more. I do not want you to steal again."

Bean shoved the change into her purse then clutched the case to her chest.

"What do you say?"

"Can I buy a toy?"

Meredith shook her head in disbelief. "I'd hoped for a thank you. You bought M&Ms. Nothing more today."

At the truck, Meredith's stomach grumbled. Dinner time neared. She'd need to give the girls something semi-nutritious to eat. She dialed Pizza Hut and ordered three large cheese pizzas as she drove to the restaurant. In its parking lot, she called Sunny, told her she'd bring dinner if she didn't snitch to Mom about its poor quality—Mom would only eat veggie pizza, her health-food version of fattening food.

She stood at the carry-out counter.

"Hello, Bean. Meredith."

Meredith turned and gazed into Parker Snow's blue eyes. Her stomach flipped, and not from hunger. His sudden appearance caught her off-guard.

Light glinted off his glasses as he smiled. "Fine minds think alike. I'm waiting for my dinner too."

"This has been a busy day. Crystal has braces. Leg braces, not teeth ones. The girls have the *important* school supplies—"

"I got a backpack. And Roxie and Crystal do too."

"Oh," Meredith said. "The school needs—"

"Look, Mr. Parker." Bean flashed her change purse in front of him. "I have money too." She opened the purse and showed him.

"You're a rich girl." He looked at Meredith.

Something in his eyes shifted. The blue warmed, and his gaze held hers. Meredith's heart sped up, *Not the time to swoon. School. Tell him.* "I tried to register the girls for school, but I need original birth certificates, and—"

"Sorry, I forgot. Call the office and remind us. We'll fax the papers that will work for now. How're the foster care classes going? You should be at number ..." He ticked down his fingers as though counting. "Week four?"

"Good memory. Eight more to go. The classes are good. Wish I knew all the information already."

"Jaynes?" The take-out clerk called.

"That's me." Meredith's face heated as she realized what a stupid thing she said. Parker knew her last name. She paid her bill and waved goodbye as Parker stepped up to the take-out window.

Parker watched Meredith and Bean walk out of the restaurant. Three large boxes of pizza balanced in Meredith's arms as Bean held the door. The late sunlight made the red in Meredith's hair glow like ... apricots? Hunger inspired his imagery. Wind whisked Mrs. Jaynes's hair as she placed the boxes on her front seat and helped Bean climb into the back. Gentleness surrounded her and exuded an unselfconscious air. *Pretty woman.*

He smiled to himself. As soon as he had his pizza, wings, and salad in hand, he'd go out to see his own pretty woman.

The door swooshed open. "What're you grinning at, Snow?" Detective Drew Carroll sauntered in with a rush of warm air. He punched Parker's arm.

"I'm not grinning." Parker pasted on a scowl which he knew didn't come off as stern.

"You're looking like a fool in love. You like the little lady with the three abandoned kids," he nodded toward the parking lot, "or the hot mortician?"

"Snow." The cashier shoved a pile of boxes across the counter.

With a parting nod, he picked up his order. Carroll's words echoed. Two different women. If he hadn't met Felicity, he would be attracted to Meredi ... Mrs. Jaynes.

Chapter 20

The sun cast its last rosy glow over Hen Waddle Hollow. Roxie and Bean's chatter became an indistinct hum, a white noise like the waves on a beach. Meredith peered into the rearview mirror. Crystal's blonde head bobbed forward in sleep. Dark crept in by the time she pulled into the driveway. The goats' bleats begged for food. And milking.

Meredith yawned as she climbed out of the truck. The girls didn't move. The night would be long and tiring.

She lifted Crystal from the car seat. Her head rolled back as she became a dead weight in Meredith's arms.

"Bean, help Roxie," She called over her shoulder.

The two didn't leave the truck until Meredith was halfway to the house.

When Crystal flopped in Meredith's arms, she nearly dropped her as she plunked her on the bed. The imp's eyes didn't flutter open, not even as Meredith slipped the new leg braces from her limbs.

"Roxie, watch your sister." She kissed both girls and tucked them in. Roxie's eyes didn't remain open past the kiss goodnight.

In the living room, Bean stretched out on the couch with the afghan over her as she channel surfed.

"You look tired. I'm heading out to do chores. Do you want to help me or watch TV?"

As though Bean had chugged a gallon of caffeine, the child jumped off the couch and raced out to the goat corral.

Meredith readied the milking pails.

Bean nabbed Mocha and pulled her into the barn and tied her to the milking stanchion, then skipped out to corral the next nanny.

Milk pinged against the pail—Mocha's udder warm in Meredith's hand. While she watched for Bean to bring in Cap, Meredith sang "Putting on the Ritz." "Do, dat, dibbidly-da-da." She bobbed her head to her scat singing while trying to maintain a semblance of the melody.

"What're you singing? You don't make sense." Bean asked as she pulled Cappuccino into the barn.

"I'm scat singing. In jazz, you can improvise with nonsense words to make it interesting.

"How do you do that?"

Meredith stopped milking and touched Bean's sternum. "You feel the music here." Then she placed her fingers on the child's lips. "The sound comes out here."

"Da-da-pa-ma Ritz." Bean giggled at her improv. "Like that?"

"Good start." Meredith tied up Cappuccino while the rest of the goats were corralled.

While Bean pitched hay, the two made up words for "Reindeer Are Better Than People."

With the last of the grain dumped into the trough, Meredith took a sweeping bow. She held the grain scoop up like a microphone. "I thank you. No encores tonight. My sweet Pearl needs to go to sleep."

"You're funny, Mama Meredith."

"Thanks, Bean-zo, girl." Meredith looped her arm around Bean. "I don't think producers will call us back for a Broadway audition, but I can make you a master soap maker if you'd like."

Bean stopped at the barn door and stared at the bike hanging on the wall. "Why don't you never use the bicycle?"

Meredith's stuttering heart surprised her, reminding her how much she had hurt before the girls arrived. She stepped toward Bean and ran her hand along the bicycle, clearing dust from the frame. "This used to be Rosemary's. We hung the bike up the last time she got sick, so the tires wouldn't wear out."

"I never rode a bike." Bean stared like a lovesick puppy.

"How about learning?"

"Really?" She flung her arms around Meredith. "I'm glad you're my mom now." Bean skipped out the door.

Riding a bike makes you happy, and now I'm your mom? Should've taught you a month ago. Meredith walked behind her feeling ancient as she watched the child caper like a goat.

While Bean splashed soap and water in the powder room, Meredith washed at the kitchen sink. By the time Bean returned to the kitchen, Meredith had pulled out the chocolate ice cream she'd made the day before. "Remember your first days here? You were surprised ice cream could be made at home, and whipped cream didn't come from a can." She scooped out two bowlfuls—one for Bean, another for her. She dug in and ate a huge spoonful.

Bean stirred her treat. The soft, homemade ice cream puddled in the bowl.

"After all our work in the barn, you're not hungry?"

Bean bowed her head, and her spoon clattered against the dish.

"What's wrong, sweet girl?" Meredith ran her fingers down Bean's arm.

Bean said nothing.

Meredith pulled her onto her lap.

"Do you think Mama heard me say I'm glad you're my mom? Would she be sad?"

Meredith stroked the child's hair and searched for the right words to say. "Not at all. I think your mama is smiling at us. She's glad you found someone to love and who loves you."

Meredith shoved her melting ice cream away. They sat in silence as Meredith caressed Bean's hair. The kitchen clock kept its steady beat.

"Time for bed. When school starts, you'll have to go to sleep early so you can be wide awake and learn all the interesting things school teaches."

"I don't want to go to school no more."

"Why?"

"I'm ..." She nestled closer. Her boney bottom dug into Meredith's lap.

Prickles worked their way up Meredith's legs. She sat still. If she moved, she'd break the spell.

Bean wouldn't look at Meredith.

"What's wrong?"

Bean wriggled back into her own chair and swirled her spoon through ice cream again. "Do you think they'll put me in kindergarten with Roxie?"

"You're too grown up for kindergarten. You'll be in third grade because you're eight. Why do you ask?"

"I'm stupid."

"Where did you come up with such a silly idea?"

"I can't read good like Roxie, and I'm older. All the letters look the same."

"You are *not* stupid. Your parents didn't teach you, but in school, you'll catch up. Aunt Sunny and I will help. I watched you count your allowance. You're good at numbers."

"Will you pray that I do good?" Bean raised luminescent eyes to Meredith.

"I will."

Bean grasped Meredith's hands and bowed her head. She didn't move but kept her eyes clamped shut.

"You want me to pray now?"

Her eyes opened wide, and she bobbed her head. "And when you pray, put one hand on my head like Uncle Blake and Aunt Sunny do."

My family. They'll rope me back into the hypocritical fold one way or another.

"Mama Meredith?"

Meredith blinked. "What?"

"Are you gonna pray?"

"For you, anything." She bowed her head and placed one hand on top of Bean's head. Her silky hair soothed like a baby's comforter. "Lord, let Bean see how smart and helpful she is. Teach her to ride Rosemary's bike. In all things, keep her safe and let her know, no matter what life brings, she has a home with me. Amen."

"A-men!" The two-syllable word rattled the light fixtures.

A warmth swelled from Meredith's gut to her head like God poured warm oil in her veins. Maybe God still hung around her. She stood. "Let's go to bed."

In Bean's room, Meredith stood back after tucking her in. Bean's sweet mouth lined with chocolate ice cream made her want to freeze this moment forever. To never lose the love beating against her chest.

Parker stood shoulder to shoulder with Felicity as they cleaned the kitchen after dinner.

"About now, I'm sorry I booked my cruise." Felicity dried the pot Parker handed her.

"Not as sorry as I am. I forgot when you leave."

"I'm meeting Laurie in Venice on the Sunday of Labor Day weekend. We wanted to explore a little before we boarded the ship."

"Don't be sorry—Greece, Morocco, Spain, then on to the Canaries."

"Sightseeing, spas, and no cooking. Or dead bodies." She laughed and reached for the lid Parker handed her.

Her fingers touched his.

Electricity jolted through his body. Parker inhaled. What did he smell? *Peaches?* He breathed in deeply. *Honey?* They finished dinner not five minutes ago, but the aroma made him hungry. He leaned over and kissed Felicity's throat.

The scent came from her.

Felicity closed her eyes and arched her neck as though begging for more.

Heat raced through Parker. He needed to pull her close, cover her mouth with his, feel the heat of her lips, to taste her. He groaned, held out his hands and stepped away. "You smell too delicious. Like peaches."

"My new perfume. Joe Malone London—on sale on the Nordstrom website."

"Nordstrom? Too high-end a store for me."

"Splurging once in a while is good. You don't want me smelling like a hayfield and milkweed, do you?"

As though her imagery conjured a scent, Parker smelled hay and molasses and sunlight in reddish-blonde hair. He turned and swiped the clean counter one last time. He couldn't think of Meredith when he was with Felicity. This woman fulfilled all the dreams he had for his forever woman.

Sophistication, career, beauty. Goats and dung and skinny women didn't fit his life plan.

Neither did being an overworked, impoverished child welfare caseworker with no family of his own.

He stepped away from Felicity as he hung the towel on the oven door handle. Life spun in crazy circles. Half the time, he didn't want what he needed. Or loved.

Chapter 20

The next two weeks flew by. Bean rode her bike. Roxie begged to learn. Bean practiced her writing and numbers. Roxie planned her wardrobe for the first day. Every day her clothing choices changed.

Now, on the eve of school, Roxie packed her bookbag with every supply she could fit. And then some. With the bag fuller than a walrus bloated with clams, Roxie crammed in Meredith's electric pencil sharpener.

"Stop. You don't need that." Meredith took the sharpener out.

"But what if I break a pencil?"

"The school has pencil sharpeners."

Crystal pounded on plastic bowls under the table.

The noise grated, felt like Crystal thumped Meredith's head. She picked up a plastic container holding the mess-free markers and one of Crystal's coloring books.

"But what if the teacher won't let me use hers?" Roxie looked like the old Roxie—the scared, silent one from two months ago.

"She'll want you to be able to write." Meredith handed Crystal the colors. She pulled off the lid of a pink marker. "Use these now. No more banging." She laid the plastic spoon Crystal used on the table. She looked at Roxie again. "If you raise your hand and ask nicely, she'll let you use the one in the classroom."

"Honest?" Roxie relaxed and looked like her usual eager self.

"Have I ever lied to you?"

Roxie shook her head.

"Now take more stuff out." Meredith removed the box of tissues and a large bottle of hand sanitizer. "I'll carry these in for you."

"But I want to." Roxie shoved them back into her pack.

Meredith grinned. She saw the knapsack explode and rain school supplies all over her farm.

Roxie tugged Meredith's sleeve. "Show me my school paper."

"You've memorized everything already." Meredith lifted her head, stepped toward the living room, and called. Again. "Pearl Solomon, come and pack your bookbag."

Roxie snatched the class assignment sheet off the fridge. While holding the paper upside down, she put on her most serious voice and recited her memorized schedule. "Roxie Harrison. Kindergarten. Room 104. Mrs. Jobe."

A door slammed upstairs.

Roxie tossed the paper on the floor and bounced on tiptoes. "Can I pack lunch?"

"You have lunch at school. Remember?"

"Oh, yeah. How about snacks? I gets hungwy."

"Go ahead. We don't want to starve, do we?" Meredith spoke as she stepped into the living room and peered up the stairs. "Bean?"

A cupboard banged behind her, and Roxie called out, "Goldfish. I takes goldfish? No. I want gummies. Maybe ..."

Crystal banged the markers on the plastic bowls.

Bean hid herself away. The slammed door meant she sulked in her room and had no intention of joining her sisters.

"Watch Crystal." Meredith stepped up one stair.

"Okay."

Crystal pounded the bowls while Roxie rattled food in the fridge.

Upstairs at Bean's door, Meredith tapped.

No one answered.

She turned the knob and stepped into the room. Frustration soured her stomach. "I called you several times." Meredith stared at the ceiling, not the child lying on her belly on her bed. "Hiding from the world won't get you ready for school."

Silence filled the room, and Meredith looked at Bean. *Did Bean's shoulders shake? Crying?*

Meredith sat on the bed. How could these girls be sisters? All three were so different. She laid her hand on Bean's shoulder. Her stiff muscles felt like rigor mortis set in. "Honey."

The tension softened beneath her hands.

As though a plug had been pulled, annoyance fled, and Meredith's own body relaxed. "I know you feel stupid, but you're not. How many times have I told you, I couldn't care for your family without you?"

"A biyon." The pillow muffled any intelligent sound.

"A what? Don't mumble."

Bean shifted to her back and stared at the ceiling. "A billion."

"See. You're smart."

"But you say Roxie could be a vet."

Meredith nodded. "Yes."

"And Crystal an athlete."

Or a stunt double. A contortionist? Definitely a wheelchair marathoner.

199

"What can I do?" Bean turned pleading eyes toward Meredith. "I can't read or write."

"We've talked about this. School will teach you. Once you learn, you can be anything you want to be."

"What am I good at?"

Meredith stroked Bean's soft curls. She twined her fingers through the strands. "You have a talent for caring for others. So, I can see you as a nurse or a social worker."

Bean sat up. "Like Mr. Parker?"

"Exactly. Maybe a guidance counselor or teacher."

"Like Aunt Sunny."

"Better than Aunt Sunny. She's *only* a homeschool teacher. Not a real one." She fought the urge to laugh. When Allison nagged her about finding a real job, Meredith told her to earn a real degree and teach in an authentic school like a trained professional. Sunny would huff and stomp away. Minutes later, she'd come back nagging Meredith on how to do something else. Her sister. She was truly her mother's daughter.

"But Aunt Sunny's smart. So's 'Nissa."

"So are you. I've watched you for two months. You're quick-witted and know how to find what you need. No one cares for others more than you. You love to give." *Especially when the goods are "free."* Meredith bit back her grin. No sense making her gem, her sweet Pearl, think she was making fun of her. "If you don't learn, you won't be able to use any of those wonderful personality traits."

Bean snuggled closer, apparently satisfied.

The silence soothed Meredith. The crisis had passed.

Then something crashed in the kitchen, and Crystal wailed.

Meredith stood and listened. Roxie's voice cooed. Crystal's sobs lessened. "I've got to check on your sisters. Come downstairs and pack your school gear."

Bean jumped on Meredith's bed.

Meredith's eyes opened a slit. No light filtered through the curtains.

"Let's go." Bean bounced and shook Meredith.

Meredith yawned. "Where would we go in the dark?"

"We gotta go to school. We can't be late for the first day."

"It's not even …" She fumbled for her phone. "Not four yet. Pearl. Go to—"

"I'm not Pearl. We got chores and gotta get Roxie dressed and Crystal ready and—"

"Come here." Meredith pulled her close. "Let's sleep…"

"No." Bean yanked the covers off the bed. "I'll start your coffee and then …" Whatever else she said evaporated as she ran down the stairs.

Meredith groaned and flung her hand over her head. *Is this kid bipolar? Last night she'd rather have a tooth pulled than go to school. Now?* She rolled over. In the next moment, something pounced on her. She swatted it away.

"Ow. You hurt me," Bean moaned. Then her whining turned to worry. "Come on. We're gonna be late."

Meredith pulled Bean next to her. "Lay here for five minutes while the coffee brews. Then we'll prep for school." She rubbed Pearl's hair. Funny, she'd rather think of this girl as her Pearl—a child of beauty and great price. A bean was a garden variety vegetable.

Pearl stilled next to her.

"Mama Mewedith." Roxie ran into the room. "School started. Wake up."

Meredith's eyes popped open, and she squinted. Sunlight streamed into the room. She grabbed her phone from the nightstand. Six-forty-five! She jumped out of bed. "Let's go, Bean."

"I told you" Bean sat up and rubbed sleep out of her eyes. "We had to get up earlier."

"I'm hungwy," Roxie said. "I dressed myself."

Meredith glanced at the child. She wore a misbuttoned, flowered shirt and tattered jeans, ones she ruined playing in the barn. Not the stylish kind kids wore these days.

"Put on the clothes we picked out for today. You tore those pants on the fence railing last week. And they're dirty." She grabbed Roxie's shoulders and turned her around. "Scoot."

"But everybody wears ripped pants."

Meredith pointed toward the door. "Skedaddle." She turned to Bean. "Go wash."

Crystal wailed downstairs.

Meredith threw on her barn clothes and ran to the kitchen. She scooped up Crystal who had scooted against the table chairs and struggled to stand. Without her leg braces, she fell each time.

With Crystal wedged on her hips, she threw Pop-Tarts into the toaster and the coffee Bean brewed into her travel mug. *Thank You, God, for free lunch at school. And Roxie's prepacked snacks.* The toaster pinged. She blew on the pastry. After strapping Crystal into her chair, Meredith handed her the Pop-Tart. "I'll feed you later." Then she plunked two more into the toaster.

Roxie, wearing a red and blue ruffled dress and a pair of cowboy boots, ran into the kitchen. Meredith opened her mouth to state they hadn't picked out *that* outfit, then stopped. Roxie looked really cute. Meredith raked a comb through Roxie's hair.

"The bus left." Roxie twisted around and pointed to the front of the house.

"That's okay." Meredith tied the child's hair back and fastened an oversized red bow on top. "I wanted to take you myself on your first day." *Not that I have any choice now. Nor will I shoot candid photos when we arrive after school starts.* She glanced at the clock. *Or at this rate, when school is over.*

The toaster popped as Bean trotted into the room.

Roxie clambered onto the chair next to Crystal.

"Eat a Pop-Tart, Roxie, and don't tell Grandma Cora—ever—that I fed you sugar on your first day of school." She pulled out a free chair. "Come here, Bean."

Bean slid into the empty chair.

With a few strokes of the brush, Meredith clipped Bean's hair, handed her a cooled pastry, nabbed Crystal, and the four ran for the truck.

The girls strapped themselves into the back seat while Meredith turned the key.

Nothing.

Tried again. The engine sputtered once, stuttered, and then stalled. She glanced at the fuel indicator. Empty.

Today of all days, why did she forget the gas?

Seven-thirty. Time for school drop-off—twenty minutes away.

"I told you we were late," Bean whined.

"We gots to go," Roxie joined the chorus and plunked her thumb into her mouth.

Hopefully, Pa Jaynes or Ma hadn't left for work. Meredith called their number.

"Howdy, Merry." Pa's cheerful voice resonated.

"I ... my ..." Tears clogged her throat.

"What's wrong?"

"I'm out of gas. I knew about school but forgot to fill up, and now the kids are late ..."

"I always have a tank for my farm vehicles. Be there in a few."

What kind of mother am I? This is why I lost Rosemary. Mills was right. Meredith banged her head against the seat rest. She closed her eyes.

"Don't worry, Mama Mewedith. God won't let us be late."

"Yeah, Mama," Bean echoed her sister. "Aunt Sunny says God's in control."

Meredith twisted her neck and gazed at her smiling children.

Bean wiped the jelly smearing Roxie's lips. In two months, they developed so much. Roxie's confidence grew, and you could understand her. Bean hadn't stolen anything in a week or ten days—at least as far as she knew. Crystal could walk if you hung onto her hands, and she wore the leg braces.

Maybe she wasn't so bad.

A truck rumbled up the road.

True to his word, Pa arrived in his beat-up Ford pick-up. After hauling out a well-used gas can, he dumped two gallons into Meredith's truck while the kids watched with eager eyes.

"Thanks, Pa. I owe you." She waved and spun out in a cloud of dust. She pushed the accelerator as much as she dared on the winding roads and reached for her coffee cup.

Nothing.

She left the cup on the counter in her kitchen.

Ten minutes later, she ran the girls into the school. At the office, she signed them in. After an eternity, the secretary led them down the hall. Slowly.

At the kindergarten door, she kissed Roxie. The child bounced into the room without a wave goodbye.

At the third-grade class, she urged Bean to enter.

The child stood as though frozen to the linoleum.

"I'll take care of her," the secretary said.

Meredith clenched Crystal closer to her and waved to Bean. "I'll take pictures when the bus brings you home."

As the bell rang, she climbed back into her truck. No relief filled her because she got them to school on time. She'd forgotten her coffee, Crystal's wheelchair, and gasoline. Then she dumped the kids in an unfamiliar school with a bunch of strangers. She laid her head against the steering wheel. *How could I oversleep on the first day of school?*

She turned the ignition, and the gas light pinged.

"I'm not forgetting gas again. Ever." She drove the few miles to the Weigel's Mini Mart to fuel up. As the pump ran, she finger-combed her hair. Strands snagged her fingers. Her face heated. She ran into school wearing barn clothes, probably with goat scat on her shoes, and a mouth smelling of morning breath.

The pump snapped off as she glanced at her shoes for goat waste. Gas spurted on her hands.

With the way this day started, nothing worse would happen.

Crystal wailed. "Hungry."

So was she.

After pulling the truck up to the store's door, Meredith grabbed Crystal. Inside, she needed to tend to necessities before anything else. She strode to the washroom with Crystal on her hip. As she shoved the ladies' room door open with her other hip, she spied a mahogany-haired woman standing across the aisle at the coffee pots.

Parker's girl.

Meredith stood with the door held open and studied the mortician.

Parker's girlfriend stood tall and straight. She hadn't forgotten to comb her hair and most likely had brushed her teeth. Straight-leg jeans fit like leggings but with enough room to be decent. A pink, flowered shirt hugged her body. She should've been on a runway, not off to drain bodily fluids from the most recent dearly departed.

Meredith bet she didn't smell like gasoline.

Maybe like formaldehyde? She could hope.

She let the door slide shut as she stepped into the restroom. While standing at the sink with Crystal squirming on her hip, Meredith prayed the woman—her name? Felicia? Alicia? No, something meaning happy like Bliss, but not Bliss or Joy or Ecstasy—anyway, she hoped Parker's undertaker would leave soon. Before Meredith left the public restroom.

Public toilets. Yuck. She looked at the floor. Could she plunk Crystal down on those tiles while she washed her hands?

No choice.

She sat Crystal on the floor then studied herself in the mirror as water ran. Her hair was worse than she imagined at the pump. Half was bedhead flat. The other half stuck out like a clown's wig. Once she washed and dried her hands, she fished in her purse for a comb.

No comb.

Crystal whined.

After a brief finger comb to her hair, Meredith lifted her daughter and washed her with a wet paper towel.

With both of them as presentable as possible, Meredith nudged the door open and heaved a sigh.

No Fiona—

Wait. Felicity. That was her name.

After grabbing a donut for Crystal and coffee for herself, Meredith headed home.

She sucked on her coffee as she drove. Through her rearview mirror, she studied Crystal. The child bobbed her head and munched her treat—the second overly sweet piece of junk in the past hour. Sugar sprinkled her nose like freckles. Cuter than any child had the right to be.

All her girls had gained weight. Crystal's braces and therapy helped her be a little more mobile.

They arrived at school on time.

They were dressed.

Fed.

Pop-Tarts count, right?

Maybe I'm not such a bad mother after all.

Her hill and her log cabin hove into sight. A silver car, possibly a Honda, backed out of her driveway.

The car—a Civic?—slowed as she came abreast of her house. The driver saluted her in greeting then sped up.

Another lost soul. Aside from Pa Jaynes, who lived up the road, no one came out here unless they were lost.

Lost or drug addicts with neglected kids squatting in someone's abandoned home.

Meredith pulled into her driveway.

Home.

She'd tend her goats and start a new batch of soap since her supplies ran low. With an unfinished education and only insurance money to supplement the foster care stipend, she needed to keep her soap business afloat. She climbed out of the truck, then remembered.

She had an overactive, non-mobile toddler. Who'd keep an eye on Crystal while Meredith kept The Merry Goat solvent? She leaned against the truck. Sunny? Mom? If she still went to Trinity, she'd call on her old friends, but she'd cut them off after she broke Lester Mills's nose.

Chapter 21

A big, yellow bus lugged itself up the hill.

They're home! Meredith clapped her hands and pranced to where Crystal played in the kitchen. She plunked the child into her wheelchair. "Your sisters are home. Let's meet them." She raced to the street. Bending over the chair, Meredith pointed to the school bus. "Look. Here they come!"

"Leddow." Crystal clapped.

"Yes. Yellow."

"Sissies." Crystal grinned and waved.

The brakes squealed as the bus crawled to a stop. With the clank of metal and the swoosh of hydraulics, the door opened. Bean bounded down the steps. "Hey, Mama Meredith. I'm hungry." She shoved her backpack into Meredith's arms and dashed toward the house.

"Wait!" Meredith turned toward Bean and held out her phone. "I need pictures, and ..."

Bean had disappeared into the house.

She shifted her attention back to the bus. While standing on tiptoes, Meredith craned her neck, desperate to catch a glimpse of her brand-new kindergartener. Movement inched down the aisle. Determined not to miss this shot, she readied her camera on her phone. At last, with bow askew and her Olaf bookbag clutched to her chest, Roxie stepped down one step. She turned and faced the bus again. "See you tomorrow, Cyrus."

Meredith snapped a picture as Roxie blew a kiss.

A kiss!

Roxie was five. How could she ...?

Roxie hopped down the last step. "Howdy, Mama Mewedith." She dropped her backpack and hugged Meredith so tight she couldn't catch her breath. With her head nestled against Meredith's side, she cooed to Crystal. "Missed you, Sissy."

"How was school?" Meredith asked.

"Good."

"And who's Cyrus?"

"My boyfriend." Without picking up her pack, Roxie skipped into the house.

Boyfriends and hunger and suddenly I'm not the center of their world.

By the time she wheeled Crystal back to the house, Bean had a jar of yogurt on the table. She scooped spoonsful into a bowl. Roxie stood on a chair by the toaster. Jam and butter crowded her as she peered into the toaster to watch the bread brown.

"What did you do today at school?"

"Stuff." Roxie's toast popped, and she busied herself slathering on the condiments.

"Bean?"

She hiked a shoulder and shoveled in another heaping spoonful of yogurt.

"Any homework?"

"Nope."

"Nah."

Meredith puffed out a breath. "I'll be in the garden. Come out when you're done eating."

No one answered.

By the empty vegetable bed used for cool-weather plants, Meredith plopped Crystal down and showed her how to yank out weeds.

The toddler giggled and babbled as she tugged greenery and dug in the dirt while Meredith turned her attention to the tomatoes.

Every few seconds, Meredith glanced from the tomatoes to her back porch. *Come on, girls. Finish eating and talk to me.*

An hour later, covered in dirt and carrying a basket of garden vegetables on one hip and Crystal on the other, Meredith returned to the house. She dropped the veggies on the counter and carried Crystal into the living room.

Bean and Roxie huddled on the couch.

The TV blared.

Meredith turned down the volume. "Too loud."

"When's dinner?" Bean asked.

"I'm hungwy," Roxie added.

"I'll start dinner in a minute." She sat between the girls with Crystal on her lap. "I'm sorry I missed the beginning of school."

"It's okay."

At least that's what Meredith thought Bean said.

"Were your lessons hard?"

Bean shrugged.

Roxie plunked her thumb in her mouth.

"I'll start cooking." Meredith returned to the kitchen. She picked up tomatoes from her basket and fingered each as she laid them on her counter. She gazed into the living room.

The girls had curled up against each other.

Laughter flowed from the TV.

Maybe they did okay. If they didn't? She turned back to her garden's bounty. *They let me know when things are bad.*

I think.

Parker pulled up to his folks' place. Lasagna night beat Pizza Hut's supreme stuffed-crust pie. He pocketed his keys and stepped into the house.

"In here," his father called from the living room.

Parker kicked out his legs as he settled on the loveseat opposite his father's recliner.

"You're early today." Dad laid his paper aside. "What gives?"

"Mom's lasagna."

As though she heard him name her, his mother entered the living room carrying a tray with a pitcher of sweet tea and several glasses. "Your brother called this morning. Guess what?" She set the tray on the coffee table and poured him a glass of amber tea.

He shook his head and picked up a glass.

"Hayes and Maggie are having another baby." She grinned. "Maybe I'll have a granddaughter."

He forced a smile which probably looked like a lopsided lemon slice. He knew what her next comment would be.

"How're things with you and Felicity?"

Parker tried to make his voice noncommittal. "Good." He slugged more tea. The sweetness turned his stomach, but he hoped with a full mouth, he wouldn't have to talk.

"Do you think—"

He clunked his glass onto a coaster. "Mom, stop." So much for being non-confrontational.

She held up her hands.

His father rattled the paper and hid behind the pages.

Parker glanced his way.

Dad bit back his grin and wiggled his ring finger behind the paper. He mouthed, "Watch out."

"You've been dating for two months," his mom said. "I'd think you'd have a sense of where your relationship is going."

"Felicity is nice, but I'm not ready to think about marriage."

"But you're not young anymore."

"Thirty's not old."

"Biological clocks don't wait forever."

He wouldn't tell her, young or old, Felicity didn't want children. He couldn't marry someone without a chance for a family.

His mother droned on about grandchildren.

Parker's thoughts drifted back to his relationship with Felicity. If he were honest with himself, what he felt for Felicity sure seemed like love. He enjoyed being with her. Loved holding and kissing her. Conversation never lagged. He'd be a fool if he let her go.

Had to be love.

A timer dinged in the kitchen. "The lasagna's done. I'll pop the garlic bread into the oven. The salad's on the table." She left the room.

His father put the paper down.

"You're no help," Parker said.

"I'm not changing your mother after thirty-odd years of marriage. Here." Dad handed him the first half of the paper. "The coach says the Vols should have a good football season this year."

"Wishful thinking." Parker didn't care about college football—but his father?

"Best talk about the Vols or your mom will natter about babies, and Hayes's kid isn't due for another six months."

Parker inhaled. Knew why Hayes and Maggie held off telling his folks.

"Dinner," his mother called from the kitchen. "Wash up and come in here before things cool."

At the table, Parker filled his salad bowl then picked up the cruet of vinaigrette.

"I almost forgot," his mother scooped salad into her bowl.

He tipped the salad dressing.

"Lily had a baby girl last week."

The dressing gushed over the top of Parker's salad.

"Parker! You've dumped enough dressing on your salad to grease a pig."

"Sorry. I'll grab the dishrag." At the sink, Parker ran the water and rinsed a cloth. *Why had Lily taken so long to realize she didn't love me?* He closed his eyes and saw Felicity. He felt her in his arms, tasted her lips. But something bothered him. He didn't want a career or stylish home and wife who could double as a supermodel. He wanted a family. Someone who needed him and someone he could actually help—unlike half the kids on his caseload.

"Parker?" his father called. "I think the washrag's wet enough."

He slapped on a smile and wrung out the cloth. "Got to make sure the cloth is clean." Parker returned to the table and mopped up his spill.

"Lily's mother said she named her daughter Darla," his mother continued, obviously unaware of—or refusing to acknowledge—his distress. "She weighed in at eight pounds, four ounces ..."

Parker shoved flavorless greens into his mouth.

The sun sat low on the horizon as Meredith and the girls finished chores.

"Can I ride?" Bean begged.

Meredith chewed her lip. They needed to prep for school. She surveyed the sky. *Still lots of light.*

"Please. I've been good."

"On the driveway so I can watch you. I have to bathe your sisters." She turned to Roxie who pushed Crystal over the lawn. "Let's take our baths."

"Lavender bubbles?" Roxie clasped her hands in front of her.

"Of course." Inside, she plopped both girls into the tub and stirred up the bubble bath as water poured in. She sat on the toilet and watched them play in the suds.

The girls splashed and giggled. Neither one looked in Meredith's direction.

"How was school?" Although she asked before, she hoped for a different answer. Maybe this time together playing in the tub would loosen Roxie's lips.

"Good."

"Did you learn anything?"

"Yep."

"What?"

"Stuff."

"Who's Cyrus."

"I tolded you."

Although Roxie's speech had become intelligible with her therapy, she now needed help in the art of conversation. "Let me wash you."

"No." Roxie protested. "Me."

"Okay." She turned her attention to Crystal and scrubbed the child.

The girls giggled as they washed, but no bicycle sounds came from the yard. Meredith peered out the window. She craned her neck and tried to see Bean. "Watch your sister."

"Uh-huh."

"Roxie. Look at me."

The child looked up.

Meredith chewed her lip some more. *No. This kid's too unfocused.* She scooped up Crystal and wrapped her in a towel. Bubbles clung to her curling hair. "Climb out of the tub, Roxie."

"Mama—"

"Now."

Water splashed as Roxie climbed out. Puddles dripped over the floor. With fingers shriveled from soaking, she grabbed the towel Meredith offered. She shivered as she wrapped it around herself.

"Dry yourself good. We'll eat a snack when you're done." Meredith pulled the stopper for the water to drain and headed to the back porch while she rubbed the terrycloth over Crystal's head. "Bean!"

Pa's cattle munched grass in the distant valley. The goats bleated to her. No Bean rode in the yard. She stepped out onto the driveway. Down the road, Bean straddled her bike and talked to someone in a gray car. "Pearl Solomon!"

Her head jerked up.

Even from the distance, Meredith could see Bean startle and stiffen. The kid knew she was in trouble.

Meredith strode toward her while the dampness from Crystal, mummified in the wet towel, seeped into her shirt. She tightened the cloth, both for security and modesty, and hugged Crystal closer.

The car drove off as Bean mounted her bike and pedaled toward Meredith.

Before Bean had a chance to pass, Meredith grabbed the handlebars and stopped her. "I'm furious. You weren't supposed to leave the yard, let alone talk to strangers."

"He was lost." Bean stood with the bike once more held between her legs.

Meredith studied the road as though she could see the car wend its way back to town. "Don't ever talk to people you don't know again. Let's go. Time to wash up for bed."

Inside, Roxie rummaged through the fridge. Water beaded her arms and her nightgown clung to her.

"Roxie, take Crystal and put her nightie on."

"I'm hungwy."

"Your tummy can wait." Meredith handed Crystal to Roxie. She turned her attention back to Bean. "You disobeyed me."

With hands hanging limply by her side, Bean stared at the floor. "Sorry."

"I'm not being mean—or cranky." Meredith knelt and held Bean's shoulder. She looked into her eyes. "Have you heard of stranger danger?"

Bean shook her head and finally looked into Meredith's eyes.

Meredith's jaws and her shoulders relaxed. She'd been unaware how tense Bean's encounter had made her, but the innocence in her sweet, blue eyes told her ignorance made the child too friendly. "Sometimes people do bad things to children. If you don't know the person, never believe them."

"But grown-ups—"

Meredith placed her index finger over Bean's lips. "Listen to me. Not all grown-ups are good. Not all want what's best for you."

"But I don't know my teacher, and you told me to listen to her."

"In school, the teachers have been checked out, and they're safe. However, sometimes a stranger seems nice and kind—like they want to help you."

Bean nodded.

"Someone might say I sent them to pick you up, or they know your family, or Parker wants to see you. If you don't know the man—or woman—run." She had to make Bean aware of the danger in the world. "I want you safe. No one who loves you would ever send someone you don't know to give you a message."

Bean blinked several times.

"Promise me you won't trust strangers."

"I promise."

"Now go wash up." Meredith shivered as she watched her go.

Bean had been left to fend for herself, to use her own wits for far too long. Did she have any sense of danger?

Chapter 22

Meredith tucked her copies of Bean's and Roxie's IEPs in her purse. Their Individual Educational Plans held no surprises. Roxie couldn't speak. Bean couldn't read. She didn't need an educator to tell her. As she headed into town, a gray car passed her. She turned her head and studied the vehicle—a Ford. Not a Honda. Not the strange man who stalked Hen Waddle Hollow. Seeing as several weeks had passed, perhaps that guy had been lost. Paranoia wouldn't ruin her day today.

Now in Walmart, Meredith shoved her buggy past displays of batteries, and bins of stuffed animals, and fried chicken under heat lamps. With no kids and ninety minutes to kill after her school meeting, she'd relish alone time.

Alone time.

Two months ago, solitude ate her like shelf fungus on a dead log. Now? A piece of heaven.

In the grocery section of the superstore, she rolled her buggy past the produce. At the endcap, Meredith skidded to a stop and stepped back.

Lester Mills, dressed in a bright orange Tennessee Vols T-shirt, bent over the onions.

She clenched her fists on the cart handle and squinted at the man.

He straightened.

She bolted.

Meredith sped past the ice cream and frozen vegetables and strode toward the peanut butter. In the aisle displaying millions of jars of peanut butter, jelly, honey, and sorghum syrup, she slowed. She released her grip on the cart and flexed the stiffness out of her fingers. With a long, slow breath, her heart quieted. She closed her eyes and inhaled one more time. She exhaled, and sanity settled once more. *Why am I running from Mills? He should avoid me.*

Still looking to where she last saw Mills, Meredith slid a jar off the shelf and into the buggy.

I broke his nose at the funeral.

She reached for another container.

I should apologize.

No way. The swine had gotten what he deserved. She refocused on the shelves, decided on a jar of all-natural peanut butter. At the end of the aisle, she turned to the right to find her baking supplies. A flash of orange caught her attention as she maneuvered her cart. She halted and turned. A few rows behind her, Les meandered.

She turned around.

Mills looked up as she approached. A smarmy smile puckered his face. "Hello, Meredith. We miss you in church."

Yeah. Right.

"Are you going to another house of worship?"

None of your business. But sarcasm wasn't why she wanted to speak to him. She studied her cart without seeing any of it. "I ..." She could hardly hear herself. "I want to apologize."

His raised brows questioned.

"At the wake ..." She cleared her throat to stop the quaver. "At the funeral," she increased her volume. She'd apologize but didn't want him to think he cowed her—even though he did. "I shouldn't have hit you—"

"No, you shouldn't have. But the doctor said the minor break would heal up well. I had no further issues."

She smiled. "I'm glad. I was distraught and—"

"Really, Meredith ..."

Was he going to apologize? Les Mills?

"Grief was no reason to lash out. We know Scripture says anger doesn't produce the righteousness God wants from us."

Her mouth dropped.

"But, of course, as nothing serious ensued, I let the issue drop."

You let? Words formed on her lips. *Shut up, Meredith.* She closed her mouth.

Mills didn't notice her shock. He rambled on. "I'd like to be able to emulate Jesus, as he hung on the cross. He forgave those—"

"Who abused him." Her words hissed. So much for being silent. She knew the direction he headed with his thoughts. Not where a Christian should go, let alone a man holding a position of authority in the church. "I am versed in Scripture. And as Jesus forgave those who accused him, who tortured him, and tried to destroy him, I forgive you for destroying so much of my life." She turned her cart.

"Forgive me, for what?"

She faced him once more, her back to her buggy. "For being a fool without a brain."

"Meredith! Don't you know the Bible says whoever says, 'You fool'—"

"Is in danger of hellfire. Well, looks like we'll be roommates."

She strode away so fast she nearly jogged. She tried to keep her back straight and her heart quiet. After careening into the baking section, Meredith leaned forward and gripped her buggy. *Meredith Jaynes, what are you thinking? Do not suffer fools.* She turned her head as though looking for Mills, then turned forward again. She saw nothing as her breathing slowed. Yes, she was wrong to have broken his nose. She was sorry—mostly because her anger put her on his level, not for the true reason she should repent. Violence was wrong. His soul and his sin were his problems. A fool had to live with himself. He wasn't her problem because once away from the dolt, his imprudence had no dominion over her, unless …

He'd only control her if she let him, and she had. For close to a year, she brought Mills home with her. Lived with him. Sanctioned the lie he told her at her family's wake. For too long, his lie eroded all she knew to be true. She did nothing to cause her grief. Losing Rosemary and John within twenty-four hours was an awful twist of fate. A cruel facet of being human. Something she had no part in causing.

But for a year, she let unforgiveness harass her. She replayed lies. Left God in Trinity Church and refused his comfort.

What would she say to her girls if a bully tormented them? *Don't let him burrow under your skin. Be confident. Believe the truth, not the lies.*

She needed to take her own medicine.

She threw baking needs into her cart and headed to the cashier.

Long lines stretched across the aisle at the regular checkout counters. At times like this, she used the self-checkout in order to exit the store before her hair turned gray and osteoporosis set in.

Lester Mills stood at one of the shorter, manned lines.

She pulled her buggy behind him.

He flinched. Did he cower? She stared at his back, now straight and his head held high.

"I do hope you accept my apology, Les. I was wrong, and I'll never break your nose again." She bit back her grin at her snarky apology.

He faced her and nodded. His eyes and lips remained impassive. He turned forward once more.

Relief didn't fill her, as Meredith expected. She studied her cart. *Sorghum? Agave syrup? Coconut flour?* She needed to think before she piled on the groceries.

"Excuse me. I have to put some items back." Meredith left the line. With a slow step and a death grip on the cart's handle, she returned to the peanut butter aisle. She replaced the container of sorghum. The section of jars was askew. She straightened them. Her fingers lingered on a jar, and her mind drifted. Doing the right thing for the wrong reason lowered her to a hypocrite's level. She returned the agave syrup. She stood, with her hand at her side, and understood the truth everyone tried to drill through her skull. *I can't let cruelty—another's or mine—define me.*

Chapter 23

Meredith was going to croak. Immediately. She hoped for sooner. A feverish trembling attacked her. The chills made her skin ache as though it would tear. She tucked an afghan around her, but still she shivered. If ever a time for one's mommy existed, today was the day.

And today, she ruined the great things they'd planned for Labor Day weekend.

No fun.

No food, except what the kids could scrounge on their own.

No boating.

In place of fun, she would die.

So much for the great Jaynes's plans.

She lay on the couch and watched Crystal tear pages in a catalog and chat to herself.

While her teeth chattered, she dialed her mother's number. The ringing hurt her head as the phone rang and rang. *Answer, Mom—*

"Meredith, what's wrong? You never call mid-morning."

"I'm sick."

"Have you taken vitamin C?"

"Don't have any." Meredith looked around the living room for another blanket or comforter or electric heater.

"Do you have a temperature?"

"Yes. 101.5. As good as 102. Do you think you can pick up the girls from school and take them to your place?"

"Of course, I will. Between Sunny and me, we've got everything they need for the whole weekend. This way you can rest, and they can stay healthy. I'm coming over right now, and I'll take Crystal."

Meredith should protest. Despite her age, her mommy comforted. Even if Mommy was Cora Crabtree. Maybe Meredith would survive.

She lay back on the couch and watched Crystal tear more pages. If only she could sleep. An active two-year-old made sleeping a non-issue.

Her head jerked. *No, I won't doze.* She scanned the room for Crystal. No tyke. Apparently, she napped long enough for her daughter to escape.

Meredith hauled herself off the sofa and took a step. She stopped as the room spun. Once the whirling ended, she stepped into the kitchen.

Crystal sat in her favorite spot under the table. She grinned at Meredith and held out her hands. "Mama, me run 'way."

"Yes, you did, you little cherub. Come here." Meredith lugged Crystal upstairs to the master bedroom. "Want to nap with me?"

"Me sleep." Crystal threw herself on the bed, curled up and clenched her hands. To prove her point, the tyke squeezed her eyes shut.

Meredith yanked blankets over them both.

The child nestled against Meredith. Crystal fake snored but squirmed. Then she giggled.

Meredith looped her arm around Crystal and pulled her closer.

Crystal stilled.

"Meredith." Someone shook her.

She jolted and tried to rise, but her hammering head wouldn't let her. Then panic seized her. "Where's Crystal?"

"Downstairs with her sisters." Her mother handed her a steaming cup. "Drink this. Turmeric tea." She held out her hand and dropped a quarter-sized tablet into Meredith's. "Put the zinc lozenge under your tongue." Her mother helped her sit up and fluffed the pillows. "The girls will be up in a minute. Roxie and Crystal are coming with me. Bean's going with 'Nissa."

"A sleepover?" Meredith sipped the steaming tea. Its peppery tang made her grimace. "Yuck." She handed the cup back to her mother.

Mom cupped Meredith's hand. Gently, she pushed the tea back. "Drink. Turmeric helps with fevers. The girls are taken care of, and the Jayneses will tend your goats after work."

"Wait. Tomorrow. Dad's taking us on the boat to see the sunken church."

"We don't need you to cruise on our pontoon. And your in-laws are coming with us too."

Meredith tried to move, but rocks rolled in her head.

"Don't worry. Ma and Pa Jaynes will return in time for goats. On Sunday, Blake's youth group is having a cook-out, and your trio is anxious to go. The kids will stay with Sunny and me. We'll bring them to school on Tuesday. You have no worries until they climb off the bus." Mom bent over Meredith and kissed her head. "Soup's on the stove. Chicken. Lots of garlic and basil." She plunked a small bottle on the table. "Dab this behind your ears."

Meredith reached for the small brown bottle. "What's this?"

"Neem oil."

Meredith plopped back against her pillows. "Neem stinks like garlic and burnt nuts."

"The oil will help." Her mother unscrewed the lid. She dabbed a little behind Meredith's ears. "You rest, and don't worry about us." With a wave, she left.

Once Mom's engine hummed and the tires crunched out to the road, Meredith climbed out of bed. In the bathroom, she scrubbed the stink from her ears then found the ibuprofen. After swallowing two, she curled up on the living room couch and turned on a Hallmark movie.

Several hours later, Meredith awoke. The television droned in low tones and flickering light. She stood. The room whirled a little, but not like earlier. When she steadied herself, she inhaled. A faint whiff of neem oil made her wrinkle her nose. She placed the back of her hand against her forehead. Cool. She turned off the TV and padded into the kitchen. After warming Mom's garlicky soup, she sat at the table and sipped a spoonful.

Garlic. Lots of garlic. Mom's favorite cure for everything was Turmeric and garlic.

Seeing as she wouldn't kiss anyone this evening, she could slurp all the stinky herb she wanted. She swallowed a little more. The seasoning and heat felt good on her throat, but after a half a bowl, her stomach churned.

She headed upstairs.

Full sun streamed through her windows when the sound of a vehicle woke her. She shuffled up in bed and swiped her hand over her forehead. Her stomach grumbled.

She grabbed her robe as someone pounded on the door. "Be right down." Meredith swept her hand through her hair and stepped into the hall. The short robe fell only to mid-thigh, but at this hour, had to be family at the door. Mom or Sunny. They'd seen her in Mom's swimming creation. This silky thing was almost a burqa compared to that.

Little feet ran up the stairs.

"How'd you get in, Bean?"

"Your hidey key."

"You know about my key?"

"Don't be silly. Everyone has one. You have to look over the door, under the mat or a planter. You keep yours under the flowerpot."

Meredith should've known. This kid had explored her house before Meredith knew of her existence.

Sunny appeared at the bottom of the stairs. "Bean doesn't want to come on the boat with us."

Meredith turned to Bean. "Why not?"

She hiked a shoulder.

The two joined Allison downstairs. Bean and Meredith settled on the couch.

"She wants to take care of you. She raised such a tearful ruckus, I promised we'd come and make sure you still lived."

"Lived?" Meredith asked. "I had a fever, not Ebola."

"E what?" Bean asked.

"Nothing."

"Mama and Danny died." Bean burrowed into her. "I don't want you—"

Meredith tilted Bean's chin. "I'm alive and will be well."

Bean scrutinized Meredith's face.

Sunny laughed. "We haven't been able to convince her you'd be here when the weekend ended."

"I love that you want to help me, but wouldn't you like to sail with Grandpa Henry and Grandma Cora?" Meredith asked. "You've been talking about seeing the sunken church since our first boat trip. With the lake level lower—"

"The church will always be there. God don't move."

"You're a wise mite," Meredith said. "God doesn't ever move."

Bean's bottom lip poked out. "I want to help you."

229

"But …"

Tears pooled in Bean's eyes as she straightened next to Meredith. "You say my gift is helping people. I want to help."

Meredith looked at Sunny who stood in front of them. With her arms crossed and her warm smile, Sunny matched her name—sunshiny patience. "I'm feeling better. I'm tired. Bean helps more than you can imagine. Let her stay."

"Yay!" Bean clapped her hands and burrowed back into Meredith's side.

"Are you sure?" Sunny asked.

Meredith nodded.

"I can make you coffee," Bean said.

"Why don't you make me peppermint tea with honey?"

The child hopped off the sofa and ran into the kitchen.

Meredith walked Sunny to her van. She squinted against the mid-morning light. "Looks like a good day for a sail."

"Call us if you need help."

"With the little imp in the kitchen, I'm in good hands."

"God knew what he was doing when he sent these kids to you." Sunny hugged her sister.

"Especially my Pearl." She waved her sister off.

The fever had broken over the night but left Meredith fatigued. In the early afternoon, she lazed in bed supposedly reading a lighthearted, mindless novel. Her thin tank top and pajama shorts felt comfortable against her otherwise bare skin. Despite the running air conditioning, she left the window open so she could listen for Bean.

In the yard below, the bicycle squeaked. Little ditties floated through the window interspersed with nonsense syllables. Bean practiced her scat singing accompanied by the clacking bicycle sounds.

Meredith drowsed. Dreams of cars driving up and down her driveway filtered through her sleep.

Silence startled her awake. She sat up and listened. Nothing.

With kids, no sound meant something bad.

She threw off the sheets and stole to the open window.

A man's lowered voice drifted up.

She pulled the curtain aside.

A silver car with puffs of exhaust flowing from the tailpipe had pulled into the driveway and blocked her view of Bean. A running car. *The* same car that'd been skulking around for a month. *Not good.* She stepped to her bedside table and yanked the drawer. Inside, she tapped in the code to the gun safe.

"Mama Meredith! Mama!" Bean's voice rose an octave and wavered in terror. "Stop! No!"

Meredith nabbed her semi-automatic and sprinted down the stairs.

"Leave me …" Terror peppered Bean's voice.

Meredith bolted out the front door.

Bean had rounded the vehicle, but the stranger gripped her arm and yanked.

"Stop!" Bean skidded against the pavement. She tripped and stumbled against the car

The man never lost his hold as he fumbled with the back door.

"Stop!" Meredith ratcheted the gun as she stepped to the end of the porch.

The man glanced her way. He lurched back a step.

Meredith jolted and glanced at her pistol. She swallowed hard and aimed. Her palms sweated against the Walther. Too late to think about her actions.

Terror shown in the strange man's eyes, and his hands jerked upward.

Bean bolted. She raced up the steps.

"Go inside. Now." Meredith kept her eyes and her aim on the stranger.

The door clicked behind her.

The man stepped toward the front of his car.

"Stay where you are."

He stopped. His hands shot upward once more.

"I'm a good shot." She snapped on the laser sight.

The stranger looked down. The laser's red light danced over his chest. He trembled.

Meredith yelled but never took her focus off the stranger. "Bean, lock *every* door, then call the cops. Call Mr. Parker. My phone's in the kitchen, and their numbers are in my contacts. *No* arguments."

The man's chest rose and fell in rapid succession. He lowered his arms and once more stepped toward the front of the car. "Let's be reasonable, lady. The girl's—"

"Shut up." She adjusted her aim and wrapped her index finger around the trigger. The laser light jiggled but never moved far from the center of his breast. "You, stay where you are, or I shoot."

The man raised his hands again. "Listen, you have my kid." His voice was warm and sounded as though tears caught in his throat. "She belongs to me. You're the one—"

"Shut up." Meredith's head spun, but she didn't waver. "This thing," she wiggled the gun, and the laser light marched up to the man's neck and back to his chest, "holds twenty rounds. One of them will meet its mark."

"But Pearl belongs to me."

How does he know her name? Bean wouldn't have told him. She squinted and studied his face. She didn't see a resemblance to Bean. "I've got custody."

He stepped toward Meredith. "You ain't got—"

She leveled the gun. "I'm not fooling."

He stepped back. "She's my—"

"Shut up." The breeze blew again, and her skin cooled. Silence fell between them.

Time crawled by.

Where are the cops? Parker?

"Bean, did you call?" She studied the man and squinted. Held her aim steady.

"Yes, ma'am." Bean's voice sounded small behind the closed windows.

Tears burned the back of Meredith's eyes. Her nose ran. Her arms ached as they held the semi. *Fake it. You'll make it. How much time has passed?*

"Look." The stranger lowered his hands, but he didn't step toward her. Or away. He smiled.

Why did he look so innocent?

"She's my daughter."

"I don't care."

Sirens. Finally.

Two cop cars swerved up to the house. One skidded in front of the stranger. The other pulled behind him. Together they boxed in his car along with him.

She lowered the gun and let her arms hang limply at her sides.

"Down." An unfamiliar officer threw open the door of the car between Meredith and the perpetrator. He drew his weapon. "Hands behind your head."

Officer Calhoun stepped out of the second vehicle with his gun drawn. "Put your gun down, Mrs. Jaynes." Calhoun stepped toward her. He kicked her gun out of the way, then stared up at her. "You held him off with an empty gun?"

She tried to smile, and her knees buckled.

Chapter 24

The security line at McGhee-Tyson Airport snaked forward. Parker wished it would slow down. He glanced at the TSA agents inspecting boarding tickets. Why had Felicity been pre-approved for check-in? He could keep her here a little longer.

Felicity ran the back of her fingers down his cheek. "I love you, Parker."

Love? Do I dare believe her? "You wait until you're leaving the country for three weeks, and then you tell me?"

"If I'd known about you before I booked this trip, I'd never have signed up."

"Say the word, and I'll kidnap you and keep you here."

She leaned in and kissed him. "Don't tempt me."

"But a Mediterranean cruise versus me?"

"A no-brainer." Felicity's eyes danced.

"I agree. Take the cruise."

They stepped closer to the checkpoint.

"I'll be here when you return. Email or text when you're able." Parker backed out of the line as Felicity stepped up to the agent.

The man thumbed through Felicity's documents.

Love. He shook his head. He felt the desire for her choke him. She filled his head with dreams and passion and fun. He didn't want her to leave him. But did he love her the way she should be loved? He opened his mouth to call the words out to her. *Stupid. Can't shout I love you at a TSA checkpoint.*

The agent finished inspecting Felicity's documents and waved her to the baggage scanner.

When she comes home, we will talk. Maybe I can propose?

Felicity turned at the conveyor belt, blew Parker a kiss, then piled her belongings into bins.

He waved. But something troubled his gut. He'd miss her. Yes. He blinked. What is love? He felt this way about Lily. But something ... He shook off the feeling. No woman could be everything to a man. Something would always be lacking.

Other travelers blocked his view of the scanners and x-ray machines. Stupid to stand here and watch strangers enter the terminal. He turned and left.

In the parking garage, he climbed into his car. After strapping his seatbelt, he retrieved his phone from the console. He had one voice mail.

He turned the ignition and backed out of his spot. Before he got to the tollbooth, Parker retrieved the message.

"Mr. Parker." Pearl Solomon's voice quavered in her message. "Someone's trying to kill Mama Meredith and steal me."

He slammed on his brakes.

"Mama needs you. Please come right away." The phone clicked off.

A horn blared behind him.

He stepped on the gas, pulled to the toll booth, and threw ten bucks at the attendant. "Keep the change." He stepped on the gas and pulled onto Alcoa Highway while calling Meredith's number. Voice mail picked up immediately. The child must've turned off the phone.

He dialed the sheriff's office. "Detective Carroll, please."

The secretary patched him through.

"Drew, what's going on with the Jaynes family?"

"Attempted kidnapping. Potential shooting."

"I'm on my way."

"No, Parker. Robin Calhoun's there with Sergeant Andrews. Stay clear until we give the go-ahead."

"But—"

"No buts.

"My wards are involved."

"Stay away. Are we clear?"

"We're clear." He pressed the off button on the steering wheel. *Stay away? No way.* Parker stepped on the accelerator.

Meredith steadied herself as she leaned on the door, then pounded. "Open up, Bean."

"Are they going to arrest me?"

Cops and this kid. She'll never be in trouble with her fear of being arrested. Laughter welled up in Meredith's chest. She bit back the nervous laugh, but her body wouldn't obey her. She snorted and doubled over while locks clicked, and the door opened a crack.

"Don't laugh at me." Bean pouted as she stepped back into the middle of the living room.

"I'm not ... I'm ..." Meredith whooped as she slammed the door behind her and sank onto the sofa. "Come here."

Bean backed away.

Meredith held out her hands. Her cheeks hurt from her grin. "Nerves made me laugh. I'm relieved."

Bean stepped forward with two hesitant steps. "No one laughs when they're nervous."

Meredith composed her face. "Sometimes fear makes you weird." She patted the seat next to her. "You're safe now."

Bean flung herself into her arms.

Someone rapped at the door. Before she could say a word, Calhoun stepped in and took out a pad. "We need a statement."

"Where's the man?" Meredith asked.

"Van Andrews has him locked in the patrol car and is waiting for the impound tow. Then he'll follow the vehicle to town."

Meredith's arms prickled in the air conditioning. She looked down at herself and suddenly crossed her arms over her torso. *I'm barely dressed.* She snagged the afghan from the floor. *I stood as good as naked in front of a kidnapper? With an empty gun?* She exhaled, slunk down, and glanced at Calhoun from under her lashes.

He settled in the chair opposite her.

She tucked the blanket around her into every space she could find between her body and the couch. "Bean, run, and find my robe."

Bean dashed up the stairs.

Calhoun's brown eyes held hers a moment and then studied the pad of paper in his hands. "We need to take a statement from you and the child. Do you need medical help?"

"I'm not hurt." She again secured the comforter around her.

"You're lucky. The guy had a gun. Had he known yours was empty ..." He jotted something down. "How could you hold him off with an empty semi?"

At that moment, Bean returned. She clutched Meredith's short, silky green wrapper.

"Excuse me a minute, Officer." She stood but kept herself swaddled in the afghan. "Bean, bring my robe to the kitchen for me."

Once out of the living room, Meredith slipped on her bathrobe which barely covered her sleeping shorts and made her look like she wore nothing. Relief pumped through her. She had another layer of cloth between the world and her nakedness. "Can you put the kettle on for tea?"

Bean picked up the teapot.

While water splashed into the kettle in the kitchen, Meredith checked herself in the powder room. She opened the medicine cabinet, grabbed a brush and elastic band, and swished her hair into a loose ponytail. She stepped out into the kitchen.

Bean clicked on the burner beneath the kettle. "What kind of tea?" Bean pulled the stepstool to the tea cabinet.

"Pepperm ..." *No. We need time so I can talk to Officer Calhoun.* "Rooibos will help. Look way in the back of a cabinet."

"Rooie-what?"

"There's a picture of a tiger on an orange box. Check all the cabinets. Start there." Meredith pointed to where she knew Bean wouldn't find the tea. "Keep looking." She stepped into the living room then called. "Sweeten the tea with the molasses. I think it's in the pantry."

With the afghan folded over her arm, she returned to Calhoun and sat. "Bean's searching for tea I hate and never use. We'll have time with her out of the room." Meredith inhaled. *Shut up.*

Her brain didn't listen to her. Words spewed faster this time. "Mom gave me Rooibos as a health-food drink. I don't think she ever brewed a cup of the nasty stuff for herself." She draped the throw over her lap. "We can talk while Bean searches for the tea." She fanned herself. "Sorry. Nerves. I'm chattering like a foolish old woman—"

"A brave woman."

Meredith's chest quieted. She stared at the officer and, finally, no words gushed. Her hands quit shaking.

"Why'd you pull a gun, let alone an empty one?" Calhoun asked.

"I heard a car. Saw that fellow go for Bean. I forgot the cartridges were locked in the bottom drawer. Didn't have time to remember. After tapping in the code to the bedside gun safe, I grabbed the Walther and ran. When I ratcheted the pistol, I realized my mistake. I had no recourse but to pretend I had a loaded gun. Prayed the whole time the noise from ratcheting the semi and the light from the laser would keep the creep from noticing."

"God heard your prayer." Officer Calhoun handed her a form. "Can you write down what happened? In the meantime, I'll need to talk to your foster daughter. What's her real name again?"

"Pearl Solomon."

As though responding to her name, Bean carried in a tray. A mug of red liquid sloshed. She set the tray on the end table then flopped onto the couch.

Calhoun turned his attention to Bean while Meredith wrote. "The man we arrested said he was your father."

"No. He ain't. Mama, my real mama, said my daddy died 'fore I was Crystal's age. I ain't never seed that man afore."

She looked down suddenly. Then glanced at Meredith.

"Tell him the truth." Meredith paused her writing. "You're not going to jail."

"I seed him one other time when he said he was lost."

Calhoun smiled at Bean. "Don't worry if you forget something. Every mistake can be fixed." Calhoun held up a pad of paper. "While you talk, I'll write down what you say. Then Mrs. Jaynes will read what I wrote and make sure everything's correct."

"Am I in trouble?" Bean's gaze flitted from Calhoun to Meredith.

Meredith shook her head.

"No," Calhoun said. "Tell me the truth. That's all I want."

"I was riding my bike when he drove up." She turned to Meredith. "I didn't talk to him. Honest." Her voice choked.

Meredith looked up from her work. "I know. Finish your story. Tell Officer Calhoun everything."

"He pulled into the driveway and stopped between me and the house. Said he was my pa. I said 'No, you ain't.' I tried to run around the car and into the house." Again, she looked at Meredith. "Like you told me. 'Stranger danger.'"

"Good girl." Meredith picked up her tea, the bag still in the cup. She sipped. The earthy flavor drenched with the smoky sweetness of molasses gagged her.

"Did I make the tea good? I used a big spoon of molasses." Hope shown in Bean's eyes.

"You made a perfect cup." Meredith put the tea back down. "Now finish your story."

"When I got in front of the car, he grabbed me and dragged me. That's when I screamed. Mama Meredith came down and tried to kill him."

Meredith blinked hard.

Calhoun laughed. "I'm glad she didn't."

"That's what happened," Bean said. "I got into the house and called you. I hid on the floor by the sofa." She pointed to the floor. "I didn't see nothing else."

"Here's my statement." Meredith handed him her paperwork as he tucked his pen into his pocket.

"And here's Pearl's." Calhoun handed Meredith what he wrote for Bean.

Meredith read Bean's to her.

Vehicles sounded outside.

She moved the curtain aside. "The tow's here."

Voices entwined with the sound of winches as Meredith finished reading Bean her account. "Do you want to add anything? Take something out?"

Bean shook her head.

Meredith handed Bean's statement to Calhoun. "Bean confirms everything I witnessed—or at least heard."

"Thanks." He stood. "If I need anything else, I'll be back."

Meredith walked him to the door.

Calhoun climbed into his patrol car as Parker Snow pulled up in his SUV.

"Are they okay?" Parker asked Calhoun, but he stared at the house.

Meredith stood on the porch. She tightened a bathrobe around her, showing off a figure her usual barn clothes hid. More curves than she generally revealed. And more leg than he'd ever seen from her. The soft green fabric accented the red in her hair. She stepped into the house.

He finally looked at Calhoun.

"Distressed as you can imagine," Calhoun said. "The two youngest are with family and weren't home."

Parker exhaled.

"Van Andrews took the perp in."

"I passed the cruiser and tow truck on the way out here."

"I think she'll be glad for company." He winked. "And you'll be glad to give her some."

Parker gulped.

The officer pulled away as Parker headed for the house.

Only Bean sat in the living room.

"Where's Mrs. Jaynes?"

Bean pointed up the stairs. "Putting clothes on."

Parker choked back his laughter. *Naked?* He wanted to see that. Parker's breathing slowed. "Are you okay?"

Bean nodded.

Parker sat. He placed his briefcase on the end table then pulled his iPad out. "I heard your sisters went boating."

"They're at Grandma Cora's and 'Nissa's."

"I'm glad they weren't here. Can you tell me what happened?" He wrote as Bean told her tale.

"Would you like a coffee or tea?"

Parker jumped at Meredith's voice. "You're a quiet one."

She stepped off the bottom step, now dressed in loose jeans and a green T-shirt. Her hair hung in soft waves around her face.

At least she kept to green. The hue heightened her coloring.

She stepped toward the kitchen. "I need a jolt of caffeine."

"Then I'll share a cup." He followed her.

"Bean, do you want to join us or watch TV?"

"TV, please."

Canned laughter hummed from the television as Meredith, her back turned to Parker, prepped the coffee. Once the earthy aroma drifted from the pot, she turned toward Parker who sat at the table. "The man said he was Bean's father."

"We haven't found her relatives. She may have been born in Memphis, but I think all of her family must be out of state—Missouri or Mississippi, probably."

"How'd he find us?"

"Drug underground. Funny, they can't show up for work or care for their kids, but they know how to find what they want."

"Any news on the younger girls?"

"Ironically, we've got a lead on Crystal and Roxie's kin."

"But they had no birth records."

243

"Right."

She sunk into the kitchen chair.

"Are you okay?" He leaned forward.

She blew out a breath and shook out her hands. "Yes. No. I don't know." She turned her head and seemed focused on the window.

Parker drummed his fingers on the table. "Calhoun thinks you've got enough grit to be a frontier sheriff."

"Why?" She refocused on him.

"Empty gun."

She stood and busied herself at the cabinets. After grabbing two mugs, she looked at Parker. Her eyes were warm and luminescent. They didn't have Felicity's exotic beauty, but a simple—pure—hue gazed back at him.

"The man said he was her father. If he is ..." She turned and filled the cups. "Can he take ...?" She didn't look at him as she doctored the coffee. She stirred the brew, then stirred some more. At last, her shoulders straightened, and she turned and smiled and placed a cup in front of him. She sat.

"No way will he be allowed custody after an attempted kidnapping." Of this, he could assure her. "He'll be jailed for a long time, so don't worry about him gaining custody."

Meredith nodded and stared at the steaming mug cupped in her hands.

"I'm glad the girls are safe."

"Me too." She looked up at him, and her eyes sparkled. "I took these kids in because someone had to. I never thought I'd come to love them so much. If the man shot me, but Bean was safe, I wouldn't mind."

"Be careful about forming strong attachments. We talked about—"

"They tell us every Thursday during foster care training that the hardest part is when the children leave."

Parker nodded and sipped.

"I have only two weeks until I can be an official foster parent."

"I think you're more than official."

"They also told us the other night adoption was sometimes possible." An unblinking determination radiated from her eyes. She leaned forward. "I dared to hope I could adopt them. Now this guy." A smile softened her face's intensity. "I figured I'd be healing these kids, but they're the ones who've fixed me."

"You're stronger than you think."

She looked startled. Her hand covered her chest. "Me?"

"You should've heard the admiration in Felicity's voice when she told me how you punched a boor."

Meredith ducked her head, but Parker saw her face redden.

She laughed and made a fist. "I'd sock him again, but I don't think it would be wise."

When Parker first saw her, he thought her fragile. "And you had guts enough to hold off a stranger with an empty gun."

"Again, my lack of wisdom."

"Don't be so self-deprecating. You know enough about guns to realize you have an empty one. You have love enough to risk your life for these girls who may leave you at any time. You give your love to them—and none of them are easy children to rear."

"No. You're wrong. These children were raised by ... can I say, incompetent parents? Addicts. Two people controlled by drugs. Healing them is easy. Rewarding. They've restored me."

At nine o'clock, after a full pot of coffee and a dinner of leftovers, Parker stood to go. "I've taken too much of your time."

They walked to the front door. The TV hummed in an empty room.

"Bean?" Meredith called up the stairs. "Come say goodbye to Mr. Snow."

"In a minute," she called down.

They stepped onto the front porch.

"Keep me posted on the parents." Meredith ducked her head. "And ..."

Parker waited.

She finally looked at him. "And let me know if they can be adopted. I'll take them all."

"You're gonna adopt me?" Bean threw her arms around Meredith.

"I didn't hear you come downstairs. You weren't supposed to hear that. Adoption probably can't happen."

"But I heard you say you would."

Parker hiked his satchel over his shoulder. "Adoption takes a long time, and if we find your biological family, they can adopt you before anyone else."

"I don't want to go with that man!" Bean backed up. The door thudded against her body.

"Don't worry. He's in jail."

She looked at Meredith.

"Honest," Meredith said. "The man's in jail, and you're safe."

She stepped forward and leaned into Meredith.

"Thank you for dinner," Parker said.

"Leftovers."

"And coffee."

"Neither of us will sleep tonight."

Bean yawned.

"But I know someone who will." Meredith leaned toward him and gave him a friendly hug.

He smelled lavender. And something else. Garlic? Certainly not Felicity's fragrance.

"Keep me posted." Meredith looked at Bean. "You. Put on your pjs and wash up for bed."

Bean stepped indoors, and the porch light snapped on.

Parker stepped to his car and backed out of the driveway.

Meredith stood on the porch and waved. The light caught the gold of her hair.

The green of her shirt made Parker remember how her legs looked in the silky robe when he arrived this evening.

He pictured that outfit long after he drove out of sight.

Chapter 25

"Pa, I'm feeling good today." Meredith wedged her phone against her ear as she scraped the peelings for apple pancakes into a galvanized pail. "Thanks for your help the last few days. I can tend my flock from here on."

"You sure? No trouble," Pa Jaynes said.

"I couldn't have survived this weekend without you, but I'm well today. Thanks for all you've done."

"Want to come to church with us this morning? Blake's preaching."

"He agreed to preach on the same day as his youth barbeque? My brother-in-law doesn't know how to say no to any request made to him."

"Like a certain sister-in-law of his. I'll keep nagging, though. Church is important. John would agree with me."

Humor laced Pa's words, unlike Sunny who nagged her to come back to Trinity. "I'll pass on church." *Or maybe not.* They disconnected

She hugged herself and grinned then called up the stairs. "Let's go, Bean-zo. The goats won't wait any longer."

Bean skipped down the stairs and skidded into the kitchen. "Can I learn to milk?"

"Sure can."

Bean raced to the barn and wrangled Mocha. She secured her to the milking stanchion and hopped from foot to foot as Meredith washed the udders.

"Let me show you."

"No. I know how." Bean shoved a pail beneath the nanny and tugged Mocha's udder.

No milk flowed.

Meredith bent over her to take Mocha's teat. "Like this—"

"I know. I seen you milk billions of times." Bean tugged again. "Mocha's not working."

Meredith fought her chuckle. Then guffawed.

Bean pouted and crossed her arms. "Don't laugh at me."

"Mocha's working fine. You can't tug. Milking is like playing a flute." Meredith squatted behind Bean, took hold of Mocha's udder, and squeezed her index finger, then her middle and worked down to the pinky. "See. You try."

She held Bean's hands and pressed each finger.

Bean shook her off. "Boring."

"Roxie doesn't think so."

"Roxie's weird. This is boring."

"Then let me." Meredith hip-butted Bean off the stool and took her place. "Clean up my soap room, then."

Bean skipped to the office off the barn.

Meredith let the last of the nannies into the pen when Bean ran back to her. "You never walk, do you?"

Bean glanced at her legs and shook her head as though Meredith was the silliest female on the farm. "You've got two hundred and twenty-eight bars of soap. That's a lot."

"You've been busy counting."

"I counted nineteen boxes. Each box has twelve bars, so you have two-hundred-twenty-eight."

"You know your multiplication table?" Meredith squinted against the morning light as Bean skipped to the door.

"Ah-duh. I go to school. Do you think I can learn to make soap?"

"You already do. Every time I work."

"No. Like design the soap and put in the smelling stuff."

"We'll start this week."

"Thanks. Do you have any treats I can feed the goats?"

"Fresh apple cores and peelings in the goat tin. You know where they are." Meredith grabbed the wheelbarrow to clean the bedding.

Bean raced out of the barn and returned a few seconds later with the pail holding the apple trimmings. She held a long curl out to Cappuccino who nibbled the scrap from her hand. Bean danced away, and Vivienne Van Goat chased her. She tossed another peeling. Soon the whole herd paraded behind her bleating and butting each other like circus clowns. Bean laughed and climbed onto the small shelter in the center of the pen. The kids, Billie Jean and Bobbi-Jo Riggs, pranced around her as she flung pieces of apple like confetti and giggled as the goats frolicked.

Meredith dumped the waste and stowed the wheelbarrow against the barn. "I'll start breakfast. I've saved the best part of those apples for us." She dusted off her hands, tossed her work gloves onto the upturned barrow and returned to the kitchen.

A half-hour later, they sat together eating apple pancakes.

"Pa Jaynes gave me a great idea for an outing today," Meredith said.

"What?"

"Church."

"You don't go to church. Besides, I want to be with you all day without my sisters."

"You've got me all to yourself. You and I can go see the sunken church if you like."

"Really!"

Meredith nodded.

"Can you drive the boat?"

"I can do a lot of things, Miss Skeptical Child, even *sail* a boat. But we don't have to take the pontoon. We'll drive there."

"You can't drive in the water." Bean wrinkled her nose as though she smelled Mom's neem oil. "You're silly."

"I think you're the silly one. We'll take the truck and follow a road to the shore. John and I used to take Rosemary for picnics there. No one else ever went to our special place." She picked up her plate to rinse. "Wait. I almost forgot. Rosie and John and I used to snorkel around the church. I've got them someplace."

"What's snorkel?"

"They're goggles and a pipe you breathe through. When you wear them, you can breathe with your head under water."

Again, Bean wrinkled her nose. "We can't breathe under water. Everyone knows that."

"Didn't I tell you I can do all things?" Meredith winked.

The two made quick work of the clean-up and snorkel search. Ninety-minutes later, they bumped down the rutted, seldom-used Bluff Road. Meredith hauled a picnic basket from the back seat of her truck. "Grab the sack with our gear."

Together, they climbed over the downed pine. "When this tree was living—tall and smelling like Christmas time—we'd sit on the soft ground. Too bad all things die." She dropped the basket.

Bean kicked off her sandals and raced toward the water.

"Back here! Put on your water shoes. The shore is rocky."

Meredith slipped off John's shirt. She glanced around as though someone could've snuck up unheard. Her only bathing gear was the one Mom gave her on their girls' day out. She might as well be naked.

Like when she held off Bean's father yesterday.

She crossed her arms and searched for other creeps. Only bird sounds and the rustling of squirrels greeted her.

Bean plunked on the ground.

Meredith helped her wriggle into the tight water shoes. After she slathered sunblock over Bean, she blew up the floaties and slipped them onto the child's arms. Finally, fortified with snorkels and towels, they picked their way over the sticks and rocks lining the water's edge. Meredith pointed. "There're the stairs leading down to the church."

"Where?" Bean looked. Her head swiveled.

Meredith stooped behind her. With her cheek pressed against Bean's, Meredith held Bean's arms with hers and pointed again. "There."

Bean squinted and leaned forward. At last, she straightened. "I see rocks." She turned her head and looked into Meredith's eyes without squirming away from her hold. "But I don't see no church."

"Those rocks are the old stairs. We can only see the top of them when the lake lowers. The building sat in a hollow and got swallowed by the water. The stairs go down to the building."

"Why do they lower the lake?"

"To prevent damage to the shoreline if the lake ices or floods." She stepped into the shallows with Bean. "Maybe they want us to see sunken churches. Put your goggles on." She helped Bean adjust them. "Now, put the tube in your mouth like this." Meredith slipped the snorkel between her lips and bit down. She took it out. "Do you see?"

Bean smooshed her lips around the tube.

Meredith wiggled the snorkel out of Bean's mouth. "Not so tight. Use fishy lips." She puckered like a kissing gourami. "You'll breathe through the tube and not your nose because your mouth is open. I'll show you." She adjusted her own breathing apparatus once more and dunked her face in the water's surface. She reemerged to see a wide-eyed, grinning girl.

"I can do that?" Bean asked.

Meredith nodded.

Bean stuck the snorkel in her mouth and bent to the water. She hesitated. Straightened and peered at Meredith.

"Go ahead. I'm right here."

Bean doubled over again. A few inches from the water, she let the goggles skim the surface. She stood again.

"Put your whole face in. You won't drown. I promise."

Finally, Bean dunked her head, keeping only her face in the water. After a minute or two, she straightened. "R off eth athing."

Meredith laughed. "Take the snorkel out of your mouth." She pulled the tube away

"I can breathe! And see!" Bean's grin stretched from ear to ear. "Everything's green, but I saw fish! Lots of little ones."

"We'll see more than that. Follow me."

They stepped over rocks and worked their way into deeper water until they stood next to the top step of the ruined church. They dunked into the warm water.

With Bean next to her, the world opened up. Shoulder to shoulder, they swam on the water's surface. Steps had fallen in disrepair. Rotting timbers rested on the stone foundation as testaments to the transience of life. She pointed to green water plants waving with the currents of the duo's paddling. Fish wriggled along the bottom. Green algae veiled their view of this ethereal world.

Ten minutes later—or maybe twenty?—Meredith and Bean edged closer to the shore and stood.

Bean shivered but grinned. "I breathed for a long time. Under water. I didn't drowned! You were right. I was scared at first. But I could breathe. Like Uncle Blake says, "Have faith. You can do all things."

Or like I said? Meredith guided her onto dry land. "Let's eat and warm up."

They slogged to their blankets and threw themselves down. Sunshine wafting through the neighboring trees speckled their skin. A woodpecker tapped on an adjacent trunk.

Bean grabbed chips and ripped open the bag. Her teeth chattered.

"Here." Meredith took the bag and rubbed a towel over Bean. She wriggled a sweatshirt over Bean's tangled, dripping hair. Bean slipped her arms into the sleeves. The fabric bunched on wet skin, but Bean shook off Meredith as she tried to adjust the shirt.

Once in dry—or drier—clothes, Meredith gave Bean the open bag of chips "Now eat." She dried herself to the crunch of chips. If she didn't know better, she'd think this kid hadn't eaten ever. "Slow down. You don't have to jam the whole bag into your mouth."

"I'm hungry."

"I see. You're growing fast and need food."

Meredith studied her foster daughter, and her heart swelled with ... pride? Nostalgia? Regret over fleeting time?

Bean no longer fit into Rosemary's or Anissa's clothes. Her face filled out, and her long, sun-bleached hair gleamed with a healthy luster. This awkward kid was going to be beautiful.

At last, Meredith slipped on John's shirt and took out their peanut butter and jelly sandwiches. She handed one to Bean. "Here. Give me the chips, and eat something healthy. You'll have grapes after PB&J. Then if you need more food, we've got cookies."

Meredith finished her lunch.

Bean pawed through the cooler. "Any peaches?"

"Only grapes."

Bean pulled out the plastic container holding the cookies, not the fruit.

"Tell me what you thought of the church," Meredith asked.

Bean popped the lid. She moved cookies around until she found the biggest. She took a bite. "I thought it would have stained glass windows and a pretty steeple like Uncle Blake's church."

Meredith picked up a small cookie. "At one time, the church did have all that."

"Where'd they go?"

"The congregation dismantled the valuable things. Then water and years and the lack of care broke the building down. The lake even wore away the stones of the foundation and the steps."

"Why?"

"Everything on earth is here for a little time. Even if we take care of things, weather and termites and natural elements break them down."

"But the stones are so hard. How can they fall apart?" Chocolate smeared Bean's mouth.

Meredith resisted the urge to wipe it away. "Given time, the world falls apart. I guess that's why God made humans. To take care of things."

"Why do they have to fall apart, though?"

"Maybe so we don't become too attached to material things and remember God instead. Seeing as he made everything, and we all go back to him when we die, we should never forget our Creator."

"Do you remember God?"

"Of course."

"Why don't you go to church like Aunt Sunny and Grandpa Henry and Pa ... What's his name again?"

"Jaynes."

"Yeah. Jaynes and Grandma Cora—"

Meredith put a finger over Bean's lips. "You don't have to name every individual attending Trinity Church. I see your point. I should, I guess."

Her answer seemed to satisfy Bean. "Can I explore?"

"Go ahead, but stay where I can see you."

Bean investigated the shoreline occasionally picking up a rock or a twig.

Meredith leaned against the fallen tree and watched. They warned her in her foster care classes about getting too attached. Why did they request something so impossible to do?

When they pulled up to her house two hours later, cars littered Meredith's driveway. "Did you invite everyone over for a party tonight?"

"No." Bean unsnapped her seatbelt and pressed her face against the window. "Looks like 'Nissa's van."

Meredith maneuvered her truck onto the lawn, around the vehicles and parked by the barn. Before she pulled the keys from the ignition, Bean bolted from the back seat.

"I seed the church," she screeched as she ran across the lawn. "Under water. I breathed under water!"

Meredith pulled bags from the backseat. No one was supposed to be here. *Why the change of plans?* She stepped into her kitchen and dumped her gear by the door.

Mom entered from the living room. With arms crossed and chin high, she scowled. "You didn't think a kidnapping was important to tell us about? We have to hear how someone tried to steal our Bean on the news?"

Ma Jaynes stepped out of the powder room. "Why didn't you tell Pa this morning?"

"Cora, Ma," Dad called. "Go easy. Let her explain." He now stood behind his wife.

Pa Jaynes, Sunny, and Blake joined them.

"We were worried to death." Sunny's voice warbled.

"If Blake prayed, wouldn't all be well?" Meredith flinched and tightened her lips. "Sorry. That came out harsher than I intended. Where are the kids?"

"Upstairs," Sunny said.

The earthy smell of coffee drifted from the nearly empty pot. She'd have a moment to adjust to her prying, well-meaning kin. While keeping her back to the crew, Meredith poured herself a cup.

"Well?" Sunny demanded more than asked.

"Are you okay?" Mom sounded more like an interrogator than a mother.

"Do you have an order of protection?" asked Dad.

"You want me and Ma to stay with you?" Pa asked.

The questions swirled. The basic idea of each query was rephrased by another person so that all voices blended into one.

Meredith smiled, but she busied herself doctoring her brew. *Let them wait. Let me compose myself.* At last, she turned and nodded toward the living room. "Go inside, and I'll tell you all that happened."

The family sat on the edges of the sofa and chairs like children waiting for their Christmas presents, half-afraid they wouldn't receive their dreams. Anxious faces, clasped hands showed their concern. Meredith's stomach warmed, and the last of her annoyance at their meddling floated off like her coffee's steam. To fortify her nerves, she took one last sip. She pushed the cup away, then gave as many details as needed. Hopefully, her meddling family wouldn't dig for more. "So, Calhoun and Andrews jailed the guy. Parker Snow will update me. The girls are safe. I didn't think I needed to worry everyone and ruin your barbeque."

"But we did worry," Sunny said.

"We heard the news from Miss Nell," Mom added.

"We could've prayed immediately," said Blake.

Meredith raised her voice over everyone else's. "You were on the boat and—"

"But we love you, and now we're worried and ..."

Once more, everyone spoke over everyone else.

Meredith picked up her coffee and sipped, more to hide her grin than to savor the cold brew. *Am I overjoyed with their concern or annoyed at the buttinskies?*

Maybe it was all the same.

Chapter 26

Graduation arrived on Thursday evening. Meredith stepped forward to receive her official letter. No one could deny her the kids because she was now a certified foster mother. She tried not to grin like a chimp, but she knew her smile showed every tooth. Her entire gumline.

She hummed Fitzgerald's "They Can't Take That Away from Me" on her way home. Tapping her fingers on the steering wheel, she improvised her own lyrics. "The way you hold Olaf, the way you crawl around, the way you help me out …" By the time she pulled up to her house, her cheeks hurt from grinning, and her throat strained against her singing.

Sunny's van sat in the driveway, and a soft light glowed from the living room. Meredith grabbed her purse and ran up the back steps holding her precious letter. She flipped on the kitchen light and opened her mouth to call that she was home.

"Surprise!" Every relative within the forty-eight contiguous states crammed into her kitchen.

She stepped back. Tears welled in her eyes. *I should've known they wouldn't let this go by without a Crabtree celebration.*

Roxie ran to her and flung herself up into Meredith's arms, twining her legs around Meredith's hips. "Can we calls you Mama now?"

"You already do." She squeezed the tyke who tightened her legs so much Meredith thought she'd be cut in two.

"No. We calls you …" She swallowed, and her lips moved silently. "We calls you Mama Mewridith." She grinned as big a smile as Meredith's must've been. "See, I says your name right now."

"Indeed." Meredith kissed her head.

"But I wants to call you Mama. Not Mama Mewridith."

"You can call me Mama." Meredith stood Roxie on the floor.

Bean leaned against the entry to the living room. She didn't smile.

"What's wrong?" Meredith stepped toward Bean.

Pa Jaynes handed Meredith a soda. "I know the kids should be in bed, but the girls wanted a party. Tonight."

Meredith took the ice-cold can and pecked his cheek. "And you've never denied a child anything—not Rosemary, not John, and not this crew."

Ma Jaynes stepped behind Pa. She held plastic bowls and spoons. "He spoiled John, that's for sure." Her lopsided smile showed her unhealed grief.

Meredith reached for Ma's shoulder, and her heart torqued. She'd been blind to Ma's pain, so focused on her own.

"Because of our John, Pa couldn't resist your sweet little Rosie." Ma's smile turned warm and loving. "Now you've given us three more girls to love."

"I hope for longer than we had Rosie." Meredith looked around.

"I have a feeling these tykes are here for good." Ma Jaynes bent down to Crystal and Owen who sat under the table. "I got you more drums to pound."

"Excuse me. I've got to find Bean. Something's bugging her." She stepped toward the living room.

"Before you run off, let's see the letter." Mom held out her hand.

Meredith nodded toward the table. "In my purse."

Bean sat on the couch with Anissa.

Phoebe and Roxie played Chutes and Ladders on the floor.

Meredith squeezed in next to Bean. "What's wrong."

"We're watching Disney channel." She shrugged and wriggled away from Meredith.

"I see that. But I saw a coconut cake on the table. If you don't eat any, I'll eat it all."

Neither girl looked her way.

She sat a minute more. "If you're not talking to me, I'm going to the party."

Neither girl said good-bye.

Back in the kitchen, everyone studied Meredith's letter. Music played from the smart speaker. Meredith ate a double portion of coconut cake. "This is Miss Nell's. No one bakes like she can."

"She made our favorite cake for you to celebrate." Sunny patted her stomach, already showing signs of baby number four. "Wouldn't let me pay, either."

The crew laughed. And talked. And ate.

Maybe the night wouldn't end.

The kids fell asleep in front of the TV. The Jayneses left around ten, Mom and Dad shortly after. At midnight, Meredith waved off Sunny and Blake and the Buchanan crew. No one would go to school tomorrow.

Time to stow her sleeping kiddos in their rightful beds. With hands on her hips, she studied the snoozing dolls. Roxie lay on the floor with her thumb in her mouth.

Crystal slept in Bean's arms on the couch. Their eyes fluttered in dreamland.

This was heaven.

Did she dare breathe?

She lifted Roxie and tucked her into bed. Except for rolling onto her side, the child didn't move—nor did her thumb unplug from her mouth.

Olaf jumped up after his mistress and curled against her back.

Crystal lay without moving in the lower trundle bed. Every limb quieted. In sleep only, did she stay still. Meredith returned to the living room and shook Bean. "Wake up. Time to sleep." She giggled at her oxymoron.

With her hand on the child's back, Meredith guided Bean up the stairs.

Bean wobbled in her walk and nearly fell into bed.

Meredith fluffed the blankets over her.

Bean closed her eyes, and Meredith straightened.

Before Meredith turned away from the bed, Bean's eyes fluttered open. She stared at the ceiling but said nothing.

Meredith sat on the edge of the bed. "Is something wrong?"

She shrugged and nestled under the blankets.

"You seemed sad when I came home from class. I thought you'd be happier that I graduated."

"I am." Bean turned away from Meredith.

"Then why so blue?"

"I miss Mama." Bean dashed away the tear running down her cheek.

Meredith turned Bean onto her back and leaned over her. "I know you miss her. No one can ever take the place of your real mother." Meredith stretched out beside Bean and took her in her arms.

The child turned into Meredith.

She pulled her close. "I never want you to forget her, but I'll try to love you as much as you love her."

Bean turned earnest eyes up to Meredith. "If I can't have Mama, I'm glad I have you." She yawned, and her eyes closed.

"When I have children," Bean mumbled through a sleepy haze, "I hope they have a foster mom as good as you."

Meredith's heart stopped. "Bean ..."

Soft breathing emanated from the sleeping child.

A deep sleep came quickly for her, as well.

The next morning, Meredith stepped into the kitchen from the barn.

"We're late!" Roxie stood on a chair by the stove and watched an empty pot burn.

Meredith grabbed the pan. "Yeow." She dropped the hot pan into the sink and ran cold water over her burned palm and into the pot. "What're you doing?"

"We gots to eat."

Something crashed.

Crystal let out a yowl.

In the living room, Crystal lay half under the coffee table. Blood gushed from a gash to the forehead.

Meredith scooped up Crystal and carried her into the kitchen. She pressed a paper towel against Crystal's head while bouncing her on her hip.

Crystal screamed.

"I'm hungwy." Roxie whined her usual mantra and jumped off the stool which tumbled one way as Roxie crumpled to the floor. "Ow. I hurt my leg."

"Bean!" *If ever a time I need her help.* "Roxie, I thought we were staying home today."

She scrambled to her feet. "No. I wants school."

"Okay."

"The bus has been here already." Bean stood before her dressed in jeans and T-shirt and looking surprisingly put together. If one didn't count her hair gathered in three ... no four different ponytails.

"Let me fix your hair."

"No. I already did."

"But—"

Bean jerked away from Meredith.

Crystal finally quieted.

"Do both of you want to go to school?"

"Yes. I'm trying out for math team," Bean beamed. "Remember?"

You never told me.

"I wants to tell my teacher you're my mama now," Roxie said.

"No. Mama's our mother. Mama Meredith is—"

"Enough. Sit at the table. Today's a cold cereal day."

"But we's late." Roxie pouted.

"Yes, but, you'll either head to school late, or you won't go at all. I won't send you hungry."

The two older children sat. Immediately.

Meredith strapped Crystal into her booster seat and plopped three boxes of cereal on the table. Lucky Charms for Crystal, who only ate the marshmallows. Apple Jacks, Mom's 'healthy' choice for the two older girls and homemade granola for herself.

Food shoved in their mouths kept them from speaking.

Meredith breathed.

Parker plopped in his cubicle and scrolled through his email knowing full well what he wanted to see. The list of new foster parents arrived.

Meredith Jaynes didn't disappoint. Four and a half couples received certifications last night.

He checked his calendar. He needed to schedule a home visit with her. He picked up his phone.

"Good morning, Parker Snow." Meredith's bright voice rang with the lilt and cadence of music and reminded him of sunshine. Background voices contrasted her voice with dissonance.

"You're perky for this hour," he said.

"Glad you didn't call fifteen minutes earlier—"

The chatter of little girls swelled.

"Girls, I'm on the phone."

Even when angry, she sounds merry. "I thought they'd be in school. Are they okay?"

"They're fine, and we're on our way to school right now. We're late this morning."

"I'd like to schedule a home visit."

"Any time."

"This afternoon? I had a cancellation, and I've got four o'clock free."

"Four o'clock?"

She paused, and he could hear the squabbling of the older two.

"Bean, do we have anything planned this afternoon?"

He waited while an indistinct voice spoke.

"My secretary, Pearl Solomon, tells me my calendar is clear. See you then."

They disconnected.

"Someone made you happy, Snow." His supervisor plunked a file on his desk.

Parker quickly recomposed his face. A grin reemerged once more. "I love when I find kids a good home."

"This update on your family in Duff will erase your grin." She walked away.

He flipped through the file. The Peters wanted to move their foster son out. He didn't blame them. Not a felicitous child.

Felicitous? Felicity.

How long until she returns? He checked his calendar. *Five days.*

He closed his eyes and imagined his body pressed against hers. *Any email?* He scanned the office. Everyone worked on papers or made calls. He picked up his cell and checked.

No new messages.

Where was she today? He scrolled through past correspondence until he found the one from two days ago. *Morocco. Casablanca.* They'd watched the movie of the same name two times before she left. After Morocco, she'd sail to the Canary Islands and fly home.

Home. He inhaled, smelled peaches. Only five more days.

His phone vibrated warning him about his next meeting. He had to head to Powell Valley. Needed to leave now.

He grabbed his briefcase and took a couple of steps. His desk phone rang. He stepped back. "Snow speaking."

"Let me know when snow melts." A baritone laugh over his stale joke said the speaker was Drew Carroll.

"What's up?"

"Got good news. We found relatives for Pearl Solomon."

Parker sunk onto his chair. He should smile. Be happy. But if this worked out, he'd break Meredith Jaynes's heart.

"That fellow Larry Solomon we arrested a few weeks back trying to kidnap Pearl?"

Parker tensed. "Go on."

"DNA proves he's the father. Originally, Solomon lived in St. Louis. His father, Guy Solomon, still lives there. From what St. Louis DCS can tell, Guy Solomon's a good man. Widowed last year. Works in the postal service. He disowned his son and hasn't seen Larry in five or six years. Guy Solomon showed DCS pictures of Pearl as an infant and up to about two years old. He had some pictures of his late wife, son, and Pearl's mother altogether. The man has a good rep. He wants to see his granddaughter."

"When can we meet?" Parker grabbed his pen and notepaper and jotted down the times the grandfather could visit East Tennessee. "Thanks, Drew. I'll get back to you with the dates." They hung up, and Parker dialed the first four digits of Mrs. Jaynes's number. He hung up.

He dropped his hand. Too cold. He'd tell her everything at the home visit. She deserved that.

"I made math team!" After bounding down the bus steps, Bean threw her bookbag into Meredith's arms.

"Mr. Parker's coming ..." she called after the fleeing child. Meredith refocused on the bus.

Roxie hopped off the steps. "I gots a new boyfriend."

Meredith's heart stuttered. *Once a week she has a boyfriend. Cute now. In ten years?* "His name?"

"Buddy." Roxie kissed Meredith, added her knapsack to Bean's and ran to the house.

Back inside, Meredith took Crystal into the living room. PT said Crystal was probably ready for gait training and gave her a new exercise for home.

Meredith sat on the floor and laid Crystal next to her. The child grasped Meredith's fingers and rolled up to a seated position. Then tugging on her hands, Crystal stood.

The toddler stiffened her legs and the pressure lessened against Meredith's fingers.

"Good girl."

"I walk." Crystal crumpled to the ground.

They repeated the exercises for several minutes. Crystal didn't stand as long each time. Finally, she plopped to the floor with all the grace of a ragdoll. She giggled.

"You go boom."

"I boom." She sat up and clapped her hands. "I done." And as though underscoring her point, Crystal scooted toward the kitchen.

"Crystal's on her way," Meredith called. "Watch her for me, girls." Meredith stood and straightened the cushions on the couch. She picked up the Chutes and Ladders pieces and placed the game back on the shelf. She double-checked the downstairs bedroom, jogged up the stairs, checked Bean's. Gave the bathroom a quick once-over. Parker couldn't see how they really lived.

Four o'clock approached. But the girls were too quiet downstairs.

She returned to the kitchen.

Had anyone ever cleaned this room?

Peanut butter, empty jars of milk, spilled honey cluttered the table. Meredith took a step, and something sticky clung to the sole of her shoe. Her sneaker squeaked as it resisted whatever she stepped in.

She turned to the sink.

Well, I suppose they did clean up.

Dishes and glasses filled the sink.

Meredith yanked open the dishwasher as a vehicle pulled up her driveway.

Too late.

She shut the door and looked around. *What would Parker Snow do, take the kids away? No way. She was certified.*

Chapter 27

The girls thronged Parker's jeep.

He eased the door open nudging Bean, who held Crystal, a micro-inch out of the way.

Crystal reached for Parker as she nearly tumbled out of her sister's arms.

He whisked her up but almost dropped her as his briefcase strap slipped off his shoulder. "You're getting ..." He bounced her up and down as though assessing her weight ... "healthy."

With the white and orange cat clutched in one arm, Roxie edged around Bean and hugged Parker with her free arm. "Mama's our real mama now."

"I read the news this morning ..."

Roxie turned and raced toward the house.

"That's why I'm here," Parker spoke to the fleeing child.

"Mama," Roxie yelled. "Mr. Parker's here."

"I made the math team." Bean grinned. "I'm smart!"

"I'm proud of you." Parker rubbed her head.

Bean took his free hand and tugged Parker toward the back porch. "Mama Meredith's making the house look good for you. She says she has to make you believe she's a good mother."

Parker chuckled.

"I know." Bean tugged as though dragging an unwilling DCS worker. "She's silly. She's a really good mother even though we live in a dirty house and eats junk food whenever we wants." Bean let go of Parker's hand and galloped up the stairs. "Mama Meredith, Mr. Parker's here." The door slammed behind her and nearly hit Parker's nose.

"Open." Crystal leaned toward the house and grabbed the air with pudgy fingers. "Bean. Open door."

"Why don't you knock."

She listed over Parker's arm and banged on wood. "Open. Bean. Now!"

Roxie flung the door wide open. The orange cat now curled around her neck like a fur stole. She didn't look at him but called over her shoulder into the depths of the house. "Bean, you knows she ain't Mama Mewridith no more. She's Mama."

At least that's what Parker thought she said before she slammed the door in his face. He stepped back and laughed. This house was crazy, but the kids felt at home.

"Roxie! Manners." Meredith swung the door open. "I'm sorry about the girls' etiquette. I was ... um, in the powder room ..."

Did her face flush?

"I couldn't stop the tornadoes from swirling into the house leaving chaos behind them." She stepped aside.

At least Mrs. Jaynes didn't slam the door in his face.

"Come on in, if you don't mind catching a fatal disease from the filth the girls leave behind."

He walked in.

"Let me finish filling the dishwasher." Meredith stepped to the sink. She grabbed the sprayer and squeezed the lever. Something stuck. Water sprayed her face and neck and soaked her T-shirt making the fabric cling to every curve.

His heart kicked up a notch.

She redirected the spray to the sink and turned off the water. "I guess distracted cleaning causes accidents." She pulled on the damp material of her tee, and the shirt fell more naturally.

Unfortunately.

She placed the last plate on the rack, dropped in the cleaner and pressed a few buttons. The machine whirred to life. As she turned back to Parker, she ran the back of her hand across her forehead. The action swiped her hair to the side.

Her hair swept her shoulders today—not tied up in her usual ponytail. Like the day Larry Solomon attempted to kidnap his daughter. Parker liked how her hair filled out her face and made her look a little wild. Uncontrolled.

Parker swallowed hard. *Not now. Think about the family. Not the pretty mother.*

"So, do I take you around the house or do you roam on your own? I think the kitchen is the worst."

Roxie materialized in the doorway to the living room. "I'll shows you my room. Me and Olaf and Crystal decorated everything ourselfs." Roxie didn't wait for an answer, and she pranced into the living room.

"I'll let the tour guides lead." Parker followed Roxie's trail to her room.

The child patted her bed. "See. My bed's pwetty." Roxie puckered her lips. Her face turned serious as her little mind worked. "I mean, *prwetty.* I speaks real good now. My teacher says I'm doing perfect."

Although far from perfect, Parker understood everything the child said. The r sound bothered Roxie the most, but if she moved to Boston, she'd fit right in.

"Why're you laughing at us?" Roxie ducked her head between hunched shoulders. Although she looked cowed, her squinted eyes told another story. They speared him.

273

"I'm not laughing." He looked around the room, more to hide his grin and to keep from chuckling out loud than to further inspect the area.

Stuffed animals sat in front of the window. The daybed was made up with a cat-themed quilt. "You like kitties, don't you?"

"Yep. But Mama says I'm 'lergic. Grwandma Cora says balderdash." Horror showed in her eyes as she covered her mouth. "Is that a bad word?"

Parker shook his head.

"Crystal sleeps there." Roxie lifted the bed skirt and showed the trundle tucked away.

"She sleeps *under* the bed?" he winked.

"No, silly." Roxie yanked on a handle. A mattress covered with a blanket with a Paw Patrol theme rolled out. "Crystal likes animals too."

"I see. Do you want to show me Bean's room?"

"Yeah!" Without waiting, Roxie raced up the stairs. At the top she turned and waved to Parker at the bottom. "Come on! Hurry!"

Parker joined her.

Roxie flung open Bean's door which crashed against the wall and half-closed once more. He stepped inside. Bean obviously tended the room on her own. The coverlet lay askew. Clothes dotted the floor of the closet. Barbies sat in a neat array against the wall.

All signs of a happy family.

Except.

Guy Solomon said he wanted to see his granddaughter. He intended to take her home with him eventually.

As was his right.

He was a good man. At least the St. Louis Social Services avowed he was a normal, well-adjusted, kindhearted fellow. Recommendations at work, an elder in his church.

Parker returned to the kitchen.

The sink now sparkled. He took his usual spot at the table where his usual coffee sat.

Bean and Crystal already sat at their places. Steam drifted from Bean's cup. A covered mug sat in front of Crystal. Not that the cover did any good. She yanked the lid off and sloshed hot chocolate over the sides of the cup, puddling onto the golden oak surface.

"Will Roxie join us?"

Meredith called. "Roxie, your cocoa's cooling." She turned her pretty—um—her eyes back to him. "So, do I pass inspection?"

"Exceptional job." He didn't look up as he tapped information into his iPad. If he didn't look at her, he wouldn't see despair replace the joy in her face. He tried to prolong his work, occasionally sneaking a peek at the family. If he typed, he wouldn't have to tell her Pearl Solomon would be leaving.

Roxie's chair scraped the floor. She reached for the bag of marshmallows set in the center of the table.

With his head ducked, he eyed the girls.

They slurped cocoa.

Crystal pilfered the bag Roxie left next to her and piled marshmallows into her cup.

Roxie slurped hers.

Bean edged closer to Meredith and gripped her arm as if she knew something was happening.

As he slipped his iPad into his briefcase, he opened his mouth to tell her they found Pearl's grandfather. Instead of speaking, he wiped his glasses on his paper napkin. He resettled them on his nose. Stirred his coffee.

"Okay. What's up?" Meredith pushed her cup aside.

"What makes you ..." *Why did he bypass the opening she gave?* He plunged into the news. "We found Bean's grandfather."

Meredith stiffened—almost imperceptibly. As though he'd been married to her for ten years, he recognized her quirks. She tried to hide them, but he saw.

"I don't have a grandfather," Bean bolted to her feet. "Only Grandpa Henry and Pa Jaynes."

Meredith clasped the child's arm. "Sit down and hear Mr. Parker out."

"Her grandfather lives in Missouri. That's what took us so long to find him. If Larry Solomon hadn't tried to take Pearl, we might never have located him."

Meredith ran her finger along the cup's rim.

"Guy Solomon wants to see Pearl again."

"I ain't got—"

"Bean." Meredith's voice was level.

Bean bowed her head but inched closer to Meredith.

"He lives in St. Louis—"

Meredith pulled Bean to her.

The child climbed onto her lap.

She hugged Bean tight. "You're not shipping her to St. Louis to someone she doesn't—"

He held out his hand. "No. The first visits will be supervised here, at the courthouse with me present. I need you to prepare yourselves. Mr. Solomon has no criminal record. He has a good job at the post office, has high recommendations from his bosses and peers. He's had no contact with Pearl's father for six years. Solomon the son won't be allowed visitation because he tried to kidnap her—"

"They could make her visit him in jail?"

He nodded. "But, because of the attempted abduction, Pearl won't have to. This is good news."

Meredith flinched. Then her face regained its serene expression. She cradled Bean and peered down at her. She smiled. "You have a grandpa. This is wonderful."

"No, it ain't." Bean thrust off Meredith's arms. "You tell Mr. Parker my grandpas' names is Henry and ... and ..." She squinted at Meredith then glared back at Parker. "One's Henry. The other's Pa Jaynes." She stomped to her feet and stormed out of the room.

"Mama." Roxie looked toward Meredith. "Is that man my grandpa too?"

"No, honey."

"Is he going take us away?"

"No. Drink your cocoa."

Roxie climbed onto Meredith's lap.

Crystal dunked her fingers in her cocoa and fished out marshmallows. She lined them on the table.

Meredith stroked Roxie's cheek. "The man is your sister's daddy's father. He's not related to you. Remember, Danny is your daddy. Larry is Bean's. Don't worry." She looked up at Parker. "When does Bean visit him?"

"We haven't set up a definite time. Right now, Mr. Solomon can come here next Friday after school. If all goes well ..." He picked up his spoon and stirred his coffee. *You've done this a million times, Parker. Quit stalling.* He looked her in the eye. "If all goes well, we'll arrange other meetings over the weekend—especially seeing as he has to travel so far. Expenses like food and lodging mount up fast."

Meredith pulled Roxie tighter, almost as snug as Roxie had clutched Olaf when Parker first arrived. "What about ..." she nodded to the two kids.

"We have a lead on Danny Harrison's kin. Beth Willoughby's a mystery." He glanced at his watch. "We're guessing their kin is out of state too. We'll let you know as soon as we have any information." He stood.

Meredith kissed Roxie's head. "Take Crystal into the bathroom and wash her up while I walk Mr. Parker to his car.

Roxie unstrapped Crystal.

"No. Mushmallows." Crystal slapped her sister's arm and grabbed a marshmallow.

"Let's go, Sissy." Roxie scooped her up and carried her to the powder room.

Meredith and Parker walked into the yard. As though humidity struck again, they trudged to Parker's jeep.

"You knew this day would come. DCS strives to unite families." He turned to her.

Straight shoulders, gentle smile. "I know." She focused on the ground. "I'm having a selfish moment. Bean's the reason I have my fam ... the girls." She ran a finger under her eye. "They told us this would be hard. I thought I understood."

He reached out and took her chin. *I shouldn't touch ...* He tilted her head so he could look into her eyes. He needed the right words to comfort her. "Look at me." His hands lingered on her face. *Drop your hand, Snow.* He ran fingers along her cheek. Soft and warm. Smooth as satin. "Steel yourself. With his stellar reputation, Pearl will be leaving."

She opened her mouth.

He touched her lips with his finger. *Too intimate, Snow. Improper. She can bring up charges against you.* After a few more seconds passed, he dropped his hand. It felt cold and empty. "You can't argue. This is the deal with foster care."

She shook her head. "I'm not thinking about her leaving or about her grandfather—but her father. Can he ever gain custody?"

"He's in jail, and there'll be an order of protection. He will be incarcerated for at least two years. From what St. Louis DCS tells me, Guy Solomon will have nothing to do with Larry unless there's a genuine, God-induced change. Bean will be safe with her granddad."

She nodded.

"This is best for Bean."

She smiled. "I know, but I do need a moment to process my pain." She gazed off into the distance. "My sorrow is a selfish longing." She faced him once more. Lines crinkled her eyes as she smiled. "My real hope is lasting love for Bean."

He pulled out of the driveway watching Meredith through the rearview mirror until she rounded the house.

In seven days, Meredith's heart will break.

Poor woman.

Wait.

In five more days, Felicity returns.

He tapped the steering wheel. The warm, smooth surface reminded him of Meredith's cheeks. Her lips.

He crossed the ethical line this afternoon.

As though he could see her, he glanced in the rearview one more time. He knew her. She wouldn't press charges.

At midnight, Meredith lay in bed in her quiet house. She stared into the dark and studied the subtle shadows on the ceiling.

Bean had been quiet all night.

Roxie put Crystal and herself to bed.

Loneliness and silence pressed down on Meredith like a coffin's lid. She inhaled. Air flowed in. Exhaled. Nothing lifted the weight from her lungs.

Why did love hurt? She squeezed her eyes shut. Hoped sleep would numb her.

She opened her eyes and stared at the ceiling once more.

Maybe Guy Solomon won't like Bean.

How could anyone not? Especially a grandfather.

I could visit her.

So far away. How often could I?

Would I be allowed?

What about her sisters? I need to ask Parker how they could separate the girls.

She turned on her side and faced the wall. Seconds later, she flipped to her stomach. Rolled to her other side and finally onto her back once more. *I'm a tumbleweed.*

She sat up and threw off the covers. *This isn't about you, Jaynes. Pearl needs her family.*

She threw on her robe and padded out to the back porch. She sat in her wicker chair and focused on the distant mountains outlined in the moon's light. She watched skunks wobble across the driveway. A possum hobbled near the goat pen. A breeze scuttled the first fallen leaves of autumn. An eon crept by before dawn skulked in.

In a week, she'd begin to lose Bean.

She could do this.

She survived the loss of Rosemary and John. Nothing could hurt her now.

Chapter 28

Meredith scrolled through her phone instead of watching for customers. Soft murmurs and faint rustling from the market stirred around her as she hit a new site. *Four. Only four.* Seeing the names made Bean's leaving too real.

"Mama Meredith, is three soaps $15.49?" Bean asked.

Meredith blinked. "Yes. You're good at math."

Bean grinned and handed the change to the customer.

"Arithmetic's easy if you know how much one is. I never changed money for three. I wanted to make sure." Bean laid the soap into the brown bag with The Merry Goat label and handed the soap, along with change, to the customer.

Meredith pocketed her cell and studied her Pearl. Grown so much. Learned so much. She closed her eyes. *Grandpa Solomon, appreciate her.*

"Make sure I counted your change good, ma'am. I'm on the math team, but I makes mistakes."

Meredith reached into her pocket and pulled out a five-dollar bill. "Take a break. Buy something from Wookie Cookie for you and your sisters."

"But you already gave me my allowance."

"This is extra because you've been so helpful."

"Can we go to Sinful Cinnamon?"

Meredith knelt so she could be eye level with Bean. "Buy anything you like for five dollars. Remember your sisters. Now is the time to make memories with them."

"Roxie, Crystal, let's go."

"How come I don't gets an allowance?" Roxie scowled.

"You're too little. When you're as old as Bean."

"Not fair."

"Enough. Watch Crystal."

The girls adjusted Crystal into her wheelchair while Meredith turned to the next customer perusing her stand. Usually, busy days kept her mind engaged. Bean's help, though, gave her too much time to think.

She sold six more bars in the next two minutes. Then the lull arrived. Only window shoppers sniffed her soaps. Comments on the scents, the packaging, the benefits of goat milk or essential oils drifted around her as she stepped back to let them browse.

They wandered off to the neighboring booth.

The lure of her Google search for Guy Solomon tempted her again. With her tap to the screen, her phone came to life. Four Guy Solomons lived in St. Louis. One in his fifties. He must be Pearl's grandf ... whatever.

She hit this Guy Solomon's name. Fifty-five. Postal worker. She clicked links and found a photo.

Her heart sank. She stared at his face. Eyes are the soul's peepholes. Why'd his have to look so kind? Brown eyes, not Bean's pretty blue. Almost bald with distinguished gray along his ears and the nape of his neck. A smile lit his eyes and made them say, "You're the person I want to speak with."

Another browser examined her wares. Meredith tilted her chin. She had a business. Needed to support two other girls.

For the time being.

If she kept busy, her heart wouldn't break.

After the first slow down, no other market lull came. By the time Meredith pulled into her driveway, she wanted nothing more than to hit the hay—and not in her barn. But duty called.

Roxie played with Crystal in the barn office while Bean and Meredith unloaded the truck.

"You were a big help today." Meredith took the last box from Bean's hands.

"I only helped when you played games."

"Games?"

"On your phone."

"Oh, I ..." She bit back her words. No need to tell Bean she was spying on her grandfather. The thought of the visit coming this Friday hung in the background throughout the day like a ghost. "Not games. Research. Why don't you ride your bike until dinner?"

"Okay." Bean raced out of the barn. She called over her shoulder. "I know, Mama, only to the Wheeler Road, and don't talk to strangers."

Meredith grinned and nodded.

Bean disappeared into the sunlight.

She called me Mama without tagging on my name.

"When can I ride?" Roxie asked.

"Soon." Meredith didn't look away from her inventory of remaining soap.

"You always promise, but I never get to."

"I keep my promises."

"No. You don't." Roxie stomped her foot. "Bean gets everything."

Meredith stopped counting soap boxes. *Do I ignore Roxie? No.* "We'll make sure you have first dibs on the bike tomorrow. I'll give you lessons."

"Yeah!" Roxie nabbed Olaf and plopped him next to Crystal on the cot.

"Watch your sister. She'll try to climb off the bed and fall."

Roxie plunked down next to Crystal. A barn cat, the one who scratched everyone but Roxie, hopped next to them.

Meredith returned to her inventory and finished counting her supplies.

They sold a lot today. Even Mom's weaving. With the season changing, she needed some more timely fragrances for her festivals. She took out her soap recipes.

Pumpkin spice.

Caramel coffee.

Hot cocoa.

All popular scents.

The girls giggled.

"Pet Olaf nice." Roxie sounded like a mother instructing her babe.

Meredith looked up from her recipes.

Roxie and Crystal sat side by side. Roxie placed her prize kitty in Crystal's lap. "You can only play with Olaf. You can't play with Shadow. He's dangerous." She gently placed the barn cat on the floor.

He jumped back into her lap.

Roxie shoved him to the side away from Crystal. "Shadow scratches everyone but me."

Crystal squeezed Olaf.

He yowled.

"No. Do like this." Roxie held Crystal's hand and rubbed over Olaf.

"Me, do." Crystal took the cat and rubbed its fur against her face.

Meredith picked up her phone and snapped a picture.

The girls nuzzled the white and orange cat. Roxie's hair draped over Crystal's as they sat cheek to cheek.

Meredith hit the record button. Soft light filtered through the window illuminating the air filled with hay bits and goat dander—almost like dandelion seeds. If Meredith could paint, how she'd capture these children. Like Renoir. Rosy cheeks and angelic eyes.

She couldn't paint if someone handed her a paint-by-number set. Cell phone pictures and videos would have to do. All her girls would leave too soon. If she couldn't keep her daughters, she'd immortalize them in more than photographs. When they left her, they'd live on in her lifeline. Her soaps. A new fragrance and color for each girl.

She bent over the 3x5 cards. Tears burned her eyes. *I will not cry. I knew this would happen.* She looked heavenward.

God, why take the one who helps me? Who makes my life possible?

She looked at her notes. *My pearl of great price.*

A white pearl who smelled, not of vanilla—too clichéd, and Bean was anything but cliché.

She needed a water-white fragrance so the soap would hold its pure ivory color. Pearl and purity.

And peppermint. What could personify winter more than white peppermint? The scent was alive. Feisty. Yet what freshened sour smells more than peppermint? Nothing made you feel more in tune with life.

This recipe would characterize Bean.

She'd call her creation Winter Pearl. She jotted down her notes before she forgot the quantities or before Crystal hurt herself.

Crystal?

Roxie?

Too quiet.

She scanned the office.

No one.

Meredith walked into the barn. Again, empty.

Out to the corral.

The goats munched hay.

Where?

She scanned the nearby fields.

Crystal and Roxie spun down the hill like tumbling logs.

"Roxie! Crystal! No!"

Roxie stopped herself and sat. She ducked, and her hands covered her head. Her terrorized looked told Meredith she alarmed the child. Roxie needed so much therapy.

"Get Crystal."

Roxie looked around. "We were playing our rolling game."

"But ..." No time to explain. She ran. "Stay where you are."

Meredith raced toward Crystal.

The duo had been playing one of their favorite games—rolling down the hill, letting gravity increase their speed. Only Crystal never looked before she rolled.

Today, at the bottom, one of Pa Jaynes's steers had escaped the pasture and watched the tumbling child with too much interest. Cavorting hooves and a two-year-old did not blend well.

"Shoo. Go home." Meredith flailed her arms and raced toward the wayward steer.

The critter looked her way then scampered off.

Crystal rolled to a stop and laughed. She spied Meredith and pointed. "Cow."

Meredith scooped up Crystal. She ran her hands over the child's head as she inspected her. Checked her arms and legs.

"Me pet cow." Crystal leaned over Meredith's arm reaching for the escaped steer who studied them with large brown eyes. "My pet."

"No, you can't pet the steers without me."

"No!" Crystal swung her head back and forth with so much vehemence, she knocked herself off-balance in Meredith's arms. She leaned back, almost parallel to the ground while her head wagged.

Meredith shifted her upright.

Crystal reached for the Black Angus. "I want pet. Like Olaf."

Meredith tried to choke down her laughter but only succeeded in cackling like a flock of Canada geese "You can't have Pa Jaynes's steer as a pet."

"I want ..."

Meredith widened her eyes. Tightened her lips. She stared.

Crystal understood the expression.

They all did.

Crystal quieted as Meredith lugged her up the hill.

Roxie sat in the grass.

"I told you to watch Crystal." Fear made Meredith sound harsh.

Roxie ducked into her turtle pose with her thumb in her mouth. "Sorwy."

"Nobody was hurt." She held a hand out to Roxie. "No one expected Pa Jaynes's cattle to escape. Take Crystal to the house."

Roxie's posture relaxed a little.

Meredith scowled as Roxie remained seated on the ground. "Get up now. I need you to hang onto your sister."

Roxie stood and held out her hands.

Crystal nearly leapt into her arms.

"Take her inside. I'll catch the steer before he tramples my garden."

Once the girls climbed onto the porch, Meredith turned back to the beast. "Mr. Beefy Bovine, Pa isn't going to be happy with you." She ran toward the steer.

It darted away.

She went right.

The steer went left.

She fisted her hands on her hips and studied the stubborn steer. *You're Pa Jaynes's problem.*

As she stood at the bottom of the hill, the heaviness in her chest lifted. *Dancing with cows. Need to dance more often.*

She clambered up the knoll toward her home. At the top of the hill, she stopped. Breathed hard. More than oxygen deprivation from chasing cows and climbing mountains weighted her. Like a heavy mantle, melancholy settled over her. Again.

Chapter 29

Life is good.

Parker stood at McGhee-Tyson Airport once more. He scanned the crowds, craning his neck to see over the people scurrying to and from the terminal. Wednesday, five p.m. finally crawled in, and Felicity's three-week idyll had ended. Her return erased any doubts he had about their relationship.

A tall, brown-haired woman exited the terminal.

Not her.

That one?

She looked up. Nope.

Eventually, a tall, slender woman exited and began her languorous descent down the main corridor.

Parker leaned forward, ready to run. He pulled back and tried to rein in his grin, but when he stopped thinking, he'd discover his toothy smile resurrected.

Elegance and beauty approached. But she carried something else. A sang-froid? Composure. He wanted her to run, to throw herself into his arms, wrap her legs around his waist. Something he could picture Meredith wanting to do. Not that she would.

At last, she let go of her carry-on and stepped into his arms. She pressed herself to him, found his lips.

Her kiss ...

Nothing existed but her warmth. Her softness, her ...

"We better stop," Felicity pulled away. "We're heating up the airport."

"But I'm chilly." Parker kept his eyes on her as he stepped back. Breathing came hard. "I can't wait for a little privacy." He grabbed her roller bag, took her hand, and squeezed.

Warm, strong fingers, long and fine, curled into his. Hand in hand they walked to the luggage carousel.

He snuck glances her way and would catch her gazing at him. Love shone in her eyes. Desire smoked in their blue irises. Did he want the grinding of the conveyor belt to break the spell? Yes. When it turned, he'd grab her bags, and they'd escape.

But no. He'd have to drop her hand, climb over strangers, beat down grandmas in order to nab her suitcase.

They waited in silence, neither one willing to shout over the airport clamor until the carousel spat out the passengers' bags.

With the luggage stowed in his jeep, they headed out to their favorite burger cafe. *Our favorites.* He glanced at her as he maneuvered onto Alcoa Highway. What other things did Felicity love? Not animals, unless to cook and eat them. Other restaurants? *The Local Goat? Nah, goats go with Meredith Jaynes. Bistros and burgers for Felicity.*

Felicity chatted. Something about Dubrovnic and the abundance of cats in the old city.

Cats. Roxie's eyes run, and she sneezes but is never without Olaf.

"Parker?"

He glanced her way. "Sorry. I was looking for The Salted Cow. I seem to miss the restaurant every time."

"I cannot wait for a bacon-jelly-burger." She took his hand. "I think Bert's kids cook better than whoever preps airline food."

"Here we are." He turned on his blinker and pulled into the parking lot. Hand in hand, they entered The Salted Cow.

A chipper hostess seated them. Another waitress delivered bread and menus and glasses of iced water with lemon.

Parker tore a piece of bread and studied the menu. He knew he wanted their rosemary-goat-cheese burger—well-done with bacon, but the other hand-crafted burgers on the menu tempted him.

The Hillbilly Burger came with a Jack Daniels sauce and fried okra.

Tex-Mex with ghost peppers and sharp cheddar? If he ate a ghost-pepper, he wouldn't feel anything near his mouth for a month. With Felicity home, his mouth needed to be in full commission.

But the goat cheese on the rosemary? No one created a better burger than this one.

Rosemary and goat cheese. Meredith. He saw laughing hazel eyes with amber highlights. He blinked to erase the image.

"What's wrong?" Felicity smoothed her napkin over her lap.

"Nothing." *Why am I thinking about ...?* Parker slathered butter on his bread. He studied his knife, swiping back and forth through the creamed butter as though he were a surgeon contemplating how to repair a vital organ.

"You haven't said more than a handful of words since McGhee-Tyson. Something's up."

"Savoring my time with you."

"What did I ask you a minute ago?"

His eyes searched the tabletop as though he could see the answer to her question. At last, he looked at Felicity. "You asked, 'What's wrong?'" He shoved another chunk of bread into his mouth.

She shook her head then sipped her water. "You're distracted."

He dropped the rest of his roll onto the plate and focused on her eyes. Beautiful. Vibrant. His tension melted. "I'm sorry. I am preoccupied.

"What's up?"

"In two days, we start reuniting Pearl Solomon—that's Meredith Jaynes's foster daughter—with her grandfather."

"Isn't this good news? You've found family, and they're being reunited."

"The situation is hard on Mrs. Jaynes." He shoved the last of his bread into his mouth.

"What did she expect from foster care? She knew DCS worked to reunite families. She should've been prepared."

Parker choked on the roll. He gulped his water, but the bread still crawled down his throat. He coughed.

Felicity leaned forward and reached for his hand. "Are you okay?"

Parker nodded. "Swallowed wrong."

"Of course, she knows these girls aren't her children. They belong to their biological families."

"Still, the children leaving sometimes feels like death. And she—"

"Let's not talk about Mrs. Jaynes." Ice coated her voice. She sipped her water. When she placed her glass back on the paper coaster, she smiled up at him. "With one less case on your workload, you should be relieved."

"You're right. I'm sorry I'm unfocused. Tell me more about your cruise. I want every detail."

He tore a second roll into bits as she chatted.

Felicity described St. Mark's in Venice, as the waitress took their orders. Her eyes sparkled, and her details rushed together.

He dropped the pieces of bread onto the plate.

"Santorini has beautiful white buildings ...

What he heard sounded wonderful. He was happy for her.

Dinner came. His burger scented the air with rosemary. Rosemary. *Poor Meredith.*

Felicity speared a French fry, which clung to the fork she waved as she described the Alhambra. She only picked at her dinner.

His own fries tasted greasy. Or too dry. Or ... He shoved them away.

They ordered a New York cheesecake slice to share as she described the last days cruising to the Canary Islands.

She ate two bites.

He ate one.

At last, with takeout boxes shoved into plastic bags, they returned to the jeep. Parker chirped the door open.

Felicity stepped up to him. "You're so quiet tonight."

"I needed to hear what you've done since you left." He placed the takeout onto the back seat.

When he turned, Felicity looped her arms around his neck. "I'll show you the best part of my trip." She pulled him to her. Every soft curve pressed against him.

His breathing quickened, and he sought her lips.

She cupped his head with her hands, and her mouth melted into his.

Her kiss. He pulled her close. Pressed against her body, he was still too far away.

Mounds of laundry stunk up Meredith's utility closet housing her washer and drier. An NFL locker room couldn't smell worse than this mildewed, soured, stench-filled cubby. She needed to wash Bean's favorite blue shirt with the unicorn tonight in order to line-dry it by Friday.

She threw in a load. "Girls, time to wash up for bed. Be sure to brush your teeth."

"Why are you washing clothes now?" Roxie asked.

"Bean needs special clothes to see her grandfather." Meredith slid the doors closed and stepped back. She stumbled. "Roxie, move." Then she looked down. "What are you doing?"

Standing in her undies, Roxie held up an armful of clothes. "Wash mine too. These are my favorites."

"I've already started the load. Put those in the hamper—"

"But ..."

Meredith pointed toward the living room. "Upstairs. Put the clothes in the hamper, then wash yourself and Crystal. Tell Bean to get ready for bed."

Little feet scrambled up the stairs. Voices argued, water ran.

Ten minutes later, she inspected faces and teeth. Combed tangles out of their hair.

Bean headed to her room as Meredith tucked Roxie and Crystal into bed. With her hand on the light switch, Meredith turned and studied the youngest two. She had done something right with the children. They glowed with health. Bad habits faded.

Except, Roxie started cowering again. Probably sad about losing her sister. Roxie was the easy child.

Crystal and Bean though? Fortunately, Bean mostly stopped "borrowing" things. Crystal could stand if she wore her braces and gripped furniture.

Good girls.

She flipped off the light and trudged up the stairs.

Why did this hurt like death? Pain knifed her, and once more, her pain told her she committed a huge sin God wouldn't forgive. How else could she explain how a botched abduction ended up with the loss of Bean?

Mills spoke truth at the funeral. She froze, one foot lifted but not yet landed on the next step. *No. What's the date?* She closed her eyes. Wednesday would be a year since Rosemary—on Thursday—John.

She'd forgotten.

She never thought she'd forget that awful day.

She waited for the ache to wash over her and weight her heart like a dull headache. How could the vitality of these three girls have healed the pain?

If the pain of losing John and Rosemary quelled, wouldn't the loss of children not her own ease?

She continued up to Rosemary's old room.

Bean sat in the far corner combing her Barbies' hair.

"You're supposed to be in bed." Meredith pasted on a smile.

"I know." Bean didn't move.

"Now." She stepped to Bean and lifted her. "Ugh. You're too big for me to do this." She tottered to the bed with the gangling child in her arms.

Bean giggled as Meredith plopped her on the bed.

"I like to hear you laugh."

"Do I really have to see that man?"

Meredith's heart strangled her breath. Her mouth dried like cotton lined it. She made her voice even. "That man is your grandpa." No self-pity sounded in the words.

"I have two already. Two's enough."

Meredith sunk onto the bed and smoothed the unrumpled blanket. "No one can ever have enough grandfathers who love them."

"He don't love me."

"You don't know that."

"He don't know me. I ain't never—"

"Shush. Listen to me." Meredith ran her hand along the side of Bean's face. "Mr. Parker knows Mr. Solomon is your grandfather. If you don't want to call him Grandpa or Pa, you can call him Papaw or Granddaddy or Grandfather Guy. Maybe he'll want you to call him Guy. It doesn't sound like a name—just 'some guy.'"

Bean didn't grin at the joke. She fingered the silky edge of the blanket.

"You never met Grandpa Guy. You may like him."

Bean's lips quivered, and she yanked the blanket over her head.

Meredith studied the lump under the covers. How could she comfort? She pulled the blanket off. "Talk to me. You're going to love this man. I promise."

"I don't want to leave you." Bean bolted upright and flung her arms around Meredith. "I want my sisters." Her voice muffled against Meredith's shoulder.

Meredith cradled Bean's head. She bit her lips, but they quivered against her will. "Shh."

Bean pulled away a fraction.

Meredith nestled her back. She closed her eyes, but a tear slipped along her nose. She inhaled to the count of five. Held her breath. Released a long, slow exhale. Tears quieted. Maybe her voice wouldn't crack. She tipped Bean's chin up. "Look at me."

Bean's luminous eyes gazed into hers.

"You'll be able to see your sisters." She mentally cursed DCS for doing what they were designed to do. She hated Parker Snow right now.

"Mama?" Bean's grip didn't lessen. "How can I see them if I'm in St. Louis. Missouri's like a hundred miles away."

Meredith chuckled. Tension eased. "A little further than a hundred. But you'll see your sisters. During the week we can Skype."

"What's a Skype?" Bean pulled away and stared at Meredith.

"The computer uses a camera so you can see people and talk to them."

Bean's eyes sparkled with something more than tears.

Hope?

"Really?"

"I'll show you tomorrow. We'll Skype 'Nissa and Grandma and Grandpa Crabtree. You'll see what they're wearing and where they are in the house like you're with them."

Bean lay back on the bed. "For real?"

Meredith nodded. "Now go to sleep." She kissed Bean's forehead. "Let's worry about tomorrow when tomorrow comes."

Meredith stepped to the door and turned out the light. She retrieved the wet wash and hung clothes on the line by the light of the moon. No katydids or tree frogs chirruped. The season had changed, and now the night offered only silence instead of summer's array of noises.

She inhaled the scent of fallen leaves. Chill goose-pimpled her skin. Bats frolicked overhead. She picked up her basket and headed indoors.

Her clean kitchen needed no more scrubbing. In the living room, only the three afghans lay askew. She straightened them. *Think happy thoughts.*

She stood in the center of the room and squinted.

I still have Roxie and Crystal.

But Bean helped so much, and—

No. Happy.

Her new soap Winter Pearl smelled divine.

But I'm going to miss ...

Meredith stomped up the stairs. She showered. The hot water poured over her, and unbidden, the tears she tried to hide from Bean poured out. She sank to the tub's floor and let the water cascade over her as she hugged her legs and sobbed. Rosemary gone. John the next day. Not fair. Now Pearl. Everything she held dear, she lost. Her tears strangled her. She held the back of her hand over her mouth, yet her moans echoed in quiet mockery against the tiles.

"God, why have you forsaken me? What have I done wrong?"

Hot water stung. The full force from the shower pinged. Her skin numbed, and the heat and the steam and the fragrance of mocha soap seeped into her core.

Her skin no longer prickled. Her heart did. As the shower cooled, she felt something other than pain. Could she dare dream for peace?

Hope?

No.

She stepped out of the shower and shivered in the cool air. She wrapped herself in a bath towel. Felt as though the arms of God held her.

Chapter 30

Meredith dusted off her hands as she left the barn. *Friday.* The sun shone warm, and humidity refused to show its face. This day should've come with rain, something miserable to foreshadow the visit.

Meredith tucked her self-pity into her breast like someone stashing a gross handkerchief. Regardless of her mood, Roxie and Bean had school.

Back in the house, Roxie and Crystal lay together on Crystal's bed. Both girls curled together. When was the last time Roxie needed Crystal's comfort?

Meredith forced a smile into her voice and kissed each child. "Good morning, girls. Time for school."

Crystal popped upright as though a second ago, she wasn't lost in dreamland. "Me school?"

"No. You doctor." She tousled her hair.

Roxie stretched but kept her eyes closed.

"Roxie, wash Crystal and yourself. Get dressed for school."

Upstairs, she shook Bean awake. "Time for school, sleepyhead." She stepped to the closet and took out the outfit they selected. Soft blue unicorn shirt and cotton slacks. With her back to Bean, she bunched the clothes to her face and inhaled. "These smell like fresh air."

"I'm sick."

Meredith hugged the clothes to her chest as she turned.

Bean had flipped to her side and pulled the blanket over her head.

Meredith peeled back the cover and felt Bean's forehead. She found exactly what she expected. After yanking the covers off, she dropped the clothes on the bed. "I'll see you in ten minutes."

In the kitchen, Roxie had strapped Crystal into her chair and busied herself in the cabinets.

"I'll cook breakfast." Meredith grabbed the milk and placed it on the table. "Drink milk, and I'll cook." Bending over, she nuzzled Crystal's head. "We see the doctor today. We think you outgrew these braces because you've gotten so big."

"I big." Crystal lifted her arms over her head. "Want flufferby."

"Maybe we'll do something other than butterflies on your braces."

Crystal shook her head so hard the booster seat forced her chair to wobble. "No. Flufferby."

Roxie shoved cereal boxes on the table.

"No cereal today. I can make eggs and bacon."

Roxie scraped the chair along the floor, so she could step up to reach the bowls.

"Pancakes would be good."

Roxie dragged the chair back and clattered three bowls on the table. "We likes cereal."

Someone woke up in a bad mood.

"Want mushmallow." Crystal reached for the Lucky Charms.

Bean stepped into the kitchen and scraped her chair up to the table.

"I'll be at your meeting, Bean. Parker said I could wait in the hallway."

"I don't wanna go." She poured Applejacks until they overflowed the bowl.

"Crystal has a doctor's appointment in Knoxville this morning. I'll be back in plenty of time."

The girls dumped milk into their cereal. Crystal picked out marshmallows from her Lucky Charms and popped them into her mouth. The other two slurped.

"Want me to drive you to school?"

"Nope."

"Nah."

"Watch Crystal. I've got to change out of my barn clothes." Meredith hauled herself up the stairs. Each step felt like gravity wanted to pull her back into the center of the universe. She hoped this day would be a celebration. Even if she lost Bean. She slipped on her favorite jeans, which smelled as fresh as Bean's clothes. She pulled her blue tee over her head, stopped, and listened.

No chatter floated up the stairs.

One benefit from the girls this morning—no conversation with her or each other meant no meltdowns would pepper the morning.

She'd miss Bean's bossing. The quarrels.

Something crashed in the kitchen.

"You stupid—"

"I'm not stupid—"

Meredith sunk onto her bed. Maybe she hoped for too much.

The orthopedic doctor stepped back from the exam cot. "Crystal's progress is beyond textbook. She may just walk."

"But you always said—"

He offered a sly grin. "I tried to keep things in perspective and not give unrealistic expectations. Now, though? With crutches, she won't have to scoot. She won't be able to walk unaided, though." The doctor peered at Meredith. His eyes danced. "You've been a godsend. I don't see children outgrow braces so soon. I hope the foster system cherishes you."

Cherishes? Meredith kissed Crystal's head. "Did you hear the doctor, Crystal? New, pretty pink braces."

"No! Flufferby."

"Can we have the same style?" Meredith asked the doctor.

"We'll try. If not, any specific color?"

"Pink."

"The office will call next week. The nurse will be in with the paperwork in a sec."

When the nurse returned, Meredith grabbed the bill and appointment forms. She fought with Crystal over control of the wheelchair as far as the checkout counter. Meredith handed the papers to the secretary.

"Pancakes." Crystal clapped her hands "Want pancakes." She pushed away from Meredith as she made the next appointment and turned her wheelchair in circles.

Waiting patients smiled.

"Funny Face." The lights on Crystal's wheeled blinked merrily.

"I remember, sweet cheeks. IHOP is our next stop."

"No. Pancakes."

Meredith chuckled and pushed Crystal.

"No. Me." Crystal bobbled back and forth to free the chair, then pushed herself. She went mostly straight. Only banged into the wall once, if you didn't count the time Meredith caught the chair a nanosecond before it hit.

Other patients grinned at her. Or pointed. All adored her lively spirit. No other word described the looks they cast her way. Adoration.

Secretly, Meredith guided the chair into the parking lot, making Crystal believe she directed herself. In IHOP a half an hour later, a full pitcher of coffee along with a French crepe lay before Meredith.

A Funny Face pancake, Crystal's food obsession, next to marshmallows, sat on the table in front of her. Ignoring her fork, Crystal scooped whipped cream off her pancake and into her mouth.

Meredith knew not to cut the pancake because she'd ruin the face. Crystal would pitch a fit until Meredith bought her an unspoiled one.

Meredith sipped her coffee. Her first cup. Heaven. She unrolled her utensils.

Crystal flung the maraschino cherry onto the table, then wiped her fingers on her shirt. She lifted her fork and stabbed at the pancake. It fell off the fork. She speared the pancake again. Clutching the fork in her right hand, she picked up the stubborn pancake with her left fingers, forced the food onto the tines of her fork and aimed for her mouth.

Most of it got in.

Meredith leaned against the tabletop. Watching Crystal eat beat any sitcom.

Then her phone rang. *The girls' school?* Her finger hovered over the answer button.

"I wuv you." Crystal beamed in Meredith's direction and then shoved another ripped piece of pancake into her mouth.

Meredith blew her a kiss as she answered the phone. "Meredith Jaynes here. Is someone sick?"

"This is Mrs. O'Brien."

The principal? Meredith's heart skipped as though the coffee in front of her was a double shot of espresso. The secretary called with mundane things—skinned knees, stomach bug. If the principal called … "What's wrong."

"I don't know how to tell you this ..."

"Tell me."

"Pearl disappeared."

Meredith clutched the phone tighter. "What do you mean *disappeared?*" Anger shrilled her voice.

"She asked to go to the bathroom thirty minutes ago. When she didn't return to class after five minutes, her teacher Mrs. Jeffers sent a girl to find her. Pearl wasn't in any of the bathrooms. We paged her. If she's in the school, she ignored our page." O'Brien's voice shook.

Meredith breathed in. Exhaled. She clenched her hand.

"We can't imagine why she skipped school. This doesn't match Pearl's personality. She's warmed up to school. Is learning—"

"I'm in Knoxville." Meredith looked at Crystal happily licking her fingers. This was supposed to be their time together. "I need thirty minutes to drive back. Have you called Mr. Parker Snow from DCS?"

"He's on his way."

"I'll be there as soon as I can." *Hopefully without a speeding ticket.* She hung up and started to rise.

Chocolate and whipped cream smeared Crystal's rosy cheeks. She sang to herself between bites.

What do I do? She sat down again.

Meredith shoved her untouched crepe aside and signaled the waitress as she dialed her mother.

"Mom, can you go to Bean's school?" Meredith explained the situation. "You can give them insight. I need a half-an-hour to get there."

"I'm already heading to my car. You finish with Crystal."

"But ..."

"Listen to me, the school, Snow, me, we're all on Bean's tail. Take care of your little imp eating a deplorable, sugar-filled pancake. You spend all your time fussing with Pearl.

The little ones feel left out. We'll find Bean. Besides, what's the difference between a half-hour or forty minutes?"

Meredith disconnected. She closed her eyes. *God, what do you want?*

Her heart stilled, and her stomach growled.

The waitress arrived with the check.

While Crystal sang and ate and banged her legs in their too-small braces against the booster seat, Meredith nibbled her crepe. She hadn't eaten since dinner. Her stomach demanded more. She ate until her daughter finished.

Crystal shoved her plate across the booth. "All done."

Meredith wiped her down, paid her bill, and scrambled to the car.

Crystal fussed with the straps to her car seat.

Meredith let her. No need to rush. Another five minutes? Pearl knew how to be safe and take care of herself. At least, her lovely parents instilled survival into her.

"You do." Crystal finally stretched the seat belt out to Meredith.

Meredith latched Crystal in, then tickled the tyke and climbed into the driver's seat.

The lack of condemnation about not rushing back to town felt unfamiliar. Lightness lifted Meredith as though Earth's gravity no longer matched Jupiter's. The whole of Jacksboro looked for Pearl Solomon. One more person wouldn't help much.

Thirty minutes later, she strode into the school office. Not bothering with the wheelchair, she perched Crystal on her hip. Holding the child would keep Meredith from punching the school officials for losing her daughter.

Or Bean for being ... scared.

The secretary smiled and pointed to the closed door of Mrs. O'Brien's office. "They're all in there. Pearl included. Go on in."

Meredith tapped at the door.

"Come in." Mrs. O'Brien sounded calm, all business.

Inside, Parker Snow, her mother, and Roxie lined up like a jury in their box. Give Mrs. O'Brien a gavel, and she'd pass as a judge.

She handed Crystal off to her mother.

Bean kicked her foot back and forth in the seat farthest from the door. Her eyes glinted.

Roxie hopped out of her chair and stood in front of her mother. She bounced on the balls of her feet. "I founded her."

"Where?" She directed her question to Bean as she moved Roxie out of her way.

"She likes the woods over there." Roxie waved her hand in the direction of town, not the woods. "I knows her secret places."

Meredith glanced at Roxie. "Shh. Have a seat."

She slunk back into her chair.

"Pearl lost recess privileges for the week," Mrs. O'Brien said.

"And all bike privileges at home." Meredith sank into the nearest chair.

"Can I ride?" Roxie asked.

"Come here, Pearl."

Bean crossed her arms.

"I am angry, but I love you. Here. Now."

With hesitant steps, Bean approached.

Meredith pulled her onto her lap. "Have you apologized to everyone?"

Bean's lower lip jutted.

"You worried us all. We deserve an apology."

Every muscle in Bean's body stiffened.

"If you don't, you will lose access to your Barbies along with your bike."

Bean's shoulders rose. "Don't matter. That man's taking me anyway."

Meredith curled her arms around the stiff child. Good thing God wrapped hearts deep inside our chests, so we couldn't lose the pieces. Meredith wanted to yell at Bean for acting so childish. For breaking rules. For scaring everyone. She knew the truth, though. She loved the child too much to make her want to stay with her and her sisters. "Pearl Solomon." Meredith tipped Bean's chin with her finger. "We love you more than you'll ever know. We need to keep you safe. We will talk at home."

Bean's body deflated. She kept her eyes focused on the floor.

Meredith looked around. "I'd like to sign her out. We need to figure out how to make this afternoon's meeting with her grandfather work." She turned to her mother. "Can you take Crystal and pick up Roxie this afternoon—"

Roxie scowled.

Why the frown? She turned her attention back to her mom. "Of course, sweetheart."

What would she do without Mom?

Or Sunny?

They made survival possible. She had to do the same for Bean.

Meredith turned to Parker. "She'll be at the courthouse at four."

Chapter 31

Meredith kissed the top of Bean's head as Parker took her hand, and they stepped into the visitation room to meet her grandfather.

He half-closed the door.

The feel of Bean's hair lingered on her lips—fairy wings. She closed her eyes and pressed the feeling into her memory.

The door stood ajar. Maybe she could watch? She stepped toward the room and peered in but only saw the end of a conference table and the dun-colored walls. Instead of acting like a Peeping Tom, Meredith sank onto a bench. She focused her eyes on the stained, dull walls as she strained to hear what everyone said in the room behind her.

"This is your grandfather." Parker introduced Guy Solomon by a too familiar a term.

Grandfather? Meredith breathed. Of course, the man had a biological right to Pearl. She needed to let go.

The deep rumble of a male voice answered. Then a pause filled the conversation.

Did Bean answer?

Meredith closed her eyes to better focus on the voices. The low murmur drifting through the doorway made a comforting sound, like her goats bedding down. The hint of a child's voice, the bass of a man's. All indistinct.

A door clanged somewhere in the courthouse. Laughter drifted in the distance. She slouched against the wall. From down the hall, footsteps squeaked on the linoleum. They approached. Passed her. Stopped.

"Aren't you Meredith Jaynes?" A man asked.

She opened her eyes.

A male about her age with short red hair and slim physique stood a few feet away. He wore a brown sports jacket over an off-white shirt with a green-striped tie and dress trousers. Something about him looked familiar. "Do I know you?"

The man doubled back and held out his hand. "Sergeant Donovan Andrews. Everyone calls me Van."

She stood and shook his offered hand.

"We've never been formally introduced. I arrested the fellow you held off with an empty gun."

"All foolish actions live on forever." Meredith grimaced. "How's a gun supposed to protect you if you keep ammo locked up in another location?"

"Maybe we should make a law. If you plan to break into a house, give the owner twenty-four hours' notice so she can prepare herself."

"I like your idea." Meredith laughed. "I didn't recognize you out of uniform."

Van's eyes sparkled. "No uniform today. Testified about a half-hour ago. Now I'm heading back to the station. How're you and the girl doing?"

Meredith nodded toward the room behind her. "Because of Larry Solomon's attempted kidnapping, they found Bean's grandfather. They're inside now."

"Good things can come from bad."

She studied the floor. Worn spots and bits of candy wrappers blurred together until she saw nothing. Reuniting Bean with her grandfather was good. Love and family could heal the child. She'd know her heritage. Meet more of her kin. Be loved forever. Why didn't she feel good?

"Are you close with the child?"

His voice refocused her on the moment. His compassion lifted her hurt a fraction. "Yes. Everyone can't help but love Bean. She's one of a kind."

"If she's lucky, her home will be good with her newfound relatives."

Meredith nodded. *If she's lucky.*

"I can't sugarcoat the issue. Sometimes the biological home isn't good."

His words should've scared her or made her angry, but his tender tone gentled the honest thought. She cocked her head. Heard them again in her mind.

"Sorry. I was crude."

"No. I like your honesty." Something in hearing truth, even an unpleasant one, made heartache easier. She could face her fears.

She studied Van's face. He had softer lines than Parker's linear ones. Despite the short hair and neat suit, he looked more casual. His easy-going, kind appearance had to make criminals trust him.

"Everyone but Parker tries to reassure me," Meredith said. "They tell me 'She'll stay with you.' 'You'll remain in touch.' 'She'll live with a loving grandfather.' They all deny the potential for bad. Should we trust Solomon?" She glanced at the wall of the conference room. "After all, he raised a drug addict."

"A problem child doesn't indicate a bad parent. You'd be surprised how many decent human beings end up with messed up offspring." Andrews pointed at the empty bench. "Can I keep you company for a minute?"

"Please. Sit."

Andrews half faced her as they sat. "I've worked with Snow a few times. He's a good caseworker. How he stays sane in his job makes no sense to me."

"Like you pulling guns and fighting off creepy, wannabe abductors? I don't see how you stay sane."

"Guns, fights, tasers, and handcuffs are all manly stuff. Not like coddling toddlers." He laughed, but something in his chuckle, in the warmth of his smile, showed Meredith his respect for Parker and his own love for kids.

His smile revealed straight, white teeth. A rusty stubble outlining a rounded jaw defied his characterization of himself and his job as manly-man. He looked more like a doting caseworker than a cop with nerves of steel. "The best part of my job is I rescue damsels in distress."

Their laughter worked like a narcotic. Taut nerves numbed, and for a moment she believed she lived in a normal world. "How'd Larry Solomon find us? Did someone give him our address?"

Van grimaced. "Addicts have their own grapevine."

She stiffened. Could they find her again? Take Roxie and Crystal?

"They find what they need when they want."

Those words didn't reassure her.

"Hey, Andrews, you're still on the clock." A uniformed cop walked by and winked. "No time to pick up pretty women."

Meredith's cheeks warmed signaling a flush darker than beets.

"Yeah, so? Fire me."

The two cops chuckled, and Van waved his colleague off. He turned back to Meredith. "Having to spend the afternoon hanging around a musty courtroom allows me a break, but ..." He stood and tugged his sports jacket. "He's kidding about being on the clock. Still, he's right. I've got to get back." He held out his right hand. "I like talking to you unarmed."

She stood and shook. Strong fingers gripped hers, and she gazed into his face. Hazel eyes. Straight nose with patches of faded freckles. A kind face.

"I hope to see you again." He still held her hand.

Its warmth soothed her frayed nerves. "Me too."

She dropped her arm to her side and watched as he walked down the hallway. His broad shoulders and slim hips reminded her of the heroes in her romance novels. She smiled.

Van's conversation, his touch filled her with optimism. And something else. She hadn't felt this way since ...

A week ago.

Only a week? Standing in the driveway with Parker, his fingers had trailed her cheek after telling her about Guy Solomon. Gentle, smooth hands. They comforted, but they also enticed her to want more, to feel his arms around her.

But John ...

Felicity ...

Meredith stared after Van. His warmth lingered on her hand. She shouldn't want this attention, but it felt so ... good.

No. She stiffened. Wasn't ready for anyone else. In five days, the one-year anniversary of Rosemary's ...

She'd no longer think of her death as passing. For the first time in a year, she didn't want to hide from the unpleasant fact. She didn't lose Rosemary. Her child died.

And John. Six days would mark a year since she felt his touch, since his body warmed her, and his arms protected. She turned her wedding ring on her left finger.

She stood in the hallway as waves of sorrow climbed up from her gut. Her lips trembled, but instead of tears, anger tightened her muscles. *Enough self-pity.*

Little steps ran out of the room. The sound sparkled like stars.

"We're done." Bean threw her arms around Meredith.

"Tomorrow morning, then?" An unfamiliar man with a bald head stepped out of the room. He was shorter than she imagined. Stockier.

Parker shook his hand. "Ten o'clock."

Guy Solomon stooped in front of Bean. "Pearl, you have no idea how blessed I am because I found you." He stood and held out his hand to Meredith. "Thank you for taking such good care of my granddaughter."

She looked at his hand. Studied his face. This thief shouldn't have such kind eyes. She lifted her arm. Dropped it. Finally, she grasped Solomon's hand. "Your granddaughter's been the joy of my life."

"We arranged another visit for tomorrow morning," Parker said.

Solomon faced Parker. "I'll give you the Willoughby address in the morning. Last I heard, though, this aunt's the only one left in Beth's family. She's unmarried with about thirty cats. Since Beth and Larry split, I haven't had much contact with them." He glanced at Bean who appeared oblivious to the adult conversation. "Not a stellar family."

"Thanks," Parker said.

Meredith stared after Solomon as he walked away.

"Can we go out to eat?" Bean tugged her arm.

Solomon disappeared around the corner.

Meredith shook her head to clear her distress and looked at Parker. "What did he mean? Do they know where the girls' family is?"

"Likely a dead end, but we have to follow every lead."

Bean tugged. "Miss Meredith. Let's go."

"I'll know more when we meet tomorrow at ten," Parker said.

"I can't be here."

"You're not expected to be."

"Bean will be ..." She looked down at Bean. "Somewhere."

Bean climbed onto the bench.

Meredith turned back to Parker. "I'll call you. With the market, I need to have someone watch Bean. Probably Sunny."

"Let me know." He stepped away. Turned back. "I like Solomon. Pearl warmed up to him fast. She didn't even correct him after the first time he called her Pearl."

"Let's go to KFC." Bean rolled off the bench and strode down the hall. She rounded the corner.

"Back here, Bean," Meredith called.

An impish blonde reemerged.

"Are you okay?" Parker asked.

Meredith twisted her ring and tried to smile.

"Miss Meredith!" Bean whined. "Come on. I'm hungry."

One visit with your grandfather, and we're back to Miss Meredith."

Chapter 32

Fortunately, the market boomed. Sunshine brought crowds. Fall veggies filled Market Square with color like a patchwork quilt. Green collards, gold pumpkins, and red apples bathed in sunshine drew in the hordes. Customers surged around everyone's booths oohing over the wares.

Meredith's Winter Pearl soap gleamed on its display easel. Samples disappeared with the crowd's interest. Any woman who sniffed the soap bought it. Meredith chatted and smiled and made change or swiped credit cards. The hours rushed by, but loneliness hovered like a bird looking for a nest. Heartache pecked her mind whenever a lull arrived. She'd scan the market searching for a wayward blonde "borrowing" cookies so she could save her allowance for something good. Bean had gotten better about shoplifting, but what would happen when she went with Solomon? She'd have to warn him about her creative accounting.

Meredith made a dozen sales in swift succession.

Then another letup. This time she saw Crystal in the face of a cherub being pushed in a jogging stroller. How the child would love to run, even if Meredith did the running instead of her. With the leads on the Willoughby family, would she be taken away before she took her first solo steps?

Clouds scudded overhead. Little ones. None bringing storms. Simply the autumn breezes stringing clouds across a pale, blue sky like Roxie leading the goats across the meadow.

Roxie?

These days, she always thought of Roxie last. No trouble. Always compliant. Too submissive? *Maybe I'd miss her most of all.*

Pearl sat close to Guy Solomon. They played coloring games on his phone. Occasionally, Solomon fingered the child's hair as though daring to believe Bean was really next to him.

Parker sat in the corner reading the day's news on his phone, only half-listening to the conversation. His gut told him Solomon would be good for Bean.

"You look like your daddy," Solomon murmured.

"I don't have a daddy." Pearl jabbed the phone without looking at her grandfather.

Guy Solomon murmured something sounding like, "And I don't have a son." His voice drifted off in the wistful manner of longing.

Pearl moved close to Solomon and almost crawled into his lap.

Solomon poked the phone.

"Stop!" Bean shoved his hand away. "I'm coloring. You're too old to color."

"Old? Fifty's the new forty."

Pearl looked up at him as though he spoke Mandarin. "Huh?"

He kissed the top of her head.

Parker leaned back in his chair and stretched out his legs. One more controlled observation and Solomon could take Bean for brief, unsupervised visits. After forty minutes more, Parker pocketed his phone. "Time's up."

"No," Pearl moaned.

"Yep." Parker stood.

"Before I go," Solomon dug into his pocket and pulled out a wallet. "Here's the address of the aunt. Annette Willoughby in West Memphis, Arkansas." He handed Parker a slip of paper, kissed Pearl on the top of her head. "See you tomorrow." With hands in his pockets, he whistled as he strode down the hall.

Back in his vehicle, Parker tossed his work folders onto the passenger seat of his jeep. He looked at the paper Guy Solomon handed him. Might as well ring her now.

Voice mail.

He identified himself, gave a brief explanation for the reason for his call and said he'd call back.

He then headed to his folks'. His brother and his wife, Maggie, were coming for a barbeque. Most important, he and Hayes would finally get out on the ATVs.

After family greetings, he and Hayes loped to the four-wheelers. They cranked the engines and without a word, the brothers raced up the side of the Cumberland Mountains. Wind whipped their faces, and dirt coated their helmets.

Hayes careened ahead of Parker. In everything they did, Parker's younger brother trumped him. Trail riding proved to be no exception. Dirt spun up from the wide tires of the ATV and coated Parker's visor. Hayes turned left. Parker knew the trail he'd take, but Hayes gave him an opening to one-up him. Finally.

Parker turned right, bounded over hills and rocks, saw Hayes to his left, stepped on the gas and edged in front. The trails merged in a hundred feet. He leaned forward, coaxing his machine, determined to one-up Hayes.

For once in his life.

He cut Hayes off. At their favorite lookout, they killed the throttles and swerved to a stop. They whipped off their helmets, dismounted, and stood side by side. "Beat you."

"Only 'cause I let you," Hayes said.

Parker punched his arm. "Right."

"I need a testosterone day. My wife ..." Hayes shook his head. "Maggie's hormones ..." He looked into the distance, and a small smile played around his lips. "Wait until you knock up Felicity. Then you'll know what I'm talking about."

"I'd have to marry. Right now ..."

Hayes jerked his head and stared at Parker. "Wait. You sound like you're unsure about marriage. Felicity's a babe."

Parker nodded. Felicity made Lily look dowdy. "I'd be stupid to let her go."

They stared at the view of Jacksboro spread out beneath the overlook.

"You should see Maggie when in-laws aren't around. She cries all the time. Won't let me near her. Says I'm never touching her again. She's mopey until suddenly she isn't." Hayes glanced at Parker, and his grin revealed his love. "You know—"

Parker threw up his hands. "Don't want to hear about your love life."

"You'll know what I feel when you marry Felicity. Let's head back. Dad's barbequing. He'll pitch a fit if we're off playing."

"Manly-man." Parker thumped his chest like a gorilla.

Hayes slipped his helmet on and turned to Parker as he fastened the strap. "We're heading to the zoo next Saturday. Want to join us? I could use some male companionship."

"Hang out with kids when I'm not working? No way." Parker latched his helmet.

Hayes eyed him. "I fear the man doth protest too loudly."

Parker cranked the ignition. Dust kicked up as they bounded over hillocks and rocks ending this conversation. Trees and curves blended. Aware of the mountainside but lost in thoughts, Parker's body vibrated with more than the power of his four-wheeler. To be married to Felicity and have her loving every night. Lovemaking. Babies.

More babies than Hayes and Maggie. And a wife to beat all wives.

They swerved around curves. Parker gave the lead. *Eat my dirt, Hayes.*

Bean bounded out of the truck.

Meredith unstrapped Crystal. They jogged after Bean into the kitchen. "How was your visit with your grandfather?"

"Good." Bean rummaged through a cabinet and pulled out chips.

Meredith snatched them. "Healthy food."

Bean stomped her foot. "You're mean."

"Because I'm a grown-up." She pulled left-over mac and cheese from the fridge. "Nuke this and feed your sister. I'll unpack from market."

"Where's Roxie?"

"She's at Grandma Cora's."

"'Kay." Bean shoved the container into the microwave.

While the microwave whirled, Crystal pulled herself up. She grinned. Let go. And fell. "I go boom."

"Crystal falls." Meredith stooped and kissed her fine hair. "Be careful. Listen to Bean and be a good girl."

Back in the yard, Meredith unloaded her truck. Stopped. Snapped her fingers. *Crystal Falls. Perfect name.*

She tended goats and thought of fragrances for her new Crystal Falls soap. Nothing minty—too close in scent to Pearl's peppermint. Something tart and sweet and alive.

Then she knew.

Bergamot. And she'd color the soap yellow. Happy, joyful yellow. Like Crystal, the happiest of the trio despite her disability.

Her angoras bleated. They needed to be shorn before the weather got too cold. She'd call Mom. Shearing these critters was her responsibility.

Maybe she called? Meredith glanced toward the darkening west. The sun set sooner these days. The cool mountain air made her shiver. She had worked longer than she intended. Bean was a responsible child but still a kid.

She stepped into the kitchen.

The TV hummed in the living room.

Meredith peeked in. "You're such a good girl. Did you have a good day?"

"Hmm-hmm."

Crystal dozed in Bean's arms.

"Where're you going tomorrow?"

Bean hiked a shoulder. "I'm watching my show."

"When this one's done, you're off to bed."

Bean growled and slunk into the chair.

Crystal shifted and mumbled in her sleep.

Bean drew her close. Kissed the top of her head.

Meredith returned to the kitchen. She checked her phone, but Mom hadn't called. Then she remembered. Parker had left a voice mail during the busiest time of the market.

Her thumb hovered over the number. She allowed her mind to dream of the possible scenarios today's visit presented.

Bean hated her grandfather. He decided he was too old to raise a child. They discovered he was a serial killer. He signed all parental rights over to her.

She hit the voice mail.

"Parker Snow here. Visit went better than expected. We're meeting at my church tomorrow at ten and then heading to Shoney's. I'll pick Pearl up at nine-thirty."

"When's dinner?" Parker called as he strode into his parents' home.

No one answered.

He stepped out onto the back deck where steam wafted from the grill. Barbecue spiced the air, and his stomach tightened. He hadn't eaten since breakfast. He stepped toward the grill, only to stop at the sight of her. Close or distant, the sight of her always heated his body.

Felicity rose from her lawn chair and stepped into his arms.

He folded his arms around her. Kissed warm lips.

"Get a room." Maggie nudged him.

Parker pulled up a spare chair and sat close.

"Here." Mom handed Hayes's son to Felicity. "Watch Ezra. I'll bring out the salads."

"Let me help—"

"You are. Keep Ezra happy."

"That's easy." She made faces at the eighteen-month-old. He giggled and reached for her nose. "Oh, no. Can't have mine." She plucked his nose then stuck the tip of her thumb between her index and middle finger. "I got your nose." She wriggled the thumb. Felicity feigned sticking it to her face.

"No." Ezra yanked her nose and shoved his palm against his face.

Both giggled and repeated the routine.

Mom returned to the patio and called to Dad manning the grill. "How much longer, Darrick?"

He lifted the grill cover. Smoke spilled into the air. "About fifteen minutes."

Mom smiled. "Good. Maggie, Felicity, you need to see the antique cradle we found in Townsend. Hayes will have to re-finish it." She continued talking as she left the deck.

Maggie and Felicity chattered as they followed, their heads nestled together.

Parker watched. Then was certain. Felicity couldn't hide the fact that she loved kids. Now he was as certain as his name was Parker Snow. Tomorrow. After Pearl's visit to church and Shoney's for lunch, he was heading to Knoxville. He needed to buy a ring.

The Sunday sun shone in glorious September warmth. Across the valley, the trees rusted—hinted at autumn. Meredith pushed Crystal's wheelchair up Hen Waddle Hollow. Lights fluttered on the wheels but paled in the creamy light of mid-afternoon. She and Crystal stopped and examined every flufferby they saw. They picked asters, inspected mushrooms growing in rotting logs. She glanced at her phone. Two-thirteen. *Soon.*

"Let's run." Meredith broke into a jog, but the wheelchair was not designed like the jogging stroller she saw in the market yesterday. Good. She hated running. Within minutes, she slowed. "Time to go home."

"No. Run." Crystal pointed. "Fast."

The sound of an approaching vehicle made Meredith pull to the edge of the road. She turned and watched Parker's

SUV. "Sissy's home." She stooped next to Crystal, and the two of them waved.

Parker pulled abreast and unrolled his window. "The visit went well. I think you'll have a happy child this afternoon."

"I'll meet you in the driveway." A happy child made Meredith's heart heavy. Every day, her mind turned schizophrenic. In two minutes, Meredith greeted Bean who tumbled out of the car.

"I bet you're hungry."

Bean held her stomach. "I'm stuffed." She grabbed Crystal out of the wheelchair and skipped into the house.

Parker leaned over the open window. "Next week Guy and Pearl go solo. Friday, they're going to the library for movie night. If that goes well, he wants to take her to Dollywood on Saturday."

Meredith blinked. "Dollywood's in Pigeon Forge …" She closed her eyes. Then looked into Parker's eyes. "Bean will love Dollywood. I've wanted to take the girls."

"Living so close, we take things for granted. Anyway, I need to run. Have to hit Knoxville before …" He glanced away. "The stores close."

Meredith waved him off and returned to the house.

Bean and Crystal sat on the couch watching cartoons.

"Want lunch?"

"I'm stuffed." Bean held her stomach. "I told you."

"I don't think I've ever seen you refuse food."

"Did you know you can eat as much as you want at Shoney's?"

Meredith nodded. "Scoot over." She wedged herself between Bean and Crystal.

Bean flicked the remote.

Meredith took the controller, then hit the off button. The TV faded into blackness. "What did you eat?"

"Pudding and Jell-O and cake."

"Anything healthy?"

"Pancakes and waffles and sausages." Bean sat up straighter and wiggled in closer. "We should eat there every day. You'd save lots of money. They have bins filled to the top with everything. When the pans empty out, waitresses fill them up again. And look." She hopped off the couch and ran into the kitchen. She returned with a napkin full of squished-together treats. "I got cake for my sisters since it's free."

Meredith opened her mouth to reprimand Bean about take-outs from all-you-can-eat buffets. *No. I'll let Guy teach her about no buffet doggie bags.*

Bean crawled onto her lap. "We ate fried chicken, macaroni salad, French toast—"

"Mama Mewredith. I'm home." Roxie charged into the living room with Olaf squeezed in her arms. "You missed me, Olaf." She skidded to a stop, turned, and looked behind her. Her mouth opened, and her eyes questioned as though something confused her.

"I didn't hear Grandma drive up," Meredith said.

"I thought you was at Aunt Sunny's." Roxie squeezed her cat and hunched her shoulders. Olaf yowled and jumped down. He strutted away. "Why're you here?"

"Me and Crystal came home yesterday. But today, I got to go to Shoney's." Bean ran down the list of foods she ate.

Roxie frowned and chased Olaf into her room.

Mom entered. "Where'd Roxie go?"

Meredith hitched a thumb toward the room.

"She's a sweetheart. Never a lick of trouble, but she's been cowering more every time she thinks she's done something wrong."

Meredith shifted Crystal as the child snored softly beside her.

"Probably stressed about Pearl moving." Mom settled across from Bean. "Tell me about your weekend."

Roxie's door slammed.

Chapter 33

A cool breeze blew the silk flowers on the tombstones in Angel Point Cemetery. Meredith pushed Crystal along the asphalt walkway. The two flower arrangements hanging from her wheelchair's handles bobbled between Meredith's legs scattering glitter as though marking the way to a happy place.

Crystal rocked forward. "Faster, Mama. Faster."

Meredith's leaden legs stuck to the pavement as though mid-summer softened the tar and glued her steps to the surface. She hadn't visited since Easter. How could she have not found time? Was she forgetting the ones she'd loved most in her life?

The thought knifed her, and she slowed.

At last. Her family's plot.

She lifted Crystal from the chair. "I'm going to visit my husband and daughter. You play right by me, okay?" How much did the child understand? She sat Crystal on the lawn.

Crystal scooted along the adjacent graves. "Pretty flowers." She'd reach for a silk petal and pulled. "Flufferby." Off she skedaddled after her favorite insect.

"Stay close."

Crystal circled back.

Meredith knelt and unclipped the faded flowers she'd placed on Rosemary's tomb six months ago and laid them next to their plot. The pink had grayed. Sprigs of green had pulled away. Their bare spots and dangling leaves matched Meredith's life. Her loss. She closed her eyes. So busy with her girls, she dared to believe life would move forward.

She lied to herself.

Hot pokers seared her heart like the day Rosie died. Fresh. Never fading.

Crystal babbled as she pulled wildflowers growing between the plots. "Pretty." Only a toddler would find the wayward asters beautiful. Holding a fistful of weeds, the child pulled herself up on a gravestone a few spaces down. She studied the flowers on the marker.

Meredith turned back to Rosemary and fastened the new spray of silk flowers to the gravestone. Bright pink and purple dahlias. Lots of glitter. And butterflies. Whenever she came here, she'd think of Crystal and her flufferbies.

She pulled a butterfly from the arrangement and tucked it into the pocket of her jeans for Crystal to play with on the way home. To hear her babble to the silk insect would be worship music.

"You would've cherished your sisters, Rosemary. Bean loves your room …" Tears choked her voice. Then she checked for Crystal, as much to bat back the tears as to check on the child.

Crystal chattered to the wind or the sun or the insects. She didn't know the meaning of unhappiness. Despite the spina bifida, Crystal epitomized sunshine. And butterflies.

Meredith ran her hand over the inscription. *Beloved daughter.*

Her fingers strayed to the next line. *Cherished husband.*

She removed John's faded flowers from his side of the shared marker. The yellow flowers had weathered poorly.

Yellow, he said, was the happiest of colors. When she got moody, he'd sing "We All Live in a Yellow Submarine" until she slapped him in jest. They'd wrestle, and he'd tickle her and then ...

She smiled. How she missed his arms, his kisses, and their lovemaking.

She lifted his new wreath in autumn hues of yellow and orange and brown.

"Sorry, Rosemary. You share your spot with Daddy. We need a color other than pink." She fingered his name on the tombstone. "John, losing you doesn't hurt like Rosemary's death. Are you mad at me for that?" Her chest tightened. "You would understand. When our Rosemary died, I saw your pain, heard your tears when you thought I wasn't near."

Pain tore her eyes from the grave, but she couldn't leave. Instead, Meredith turned around and leaned her back against the headstone. She pulled her knees to her chest, then looped her arms around her jean-clad legs.

Crystal made no noise. Silence spelled trouble.

A few plots down, Crystal grasped the side of a memorial and pulled herself up. She moved her leg forward. She let go of the stone. Wobbled. Collapsed onto her butt with her back to Meredith.

Meredith clapped. "You're walking!"

Crystal faced Meredith and grinned. "I walk. Like Sissies." She pulled herself up.

Hope and a future showed in Crystal as she once more worked to take a step. Over and over. Crystal moved forward only a step—maybe a half-step, but she worked. Then she stumbled and whacked her head against a grave.

Meredith scrambled to her feet and scooped her up. She moved the child's fine hair from her forehead. A small scrape oozed blood. Tissues pressed against the cut stopped the bleeding. Kisses wiped the tears away. "Ready to go home and see your sisters?"

Crystal beamed as Meredith swiped an errant tear from the toddler's cheek. "Home. Sissies." With her injuries forgotten or ignored or accepted as a part of life, Crystal babbled as they returned to Meredith's truck. Life, once more, became joy and light.

Chapter 34

On Saturday morning, a crack of lightning lit the predawn darkness. Thunder loud enough to wake John and Rosemary in their graves jolted Meredith out of a deep sleep.

Like turning on a faucet full force, the rain pummeled the house. *Poor Bean wanted to go to Dollywood.* She leaned against her headboard. Waterfalls ran down the windowpanes. She closed her eyes. No farmers' market in this weather.

Maybe she could do something special with Roxie and Crystal after bringing Bean to her grandfather. What could they do in his downpour?

After chores, she grabbed a towel and plopped onto a kitchen chair. Water dripped from her hair into her eyes.

"Mama Meredith!" Bean ran into the room and threw herself into Meredith's arms. "I'm supposed to go to Dollywood." She buried her face in Meredith's chest and sobbed. "I ain't never been to Dollywood before."

"I'm sure your grandfather will have other plans."

"But—"

Meredith shook a finger.

Bean climbed off her lap. She flopped down in an adjacent chair.

Meredith pinched Bean's bottom lip. "Quit scowling. I could place a bowl on this shelf."

Bean slapped Meredith's hand away.

Little feet padded on hardwood floor. Roxie stumbled into the kitchen with Crystal clutched in her arms. Roxie's hair lay matted, and Crystal rubbed her eyes with her fist.

"Eat cereal. We have to take Bean to town to meet her grandpa."

With a crack of lightning, Parker's eyes popped open. The clap of thunder sounded as though the lightning may have hit next door. He lay without moving. The rain's intensity built as the storm moved in.

He stretched. *Pounding rain doesn't matter.* Today he was off.

He sat up and opened the drawer to his bedside table. He took out the black velvet box and flipped up the lid. The ring didn't reflect light in this gloom. Still, the cut and setting displayed beauty. Like ... Felicity? He slipped the ring on his pinky as far as his second knuckle. He held his hand out to the bedside lamp, and the ring sparkled.

Contentment warmed him. Even when thunder clapped again, his pulse stayed steady. No storm or peril or unexpected phone call from work would shake this peacefulness.

He fingered the gems in the setting. Parker didn't know their names. Lily could identify them. And surely Felicity. From experience, he knew the jeweler would fit the ring to Felicity's finger. Sadly, from experience, once altered, it was non-returnable—except to the former fiancée.

He was now the proud owner of two engagement rings.

He returned the ring to the box, snapped the lid shut, and headed to the kitchen.

As coffee dripped into the carafe, he stared out the window. After the initial burst, the downpour slowed to a drizzle saturating the ground.

Tonight, he and Felicity would head to Knoxville and Shuckers Seafood Café perched along the Tennessee River. They'd grease up their hands with buttered mussels and clams and lobster in clarified butter. They'd head to Lakeshore Park, stargaze, and then ...

But the day would be wet and cloudy. He'd have to think of something else.

His phone rang with an unfamiliar number. "Parker Snow here."

"This is Miss Annette Willoughby's home health aide. You called a week ago."

Parker raked his hand through his hair. He'd forgotten he was waiting on the callback. "She got my message, I assume."

"That's why I'm calling. Sorry for the delay. I just found her cell in the bathroom cabinet when I went to put towels away."

"She's not in any shape to take on any children."

"On good days ..." she lowered her voice, "no. Forget about the bad days."

"When would it be a good time to send Social Services to talk to her?"

"I'm here every morning except Sunday and Monday. I work seven to two."

Parker scribbled down the info he needed. He hung up a happy man. One more lead tracked down. Closer to closing the Harrison kids' case. And a few hours away from being engaged.

Then came the next call.

"Sweetheart, bad news."

Parker's heart sunk at Felicity's tone. "What happened?"

"Kit's daughter wrecked her car in the storm."

"Is she—"

"She's being airlifted to Nashville, and Kit's driving out to be with her. Unfortunately, he has two funerals tonight. Can we take a rain check?" Her melodious chuckled filled the line. "Sorry. Bad pun."

"Of course. We'll talk when you have a break."

Parker clasped his phone. He didn't want to be alone.

I know. He snapped his fingers. *Surprise Hayes and Maggie at the zoo.*

"I want to go to Dollywood!" Roxie kicked the back of Meredith's driver's seat as Bean dashed through the drizzle and climbed into Guy Solomon's car.

"What'll you do in the rain?" Meredith asked Guy through her open window.

"I don't care about rain. Dollywood's fun," Bean whined.

Guy leaned toward Meredith. "My weather app says the rain's passing through." He craned his neck and smiled at Bean. "If you don't mind being wet, neither do I—but a lot of rides will be closed."

"Don't care." Bean slunk down in her seat.

He smiled at Meredith. "If nothing else, the weather will keep the crowds away."

His warm laugh reassured Meredith. Then a twinge of jealousy pierced her. She tried to keep her face from grimacing. Why did she like this man?

She watched as he pulled out of the parking lot.

A kick to her seat from Roxie brought her back to reality. "How come Bean gets to do everything?"

"Let's go to the zoo."

Roxie leaned forward. "Do they have lions and tigers?"

"They do."

"But what about the rain?"

"I've got umbrellas, and the animals don't care. We won't leave Zoo Knoxville until we've seen them all."

"You promise?"

"I do."

Halfway to Knoxville, Meredith's gas light pinged. She pulled off the highway and into a station.

"Why're we stopping. This ain't the zoo."

"Need gas." Meredith climbed out of the truck.

Roxie hopped down.

"Where're you going?"

"Taking Crystal to the bathroom." Roxie leaned into the truck and lifted Crystal out. "Don't worry, Mama. I'll be careful."

A few minutes later, Meredith slid the gas hose back into the pump and waited for her receipt.

The door to the service station flew open. "Ma'am!" A middle-aged man strode toward her. "Do you have two kids?"

Meredith nodded, frozen in place if she didn't count the hammering of her heart.

"One of them fell against the sink in the bathroom. She's bleeding a lot. My wife's in there with them."

Meredith ran. Thought nothing until she shoved open the door to the ladies' room and found Roxie slumped on the floor, coiled into herself. Blood oozed through Crystal's hair and into her eyes.

"What ...?" She stepped toward the lady tending Roxie.

"I think she'll need stitches." The woman stood still, holding a wad of blood-soaked toilet tissue.

"Thank you." Meredith stooped and gingerly brushed aside Crystal's hair with her fingers. A few tears clung to the silent child's lashes, and she sucked her thumb. "Roxie, get me paper towels."

Roxie didn't move.

"Roxie!"

Still, she sat with her head against her knees, arms wrapped around her legs.

A shiver coursed down Meredith's spine. Frustration hardened her voice. "We need to go to the hospital."

"No. You promised the zoo."

"After the hospital. Come."

Roxie didn't move.

"Wait here." Again, the unintended harshness her voice made Meredith recoil. While pressing the rough, brown paper towel to Crystal's head and clutching the child against her shoulder, Meredith ran to her truck—still in front of the pump with the receipt hanging from the pump, flapping in the breeze. The door was open, her purse inside. After strapping Crystal in and commanding her to hold the towel to her head, Meredith ran back to the bathroom.

"Let's go."

Roxie looked up with hopeful eyes.

"Not the zoo. First the hospital."

Roxie ducked.

Meredith lifted her—the gangling child a dead-weight.

At last, Meredith plopped Roxie in the back seat. "Strap yourself in."

Roxie didn't move.

Meredith looped the seat belt around the child. She poked Crystal whose head bobbed in sleep. "Don't let Crystal doze. She might have a concussion."

"I'm sorwy." Roxie's soft voice told Meredith the child relented.

"I know."

Fortunately, the hospital was only ten miles out, but the stint in the ER? Interminable. While a physician assistant applied Steri-Strips to Crystal's wound, Meredith called Parker. He had to be apprised of the accident.

Four hours later, with six real stitches put in after a CT scan confirmed a mild concussion, Meredith pulled into her driveway.

Roxie pouted in the backseat.

Crystal dozed.

"How about we play games and watch movies?"

Roxie scowled.

"Not interested?" She walked away

Roxie scrambled out of the truck. "Wait for me. Can we play Greedy Grandma?"

"Set up while I settle your sister down for a nap."

They were in the midst of their third game when a vehicle rumbled. Loud. Like a motorcycle. Then the engine quit.

Roxie ran to the window. "Mama. There's a strange man outside. Does he wants to kidnap me?"

"I doubt that." Meredith rubbed Roxie's hair as she peered over the child's head.

On the front steps stood a good-looking man with rusty hair, helmet in hand, scuffing his foot like a schoolboy.

Meredith flung open the door. "Van. What brings you here?"

"I was in the area."

No one's 'in the area' out here.

"I wondered if you'd like to go for a ride." He nodded toward the bike.

"I'd love to, but …" She stepped aside. "With two munchkins and a promised night of games, no chance. But come in."

"I don't want to intrude."

Meredith turned toward Roxie. "Do you mind another player?"

"No. We're playing Greedy Grandma. It's fun. Especially when Mama screams."

"Screams?"

"I'll tell you as we stuff plastic cookies into the game's granny." She grabbed his hand. "Now get into the house before all the flies and mosquitoes invite themselves in."

His face flushed.

Why hadn't she noticed how shy the sheriff was?

Time at the zoo with Hayes, Maggie, and Ezra flew by. And who could pass up an after-zoo dinner at the Texas Roadhouse with family? Now exiting the interstate, Parker didn't want to go home.

On a whim, he took whatever turn he felt like and explored roads he hadn't been on in ages. He made a turn. The road looked familiar. *Why am I on Hen Waddle Hollow?*

Crystal. She was the reason. He had to see if she was fine.

He pulled by Meredith's house.

A motorcycle parked in the driveway. A Harley ... big one.

Should he stop?

He slowed.

Studied the house as he passed.

No activity.

A quarter mile later, he made a U-turn in a farm's driveway and headed home.

A sudden ache of loneliness hit him. He wanted to see Felicity, to hold her in his arms.

Like Mr. Harley-Owner probably held Meredith.

Bean bounded into the house at seven.

Mom ran in after her like a mother goose trying to corral her gosling.

"Dollywood was so fun!"

Meredith clambered to her feet. She grinned and swooped Bean into her arms.

"Tell me everything you did."

Bean squinted at Van. "Who are you?"

"I'm Van Andrews. I helped your mom when your father tried to take you."

"Oh." She turned to Roxie. "Wait until you go to Dollywood. It's so fun." Bean scampered up the stairs.

"Thanks for bringing her home, Mom." She turned to Van who stood. "This is Officer Donovan Andrews."

He offered his hand.

Mom shook. "I'm Cora Crabtree. Aren't you the one who arrested that awful Larry Solomon?"

"Part of the team." Van's smile accented his dimples.

Mom glanced at Meredith, and she mouthed the words, "Nice guy." Her quirked eyebrows left no doubt about her opinion. Cora Crabtree, fabric artist extraordinaire, would, in another life, be matchmaker extraordinaire. "I'm putting on the tea water." She left the room.

Van picked up plates from the floor. "Hey, where'd the Greedy Grandma champ go?'

"I don't know. Probably to her room." Meredith picked up napkins and whispered. "Now we'll see if you pass the Crabtree test."

Chapter 35

On Monday morning, Parker arrived late at the office. Seeing as he had enough comp time to vacation for a year, he shouldn't have. Sadly, issues didn't stop for comp time.

He slid into his swivel chair, swigged a coffee, and dreamed. Where would they go for their honeymoon? Hiking Yosemite? Glacier National? Right. Not Felicity. Las Vegas with its shows and buffets and swanky hotels. Life was good.

He tossed his paper cup into the trash and checked his inbox. He deleted most. He paused at Guy Solomon's message. Full Custody of Pearl?

He read the message.

We had a wonderful weekend. Was wondering how soon I can take Pearl home. Having to disown my son, her father, and the death of my wife ..., Pearl healed my heart.

Parker had seen Solomon and Pearl at church yesterday. The child had clung to Solomon's hand and chatted throughout the service. The man puffed out his chest as though he'd won a grand prize.

He dialed Meredith. "Can you talk?"

"Crystal's in PT, and I'm reading ancient copies of *People*. Please talk to me."

"How'd Pearl react to her independent visits with her grandfather?"

"Unfortunately ..."

He stiffened. Waited for her to continue. Her one word hung in the air. Could he have misjudged Solomon?

"Sorry about the silence. I needed to step outside. Too many bored people in the waiting room. They'd love to hear what I have to say, which would be far more fascinating than the receptionists making appointments over the phone."

Her laughter soothed like windchimes.

"The visit went better than I could've dreamed. The man's good. Bean loves him. I wanted him to be a miserable creature, so I could keep …" She coughed. "Sorry. Wrong attitude."

"I'm glad Pearl and Guy enjoy each other. This case is beyond textbook perfect."

She paused, then asked, "Will they visit again this weekend?"

Here came the happiest and the saddest part of his job. A good and loving foster family would have to say good-bye to their sweet charge.

"Parker, do you have something to tell me?"

"I'm calling Guy once I'm off the phone. We'll be setting up a day he can take custody."

"How soon?"

"This week."

Silence.

"Meredith?"

He was about to hang up and call again when Meredith coughed. "Bean will be happy." Her voice remained neutral, no joy or sorrow or worry.

Parker tried to keep his voice the same. "Parental custody is a good thing. What we hope for."

"I understand. Let me know when."

Custody. The word sucker-punched Meredith, and she leaned against the brick wall of the rehab center. A cool breeze caressed her face. The sun shone warm in a pale blue sky. Bean would leave. This week. At most, she'd have seven days to prepare herself. She'd never be ready, though. For three months, she'd known this day would come. Knowing the truth didn't prepare her for this ache she felt.

Disinfectant scents made her grimace as she stepped back into the waiting room. How she wished she could swipe her emotions with Clorox and be free.

"Mama." Crystal wheeled herself out of the treatment rooms. She let go of the chair and waved chubby fingers.

"She's taking steps with the use of the bar and gait trainer," the therapist said.

Meredith stooped in front of Crystal. "You're walking!"

The therapist gripped the chair as Crystal tried to wheel herself again. "One or two steps, not ready for a run."

"Will feeling come back to her legs?"

He shook his head. "What she feels now will never change, but she has enough nerve function to sense leg pressure and to balance herself. Once she's old enough for crutches, no one will stop this kid."

Meredith looked up at the therapist. "When will that be?"

"In about five years. Kids can't coordinate crutches much before they're seven."

"Thank you for your work. Crystal's pure joy."

"This kid's aptly named. She sparkles in everything she does. Reflects light. Everyone wants to work with her."

"And, dare I say, Crystal proves the New Age flimflam. A Crystal does have healing powers." She kissed Crystal's cheek. "My little superwoman."

"No. Me Crystal.

Meredith laughed with the therapist.

As she settled Crystal in the truck, her phone, buried in her purse, rang. She rummaged through the garbage in her bag and shoved the phone to her ear moments before voice mail would've picked up. "What's up, Parker?" She clicked Crystal's seat belt.

"I got in touch with Solomon."

She gripped the back of the car seat. This meant only one thing. "That was fast."

"Solomon's coming on Wednesday. We'll arrive at your place around nine and pick up Pearl and her things."

Meredith's mouth dried as though the word Wednesday stuffed her mouth with sand.

"Are you there?"

"She has a bike. Can he ...?"

"He'll bring his pickup. He has lots of room."

"I'll tell the girls tonight." She climbed into the truck as she disconnected. Her hand shook as she grasped her keys. They wouldn't slide into the ignition. Meredith stared through the windshield. Cars rumbled down the four-lane. Clouds climbed the Cumberlands. Life went on.

She blinked.

Crystal kicked the passenger seat, over and over and over. "Go, Mama. Go."

"Yes, ma'am." She turned and saluted, then started the engine. After she pulled onto the main road, Meredith checked on Crystal in the rearview mirror.

Breezes played with her hair from the partially opened window. Crystal had no idea what would happen in two short days.

Would she grieve?

She was young. She'd cope with the loss of her sister. The sad thing was, she would be too little to remember Bean. She'd grow to adulthood with no memory of the little girl who protected her so fiercely when her parents didn't care.

Even a deep sigh didn't lessen the pain. *You're only a foster mom, Meredith Jaynes. Foster moms don't keep the kids.* She frowned. *Don't think about loss. Think about driving.* Meredith focused on the traffic as she turned up the backroads.

How could she make Crystal remember her sister?

Skype. She'd see Bean online.

However, the computer couldn't replace Bean's hugs and kisses. They wouldn't be able to curl up together while Roxie read stories to the three of them.

What about Roxie? She'd been acting weird lately. She attached Olaf to her face and buried her nose in his fur. No one but Mom understood everything the child said with her speech impediment and her allergies congesting her.

Meredith trudged into the house.

Her garden's fall bounty cluttered the counters. Chores would keep the sorrow at bay. While Meredith froze collards and canned pumpkin, she practiced telling the girls about Bean's move. "I've got happy news."

No.

"Sissy Bean has a new home," Meredith told Crystal over lunch.

The child shoved a banana in her mouth.

Meredith sang about the move when she laid Crystal down for her nap. Told each goat. Each time, self-pity choked her words. How could good news hurt so much?

After school, the girls ran into the house.

Bean buried her face in the refrigerator.

"I've got news—"

"Do we have anything besides fruit?" Bean didn't look away from the fridge's interior.

"Bananas," Meredith said.

Bean turned and stared her down. She twirled her finger toward her head.

"On Wednesday—"

"I'm sharing my banana with Crystal." Ripping the fruit from the bunch, Roxie ran into the living room where her sister played. "Hey. She's wrecking my game."

Crystal wailed.

"She ruined Greedy Grandma."

In the living room, Roxie clutched her game to her chest. The box was flattened and torn. Crystal's love of shredding paper didn't spare Roxie's favorite game.

"Not ruined. I'll tape the box. Pick up the pieces."

Roxie piled all the fragments of the game onto the kitchen table. Along with her banana peel and Crystal's half of the fruit. She ran out of the door to join Bean. "Can I ride?" She called to her sister.

The bike's horn sounded. "Okay. But only until I finish multiplying by four. I can multiply up to four times twelve now."

Bean and math.

The girls and their bike. On Wednesday, she'd buy one for Roxie. She stepped onto the back porch. She opened her mouth to call them but pinched her lips together. *I'll tell them about the move after their bike ride.*

At dinner, the girls ate like they hadn't been fed an hour and a half ago.

"I talked to Mr. Parker today—"

"Hey, pass the ketchup." Bean reached over the table before anyone could hand her the bottle.

Meredith shut her mouth and pushed her food around.

"Can I have your hamburger?" Bean asked.

Meredith looked down at her plate. She had rearranged her food, eaten a forkful or two, but every mouthful stuck like a wad of cotton. Without a word, she lifted her burger.

"Me. I want more," Roxie said.

Meredith cut the burger in two and gave Roxie half.

"She got a bigger piece. The side you didn't bite into," Roxie said. "You always give her more."

Meredith closed her eyes and waited until she knew her voice would sound calm. "Tomorrow, Roxie, you choose first. All day. Anything you want."

"Hey."

"Pearl Solomon." Meredith leveled her eyes.

Bean sat back and smirked.

Meredith groaned. "After we clean up, we need to have a talk."

"Did we do something bad?" Bean asked.

Meredith willed happiness into her voice because this truly was good news. "Not at all. I have exciting news to share."

After clearing the table and filling the dishwasher, the girls piled onto the sofa and clicked on the television.

In the kitchen, Meredith polished the stovetop and refrigerator and microwave. She searched the kitchen for something else to clean but knew she had to bathe the girls.

And tell them.

Pearl would be too excited to sleep.

Roxie? How would she survive without Bean?

She couldn't delay any longer. Back in the living room, Meredith wiggled between Roxie and Bean, took the remote. and clicked off the TV. "Guess what I found out today?"

The girls crowded closer while Crystal tore catalogs on the floor.

"Bean's grandpa is going to take her to St. Louis."

"We know." Bean's voice sounded like Grandma Cora's, all obviously aware.

Roxie stared into space.

"You're moving on Wednesday."

Bean straightened, and her brows knit. "In two days?"

Meredith nodded.

"But we have school then."

"I know."

"For how long?" Bean asked.

"How long? What do you mean?"

"How long will I stay at Grandpa's? We have a math competition on Friday."

Meredith licked her lips. "You're moving there."

"Forever?" Bean's face paled.

Meredith nodded. She forgot how little eight-year-olds understood. "Remember? He's been visiting so he could take you home with him."

"I thought I'd move a long time from now. Like next month or Thanksgiving."

"Wednesday."

Roxie stuck her thumb in her mouth.

"But what about Roxie and Crystal? Are they coming?"

"No."

"Why not?"

"Grandpa Guy's not related to them. Remember? He's your father's daddy. He's only taking you."

"I don't want to leave my sisters."

"We'll Skype and write and text."

"What if Grandpa Guy won't let me?"

"He already promised you could. Mr. Snow said you wouldn't leave if you couldn't keep in touch with your sisters."

"I don't want to go."

Meredith looped her arm around Bean.

Roxie stiffened at her side.

"Talk to me, Roxie."

She shrugged.

"Do I have to move forever?" Bean asked. "I like Grandpa Guy, but I love you."

"There you are!" Roxie hopped off the sofa and charged after Olaf. She swooped up her cat and ran into her room.

"Roxie, where are you going?"

The door slammed behind her.

Meredith would deal with her later. She turned back to Bean. "Remember when you first came here, and you wanted your mama?"

Bean nodded.

"You didn't love me then. And you never stopped loving your mother. God is being good to you. He's giving you another person to love and a home you'll never have to leave again."

A small smile played on Bean's lips.

"Can I take my bike?"

Meredith nodded.

"And my clothes?"

"Yes."

"And—"

Meredith kissed the top of her head. "And your Barbies and floaties and shoes and underwear—"

"Ew. Underwear." She giggled.

"You can take everything you own."

Bean picked up the remote.

Meredith grabbed Bean's hand holding the remote. "Go take a bath. Later, when we bathe Roxie and Crystal, I'll show you pictures of St. Louis. They have a beautiful arch next to the Mississippi."

"St. Louis is near the M-I-S-S—"

"Enough." Meredith placed a palm over Bean's mouth. "Take your bath."

Bean trotted upstairs. She sang the Mississippi spelling song. Giggled, as usual, at the I-P-P-I, then started over again.

Water ran in the tub.

Meredith inched the door open to Roxie's room.

Roxie sat on her bed with the chapter book they were reading together at bedtime held upside down. She murmured to Olaf. "And the poor princess sat in her tower. She was very lonely except for the handsome prince Olaf."

"Want to talk?"

Roxie glanced her way. "No. Me and Olaf's reading.

Chapter 36

Tuesday, twelve hours left.

Meredith's mouth dried. She waved off the Buchanans and the Jayneses while Mom and Dad fussed over Roxie in the living room.

Silence haunted her kitchen. Five minutes ago, a laughing, crying, loving mix of people crowded the room as they celebrated Bean's going away party. Now only dirty dishes and leftover food hinted at the chaos. She stepped into the living room and steeled her voice. "Time for bed, girls."

Roxie sat on Mom's lap. She'd clung to Grandma Cora all night, never more than a few inches away from her.

Bean raced up the stairs. Her giddy grins and chatter contrasted with the subtle ache of Meredith's family.

Guilt clung to Meredith like dust. She should be rejoicing, not mourning. Pearl left for a good life with a family who loved her. She'd never have to move again. In her new school, she'd make new friends and join new clubs. In St. Louis, Pearl would be reborn to those who shared her DNA.

"I'll put Roxie to sleep in a half-an-hour," Mom said. "Crystal will be sound asleep by then, and I won't wake her."

"Thanks." Meredith smiled and watched Roxie color on the app on Mom's phone. "Come here, Crystal."

The child lifted her arms.

As she scooped Crystal up, Meredith twirled her around and took her to the powder room off the kitchen.

"Bean bye-bye 'morrow." Crystal grabbed the washcloth once Meredith sat her on the closed toilet lid. "Me do." She ran the damp cloth over her face and managed to miss every dirty spot.

Meredith chuckled. She looked too cute to fix. After brushing Crystal's teeth, Meredith tucked her into bed. She smoothed the covers and bent to kiss the child.

"Want Roxie."

"Grandma Cora will bring her in shortly."

"'Kay." Crystal rolled over.

Meredith stood at the doorway before flipping off the light. Her heart warmed, and taut nerves unwound. At least this little chickie wouldn't leave her.

Upstairs, Bean lay on her bed. Every light in the room shown.

"Goodnight."

Bean didn't budge. Her closed eyes and relaxed posture said sleep had claimed her. This kid had no anxiety about tomorrow. Meredith studied the child, her gift. The peace she'd found in Crystal's room downstairs evaporated. Meredith trembled as she lingered in the darkened room. So sweet to love this girl. So bitter to lose her. So unfair.

She closed her eyes. No, not unfair. Pearl didn't belong to her. She never did.

Leaden feet led her body back to the living room. Her heart stayed with Pearl.

Mom kissed Roxie's head. The child slid off her lap as Mom stood. After settling her feet on the floor, she patted Roxie's derriere. "Time for you to wash for bed."

"But Grwandma ..."

"I'll tuck you in."

"'Kay." Roxie trotted to the powder room.

Dad stood. "I'll meet you in the car, Cora."

He hugged Meredith. His strong arms anchored her breaking heart. Pearl would know this kind of strength. A father's love. And she needed her heavenly father now, more than her earthly one.

"We'll be praying for you tomorrow." He broke his hug and kissed her cheek.

When the door closed behind her father, Mom turned to Meredith. "Sweetheart, you've forgotten about Roxie."

"What do you mean?"

"You don't pay attention to her."

"Yes, I do." Anger curled in Meredith's chest.

Mom didn't smile. She tilted her chin and held Meredith's gaze. "Not intentionally, but she's left out."

"How?" Meredith didn't need a lecture. Not tonight. She snatched a stray coffee cup from the end table, bent to grasp another.

Mom grabbed her hands. "Put those down and listen."

Meredith obeyed.

Mom pointed to the sofa. "Sit."

Meredith rolled her eyes. "Not tonight. I don't need a lecture."

Her mother's gentle hands gripped Meredith's shoulders. Her eyes softened. "Hear me out."

Her mother's soft voice weakened Meredith's resolve. She sank onto the sofa as though her legs would no longer hold her.

"Crystal has therapy three times a week."

"Oops," Meredith started to rise. "I need to make a note to cancel tomorrow's session."

"Not now. Sit."

Meredith knew not to disobey when her mother used *that* tone. She settled back onto the couch.

Mom exhaled a long breath and steadied her gaze on Meredith. The tilt of her head and the softness of her eyes spoke of kindness, not anger or judgment. "Where do you and Crystal go after each PT session?"

Meredith shifted away from her mother. "Dairy Queen." Her voice came out surlier than she intended. "Is this a sugar lecture?"

Her mother took Meredith's chin in her hands and gently turned Meredith to face her.

Again, the love and gentleness in her actions softened Meredith, made her listen. Made her yearn for her mother's love.

"Who do you fuss over every day since Guy Solomon showed up?"

Meredith knew she didn't need to answer.

"As grown-ups, we understand the adult's loss. But this isn't about you. Think about the three little girls who need so much love."

Meredith tightened her lips.

Little feet padded into the living room. "I'm all done, Grwandma Cora."

"I'll kiss you goodnight in a minute."

Mom watched Roxie run to her room until the door closed softly behind her. She turned back to Meredith. "When a crisis arises, does Roxie create the problem? Is she ever the object of the emergency?"

Meredith said nothing.

"The trip to the zoo didn't happen because of Crystal's accident. Bean owns the bike, and you give her the lessons. Roxie's promised one tomorrow. You have soap named after Pearl and Crystal. Still none for Roxie."

Did Meredith's heart beat? She wasn't sure. Words wouldn't form as Mom waited for the answer Meredith couldn't articulate.

"The good girl, the easily-cared-for one, hurts. The one who learns easily gets the help she needs at school, so your attention focuses on the other two."

Meredith rose and paced the length of the room while Mom continued. She didn't want to hear the words but needed to listen to every syllable.

"Roxie waits for everyone else's—"

"But—"

Mom stood and pulled Meredith into her arms and whispered into her hair. "You're *not* doing a bad job. Raising three abused children by yourself while self-employed with a field full of goats ..."

Meredith stepped away and ducked her head.

"Everyone in this family knows you treasure Roxie as much as the other two. Everyone but Roxie."

Mom's truth settled deep into Meredith's chest. The good child wouldn't understand why she got shunted aside. She was only five. A baby.

Once more, her mother hugged her. Meredith finally relaxed in the embrace and trembled. This time she relished the softness of Mom's body, felt like a little girl again.

Mom ran her hand over Meredith's head. "Roxie's losing the sister who's been more than a mother to her. Lay your pain aside. Quit obsessing over Bean's move, your loss of John and Rosemary, over Deacon Mills—"

Meredith yanked away. "Mills has nothing—"

"Then why have you ditched church?" The words held no condemnation or harshness. "You don't see your expression every time his name comes up in conversation. Like him or not, you need to forgive the boor." Mom eyed Meredith. "You don't know how long you'll have these other two girls. Cherish the moments. Quit sulking. Your faith is what Roxie needs. But more than forgiving Mills, the pompous Pharisee, forgive God."

Meredith looked into her mother's eyes. Love showed in their tender gaze. Her heart, which had been pounding hard against her ribs, quieted. Mom was right. God had been gentle with her over this last year. He talked to her, directed her even when she didn't want to listen or when she believed he hated her. Why she suffered, she didn't know. But her girls suffered more. Lots of the world endured worse pain in a year than she had in her lifetime. She needed to beg the Lord for forgiveness.

A horn honked outside.

"Dad's not so patient." Mom kissed Meredith's cheek. "Call me when Pearl leaves. I'll be here if you need me. But first, I promised Roxie I'd tuck her in."

Mom stepped into Roxie's room. Soft murmurs drifted through the open door.

Meredith sunk onto the couch. With closed eyes, she felt the tone of Mom and Roxie's conversation—tender, loving. At the moment, Roxie knew she was the center of her mother's universe.

Then, too soon, with a last peck on Meredith's cheek, Mom sailed out the door and rejoined Dad.

Meredith stepped into Roxie's room. Both she and her sister breathed lightly. Occasional snores serenaded her.

Everyone slept but her.

Her hands itched, and she tapped her foot. Too anxious to sleep, she scoured the kitchen and living room until they gleamed. Bean's belongings piled near the front door. Gifts of cookies and new clothes and new bike helmet piled on top of the suitcases. Meredith stepped out to the barn and found the wrapped gift she saved for Bean's departure. She placed the package in a kitchen cabinet in the silent house.

Midnight arrived.

Meredith sat on the edge of her bed. Cool air blew through the open window. She shivered and stared into the dark.

"Mama?" Roxie tiptoed in with Olaf in her arms.

"What's wrong?" Meredith patted the bed next to her.

"Olaf can't sleep." Roxie climbed onto the bed and nestled next to Meredith.

"Olaf, huh?"

She nodded.

"Would he sleep if he lay in my bed?"

Roxie didn't say a thing. She wriggled to the far side and pulled the covers over her and her cat.

Olaf yowled and hopped down.

Roxie sat up to grab him.

"Wait." Meredith stretched out next to Roxie. "I'll take his place, okay?"

She pulled the covers over them and cradled Roxie in her arms. Old enough to be aware of what was happening. Too young to articulate her pain.

Mom spoke truth.

"Sing to me," Roxie said.

Meredith thought a moment—her bluesy-jazz songs weren't appropriate for one so young. Instead, she reprised "Reindeer Are Better than People."

"No," Roxie interrupted before Meredith finished the first verse. "Not baby songs. Do your funny words."

"My scat singing?"

Roxie nodded and moved in closer.

Meredith jazzed up the *Frozen* tune. She scat sang and improvised until Roxie slept.

Olaf, as though assured he wouldn't be suffocated by needy arms, jumped onto the foot of the bed and slept too.

In the quiet night, only children dreamed. Meredith counted the quiet creaking of the house. Counted the minutes remaining until Bean left her.

No more self-pity, Jaynes.

She wouldn't cry.

Couldn't sleep.

The next thing she knew, the sun peaked its head over the horizon.

Today.

By eight o'clock, Bean sat on the top step of the front porch as though keeping watch for Santa.

Roxie clung to Meredith's legs.

Crystal drummed on her bowls under the table.

And Meredith's heart stretched tighter than the skin of a real drum—ready to be torn to pieces.

"Mama, does Bean have to leave?"

Meredith unwound Roxie's arms. She used the moment to steady herself. Instead of speaking, she nodded.

"Why?"

They'd been through this. Meredith scooped up Crystal and held a hand out to Roxie. "Let's go sit with Sissy."

Roxie pulled them out to the porch.

The world was cool and quiet here. She handed Crystal to Roxie then returned to the kitchen and slipped the hidden package from the cabinet.

Back on the porch, they sat. "I have one last gift."

Bean's eyes lit up. "Really?"

Roxie melted into herself a mite.

Meredith looped her arm over Roxie and pulled her close.

Bean tore into the paper. Crinkled her brow. "Soap?"

"Not any old soap. Winter Pearl." She picked up a bar of pearly-white soap tied with ivory ribbon. "And look." She turned the bar over. "Here's my address, phone number and email. Each one has this information. With twelve labels, how can you not find me if you ever need me?"

"Silly, Mama Meredith. I know where you live. And I know our phone number."

Meredith nodded. They sat in the cool September sun.

Roxie moved to the bottom step and let Crystal scoot after bugs in the grass.

Parker's jeep and a four-door pick-up pulled into the driveway.

Meredith stood.

Bean stayed seated.

The two men strode across the lawn. Guy grinned like the sun shone inside his heart.

Parker looked like Parker. In control. Compassionate. Yet, distress showed itself when he took off his glasses to clean them. His "tell."

"Ready, Pearl." Guy's smile warmed like sunlight.

Bean leaned back.

Guy held out his hand. "I'll help you carry your—"

"No! I changed my mind. I ain't going."

Guy Solomon stepped back. Shock showed in his wide eyes.

Before anyone could move, Bean bolted. Ran across the yard. Without looking for traffic, she sprinted into the overgrown field across the road.

Solomon stood frozen. "What ..."

Parker started to run after Bean.

"No," Meredith cried.

He stopped as if her one-syllable word lassoed his legs.

"Watch Roxie and Crystal for me." She glanced at Solomon. "She's not afraid of you. Pearl has been looking forward to this. Reality has given her cold feet. I know where she went. I'll find her." She ran. Within seconds, she passed Parker and crossed the street.

The old path to the Wheeler Road had grown over. Blackberry thorns tore at Meredith's jeans. She ran along the path—only discernable because no trees or shrubs had sprung up yet. Pearl had to have gone back to the dilapidated Wheeler house. Meredith ran until she wheezed. She gulped air as deep into her lungs as she could and pushed on to the worn road. She turned and ran until her chest ached.

The house came into view, but no child.

"Bean?" She ran around the back and scanned the wooded lot. Briars and brambles and poison ivy and trees crowded the space. Never had she seen a trail in this thicket, even when she discovered the girls lived here, so Pearl hadn't run into the woods. Meredith stepped into the house. The place deteriorated more in the last three months. The ceiling in the corner of the kitchen by the shot-out window hung in dusty fragments of sheetrock. The mold made her cough. "Bean?"

Something moved upstairs.

Meredith strode into the living room. She rubbed her hands on her pants legs then climbed the stairs. The rickety one from her last foray here had completely rotted out. How soon man's creation fell apart. With a wide step, she skirted the missing tread and reached the landing.

In the bedroom to the right where they'd found Beth Willoughby's jewelry, she located Bean.

She hunkered down against the wall on the rodent-infested mattress. Her arms wrapped around her legs. Her head buried against her knees. Sobs racked her little body.

Meredith sat next to her. She pulled Pearl close and held the weeping girl. How she wanted to cry too. Curse the fact they lived here, not in St. Louis. Or better, to run away and live happily ever after like one of Roxie's fairy tales. But this wasn't her time of sorrow or her fairy tale. She had to make this good for Pearl. Then help her sisters live without her.

The child's tears turned to sniffles. Bean wiped her nose against the back of her hand but wouldn't look at Meredith.

"This is hard, sweetheart." No sense in sugar-coating what couldn't be changed. "I can assure you, though, with time, you'll be happy."

"I don't want to go."

Meredith raised the edge of her T-shirt and wiped Bean's face. "Here. Blow." She lifted a dry edge, and Bean looked at her like she was crazy.

"You want me to blow boogers on your clothes? Gross."

They chuckled.

"Blow. I'll change later."

Bean obeyed.

"You got scared, didn't you?"

Bean nodded.

"Moving to a strange place with a man you don't know well is a very scary thing. Things will be hard at first, but remember the fun you had with Grandpa Guy?"

Bean looked up at Meredith. The child's red and puffy eyes held a world of sorrow.

"Visiting him was fun because you knew you'd come home. Then we all shared your adventures. There's no reason you can't come visit."

"Can I?"

"I believe so." Meredith paused. *Lord, let her be able to visit her sisters.* "Until then, we'll video chat. Grandpa Guy already promised."

Bean's muscles softened under Meredith's arm.

"We'll send you presents in the mail."

"Really?" Bean grinned.

"But you have to move so we can mail them."

"I ain't going with Grandpa Guy. I'm gonna live here again. Ain't nobody gonna find me."

Meredith arched a brow and smiled.

Bean slunk a little lower against the wall but snugged up to Meredith.

"If you stay here, you can't see all the things in St. Louis. You can't climb the Gateway Arch or see the M-I-S-S-I-S-S-I-P-P-I."

Bean giggled.

"Besides your Barbies and bike are all packed in Grandpa's truck."

Bean blinked. Her lips moved as though she wanted to speak.

Meredith stood and held out her hand. "Let's go."

Bean stared at her legs and mumbled something.

Meredith still held out her hand. "What did you say?"

She peered up at Meredith. "You promise we can Skype?"

She nodded.

Bean stood and took her hand.

They walked back in silence. When they returned, the men were tying a tarp over the bed of the truck.

Crystal sat on Roxie's lap on the bottom step of the porch. Both girls silent.

Guy Solomon dropped the straps he tightened and stepped toward Pearl. He stooped to his granddaughter and held out his hand. "You scared me."

Bean stood with arms at her sides and didn't approach.

"I'm glad you came back," Solomon said.

"Can Mama Meredith and my sisters visit?"

"Of course."

"You promise?"

Solomon nodded and stood. He pointed at his truck. "We packed everything back here." He stepped to the truck bed and gave the rachet strap one last tug. "But we put the overnight bag and Barbies on the back seat." Solomon walked with Pearl to her sisters on the porch. "We'll go to Shoney's for lunch."

"But we just ate breakfast," Bean said.

"Three hours from now when we reach Nashville."

"There's another one?"

Grandpa Guy smiled and nodded.

Parker joined them. "This going away hurts. I know. Your grandfather loves you. He wants you to be happy."

Solomon held out his hand.

Bean clasped hers behind her back.

"And the Nashville Shoney's has an all-you-can-eat buffet too," Parker said.

Pearl turned to Meredith.

"He's right," Meredith said. "I bet they even have a Shoney's in St. Louis."

"For real?" Bean glanced at her grandfather. "Can we go there?"

"I promise I'll take you," Solomon said.

Sunlight or compassion shone in Parker's eyes. He stepped back as though to let Meredith and Solomon take control.

Meredith threw her arms around Pearl and hugged. The child lingered warm in her arms. Letting her go felt like watching Rosemary die. Meredith released her. "Kiss your sisters."

Bean lifted Crystal from Roxie's arms. She twirled her around. The child leaned back and let go while Bean clung to her legs and hips and spun her.

"I fly." Crystal held her hands out and closed her eyes and giggled.

Bean handed her to Meredith. "'Bye, Roxie."

Roxie stayed on the bottom step.

Bean bent over and hugged her sister.

"Time to go." Meredith handed her off to Guy.

Bean took slow steps to the truck.

Guy's body blocked Meredith's view. She forced a smile. "Girls, wave goodbye to your sister." She waved and forced a smile and joy into her voice. "We'll see her on the computer and have so much fun."

Tears streaked Roxie's face.

Crystal leaned across Meredith and held out her hands to Roxie. "No cry." She patted Roxie's cheek.

An engine started, and Meredith looked up. She held her smile and gave one last wave.

Bean pressed her face against the window. Even from this distance and the tinted windows, the tears were obvious. She didn't need to hear Pearl who clung to the window with splayed fingers as though she could press through the glass and touch her family. Her lips said, "I don't want to go, Mama."

And then she was gone.

Meredith's heart had healed enough with the girls to be shattered.

Into shards.

Chapter 37

The day stretched long and silent. Only one child left her life. Only one empty spot in her house. Still, she felt alone. Then Meredith's phone rang. She let voice mail pick up. How could she survive this loss? Mom was right. Meredith's life revolved around Bean. Because of her, she took in the sisters when Parker needed to find a home for them. Because of her, the burden of mothering three little girls was easy. Or, at the least, doable. For an eight-year-old, Bean was a reliable child.

Roxie wandered outside. She clung to Olaf and leaned against the fence to the goat pen but ignored the goats. She stared down the hills toward Pa Jaynes's pasture or past the fields to the Cumberlands, or maybe she was trying to see her sister driving to St. Louis.

"Lunch, Roxie," Meredith called from the kitchen.

Roxie didn't move.

Meredith opened her mouth to call again when Olaf leaped from Roxie's arms. The child shifted then trudged toward the house as though she headed for a funeral.

Crystal ate with two-fisted relish. Cream cheese and jelly sandwich in her right hand, carrot sticks in the left.

Roxie nibbled.

"What do you want to do with the rest of the day?"

Roxie pulled the crust off her bread.

Meredith poured herself coffee. "Want to play games?"

Bits of shredded bread fell into Roxie's plate.

Meredith stirred her drink, over and over. She watched the girls in silence. Her coffee tasted bitter. She dumped it out.

Naptime. Dinner. Baths. Bedtime. Sorrow sewed their lips closed. Even the goats refused to bleat.

When Crystal slept, Meredith took Roxie aside. "Do you want to talk?"

"Am I going to school tomorrow?"

"Of course."

"Good. I'm tired. I'm going to bed."

Meredith sat on the end of Roxie's bed and read their current chapter book for five minutes, no longer. Roxie's eyes shut.

Dark descended.

Meredith climbed the stairs to her room.

Pearl's door stood open. Meredith stepped into the doorway and held the knob. Bean had made her bed. Rosemary's Baby Alive doll sat on the pillow. She inhaled. Lavender. Her girls' smell. Not Rosemary's. Her own little girl said lavender stunk like armpits. She liked roses and lilies.

The room spun. Meredith clutched the doorframe until her vision cleared, then shut the door with a click. She changed into sleepwear and lay on her bed. Closed her eyes.

Her body took on a will of its own and trembled. Meredith stiffened to quell the shuddering. Tears welled. She blinked. *No. I will not ...* Like a flood, tears demanded their way. She turned on her side and fisted the blanket into her mouth to silence her cries. Sobs wracked her body until every muscle ached.

When the tears dried up, she lay staring at nothing. At last, she unwound her taut limbs and climbed out of bed. In the bathroom, Meredith washed her face. With the towel clutched in her hands, she leaned against the sink. Loss bent her like an old woman.

She forced herself to brush her teeth and comb her hair. Finally, she slumped on the edge of her bed but didn't want to sleep—far too early anyway. The solace of the rooftop beckoned her. Meredith climbed out onto the rough shingles.

The moon rose behind the house. Its feeble light dispelled a bit of the dark. She clasped her knees in her arms and gazed at the sky. High overhead Vega shone brightly—the brightest star tonight. She studied it as it sparkled like Bean's laughter. It shone like Rosemary's eyes or John's love.

One star illuminated three losses.

No.

Four.

She had ditched God. Or he forgot her.

What did I do wrong?

John used to chide her about her introspection. Had he lived, he would've applauded her punch to Lester Mills's nose.

She smiled. Her body relaxed against the dormer. Something told her Crystal and Roxie would be okay whether they stayed with her or if they found their kin. Bean was happy. She knew it.

Guy Solomon appeared to be an honorable and loving man.

Her own life needed to change, though. Her attitude refused to see anything bright since Rosemary and John's death. Lots of good happened, but she contented herself in misery. What right did she have to turn her back on God in the time of her loss? He wasn't to blame for her misery.

When she took in the waifs, she'd known the solution was temporary. Had hoped for a short-lived transition to their permanent home. They had a family they belonged to somewhere. Probably people who loved and missed them dearly.

Could their kin love them more than she did?

Meredith had to accept the fact the girls only sojourned with her, lent to her for a moment of time.

She closed her eyes and felt a breeze caress her body. In the depths of prayer or contemplation, wisps of wind always made her think of God's love.

The Creator loved her. Even though she threw a fit, he never turned his back on her. She was the one who ditched him.

He loved her like a father—or mother. Only more perfectly. Nothing would keep her from loving her girls—not Bean's pilfering and lying, not Roxie's insecurity, not Crystal's inability to walk. Always, she'd love them. She'd cherish them long after they found their permanent homes. Like her love for John and Rosemary.

Memories of them, all of them—foster and biological—memories of laughing and crying and arguing swelled in her mind. She loved every minute of her life with them.

If she loved her people this way, nothing she ever did or ever would do would make Jesus not love her.

Vega continued to sparkle overhead like it had for thousands of-years. Its rays twinkled in the shape of a cross. Faithful. Like God.

She hugged her knees closer. Life didn't last forever. Everyone born was only lent to those who loved them for a period of time. Borrowed lives. God loaned John and Rosie to her. In time, their Creator asked for them back, wanted everyone to come home to him.

Pearl, Roxie, Crystal, too, were borrowed. Not owned.

How selfish she'd been.

We had a time to be born.

A time to die.

A time to love a lonely girl and pour into her spirit.

Why had she not poured Christ into Pearl? "God," she whispered, "forgive me for my year-long sulk."

Now she needed to choose. Would she forever live in sorrow over her loss, or would she take off the cloak of grief and put on dancing shoes?

"Mama? Where are you?" Roxie poked her head out the window.

Before Meredith could stop her, Roxie climbed out of the window and wobbled on the roof's shingles.

Meredith grasped her arm and sat the child down.

"What are you doing out here?"

"Talking to God."

"Don't you have to be in church to talk to him?"

Meredith chucked Roxie's nose. "Nope. God can speak to you anywhere."

"Are you talking about Bean?"

"A little. I've talked about you too. Mostly, I've apologized to God."

"Why?"

"I've ignored him because I lost my little girl and husband."

"And Bean?" Roxie snuggled close.

"Yes."

"Do I have to move too?"

Meredith studied Roxie. Only five-years-old, but she understood more than children her age should. "Maybe. If Mr. Parker finds your grandpa or an aunt, you'll ..." She wanted to say 'have to.' Those words, though true, were too harsh. "If your kin is found, you'll live with them."

"But I like it here."

"And I love having you with me."

"What if I don't want to move?"

Meredith pulled Roxie tighter. "Change is hard."

"I want to live here forever."

"And I want you here for longer than forever."

"Silly, Mama. I'd be all grown up and have my own farm. Only I want to raise unicorns instead of goats."

"Unicorns?"

She nodded. "And zebras and giraffes."

"Every animal in the world?"

"No!" Roxie shook her head vehemently. "Not crocodiles or iguanas. They'd eat me."

"I don't blame you. We'll wait before we buy you a zebra. If you have to move, bringing a zebra might be hard."

"It wouldn't fit in a truck."

They sat a moment or two and stared at the sky. Meredith pointed to Vega. "See that star? The brightest one overhead."

Roxie nodded.

"If Parker finds your family, they'll want you to live with them because they love you. No matter where you live, all you have to do is look overhead and find a really bright, sparkly star—we'll name it Roxie-Star. You'll see Roxie-Star and know I'm looking at it, too, and it's shining all my love down on you."

"And Bean?"

"Yes."

"Crystal?"

"The three of you."

Roxie laid her head against Meredith's breast.

"If Mr. Parker finds relatives, they'll love you more than I."

Roxie ducked her head. "Will you give me my own soap too?"

"I certainly will."

"What will it smell like?"

"I've been thinking about its scent. I'd call it Roxie-Star, and I'd make it with vanilla and chamomile."

"Huh?" Roxie shifted and tilted her head toward Meredith.

Although dark, she could clearly picture the question in the child's eyes.

"Chamomile and vanilla are calm and irresistible fragrances. Their scents soothe, so animals will be comfortable coming to you—even if you decide you want a python."

"Yuck. I don't like snakes."

"If they're poisonous, I agree."

"And I don't want no dinosaurs."

They sat cuddled together as the stars shifted overhead. "Roxie-Star soap will be like you—peaceful and tranquil. Like the night sky," Meredith said.

"Huh?"

Meredith ran her hand over the silky strands of Roxie's head. "You are so good and smart and kind. No one ever worries with you around. Animals love you because they recognize your gentleness. That's why I want chamomile. The vanilla, though. Everyone loves vanilla. No one gets enough of it, like you."

"Okay. Can my soap be purple?"

"It can. I'll put ivory stars in it to remind you of Bean and this night sky. After it's in the mold, I'll swirl the purple with pink, Crystal's favorite color. When you use the soap, you'll always think of your sisters."

Roxie clapped her hands. "I like it."

"It took me a while to come up with the absolutely, most perfect soap for my absolutely, most perfect little girl." She paused and smiled. "Like Bean's, it'll have my address and phone number so you can always find me."

"If I have to move, can I take Olaf?"

Could she? Surely no one would be so cruel as to separate them. Meredith had spent a year lying to herself about God, and about Mills's accusation that a huge sin of hers caused

Rosemary and John's death. She wasn't going to ever lie again. "If I have any say in the matter, nothing will separate you from your cat."

Roxie relaxed against Meredith.

In the distance, a train rumbled, a lonely sound of freight being hauled to a distant location.

Roxie lay limp against Meredith.

She had Roxie for this time. She'd savor it.

And pray.

Then again, they hadn't found any relatives after three months except for the crazy cat lady. She'd live today as though Roxie and Crystal would never leave her.

Chapter 38

Parker filed his last form. He grabbed his jacket as he stepped toward the door. Six o'clock. Dinner with Felicity at seven. If he ran home and rushed his shower, he'd grab the ring and make it to Felicity's before dinner molded.

His office phone rang.

After hours. He'd ignore it. Should ignore it. He took another step toward the exit.

It rang again.

Why couldn't he let work slide? With three long strides, he returned to his desk and grabbed the white work phone from its cradle. "Snow here."

"This is Peggy Main from Crossville DCS. Glad I caught you before the workday ended."

"Technically it's over here. Eastern time zone."

"Oops—in our central time, we're nearing five."

"No problem." Parker sank into his chair while tapping his computer to bring it out of hibernation. "What's happening?"

"We found the grandmother of those two Harrison girls. Daniel Harrison's mother."

"Wonderful." Although his words sounded cheerful, a picture of Meredith Jaynes flashed through his head. Large eyes holding back tears. A forced smile. Hugging a tearful Pearl. So much info in a flickering thought. "Where is she? Does she want custody?"

"She's in Cumberland County jail. Will be there for ten more months on meth possession and prostitution charges, but ..."

Parker knew what she wasn't saying. Parental rights didn't care whether mommy or daddy was incarcerated for prostitution. Laws forbade DCS from violating their familial rights.

Peggy Main inhaled. When she spoke, her voice denoted professionalism. It held no judgment about the grandmother. "Venita Barnes wants visitation. Custody when she's released."

He closed his eyes. Not the happy ending he wanted.

"We can set up a time to visit next week. Visiting hours run Monday through Friday, nine to six. The good part is the visit's non-contact. The girls will sit behind a plexiglass partition. Distance should make it easier on them."

"Make an appointment ..." He calculated travel and time change as he checked his calendar. "Somewhere between nine and three, any day but Wednesday or Thursday."

"Will do. I'll email the details. Enjoy your evening."

At seven, Parker knocked at Felicity's door. He smoothed his hand over his pocket. The bulge of the black box in his jeans calmed his stomach's jitters. He hadn't lost it. No one died unexpectedly, so Felicity didn't have to work. No more calls wrangled him at the office. With no interruptions in sight, they'd share one of her fabulous meals.

"Door's open."

He stepped into the immaculate home. Fall quilts in gold and green replaced the ones from summer. Pristine wood glistened. He inhaled to calm his nerves, smelled the pine of the polish beneath the scent of fresh bread. Harsh and pleasant smells.

"I timed this perfectly for your tardiness." Felicity held baked spaghetti in her mitted hands. She wore jeans and a green blouse flowing out at weird angles, making her look angel-like. Her dark hair hung in waves around her shoulders. "How'd I know you'd be a half-an-hour late?" Her laughter told him his delay didn't matter. More than likely, she, too, fell behind schedule. She placed the casserole on a hot plate on the table and turned to him. "We need a proper kiss." She looped her arms around his neck.

Warm lips didn't loosen his tense muscles.

She pulled back. "Is something wrong?"

He half-smiled. Was there something wrong? No. His stomach rumbled, but something else stirred.

"You sound hungry. Sit."

He took his usual place at the table. The box in his pocket pressed uncomfortably against his thigh.

The smell of cheese and pasta drifted up from the table. Crystal gleamed. Embroidered napkins sat beside each plate. Always, he hated to mess up her table by eating. He half-smiled. Not like Meredith's home.

He shook the thought away.

"How'd work go?" Felicity slid the steaming, homemade Italian bread onto the table and sat.

"They found the Harrison girls' grandmother."

"Will this affect …" She looked away and squinted. She perked up and smiled. "Bean? Her grandfather has custody. Will it interfere?"

"Venita Barnes is Danny Harrison's mother. She's not related to Pearl. And it appears the Willoughby line—the girls' mother—is not going to factor in their life." He cleaned his glasses with the cloth napkin.

She sliced two pieces from the fragrant bread. "What do the other three girls ...? Or is it one?" She sighed in exasperation. "I can't keep track of your cases. What does the Hen Waddle crew think about this?"

He drew in a deep breath. *Why doesn't she remember?* He shook his napkin and placed it on his lap. *But why should she?* With his caseload, he was lucky he remembered everyone's name. The names of those she buried never stayed in his mind. "I haven't told them yet."

"You'll be setting up visitation, I assume." She held up her hand to make him pause. "Forgot something." She walked to the fridge and rummaged through it. She returned to the table with a bowl of grated cheese. "Fresh grated Parmesan— SarVecchio."

From her tone, he knew the cheese was high-end. Everything about Felicity spoke perfection.

He sprinkled some over the baked spaghetti and lifted a forkful. It tasted like Food City parm.

"Good, right?"

He nodded.

"SarVecchio is worth the price." She sprinkled a little over her salad. "Work was mundane today. I transported a body from UT to Stanford's Crematorium. We'll pick up the cremains early next week. Talked to the family. Sad. Cancer took a young mom. Her kids are teens. The eldest a senior. Her mom's going to miss prom and graduation and college send-off."

He nodded and shoveled more spaghetti into his mouth.

"You're awfully quiet." She dabbed her mouth with her cloth napkin.

"A little concerned. The girls' grandmother's in jail."

She put her fork down. "They allow visitations in jail?"

He nodded.

"Poor girls." She lifted the crystal pitcher of water. "Do you need a refill?"

He held out his glass while she poured. Then he knew, beyond all doubt. If he had made a checklist of the perfect woman, Felicity would tick off almost every box.

Almost.

Mundane conversation filled the dinner hour. They chatted as they cleaned up.

Felicity put the last pot away. "Do you want coffee?"

The box in his pocket provoked him. Parker shook his head. "Let's talk."

She raised a brow, and they stepped into the living room. "What's up?"

He sunk onto the sofa. "Felicity, you're beautiful and talented and loving."

She stepped back and frowned.

She knows what's coming.

"But ...?"

"I do love you." He held his breath. He sounded like Lily had a year ago.

She crossed her arms and sat in the accent chair across from the sofa. "Don't hedge. Your words say this is a 'it's me, not you' breakup." Her eyes hardened.

He leaned forward and clasped his hands between his legs. He studied his fingers. "I don't believe we have a forever kind of love ..." Words froze. His chest constricted.

Lily.

She felt this way a year ago. Breaking up with someone hurt almost as much as being dumped. *Lord, forgive me for my bitterness.* He looked into Felicity's eyes.

She shifted her legs to the side. Her lips pressed tight. Aside from those two small movements, she sat motionless.

"I thought we were perfect for each other, and truly there's nothing wrong with you."

She stood. "Spare me." She pivoted and strode upstairs.

He followed. His stomach churned as he stood before her in the hallway. "You're most men's dream."

She turned from him. The sorrow in her eyes took away his ability to breathe.

But he had to do this. Now. He caressed her forearm.

She shook him off, crossed her arms but didn't step away.

"You're beautiful, talented, dedicated to your job and your friends. In our work, we're the same. But ..."

Her glare told him to shut up.

He couldn't. He had to do this. "You're too perfect. I'm low-class, overworked, underpaid. I love four-wheeling, and if I could finagle the time, I'd be camping and fishing and ..." *goats?*

She dropped her arms to her sides.

"In the end, this is kindness."

"Kindness?" Her voice hissed like a cat ready to claw. "You keep tonight's date as though nothing's wrong. Small talk. Chat mindlessly while we clean up. Act all normal. Then you break off with me. Is this kindness?"

"I didn't realize ..." He couldn't tell her he had intended to propose until he understood how cruel that would sound to her. "No. My technique is crude and mean. I didn't come to a full understanding of what was right until ..." The pressure of the ring box made him wonder if she could see its bulge. He restrained himself from patting the lump, drawing attention to the obvious bump.

"Is there someone else?"

He shook his head.

"Not the pretty girl up at Hen Waddle Hollow?"

"No." *Yes.* Suddenly he understood. He could love Meredith Jaynes forever. Love her more than Lily and Felicity. Why? His shoulder hitched. Aside from the small movement, he made no other.

He stepped to Felicity and took her in his arms.

She felt like a cold mannequin.

He stroked the back of her hair.

She softened, and her body pressed against his. After dashing a tear, or two, away, Felicity buried her face in his shoulder.

A few moments passed. Felicity stepped away. "I'll miss Samantha and Darrick."

"There's no reason not to visit."

"I couldn't ..."

"If you won't visit my folks because of me, then I'll make sure I'm never there when I know you're visiting."

"Even Thanksgiving and Christmas?" She chuckled sadly.

"I'd even give up turkey legs and Mom's gifts of new ties." He paused. "Felicity, everything about you is good. We can be friends."

She turned away, strode into her bedroom. The door clicked behind her.

Meredith would've slammed the door.

Or maybe not.

There was so much he didn't know about Meredith Jaynes, but he wanted to learn.

Meredith's phone rang as she sat on the toilet watching Roxie and Crystal play in the tub.

"Good evening. Did I catch you at a bad time?" a man asked.

Meredith looked at her phone—an unidentified caller. "I'm sorry. Who's this?"

"Donovan Andrews. You gave me your number last week. I guess I never gave you mine."

"I have your number now." Meredith smiled as she leaned back against the john. "When I hang up, I'll add you to my contacts."

"I made the big time." His laughter mingled with the girls'—merriment in stereo.

"I've got the day off tomorrow. Do you and your three girls want to go off-roading?"

She'd love to ... but ...

"Meredith?"

"Sorry. First, we're down to two kids. Bean moved Wednesday."

"I'm sorry." He paused. "Or should this be good news?"

"Good, but hard. Also, I've got to work at the market."

"What time are you done?"

"Four-ish."

"How about I pick you up at five. We'll cruise Eagle Bluff, then eat dinner. Have you ever been to Piggy's Barbeque? Supposed to be messy and delicious."

"Sounds like fun."

A video call rang. Bean! "I've got to take this."

"I'll pick you up at five."

"See you then." She hit Skype. "Pearl Solomon, you got us at bath time." Meredith turned her phone toward her sisters all soap slathered and immersed in bubbles.

"Hi, Roxie and Crystal." Bean's happy voice rang against the tiles.

The two in the tub waved and giggled.

"Sissy!" Crystal pointed a bubble-coated arm at the phone.

Roxie snatched the cell which she promptly dropped in the tub.

Meredith grabbed for the sunken phone. She nabbed the slick case, but it slipped from her fingers. Bubbly water hid the phone from view. She grabbed wildly. Roxie looked up with terrified eyes.

Meredith snatched the phone. Slicked with soap, it slipped again. At last, she pulled out her cell. Water dripped from a blank screen.

What would Bean think when she didn't call back?

Chapter 39

Saturday morning sunlight streamed through the window. Parker stretched and lay in the sunbeams. He didn't have to get up. Had nowhere to go. He stared at the ceiling but only saw the hurt in Felicity's face. He knew how she felt. Lily taught him. How many months had he wallowed over his loss of her? What a fool he'd been. How much of his life had he wasted?

Yard work piled up outside. Instead of moping, he dressed and then raked the leaves he ignored on zoo weekend.

By three, yard litter clung to his hair and under his nails rather than on his lawn. Perhaps Meredith headed home from market. If his dreams about her were to come true, he'd have to act. He dialed her number which went straight to voicemail.

"Snow, here. Give me a call."

He disconnected. Winced at his message. He sounded too ominous. He hit redial.

No. He wouldn't call again like a lovesick Romeo.

Instead, he showered and changed into clean jeans. He grabbed one of his favorite blue T-shirts.

Felicity loved him in blue.

Lily's favorite color.

He pulled on his orange Tennessee Vols shirt. Maybe Meredith returned his call.

Three voice mails arrived in the span of one shower. All from Mom. No surprise. He deleted each message without listening to them. He'd talk to her tomorrow.

He dialed Meredith. The cell rang the usual length of time but once more went to voice mail.

"Me again. Sorry to bother you on market day. Nothing ..." What could he say? Nothing serious? With the girls' visit to their incarcerated grandmother looming, anything he said to Meredith would be serious. "I'll catch you early next week." He stared at his phone after he disconnected. The uneasiness that plagued him this morning returned. His finger hovered over the contact. Time to repent of the sour spirit he nurtured for more than a year. He pressed her name.

Lily.

"Parker? Is something wrong?" Anxiety colored Lily's voice.

"No."

"Then why are you calling?"

"Yes. Yes, something's very wrong ... Well, not life and death. With me." He swallowed hard. "Sorry. Not serious. I need to apologize."

"For what?" A baby cried in the background. "Honey, can you get Darla?"

"I understand the kindness of your heart when you broke off our engagement." He chuckled. "Although, I wish you'd told me a little earlier—"

"I—"

"No. My statement isn't an indictment. I'm calling to apologize. My bitterness colored my thoughts about you. I want to congratulate you on Darla. On your marriage."

"Oh, Parker, you are so sweet."

"I will pray for your family."

They chatted a bit longer about Darla, her husband, God's work in their lives. Good things. When they disconnected, Parker felt ... different.

Light.

Clearing bitterness from his life, making the decisions God wanted did miraculous things to one's mood.

Life was too good to sit around the house. He'd go for a ride.

In the jeep, he turned the ignition. No sooner had the Cherokee turned over than the gas light dinged.

Fill up now. Cruise after.

As he pumped gas at Weigel's, a stripped-down, orange Rubicon pulled into the next lane. Two blonde-headed girls bobbed in the back. A pretty woman with tousled hair sat in the front.

His breath hitched.

"Hey, Snow." Van raised a hand then grabbed the gas pump.

Meredith turned and shot him her warm smile.

"Mr. Parker," Roxie leaned through the missing back window. "We ate at a Pig place."

"Piggy's Barbeque," Van said. "You've got to go there."

"Good chow?" Parker kept his eyes on Meredith.

"Oh, yeah." Van slapped his stomach, then turned to insert the pump into the gas tank.

Parker grabbed his receipt and climbed into his Cherokee.

The passenger door of the Rubicon flung open. "Wait." Meredith jogged over to Parker's vehicle. She leaned into the driver's window with her phone in her hands.

He inhaled the scent of earth and flowers.

"Do you have Bean's new number?"

He shook his head, not only to tell her he didn't but to clear his head of ... her.

"A little …" she leaned forward, so close he felt the heat of her body. Meredith lowered her voice as though anyone else could hear her, "… klutz dropped my old cell into the bathwater. Prayers and rice and a blow drier couldn't save the phone. Nor did my prayers save her number." Her hand holding her phone brushed his.

He tried not to move, to keep her fingers touching his hand. "Her number's in my office. I'll text it to you on Monday."

"The one benefit," she lifted the shiny cell enclosed in a glittery case with a picture of a goat on the back, "I've got the latest Galaxy." She turned away, then stopped. "Off to see Felicity?"

He shook his head. "We …"

Meredith stepped back to his open window. "We what?"

"Broke up last night."

Shock showed on her face. "No." She leaned back into the window and laid her hand on his shoulder.

He stared at her lips. Wondered at their taste.

"I'm so sorry."

Did he imagine things, or did her hand rest on his shoulder longer than it should? If he spoke or moved, she'd let go and run back to Van.

"What happened?" Her hand slid down his arm and lay on the opening of the window. Fingers so close to his skin.

He stared at them. "My choice."

"Ready, Meredith?" Van called as he ripped the receipt from the pump.

"I'll keep you in prayer." She stepped away, but her eyes stayed trained on him. "God and I made up."

"What do you mean?"

"Bitterness turned my life sour. I decided I liked sweetness better."

He smiled. *We've got a lot in common.*

"Jesus and I chatted long into the night on the day Bean left. Her time in my home taught me things my loss of John and Rosemary didn't. I will pray for you." She lifted a hand in farewell and walked away. Her feet took her back to Van, but her eyes focused on him.

A feeling like panic gripped him. How could he keep her near? Keep her away from Van? *The visitation!* "Wait."

She had turned and climbed back into the Rubicon.

Monday would be soon enough to tell her about Venita Barnes.

Chapter 40

Sunday morning, Meredith pulled her truck into Trinity Church's lot. *Why did I give in to Roxie's pleading and come here?* Her hands clenched the steering wheel as she stared at the brick building ahead of her. Every muscle in her body stiffened.

Smiling congregants strode into the building. The late morning light glinted off the stained-glass windows. She knew these people.

Worse. They knew her.

Would judge her for her year's absence.

With sweating palms, she shifted the running truck into reverse. They'd go somewhere else. God went to a million different churches.

Roxie leaned over the seat. "Come on. We're going to miss the songs. After two of them, I go to kids' church."

Thanks to her family, Roxie knew Trinity's routine.

The child bounded out of the truck.

"Wait!" Meredith shifted into park and turned off the ignition. "Back here, Roxie-Star."

The child skidded to a stop. She tilted her head—the picture of sweetness and compliance. Not the dragon-child of recent weeks.

After their rooftop chat, she promised God she'd make sure her Roxie-Star would get top billing more often. "I guess you made my choice for me." Meredith climbed out and rounded the truck. "Get Crystal." She pulled the wheelchair from the truck bed.

Roxie climbed onto the rocket panel and unhooked her sister. "Hurry. All the people are already there." She waved her hand toward the building.

With Crystal firmly strapped in, Meredith straightened her shoulders. She stared at the entrance to Trinity like a condemned woman eyed the execution chamber. "Hold onto the wheelchair. This parking lot gets busy."

Roxie yanked them forward.

Meredith pulled back. Like a slow-motion film, she pictured every eye on her. She imagined their thoughts. The sinner returns.

She jerked to a stop once she got to the sidewalk.

No.

Les Mills stood at the front door with a stack of bulletins in his hand.

Roxie let go and ran for the doors. Before Meredith could call, the child skipped into the narthex.

Meredith looked behind her. Wanted to run. Anywhere but here. When she faced forward once more, Mills held Roxie in his arms. His smile, seen through glass doors, sparkled and took years off his face.

He put Roxie down as Meredith stepped inside.

Roxie grinned at Meredith. "Mr. Mills is my new boyfriend." Before Meredith could respond, Roxie turned. "Phoebe!" Without asking, she ran toward the sanctuary door where her foster-cousin waved to her.

"Welcome, Meredith." Les Mills turned somber as he handed her the sermon notes. When she took them, he offered her his hand. "I'm glad you decided to come back to the Lord."

His implied judgment lodged in her stomach. Meredith gritted her teeth. She stared into his face. Smiled. Ignored the proffered hand and pushed Crystal off to the nursery.

In the toddler classroom, she signed in Crystal with a woman she hadn't seen before. With a kiss to the top of Crystal's head, Meredith returned to the nearly empty narthex.

Mills paced near the entrance. His back faced the sanctuary doors.

She stared his way. *The fool.* The four-letter word needled her. *My judgment of Mills rivals his moralistic attitude.* She pushed open the swinging door. Her heart stuttered. She stood half in and half out of the auditorium.

Incomplete repentance meant nothing.

She let go of the door which bounced shut behind her as she strode across the foyer. "Lester."

He gave her his smarmy smile. "What can I do for you?"

"I need to apologize."

"You did. In Walmart."

She shook her head. "No. This no longer concerns your nose or my anger. Bitterness toward you consumed me because you hurt me more than you can imagine at the funeral."

"I—"

She held out her hand. "No. Listen. I was wrong to hit you." She bit back her smile. The picture of smacking his nose still made her grin. God would have to work that bit of unrighteous satisfaction out of her later. "What I need to ask forgiveness for is the anger I held toward you. It in no way demonstrated my faith nor honored God." She stuck out her hand. "Will you forgive me?"

His unctuous grin spread. He puffed his chest and straightened to his full six feet. "Apology accepted." He shook her hand. "I'm glad you've seen the light."

She shivered. Then smiled. She had no need to associate with him. She didn't need to cast her pearls before swine. Lester Mills was a child of God. Thus, she could not hate him. But she didn't need to be his friend.

Parker kicked up his feet and opened the newspaper. Good service, quiet Sunday. Pleasant life.

Until Peggy Main called. "I've got a date for the girls to meet their grandmother. You won't like the timing."

"Do we have a choice?"

"Seeing as Venita Barnes has a meeting with her lawyer on Tuesday for her court date Friday, the only time we could arrange a visit this week would be tomorrow."

"Tomorrow?" Parker inhaled a deep breath and stared out his front window. "Can't we visit next week? This way, the foster family will have time to prepare."

"I go on vacation to Vermont next week. The peak colors will hit the Northeast. My husband and I will be out of town for two glorious—no cell phones with us—weeks."

Parker smiled. He understood.

"If you or the family can't make tomorrow, the soonest we have is—"

"Tomorrow should work. Why delay the inevitable? I'll call the family and get back to you." He disconnected. With phone in hand, Parker paced his living room. *Tomorrow. No notice. No time to prep for this.*

He called Meredith.

"Where? No way!" Meredith pulled the phone from her ear. *Why couldn't you slam a cell?* She paced her kitchen where the girls chowed down on leftover pulled pork and spareribs.

Parker's voice drifted in soft murmurs from the phone held at her side.

A perfect Sunday. Repentance. Great worship. And now, this.

She lifted the phone. Inhaled to calm her voice. "What, in the name of sanity, is wrong with DCS? Their grandmother ... grandmother, mind you ... is incarcerated for prostitution and drugs. An old-lady hooker has the right to see the children? In prison?"

"Jail. Not prison. She does have the right. I will pick them up—"

"You give me no notice to prepare them? How long have you known?"

"Five minutes."

Again, she dropped her hand and gripped the phone at her side. *Things move at a snail's pace with DCS, but not this bombshell.*

A questioning voice drifted from the phone.

She lifted the phone back to her ear. "What did you say?" She studied the children as they chatted at the kitchen table.

"I'll come for the girls at eight in the morning."

"No, you won't—"

"Meredith, you have no say in the—"

"Do you think I will let them travel to Crossville, go into a jail, then let them drive all the way home without the security of someone who loves and understands them? I will drive them to Crossville."

"You can't go in."

"I don't care. I'll sit in my truck, wait for the visit to end, then I will pick up the pieces of their frightened, broken hearts."

"Do you want to ride with me?"

"No!" No way would she ride with this destroyer of children's homes.

"Do you need directions?"

"I'm sorry for being rude. I know this isn't your fault." She glanced at Roxie who wiped Crystal's mouth. "This is cruel to the girls."

Roxie smiled and cooed to her sister. For a moment, she looked like Bean.

Bean. What did she think with the aborted Skype chat and no return call?

"If I drive, we can have a mini-vacation after the visit. The girls are going to be ..."

Roxie looked up at her. "What's wrong?"

Meredith placed a finger over her own lips. "I need to finish this conversation." She turned her back to the children. "My phone comes with Google Maps. I can find the jail."

"You need to be there by nine Central time."

"Under one condition."

"Meredith, this isn't up for discussion—"

"You get me Bean's phone number." She tossed the phone aside. "Roxie, when you're done, watch Crystal for me."

Meredith stepped into the living room and collapsed onto the sofa. She dropped her head into her hands. *Lord, our world's insane. A fifty-year-old meth-addict prostitute has more rights than two little girls?*

She clenched her hands. Loosened them. *If my time is up with them, God, help me pour into their lives.*

Little feet padded into the room. "What's wrong?" Roxie sat Crystal on the couch and hopped next to her.

Meredith pulled the afghan off the back of the sofa and made Crystal lie down for her afternoon nap. Then she tugged

Roxie onto her lap. Whether she was ready or not, she needed to tell her. "Tomorrow, we're taking a field trip."

"Where?"

"Mr. Parker found your grandmother."

"I don't want to move." Roxie jerked away.

She pulled her closer. "You won't be moving any time soon. You have to visit your grandmother. She's in jail."

"I don't want to go to jail." Roxie buried her head in Meredith's chest.

Meredith pulled the trembling child tight and spoke into her hair. "You'll have a little visit. You'll be with Mr. Parker."

"What about you?"

"I can't go in. I'll wait for you outside. Right after your visit, we'll go to Nashville and see their zoo."

Roxie pulled away.

Meredith tugged her back.

The two cuddled as soft breaths came from Crystal.

"We'll stay in a hotel in Nashville. Eat at Shoney's. We can Skype with Bean if she's home—maybe we'll call her from the restaurant.

"Okay." Roxie hopped off the couch. "I'm gonna go tell Olaf."

If only adults could put off sorrow the way kids did.

Chapter 41

Meredith climbed down from her truck outside the Cumberland County Jail. The squat, brick structure looked more like a school complex than a detention center. And like a school, a short distance from the front door, a furtive cigarette smoker leaned against the wall. The smoking guard chatted with Parker Snow.

Parker strode toward her. His legs took long strides as if he was all business. His eyes, though. What did she see in them?

He stooped to the girls' height. "Ready?"

Crystal held out chubby hands.

Roxie grabbed Meredith's legs.

"You'll get to meet your real grandma, Roxie-Star. She's going to love you." As she unwound the child's arms, Meredith prayed she spoke the truth. She forced the largest smile she could find.

Parker took the wheelchair and pushed past the smoking guard.

Meredith focused on the trio until the door closed behind them.

She couldn't sit. Couldn't wait. She paced the length of the jail. If she prayed like the Israelites did when they marched around Jericho, would the walls of her pain disintegrate?

Electronics beeped as Parker and the girls passed metal detectors. Heavy iron doors clanged behind them. No outside light filtered into the institutional gray hallways. The smell of powdered eggs and dirty bodies filtered through the gloom. He gripped the wheelchair tighter. "Are you okay, Roxie?"

The child's knuckles turned white where she grasped the handle of the chair. She couldn't hug it any closer without climbing into the seat with Crystal.

The visitation room held lines of stations. A round speaker sat in the middle of each plexiglass partition. The plastic was scratched by a multitude of visitors.

"Here you go." His guard pointed to a single chair. "Barnes'll be out in a minute." The guard turned. Leather scuffed against the tile as he walked away.

Parker wheeled Crystal, so she faced the window. He pulled Roxie onto his lap.

After a few minutes, a woman with hair pulled into a ponytail stepped to the window. Gray roots sprouted beneath dark brown hair revealing the months Venita Barnes had lived behind bars. She smiled. Her grin showed teeth rotted from meth. Several front teeth were missing. Some were discolored with rot. He could imagine what her breath smelled like.

"Girls, Mrs. Barnes is your …" He couldn't choke out the word grandmother. "Mrs. Barnes is your father's mother." He looked up at Barnes. "Venita, this is Roxie," Parker patted her head. "And this one's Crystal."

"So, these are my baby boy's kids." She stared at Parker with somber eyes. "My boy." She patted her chest as though to soothe a heartbreak. "He was the whole world to me. So how old's my grandbabies?"

Parker pointed at Roxie. "She's five. Crystal's two."

"What's wrong with that one?" Venita Barnes pointed at Crystal. "She ain't in a regular stroller."

"She's got spina bifida."

"What's spinal beef-a-da?" Barnes asked.

"Her spine didn't close up properly."

"What's that mean?"

"She can't walk without help."

"She's a cripple?" Venita Barnes grimaced. "My boy had a gimp for a kid?" She turned to Roxie. "Your daddy was my only son. You got a aunt out in Fort Campbell somewhere."

Roxie hunched her shoulders.

Barnes looked at Parker. "Why don't she look at me?"

"She's shy," Parker said.

Barnes turned her attention back to Roxie. "I ain't gonna bite you. What's wrong, girl?"

"Nuffin.'"

Venita squinted and looked at Parker. "What she say?"

"Nothing."

"She said something. I heard her."

"She said the word nothing."

"Didn't sound like that." Venita Barnes looked back at Roxie. "Tell me about school."

"I'm in kwindegawten."

Again, Barnes looked at Parker. "Can this girl speak English?"

Parker forced in a breath. No matter who he served, he had to show respect.

"You deaf. What's wrong with my son's girl?"

"Roxie has a speech impediment. The school gives her therapy. When Roxie gets nervous, she can't focus on her speaking."

"So, I finally get some grandkids I'm allowed to see, unlike my ingrate daughter's boys, and all I get is a cripple

401

and a retard?" She stood. "My boy." Once more, she clutched her heart as though having a heart attack. "My boy deserved better. I got enough problems. I ain't able to deal with two defective retards."

If Roxie's stiffened posture was any indication, she understood every cruel word Venita Barnes hurled.

"Guard." Barnes turned. "I want to go back to my cell."

"Wait," Parker called. "Your daughter. The girls' aunt. What's her name and where does she live?"

"I ain't got nothing to do with that witch." She stepped away.

Parker lifted Roxie and steadied her on her feet. Then he stood and placed a palm against the window. He called after the departing woman. "Please tell me her name. She needs to know about her nieces."

Venita glowered at him. "Lisa Simpson. Married a Todd Simpson. They live near Fort Campbell. He's some sorta army guy. I ain't got an address. They think they're too good for me."

A door clanged.

"Ready?" a guard asked.

"One more thing," Parker said. "Do you want to give up all parental rights to the children?"

"What use do I have for two defectives." She walked to the guard.

"I'll get the papers to your lawyer."

The door resounded behind them.

After five minutes, the visit ended.

Only one more lead to track down.

Sunlight slapped Parker as he stepped out of the jail. He squinted against the light blurring his vision.

Meredith ran toward them clutching the cell phone she talked into. She threw her arms around Roxie. "You're done already."

Roxie grabbed the wheelchair handles. "The lady didn't like us. Can we go to the zoo?" She pushed Crystal toward the truck.

"Stay on the sidewalk," Meredith called after Roxie.

"I know." Roxie broke into a jog.

Crystal squealed in delight.

Meredith held out a finger to Parker. "One moment." She lifted the phone. "I'll talk to you tonight, Van." She tucked the phone into her pocket and looked at Parker. "What happened?"

Parker gave her the rundown.

"I told you this was a bad idea." She strode after the children.

Parker had the rest of the day free, sort of. He wasn't far from the army base in Kentucky. Maybe ...?

He called Peggy Main. After two hours in her office, he was back in his jeep and on his way to Fort Campbell.

He pulled into the driveway of a semi-attached brick ranch. Typical army housing. He knocked at the door. Tapped his fingers at his side and hitched his briefcase more securely onto his shoulder.

The curtain moved behind the living room window. Seconds later, the door opened a fraction. "Yes?" A petite woman with sand-colored hair asked.

Parker held up his credentials. "Parker Snow from Campbell County DCS. We talked earlier."

She opened the door wider to take the card he offered.

Parker polished his glasses as she studied his credentials.

She returned the identification. "I told you earlier—I don't know about any nieces." She glanced at her watch. "I need to be at work in thirty minutes."

"I'll be as brief as possible. Did you …" He coughed. He talked of Harrison in the past tense. "Do you have a brother Daniel Harrison?"

Her lips tightened.

"He passed away from a heroin overdose about three months ago. He had two daughters. I need to talk to you about them."

"Come in." With a stiff back, she stepped away from the door. Her expression remained stony. "Can I get you anything?"

"No, thank you."

"Have a seat." She indicated a tan easy chair with a colorful afghan thrown over the back. Inexpensive, pleasant art hung on the walls. In the corner, a small cubby shelf held trucks and cars and LEGOS.

"You have two sweet nieces in Tennessee." Parker described the girls.

As he talked, Lisa Simpson's posture softened. She leaned against the matching sofa and clutched a throw pillow. She fingered its edges. "They're sweet, you say?"

He nodded. "I understand you don't have anything to do with your mother. Is there any other family?"

She shook her head. "No. Danny was my only sibling. We didn't get along. His overdose doesn't surprise me."

He waved toward the shelf of toys. "You have children?"

"Two boys. I already took them to my friend's. She watches mine when I work. I watch hers."

"Military wives?"

She smiled. "My husband's deployed. Not due back for two more months." She stood. "Let me call work. I'll go in late. Then tell me about my nieces."

"Hey, Bean," Meredith spoke to the child when her image showed up on the Skype call. "Guess where we are?" Meredith flipped the phone's camera so she could see Shoney's buffet across the aisle. Roxie had insisted they sit next to the counter so she could get her free food.

"Why'd you hang up on me," Bean asked when Meredith turned the camera back to her. "And you never answered when I called."

"Well—"

Roxie snatched the phone. "Lookit. We're at Shoney's. In Nashville." She skipped up to the buffet.

Meredith eyed her. *Do not drop my phone in the Jell-O salad, please.*

Roxie waved the phone toward the buffet as Meredith cut Crystal's chicken fingers into small pieces.

A bad day turned out good. She knew nothing would ever go wrong with this family again.

Chapter 42

Parker whistled as he pulled up to Meredith's house on Tuesday. Once more, a phone call would've met his purposes, but—

He ended a relationship.

He healed another.

Found the last of the girls' family.

Batting a thousand, he was sure he'd nail this home visit.

"Parker." Meredith pulled gardening gloves from her hands. She strode toward him. Frowned. "What's wrong. The grandmother—"

"Nope. Barnes will sign all the paperwork. No worries about her."

"Come. Sit." They settled into the wicker chairs on the porch. Her cell lay face up on the table between them. "Why are you here, then? Roxie doesn't get home from school for another hour. Crystal's napping."

He tried to bite back his grin and knew he failed.

"You look self-satisfied."

"I found Lisa Simpson. The last of Roxie and Crystal's family."

Meredith bit her lips.

He wanted to kiss them. "Simpson's a nice woman—about our age. Two boys. Her husband's in the military."

"Go on."

"She wants to meet the girls."

Meredith stared at her hands clasped in her lap.

"Someplace neutral." His grin spread. Teasing didn't come naturally to him. "She works as a nursing assistant. Her husband's deployed in South Korea where the family may join him."

"The girls will—" Meredith stared away from him.

"Let me finish. Lisa Simpson wants to meet Roxie and Crystal. And you. She says ..." he leaned forward. "Look at me."

Meredith turned.

"If Simpson's family can have visitation—not big holidays, and not all the time—and an open adoption, so she can see the girls ..."

Meredith leaned forward. Eagerness shone in her eyes.

"If you're a suitable guardian, she'll relinquish her custody rights."

Meredith's mouth dropped open. She stood and paced to the end of the porch. Turned. She beamed as she leaned against the railing. If anyone looked like an angel, Meredith did.

Her phone rang.

Parker glanced at the phone as the screen pulsed with Van's name. He stood.

The phone rang several more times.

"Do you want to answer?"

She shook her head. Her eyes glistened. "Van'll leave a message."

He swallowed the lump in his throat. "Are you two serious?"

She scoffed. "He's the first fellow I've dated since John. We've only been out a couple of times. Talk on the phone. I'm not ready for anything serious."

"So, you're not exclusive?" He looked into her eyes. They sparkled with unshed tears.

"No, Parker Snow." She stepped closer. "I do have a question." She was so close he could smell the lavender on her.

Did she look coy? Did she feel the way he did?

"When will Simpson visit? How long until I can adopt them?"

Just when he thought he'd be able to kiss her or at least ask her out, she paced to the far end of the porch once more.

"Adoption through foster care can take years. I'll put in the paperwork." He took off his glasses to clean them.

"I know that look, Mr. Snow."

He put them back on. "What look?"

"You wipe your glasses when you're nervous." She took a few steps back to him. "Why are you worried?"

"You know why." Surely, she understood his feelings.

"Scared I'd be hurt if the adoption failed?" She straightened and licked her lips. "Or is there something else?"

Parker reached out. *Now or never.* He caressed her hair. "There is something else."

"Mama." A wail followed Crystal's call. "Mama."

"We'll have to continue this conversation, Parker Snow." She tilted her head. Did her lips pout? Beg to be kissed? "You'll have to excuse me. My daughter needs me." She tossed a smile as she stepped into the house.

Oh, we'll continue our talk. Van's not making you love him. He sank back into the wicker chair. He'd wait as long as he needed. Do what needed to be done. Two other times he found the almost perfect woman. This time?

He nailed it.

And Meredith Jaynes knew.

About the Author

CAROL MCCLAIN'S an award-winning author and a passionate Christian. Her stories show the redemption of the unredeemable. Although themes range from forgiving the unforgivable to escaping the trauma of the past, all her stories are told with humor and compassion. They will make you laugh and cry.

If you've enjoyed this book, Carol would love for you to leave a review on Amazon. A review need not be long—a sentence or two is perfect! Below is a link to copy to take you to Carol's author page to leave the review. Thank you for reading *Borrowed Lives*.

HTTP://BIT.LY/4PUPPBM

www.ingramcontent.com/pod-product-compliance
Lightning Source LLC
Chambersburg PA
CBHW072257020726
47501CB00002B/295